Praise for

Lonely Castle in the Mirror

Publishers Weekly **Best Book of 2022**

"A gorgeous, wrenching fantasy that lays bare the anxieties and desperation—as well as the small triumphs—of adolescence."

—*Locus Magazine*

"[A] moving psychological journey. . . . Tsujimura is a master at projecting these young anxieties onto the page, offering hints and shadows and silhouettes of what the world might be like once we finally grow up, and how difficult it is to take that first step."

—Tor.com

"This sweet, kindhearted, and deeply sympathetic magical realist novel about middle school dropouts pulling each other back from the brink will resonate with readers of all ages."

—*Publishers Weekly*, **Starred Review**

"A moving, reflective, and surprising novel. . . . Anyone who has ever struggled with feeling isolated, had difficulties at school, or had mental health struggles, will find this novel to be a cleansing balm."

—*Culturefly*

"[A] respectful, moving novel about teenage bullying in the Tokyo suburbs. . . . Tsujimura shows how easily misunderstandings and miscommunications can escalate, and treats everyone—even the bullies—with nuance."

—*...an Times*

"An innovative and tender blend of social commentary and magical realism."

—*The Japan Society Review*

"Genuinely affecting. . . . [A] story about collaboration, empathy, and sharing truths, a modern, all-ages fairy tale that should appeal to fans of Neil Gaiman and Studio Ghibli animations."

—*The Financial Times*

"In a world where there is so much untruth, so much altered reality, so many superficial existences forming even more superficial relationships, this book turns back the clock and reminds us of what is real, and what truly matters: compassion and kindness, the strength in our bonds, and how we can find those right beside us."

—*The Yorkshire Times*

LONELY CASTLE IN THE MIRROR

Mizuki
Tsujimura

Translated by

Philip Gabriel

Erewhon Books
Kensington Publishing Corp.
www.erewhonbooks.com

EREWHON BOOKS are published by:

Kensington Publishing Corp.
119 West 40th Street
New York, NY 10018
www.erewhonbooks.com

Erewhon and the Erewhon logo Reg. US Pat. & TM Off.

KAGAMI NO KOJŌ
LONELY CASTLE IN THE MIRROR
Copyright © 2017, 2023 by Mizuki Tsujimura
First published in Japan in 2017 by POPLAR Publishing Co., Ltd., Tokyo
Revised edition published in Japan in 2021 by POPLAR Publishing Co., Ltd., Tokyo
English translation rights arranged with POPLAR Publishing Co., Ltd., through Japan UNI Agency, Inc., Tokyo

English translation copyright © 2023 by Philip Gabriel
First published in the UK by Transworld Publishers, a division of the Penguin Random House Group Ltd

This edition published in North America as *Lonely Castle in the Mirror* by Erewhon Books, an imprint of Kensington Publishing Corp., in 2023

All Kensington titles, imprints, and distributed lines are available at special quantity discounts for bulk purchases for sales promotions, premiums, fundraising, educational, or institutional use. Special book excerpts or customized printings can also be created to fit specific needs. For details, write or phone the office of the Kensington sales manager: Kensington Publishing Corp., 119 West 40th Street, New York, NY 10018, attn: Sales Department; phone 1-800-221-2647.

Library of Congress Control Number: 2022942291

ISBN 978-1-64566-074-3 (paperback)
eISBN 978-1-64566-041-5 (ebook)

Cover art by Shoko Ishida. Cover design by Dana Li. Interior design by Cassandra Farrin. Author photograph by Yoshihiro Kamiya.

First US Edition: August 2022

10 9 8 7 6 5 4 3 2 1

LONELY CASTLE: (1) A castle situated off by itself. (2) A castle surrounded by enemies, with no hope of relief forces arriving.

—Daijirin dictionary

I SOMETIMES FIND MYSELF DREAMING.

A new transfer student has started at our school, and everyone wants to be friends with them. The most cheerful, kind and athletic person in our class. And smart, too.

Out of all my classmates this new student picks me out with a generous smile, as dazzling as the sun, and says, "Kokoro-chan, it's been such a long time."

The other students can't believe it. "What?" they say, looking at me meaningfully. "Do you two already know each other?"

In another world, we were already friends.

There's nothing special about me. I'm not athletic, and I'm not smart. There's nothing about me anyone would envy.

It's only that we had the chance to meet before, and form a special bond.

We go everywhere together: when we move to a different classroom, when we go for break, and when we walk through the school gates at the end of the day.

Sanada's gang may be dying to be friends with them, but all the student says is, "I'm with Kokoro-chan."

So I am no longer alone.

I've been hoping something like this will happen for such a long time.

Though I know it never will.

FIRST SEMESTER:
WAIT AND SEE

May

BEYOND THE DRAWN curtains floated the sound of the little truck from the local supermarket coming to sell produce. "It's a Small World"—the song from Kokoro's favorite ride at Disneyland— boomed from the large speaker on the back, reminding her of the world of laughter and hope that lay just outside her window. Ever since she could remember, it always played the same song.

It was abruptly cut off, and an announcement followed. "Hello everyone. This is the produce truck from Mikawa Market. We have fresh goods, dairy products, bread and rice for sale!"

The supermarket along the highway was far away, and you needed a car to get there, so ever since Kokoro was small the Mikawa Market truck had driven over every week, and parked behind her house. Its melody was the signal for old people in the neighborhood, and mothers with small children, to come outside and buy their provisions.

Kokoro had never gone to shop there herself, though her mother apparently had. "Mr. Mikawa's getting on in years, so I wonder how much longer he'll keep coming," she'd said.

In the past, before the supermarket appeared in the area, it really had been convenient for the truck to drive over, and plenty of families bought its produce. But it was beginning to lose its customers. Some people even complained about the loudspeaker, calling it noise pollution.

Kokoro didn't think it was a nuisance, but whenever she heard the melody she became, like it or not, aware that it was daytime, and a weekday. *Forced to be* aware of it.

She could hear children laughing.

It was only after Kokoro stopped going to school that she discovered this was what eleven o'clock in the morning was like in her neighborhood.

While in elementary school, she only ever saw the Mikawa truck during the holidays.

She'd never listened to it so intently—on a weekday, in her bedroom, curtains drawn, her body rigid. Not until last year.

She watched TV with bated breath, the sound on mute, hoping the light from the set wouldn't filter out through the curtains.

Even when the Mikawa truck wasn't there, there were always young mothers and children playing in the park beyond their house. Whenever she spied the strollers lined up by the park benches, colorful bags hanging from the handles, a thought came to her: *It's not early morning anymore.* The families who gathered between ten and eleven always disappeared by midday, heading home to have lunch.

And then she slid open her curtains a tiny bit.

Spending so much time alone in her bedroom—gloomy during the day despite the orange curtains—feelings of guilt welled up in her. She felt she was being blamed for being slack and lazy.

At first she'd enjoyed being at home, but as time passed, though no one said anything, she knew she couldn't carry on like this.

There were good reasons why set rules existed.

Rules like: you should open your curtains in the morning.

And all children should attend school.

TWO DAYS AGO, she and her mother had visited a private alternative "School" (they used the English word), and today she'd been sure she could make a start there.

Yet when she woke up, she realized it wasn't going to happen.

As usual, her stomach was killing her.

She wasn't faking it. It really did hurt.

She had no idea why, but in the mornings, her stomach, and sometimes even her head, pulsed with pain.

Don't force yourself to go, her mother had said.

So when she went downstairs to the dining room, she wasn't worried about her mother's reaction.

"Mum, my stomach hurts."

Her mother had been preparing some hot milk and toast, and when she heard this her face went blank.

She wouldn't meet her daughter's eye.

As if she hadn't heard, she looked down and carried a mug of hot milk over to the dining table. "*How* does it hurt?" she asked.

Then her mother yanked off the red apron she was wearing over her work clothes—a trouser suit—and draped it over a chair.

"The same as always," Kokoro said in a small voice, but before she'd managed to finish speaking, her mother interrupted.

"*The same as always?* But you were fine until yesterday. The School we visited isn't like your public junior high, you know. You don't need to go every day, there are fewer children in each class, and the teachers seem so kind. You said you'd go. But now you're telling me you won't?"

Her mother obviously wanted her to attend. The sudden accusations made that clear enough. But Kokoro wasn't feigning illness. Her stomach really *was* killing her.

When Kokoro didn't reply, her mother shot an irritated glance at the clock.

"Ah—I'm going to be late," she said, clucking her tongue.

"So—what do you want to do?"

Kokoro's legs felt paralyzed.

"I can't go," she said.

It wasn't simply that she didn't want to go. She *couldn't*.

When Kokoro was finally able, with great effort, to mutter a response, her mother let out a huge sigh and grimaced, as if she too felt a twinge of pain.

7

"Is it only today you can't go? Or are you never going to go?"

Kokoro couldn't say.

She wasn't going today, but she had no idea if, the next day, she might not have a stomachache again.

"OK then," her mother said, and rose to her feet. She picked up the plate with Kokoro's breakfast and threw it in the triangular waste collector in the corner of the sink. "So no milk either? And after I heated it up for you," she added, and poured it down the drain without waiting for a reply. A burst of hissing steam rose up from the hot milk, quickly vanishing under the sound of tap water.

Kokoro had planned to eat it later, but before she could get a word out the toast and milk were history.

"Could you please move?" her mother said, brushing past Kokoro, sitting motionless in PJs. She disappeared into the living room. After a few moments, Kokoro heard her talking on the phone. "Good morning, this is Mrs. Anzai." Her earlier testiness had gone, replaced by a formal, polite tone.

"Yes, that's correct," she heard her mother say. "She says her stomach hurts. I'm so sorry. When we visited the School, she seemed so enthusiastic to start. Yes, that's right. I apologize for any trouble."

The School that her mother had taken her to was called *Kokoro no kyoshitsu*—literally "Classroom for the Heart," a sort of children's counseling center and alternative School. Above the entrance were the words *Supporting Children's Development*.

It was situated in an old building, a former school or perhaps a hospital, and when they'd first arrived, Kokoro had heard children's voices coming from upstairs. Elementary age kids, she thought, from the sound of them.

"You must be a little nervous, Kokoro, but let's go in," her mother had said, smiling. She looked more on edge than her daughter but nevertheless gave Kokoro's back a tiny, encouraging push.

Kokoro had felt awkward that she and the School shared the same name—*kokoro*, "heart."

8

Her mum must have noticed the coincidence, too. It wasn't as if she'd named her that just so she could bring her here. Even thinking such a thing brought a pang of pain.

This was how Kokoro learned for the first time that the so-called *non-attendee* children had somewhere else to go, other than normal school. Back in elementary school, no one in her class ever refused to go to school. A few kids might fake a sick day or two, but there hadn't been a single child who would have to go to a school like this one.

Even the teachers who greeted them all referred to the alternative School by the English word "school."

Kokoro felt a bit strange in the open slippers she'd been given, and as she sat waiting, she nervously curled up her toes.

"So Kokoro, I understand you're a student at Yukishina No. 5 Junior High School?" The teacher was smiling gently as she checked all her information was correct. She was young, and reminded Kokoro of those cheerful, ever-smiling older girls who danced and sang on children's TV. The woman had a sunflower-shaped name tag on her blouse, with a tiny portrait of her, undoubtedly created by one of the children at the School, and the name Kitajima written on it.

"Yes," Kokoro said. Despite her efforts, her voice came out sounding weak and muffled. She wondered why, but at that moment it was the only voice she could manage.

Ms. Kitajima smiled broadly.

"I went there too," she said.

"Oh."

Their conversation stalled.

Ms. Kitajima was actually a beautiful young woman, her short hair giving her a vivacious look. And she had the kindest eyes. Kokoro immediately liked her, and she envied her no end that she had long since graduated and no longer had to attend the junior high.

It was hard to say that Kokoro herself was actually *attending* junior high. She had only just started school in April, when the new academic year began, had only gone to lessons for the first month, and then stopped.

"I CALLED THEM to let them know."

As she reappeared in the dining room, her mother's irritated tone had resumed. She looked at Kokoro, who hadn't moved an inch the entire time, and frowned. "Look, if your stomach still hurts, you should go back to bed. I'll leave the lunch I made for you to eat at school, so if you feel like eating, go ahead." Her mother spoke without so much as a glance at Kokoro, and started to get ready to go out.

If only her father were here, Kokoro thought painfully, he'd stand up for her. Both her parents worked, and since her father's job was further away, he left early in the morning. Most days when she woke up, he was already gone.

If she just stood here, she'd most likely get told off further, so Kokoro started to climb the stairs. From behind, like a final stab, she heard her mother let out another loud sigh.

BEFORE SHE KNEW it, it was three o'clock.

She had left her TV on, and it was now airing an afternoon talk show. After a segment highlighting celebrity scandals and news, it switched to an infomercial, and Kokoro finally hauled herself out of bed.

Why was she so sleepy? When she was at home, she always felt so much sleepier than she did at school.

She rubbed the sleepy dust from her eyes, wiped away the trace of drool from the corner of her mouth, turned off the TV and went downstairs. As she stood at the kitchen sink and washed her face, she realized how hungry she was.

She went to the dining room and opened the bento lunch her mother had made for her.

As she untied the ribbon holding the checked cloth around it, Kokoro thought of how her mother must have pictured her as she wrapped the bento, how she saw her enjoying the lunch at the School. Her chest tightened at the thought, and she wished she could apologize to her for not going.

There was a small Tupperware container too, on top of the bento, and when she opened it Kokoro found slices of kiwi fruit, one of her favorites. The bento itself was something she loved: three-colored *soboro* rice, minced cooked cod, ground chicken and egg in a lively design.

She took one bite and hung her head.

When they'd first visited the School, it had seemed like a fun place, so why couldn't she bring herself to go? This morning she'd thought that her stomachache had prevented her from going today only, but now that she'd wasted the entire day, she'd lost all desire to go at all.

THE KIDS AT the School were of both elementary and junior high age.

They all seemed like normal children, and none struck her as the sort who couldn't get on in public school. None of them were especially overweight or particularly depressed, and none of them seemed like losers no one wanted to hang out with.

The only difference was that the junior high kids weren't in school uniforms.

Two girls a little older than Kokoro had brought their desks together, facing each other, and the snatch of conversation she'd overheard—*That totally sucks. For sure, but you know . . .*—seemed no different from the chat at her junior high. When she overheard this little scene, her gut started to ache again, though she also found it strange that girls like these, seemingly so normal, had dropped out of school.

As Ms. Kitajima showed them around, one child came up to her complaining that "Masaya hit me!" The child had charm, and Kokoro imagined herself playing games with him if she started at the School. She could see it clearly.

Her mother said she'd stay in the office downstairs with the head of the school, while Kokoro went on a little tour.

Her mother never mentioned it, but Kokoro got the distinct impression that she'd been to the School a number of times herself, before Kokoro made her visit. The way the other teachers greeted her mother made it clear they'd met before.

Kokoro remembered how awkward and uncomfortable her mother had been when she first broached the topic of visiting the School, and realized how her mother, in her own way, was trying her best to be sensitive to Kokoro's feelings.

When Kokoro stood outside the office where her mother was waiting, she heard what she took to be the voice of the head of the school, saying, "Elementary school is such a pleasant, comforting place for most children, so it's not at all unusual for many to have trouble fitting in when they make the transition to junior high. Especially with a junior high like Yukishina No. 5, which has grown so large, what with other schools merging after the school restructuring. They now have one of the largest number of students."

Kokoro took a deep breath.

At least they're not touching on painful subjects, she thought.

And it was true—when she'd entered junior high, she'd suddenly gone from a school with two classes in each year to one with seven, and it had definitely thrown her. She barely knew anyone in her homeroom.

But that wasn't it.

That wasn't the reason why she *had trouble fitting in*.

This woman has no idea what I've been through, she thought.

Ms. Kitajima, standing beside Kokoro, seemed completely unfazed by what they'd overheard, and knocked firmly at the door. "Excuse me," she announced. The older head teacher and Kokoro's mother, seated opposite each other, turned simultaneously to face them.

Her mother was clutching a handkerchief, and Kokoro hoped she hadn't been crying.

IF SHE LEFT the TV on, she would end up watching it.

And if she did, she'd feel she'd accomplished something, even though she'd wasted the entire day.

Even if she was watching a program with a plot, a drama for instance, she realized that most of the time she couldn't recall the story. *What am I doing?* she'd wonder, and suddenly find the day drawing to a close.

On the screen they were interviewing a housewife on the street, and when she casually made the comment that she was out "while the kids are at school," Kokoro felt like this was a barbed rebuke directed straight at her.

KOKORO'S HOMEROOM TEACHER at Yukishina No.5, Mr. Ida, was a young man who still stopped by their house to check on her from time to time. Sometimes Kokoro would come downstairs to see him, sometimes not. "Mr. Ida's here," Kokoro's mum would announce. "Do you want to see him?"

Kokoro knew she really should talk to him, but on days when she told her mother she didn't want to, her mother never got upset. "All right, I'll talk to him today," she'd say, and show him into their living room.

"Today's really not a good day for her . . ." her mother would apologize, and Mr. Ida would say, "That's fine. No problem at all."

Kokoro hadn't expected them to let her get away with it, and it left her confused. She'd always believed she had to do what her teachers, her parents and other adults told her, but how they readily assented to her now made her finally understand: this was a real emergency.

Everyone's walking on eggshells because of me, she thought.

Occasionally her classmates from elementary school, Satsuki-chan and Sumida-san, would also come by to see how she was doing. They had moved into different classes now, and maybe their teacher had asked them to visit. But Kokoro felt embarrassed about skipping school, and she refused to see these long-time friends when they stopped by.

She really did want to see them—she felt there was so much she wanted to say—but making them feel obliged to come over made her uncomfortable, and that's how it turned out.

WHILE SHE WAS eating the bento, the phone rang. Just as she was wondering whether to get it, it clicked on to the answering machine.

"Hello? Kokoro? If you're there, will you pick up?"

Her mother's voice. Kind and calm. Kokoro hurriedly picked up the phone.

"Hello?"

"Kokoro? It's me."

Her voice was gentle now, not like this morning. She heard her mother laugh. Where was she? It sounded quiet around her, so maybe she'd stepped out of the office.

"You made me worried when you didn't answer. Are you all right? Are you eating the bento? How's your stomach?"

"I'm OK."

"Really? I was thinking that if you were still feeling ill, maybe you should go and see the doctor."

"I'm OK."

"I'll come home early today. It's going to be all right, Kokoro. We're just learning how to deal with this, so let's do our best to work through it, OK?"

Her mother sounded so cheerful, but all Kokoro could manage was a muttered "Sure" in response.

Her mother had been so cross this morning. So what had happened since? Maybe she'd got advice on the situation from one of her colleagues at work? Or perhaps she was having her own second thoughts about her earlier outburst and thought she'd call.

Do our best. Kokoro had no idea if she could live up to her mum's expectations, but she went ahead and agreed with her anyway.

IT WAS AFTER four now, and she couldn't stay downstairs.

The curtains in her room upstairs were, as in the morning, still closed.

As she waited to hear the now-familiar sound, she began to tense up. She could never get used to it. She tried watching the TV, with the sound turned down, to take her mind off it, but nevertheless she sat on her bed, anxiously waiting.

Any minute now.

There it was. She heard the mailbox in front of their house swing shut with a clang as someone dropped a letter inside.

"Ah—Tojo-san's here," she said to herself.

Moé Tojo-san, a girl from her class.

Tojo-san was a transfer student who'd joined their class at the end of April, after the semester had already begun. She'd arrived late due to some formalities to do with her father's job, apparently.

She was a pretty girl, good at sports too, and her desk in class was right next to Kokoro's. Moé's athletic build and long lashes took Kokoro's breath away—she reminded her of one of those beautiful French dolls people used to collect. Tojo-san didn't have any foreign blood, apparently, though she did have the attractive features often found among Eurasians.

The teacher assigned her to sit next to Kokoro for a reason—they were neighbors, with Tojo-san's house only two doors down from Kokoro's. His aim was that, as neighbors, they should get to know each other, and Kokoro hoped they would. And in fact, in the first two weeks after she began school, Tojo-san asked Kokoro if she could address her by the informal *Kokoro-chan*. They also walked to school and back home together.

Tojo-san had even invited Kokoro to come over to her house.

Her home had the same basic floorplan as Kokoro's, though she got the impression it had been designed with Tojo-san's family specifically in mind. The building materials were the same, as was the height of the ceilings, yet the ornaments on display in the hall, the pictures hanging on the wall, the light fixtures and color of the carpeting were all different. The identical construction and layout made these differences stand out all the more.

Tojo-san's home was so smart and stylish, with paintings just inside the entrance based on the fairy tales her father was apparently fascinated by.

Tojo-san's father was a college professor researching children's literature. On the wall, he had framed line-drawings from old illustrated books he'd picked up while in Europe. Scenes from stories Kokoro was familiar with: *Little Red Riding Hood*, *Sleeping Beauty*, *The Little Mermaid*, *The Wolf and the Seven Young Goats*, *Hansel and Gretel*.

"Pretty weird scenes, aren't they?" Tojo-san said. By this time Kokoro was addressing her, too, more familiarly, as Moé-chan.

"Papa collects drawings by this artist, including their illustrations for the Brothers Grimm books and illustrations from the Hans Christian Andersen stories."

The scenes didn't strike Kokoro as *weird*, exactly. The one from *The Wolf and the Seven Young Goats* was the well-known episode where the wolf breaks into the young goats' house and they scramble to escape. The drawing from *Hansel and Gretel*, too, was one of the more famous ones, where Hansel is walking in the forest, tossing out breadcrumbs. There was a witch in the picture, but that alone told you which story it was from.

Their houses were the same size inside, but for some reason Tojo-san's house seemed much more spacious.

In the living room were shelves lined with books in English, German and other languages.

Tojo-san took one out. "This one's in Danish," she said.

"Wow," said Kokoro. She could understand a bit of English, but Danish was totally alien.

"Andersen was a Danish writer," Tojo-san explained bashfully. "I can't read it either. But you can borrow it if you're interested."

16

Kokoro was thrilled. She might not be able to read Danish, but from the illustration on the cover she knew it had to be *The Ugly Duckling*.

"And there are lots of books in German, too," Tojo-san said. "The Brothers Grimm being German and all."

This made Kokoro even more excited. She knew many of the Grimms' fairy tales, and these foreign picture books seemed so stylish and cool.

"You should come over to my house next time," Kokoro said. "We don't have anything nice like these, though . . ." Kokoro really thought it would happen. At least she thought it should.

So why did things turn out the way they did?

Tojo-san ended up turning her back on Kokoro.

KOKORO QUICKLY WORKED out that Sanada and her little cohort had said something to Tojo-san about her.

One day in class, Kokoro went over to her. "Moé-chan?" she said, and Tojo-san looked up, obviously annoyed. *What do you want?* her expression said.

It was clear Tojo-san found Kokoro a nuisance. She no longer wanted to be in Kokoro's company, especially not in front of Sanada and her gang.

Tojo-san and Kokoro had been discussing which after-school club to join. But when the time came to meet, as they'd promised each other, Tojo-san strode right out of the classroom with Sanada and her crew. When they were out in the hallway Sanada said, loudly enough for Kokoro to hear, "I feel so sorry for those loners!"

As she slowly packed away her schoolbooks, ready to go home, she noticed the stares from the other kids, and Kokoro finally understood: the comment had been meant for her.

Loner, loner—the word whirled around in her head as she left the school building. She intentionally avoided the other kids' eyes. If that gang was going to be there, it was enough reason for her to lose all desire to check out any clubs.

Why did they pick on me like that? she wondered.

They gave her the silent treatment.

They whispered about her behind her back.

They told other girls not to have anything to do with her.

They laughed.

Laughed and laughed.

Laughing at her, Kokoro.

Her stomach ached and she locked herself in one of the toilet cubicles. She could hear Sanada giggling just outside. Break was nearly over, but she couldn't leave while they were outside. She was on the verge of tears, but steeled herself anyway, and emerged only to hear a little exclamation from the adjacent cubicle, as Sanada was coming out. She looked directly at Kokoro and grinned.

When she later heard from a classmate what she'd done, Kokoro blushed with shame. Wondering why Kokoro was taking so long, Sanada had crouched down in the adjacent cubicle and was watching her from below. When she pictured the scene that Sanada must have witnessed—her squatting there, underpants around her ankles—Kokoro thought she felt something collapse inside her.

The classmate who'd informed her, while lamenting how *horrible* it all was, also made Kokoro promise never to reveal that she'd been the one who told.

Kokoro stood there, frozen, dazed, totally crushed.

She had nowhere left to go where she could feel at peace.

This happened again and again—until *the incident* took place, and Kokoro made the fateful decision.

She stopped going to school.

EVEN AFTER KOKORO had dropped out, Tojo-san would stop by to deliver leaflets and notices from school.

She did it very matter-of-factly.

Kokoro had hoped they would still be friends, but Tojo-san merely placed the papers in her mailbox and never once rang the doorbell. Kokoro had witnessed this any number of times from her upstairs window; Tojo-san dumping the leaflets, as if fulfilling a duty, then hurrying off.

Now she watched idly as the figure in school uniform, a shirt with a blue-green collar and a dark red scarf, appeared. The same uniform she herself had worn in April.

Kokoro felt relieved at least that Tojo-san came by alone on her errand, probably because the other girls lived elsewhere.

Her teacher had probably told Tojo-san to stop by and see Kokoro, and Kokoro decided not to think about the possibility that Tojo-san was intentionally ignoring these instructions.

The mailbox clanged shut and Moé-chan left.

THERE WAS A full-length mirror in Kokoro's room.

She had got her parents to put it up as soon as she had chosen her room—an oval-shaped mirror with a pink stone frame. When she looked at herself in it now, she looked sickly, and she felt like crying. She couldn't stand to look at it anymore.

She quietly lifted a corner of the curtain to make sure that Tojo-san had left, then collapsed in slow motion back on her bed. With the sound down, the glow from the TV struck her as overpoweringly bright.

She thought about how, now that she'd stopped going to school, her father had taken away her video game console.

"If she doesn't go to school but still has video games, she'll never do any studying," he'd said to her mother. It looked like the next step was to take away her TV as well, but her mother had cut him short.

"Let's just wait and see," was her verdict.

At that moment, Kokoro had hated him, but now she wasn't so sure. She had the feeling he might be right—that if she did have video games to hand, that would be all she did all day. She certainly wasn't doing any studying at this point.

Keeping up with schoolwork in this new school—junior high—wasn't going to be easy. She felt lost, not knowing what to do.

The glow in her room was becoming really bright.

She casually raised her head from her pillow, thinking she should switch off the TV, and gasped.

The TV was not on.

She must have turned it off without realizing.

The light was coming from the full-length mirror near the door.

"What the—?"

She got off her bed and walked over to it without really thinking. Light seemed to be radiating from inside the mirror; it had become so blinding she could barely look.

She reached out a hand to touch it.

She realized a beat later that it might be hot, but the surface was still cool to the touch. With a flat palm, she pushed a little harder.

"Oh my god!" she screamed to herself.

Her palm was being sucked right into the mirror. The surface was soft, as if she were pushing against water. She was being dragged to the other side of the mirror.

In an instant, her body had been swallowed up into the light and was moving through a tunnel of chilled air. She tried calling her mother, but no voice emerged.

*   *   *

SHE WAS BEING dragged somewhere far away. Up or straight ahead, she couldn't tell.

"Hey you, wake up!"

The first sensation was of a cold floor beneath her cheek.

She had a splitting headache, and her mouth and throat were parched. Kokoro heard the voice again, but couldn't lift her head.

"Come on, wake up."

A girl's voice, a girl from the lower grades of elementary school by the sound of it.

Kokoro didn't know anyone that age. She shook her head, blinked, and sat up. She turned to look in the direction of the voice and gasped.

A weird-looking child was standing there, hand on hip.

"Are you awake now? Kokoro Anzai-chan?"

She was looking at the face of—a wolf.

The girl was wearing the sort of wolf mask usually found at temple festivals.

She was wearing an outfit that clashed with the wolf mask—a pink, lace-trimmed dress, the kind a girl would wear to her own piano recital, or to a wedding. She was like a live version of a Rika-chan doll.

And she—knows my name.

Kokoro's eyes darted around.

Where am *I?*

The shining emerald floor reminded her of something from *The Wizard of Oz*.

She felt perhaps she was in an anime, or in a stage play. Then she noticed a dark shape looming over her. She looked up and took a huge, deep breath. Her hand flew to her mouth.

She seemed to be in some sort of castle. A castle from a Western fairy tale, with a magnificent gate.

"*Congratulaaations!*" a voice sang. Behind the mask, Kokoro couldn't read the little girl's expression, or see her lips move.

"Kokoro Anzai-san, you have the honor of being a guest in this castle!" She spread her arms out wide and spun around.

The magnificent iron gate began to creak open.

KOKORO'S MIND WENT blank with fear. She had to get out.

The wolf girl continued to gaze at her, inscrutably. Kokoro hoped that, if this was some sort of dream, then the next time she looked, the girl would have vanished.

Something caught the edge of her vision. Kokoro slowly turned around: a mirror on the wall was shining.

Not the same oval-shaped mirror as the one in her bedroom, though it seemed a similar size. Its frame was ringed with multi-colored, teardrop-shaped stones. Kokoro scampered towards it. This mirror must surely connect up with her room, and if only she could pass through it, she might be able to go back.

Kokoro suddenly felt the weight of the little wolf girl clinging to her back, tackling her from behind with her spindly limbs. The force of her charge sent Kokoro tumbling face first back on to the emerald-colored floor.

"Don't you dare run away!" the little girl shrieked in her ear. "I've been interviewing six others all day, and you're the last. It's already four o'clock and I'm nearly out of time!"

"I really don't care!" Kokoro found her voice.

She was sure she sounded extremely harsh to this girl, so much younger than her, but Kokoro was feeling panicked.

Lying on the floor, she tried to pry the clinging girl off her back. She twisted her head sideways for another look at her surroundings.

It was like a Disney Cinderella castle, ripped from some fantasy.

This has got to be a dream, she thought. But the girl now pinning her to the floor with her legs around her waist had tangible weight and substance.

She continued crawling towards the shining mirror, when she felt the little wolf girl begin to pound her with her fists.

"What's *wrong* with you? Don't you want to know where you are? You could be on the brink of an adventure, and you're telling me you *really don't care*? Use your imagination for once in your life!"

"*I will not!*" Kokoro shouted back, nearly in tears. In her head she was thinking she could still get back. Pretend it never happened.

But she was becoming more certain: this was no dream.

The girl tightened her grip around Kokoro's waist, squeezing her sides so hard Kokoro could hardly breathe.

22

"As I was saying—we'll grant you a single wish. It will come true, even for a dullard like you. So listen to me!"

As I was saying, the girl had said, but this was the first time Kokoro had heard anything about a wish. She was too out of breath to respond. She tried as hard as she could to shake her off, shoving the wolf girl's snout away from her shoulder, where it was rubbing on her neck. Visible above the mask, the girl's hair was so soft, the head Kokoro had pushed against so tiny, it surprised Kokoro how much it really did feel like a very small child. Nevertheless, she gritted her teeth and shook her sideways to the floor.

She crawled further, then struggled to her feet, and reached out to touch the shining mirror. Within seconds, her hand was being sucked into the surface, as if passing through water.

"*Wait!*" a voice shouted, and she held her breath. Shutting her eyes, she pushed against the mirror with her whole body, and leapt into the light.

"Hey! You'd better come back tomorrow!"

She was assailed by a deafening, blurry noise. Then it faded away.

*　　*　　*

SHE BLINKED SEVERAL times, and found herself on the floor back in her room. The TV, her bed, the stuffed animals lined up along the window, the bookshelf, desk, chair, dressing table with hairbrush, clips, comb. Everything was in place.

She looked behind her—the full-length mirror was still on the wall.

It was no longer glowing.

It merely reflected her dazed expression.

Her heart was racing.

What on earth had happened? She instinctively reached out to the mirror, then quickly pulled her arm back. Perhaps someone was watching her from the other side. Maybe that little wolf girl's skinny hand would reach out and pinch her. She shuddered.

But the mirror remained still and mirror-like.

She glanced at the clock on the wall above the TV and drew in a quick breath. Her favorite soap had already started. More time had passed than she'd realized.

Perhaps it was just the clock that was fast? But sure enough, when she turned on the TV, the soap had been airing for some time. The clock was definitely not wrong.

What is going on?

She silently bit her lip. Then she stepped backwards from the mirror for more perspective, and gazed steadily into it.

Is it real?

In her PJs, she could still feel someone squeezing her sides.

Keeping her feet at a distance, but with arms outstretched and bending from the waist, she turned the mirror around to face the wall.

Her fingers were trembling.

"What is going on?" she said aloud. She remembered shouting at the top of her voice. She didn't talk to people much, so her voice was usually a little hoarse, but she remembered how clear it was, like a bell.

Is this what's called a daydream?

Or am I losing it?

AFTER SHE'D CALMED down enough to think, she realized what was a distinct possibility. *Oh no, oh no, oh no! What if staying at home all day is making me hallucinate? Then what?*

Your wish will come true.

The little girl had said: *As I was saying—we'll grant you a single wish. It will come true, even for a dullard like you.*

The words came back to her, loud and clear. Too distinct to be some hallucination.

"Hi, I'm back!"

Her mother's voice at the front door.

She'd be annoyed if she found her daughter watching TV, so

Kokoro grabbed the remote and switched it off. "Hi, Mum!" she called. Her mother had told her on the phone that she'd be back early, and sure enough she was.

Kokoro was about to go downstairs when she shot another glance at the mirror, but it was no longer shining.

HER MOTHER WAS in a good mood.

"I know you like gyoza, so would you like to help me make some from scratch?" Her mother placed her shopping bags on the floor. They were full of cans of milk, coffee, yoghurt, fish, sausage. She had been complaining that, with Kokoro at home so much, she had to restock the fridge more often.

"Mum?"

"Hmm?"

Her mother, decked out in business wear, slid off her shoes, unclipped the silver barrette in her hair, and headed into the kitchen.

Kokoro wanted to share what she'd experienced earlier, but as she contemplated her mother's back she knew she couldn't. It would probably ruin her mother's good mood, and anyway she wouldn't believe her. Kokoro herself still couldn't believe it.

"Um . . . never mind."

Kokoro skidded on the floor towards the kitchen to help put away the shopping.

"Don't worry," her mother said. And she gave her a gentle pat on the back. "I'm not upset about you not going to the School today." Kokoro realized with a start that her mother thought Kokoro was feeling guilty.

"It was your first time today, after all. But I do think it's a lovely place, so whenever you feel up to it, let me know. When I called this morning, the teacher you met said to come in whenever you're ready. She's really very nice, I think."

The events earlier had stirred Kokoro so much she'd completely forgotten about abandoning school.

It was now clearer than ever that her mum really hoped Kokoro would decide to go, and Kokoro began to feel extremely guilty.

"They said their next session is on Friday," her mother said.

"OK," Kokoro managed to say.

HER MOTHER HAD probably called her father, because he came home earlier than usual too, in time for dinner.

He didn't mention the School. "Wow, gyoza!" he said, as he sank down in his usual chair at the dining table.

"Darling," her mother said, "do you remember when Kokoro was little, how all she could eat whenever we had gyoza were the wrappers?"

"I do! She'd take out all the filling and I ended up eating the rest."

"So I started making the skins from scratch. I thought if she doesn't eat the filling, at least I could make some delicious wrappers for her."

Kokoro picked at her bowl of rice.

"Do you remember that, Kokoro?" her father asked.

Of course not. All she knew was the story they had made out of it, which they repeated every time they had gyoza.

"I don't remember," Kokoro said. She'd told her mother so many times that she couldn't eat such a huge portion, but she still insisted on loading her rice bowl to the brim.

Did her parents always want her to be the kid who only ate the skins of the gyoza?

They want me to be how I was before I became the girl who won't go to school.

KOKORO WONDERED WHAT she should do if the mirror began to glow again, but no light seemed to come from it now that it was turned towards the wall.

She felt a surge of relief. And yet, with the mirror lurking in the corner of her eye, its presence still weighed on her. Even after she'd gone to bed and closed her eyes, she turned over a few times to snatch a look.

I must be hoping for something, she thought vaguely as she drifted off.

You could be on the brink of an adventure, and you're telling me you really don't care? the little wolf girl had said, and truthfully Kokoro *was* hoping for something—at least a little. Hoping that this would be the beginning of something special.

The Chronicles of Narnia, which sat in the bookcase downstairs, crept into her mind. How could a portal into a different world *not* be appealing?

Maybe she shouldn't have run away. She may have wasted an opportunity. Of course, she would have preferred it if a rabbit had shown her around, like in *Alice in Wonderland,* not some shrill girl in a wolf mask.

She was beginning to feel expectant. So what *did* she want to happen, anyway? Now that the mirror wasn't glowing anymore, she suddenly began to regret what she'd done.

What if . . .

What if the mirror started to shine again?

Then she might decide to enter it one last time.

With these thoughts in mind, she melted into sleep.

THE NEXT MORNING, the mirror still wasn't shining.

Feeling a bit bolder, she gently turned it around to face her, but all she could see was her own reflection—in her PJs, with her messy bed-head hair.

As usual, Kokoro had breakfast with her mum before she left for work; she then washed up, before heading back upstairs. She would often spend the entire day in her PJs, but today she decided to change and even made an attempt to tidy her hair.

At nine o'clock the mirror began to shine.

It glittered like a pool of water reflecting the sunlight.

Breathing slowly, she reached out and slipped her hand inside. She pushed further until her whole body had been sucked in.

Her vision turned a dazzling yellow, and then white, as she passed into the other world.

*　　*　　*

INSTEAD OF THE emerald-green floor and the mighty gate of the previous visit, what she saw as her vision gradually cleared were two staircases and a large grandfather clock above them.

She blinked slowly.

It looked like the set for a Hollywood film: a grand foyer inside a mansion, with thick carpeted stairs like the ones Cinderella ran down in the film.

The staircases led up to a landing with the tall grandfather clock halfway along. Inside it, a large pendulum swung gently back and forth, revealing a sun and moon design.

Kokoro knew it—this was exactly the same castle she'd been to the previous day.

A group of people were gathered at the bottom between the staircases. She blinked at them in astonishment. They stared back in silence.

There were seven of them, including Kokoro. They appeared to be of a similar age.

"So you came."

The little wolf girl came bounding towards her, wearing as before a mask and a smart dress. She stood with her legs hip-width apart in front of Kokoro, her expression unreadable.

"You ran away yesterday but now you're back, eh?"

"Well, the thing is . . ."

With the others there—a mix of boys and girls—she felt less intimidated. She noticed how one of the boys, head bent, was holding what looked like a game console. Beside him stood a girl with glasses, and a plump-looking boy. Another boy leaning against the wall under the clock seemed at first glance quite good looking. Even in his sweats, he looked a bit like a celebrity.

As Kokoro inspected them, she began to feel as if she'd seen something she shouldn't have, and dropped her eyes quickly.

"Hello," a voice said, and she looked up. A tall girl with a ponytail was smiling at her. "We've also just arrived. We heard you ran off yesterday, so this child told us to wait here for you, so you wouldn't run away again."

"This child?"

"Call me the Wolf Queen," announced the child stiffly.

"OK, OK," the girl said. "The *Wolf Queen* told us to wait for you. She said there would be seven of us."

"You're the only one who ran off," the little girl—the Wolf Queen—said. "I thought it would be too chaotic if you all arrived at the same time, so I got you in one by one."

"But . . . what *is* this place?"

The girl gave a haughty little laugh.

"Well, I was trying to explain things to you when you ran off like a dumb fool."

"We're in the same boat as you," the ponytailed girl said. Kokoro had thought they were about the same age, but this girl sounded older. Calmer and more grown-up.

"She told us we're all in a castle that can grant us a wish."

This from someone else, a sharp, high-pitched voice. A sort of actorly voiceover tone that Kokoro might normally have found off-putting.

Kokoro turned to see the girl in glasses, sitting on the bottom step of one of the staircases. Her hair was in a bowl cut, and she wore a beige parka and jeans.

"Correct!" the Wolf Queen trilled loudly.

Kokoro thought she could hear a distant howl ringing in her ears. It made her freeze.

Eyes widening in alarm, they stared at the Wolf Queen.

29

Unconcerned, she carried on. "Deep inside this castle is a room none of you is permitted to enter. It is a Wishing Room. Only one person will eventually have access. Only one of you will have your wish come true. One Little Red Riding Hood."

"Little Red Riding Hood?"

"You are all lost Little Red Riding Hoods," the Wolf Queen said. "From now until next March, you will need to search for the key that will unlock the Wishing Room. The person who finds it will have the right to enter and their wish will be granted. In the meantime, every one of you must hunt for it. Do you follow me?"

Kokoro did not know what to say. The others exchanged silent glances.

"Don't expect someone else to answer!" the Wolf Queen squealed suddenly. "If you have something to say, then speak up!"

"I do." It was the bold, ponytailed girl who'd first welcomed Kokoro. "I'd like a bit more on this," the girl said. "How can a wish come true? Also, I just don't get it: why have you even called us here? Where *are* we? I mean—is this real? And who are *you*?"

"Yeeee!" The Wolf Queen covered her ears at this sudden barrage of questions. Not the wolf ears, but her own, human ears. "You people have no imagination. At all. Can't you simply be satisfied that you've been chosen as heroes in a story?"

"It has nothing to do with being satisfied."

This not from the ponytailed girl but from one of the boys. Since Kokoro had arrived, a boy had been perched on the left-hand staircase, absorbed in his game console. He had a booming voice, and a defensive look in his eyes behind thick glasses.

"I also don't get it," he said. "Yesterday the mirror in my bedroom suddenly started to shine and now we've ended up here. You need to tell us what's going on."

"Ah, a boy has finally found his voice," the Wolf Queen cackled. "It takes boys longer to open up. So now I'm expecting great things of you."

The boy frowned and glared at her. The Wolf Queen was unfazed.

"We make selections periodically," she said, trying to sound managerial. She gave a forced cough. "You're not the only ones to have entered the castle. At various times we've invited other lost Little Red Riding Hoods. And quite a lot of them in the past have had their wish come true. You should consider yourselves lucky to be selected."

"Can I go home?"

A boy at the top of the stairs who'd remained silent until now had stood up. A lean, quiet boy, his pale face and freckled nose reminded Kokoro of Ron in *Harry Potter*.

"No, you cannot!" the Wolf Queen shrieked, and the air was disturbed by another howl. The boy suddenly leaned backwards, as if struck by a blast of air.

"Let me finish," the Wolf Queen said, glaring at him. "Hear me out before you decide to do anything. First, your entry and exit will be through the mirrors in your bedrooms or in the castle. From now on, you'll come straight here, to this foyer. To prevent anyone from attempting to flee."

The Wolf Queen looked meaningfully at Kokoro, and she felt everyone's eyes on her. A wave of shame flooded through her.

"The castle will be open from now until the thirtieth of March. If you don't find the key by then, the entire castle will vanish and you will never have access ever again."

"So—what if we *do* find it?"

This was another new voice, and the Wolf Queen turned towards it. The boy gave a small yelp and crouched behind the banister of the stairs. Only his chubby fingers were visible.

"So if someone finds the key and their wish is granted, then the mirrors won't connect up here anymore?" he carried on bravely from his hiding place.

"Once the Wishing Room has been unlocked, it's game over. The castle will immediately close down." The Wolf Queen nodded sagely at her own words. "I should add that the castle is open every day from

9 a.m. to 5 p.m., Japan time. So you absolutely must get back through the mirrors by five. If you stay in the castle any later, you'll face a truly horrible penalty."

"A penalty?"

"A simple punishment. You'll be eaten by a wolf."

"*What?!*" The group gaped at the Wolf Queen.

You're joking, aren't you? Kokoro wanted to ask but couldn't.

"Eaten? You mean—by *you?*"

A chilly silence fell over them.

With a moment to think, a new possibility occurred to Kokoro. Yesterday the Wolf Queen had said to her, *It's already four o'clock and I'm nearly out of time.* When she got back home, her favorite TV soap had already started. The hands on her clock had moved forward. Meaning that while they were in the castle, time had passed in the real world as well.

The castle was open from nine to five. Until 30 March.

It sounded a lot like a school timetable.

Kokoro scanned the faces of her peers:

The handsome boy in the sweats.

The girl with the ponytail who seemed to have her act together.

The girl in glasses, with the high-pitched anime voice.

The brash boy absorbed in the game console.

The quiet boy with freckles who reminded her of Ron.

The meek, chubby boy hiding behind the banister.

Seven of them altogether.

Kokoro thought about the question posed by the ponytailed girl. *Why have you even called us here?* Kokoro didn't know, but she was sure everyone here had one thing in common.

Not a single one of them was going to school.

"ABOUT THAT—PENALTY you mentioned."

It was the ponytailed girl.

"Being eaten by a wolf." She seemed much calmer than the rest. "When you say *eaten*, do you mean this literally?"

The Wolf Queen gave an exaggerated nod. "That I do. You'll be swallowed up whole. But don't be tempted to do anything you've read in a story, such as calling your mum to come and rip open the wolf's stomach and stuff it with rocks. Just make sure you're very, very careful."

Her words only confused them further.

"Are *you* going to eat us?"

"I'll leave that to your imagination, but a huge wolf will indeed appear. A powerful force will punish you. And once it's triggered, there's nothing anyone can do to stop it. Not even me."

The Wolf Queen looked at each of them in turn.

"And if one of you is punished, each of you will be held equally responsible. If one of you is barred from going home, then none of you can leave. So watch your step."

"Are you saying all the others will be eaten, too?"

"I suppose I am," the Wolf Queen said vaguely and with a small wave of the hand. "Anyway, stick to the opening hours. Don't sneak in here when the castle is closed to search for the Wishing Key."

As the Wolf Queen continued to lecture them, it seemed more and more as if the wolf lips on the mask were actually moving.

"We've barely met, but we're still supposed to be responsible for each other?" the girl with the glasses and bowl cut said in her high-pitched voice. "We don't actually know each other, but we have to trust everyone?"

"Correct. So do your best to get on. I leave it up to you."

Silence.

"Will you be here when the castle is open?" Kokoro screwed up her courage to ask a question for the first time. The Wolf Queen spun around, stared at her, and Kokoro flinched.

"I'll be here, and not here. I won't be here all the time. Call on me and I'll come out. Consider me your caretaker and supervisor."

Kind of an arrogant supervisor, thought Kokoro.

Someone asked another question.

"The thirtieth of March is a mistake, isn't it? There are thirty-one days in March."

This was from the boy in sweats, the only one who hadn't spoken yet. The boy that Kokoro had secretly thought so good looking. Like a character in a manga for girls.

The Wolf Queen shook her head several times.

"No, you heard correctly. The castle will remain open until the thirtieth of March."

"Why?" the boy asked. "Is there a reason?"

"Not really. If anything, the thirty-first of March is when the castle closes for maintenance. You see that sometimes, no? *Closed for Maintenance?*"

The castle was the Wolf Queen's home, yet she seemed so detached from it. The handsome boy seemed unconvinced, and was about to add something, but then he looked away and muttered, "OK."

"Is that actually real—a wish coming true?"

This time it was the boy fiddling with the game console. He turned his body moodily towards the Wolf Queen. Kokoro looked curiously at the game console, since she didn't recognize it, though she couldn't tell for sure from where she was standing. The boy's tone had a scathing ring to it.

"You're saying if we find the key, *any* wish can come true? We can use the kind of weird supernatural power that got us here to make it come true? Like we can become a wizard, or enter a video game or something? Is *that* what you're saying?"

"I am, though I wouldn't advise it. I don't know anyone happy who wished for any of those. Enter the world of a game, and the enemy might kill you in an instant. But if that's what you want, feel free."

"You're so downbeat, aren't you? If I go into Pokémon, it won't be me doing the fighting, it'll be a monster."

Still clutching his game console, the boy said this so matter-of-factly it was hard to tell how serious he was. He nodded to himself.

"And then there are certain things you need to be aware of while you're in the castle," the Wolf Queen continued, surveying her group a little more closely.

"Only the seven of you are allowed entry. If you try to bring someone with you, they won't get in. So don't attempt to get any outside help to find the key."

"What about telling other people about the castle?"

This, again, from the good-looking boy. The Wolf Queen turned to face him. She'd answered all their questions so smoothly, but this one seemed to stump her.

"If you think you can talk about it with others, go ahead and try." She paused. "If you think anyone will ever believe you. The problem is, people will think you're weird. You're the only ones who can get in, so it will be very hard to prove it exists."

"But we can go through the mirror in front of someone, can't we? If someone actually saw their kid disappear into a shining mirror, they'd be worried enough to believe it's true." This from the boy with the game console.

The Wolf Queen sighed. "You said *kid*. So you're talking about getting your parents to help you. Not your friends, but adults?"

"Yeah."

"In that case, when you get back home the adults will probably smash the mirror. Or else they will forbid you to go through again. And if they do, then it's over for all of you. None of you will be able to come here again, and the search for the key will be terminated. For my sake, I'm not in favor of you using the portal in front of anyone else. As a security precaution."

"You're saying that when someone else is around, we shouldn't enter the mirror?"

"Well put." The Wolf Queen nodded emphatically at the handsome boy's question. Her large wolf ears flapped. "As long as you stick to the rules, then you can do whatever you want while you're here. Talk, study, read books, play video games. And I'll permit you to bring in lunch and snacks."

"Y-you mean there's nothing to eat here?"

Kokoro was surprised to hear the chubby boy hiding behind the banister speak.

He did look overly fond of food, but she was amazed that he was brave enough to ask about it.

"No, there isn't," the Wolf Queen said. "The truth is, you're all food for the wolves. So eat up and put a little meat on your bones."

The Wolf Queen gazed silently for a moment and then jerked her chin up.

"Introduce yourselves," she ordered. "Over the next year you'll be seeing a lot of each other. So go ahead and get to know each other."

Easy to say, Kokoro thought, and they all exchanged looks.

She was anxious that the Wolf Queen might scream at them again not to *look to each other for answers*! She ducked her head, fearful that the Wolf Queen would let out another howl.

"Wolf Queen, do you think you might leave us alone for a moment?" the ponytailed girl said. "We'll get on well, don't worry. We've all been thrown together here, so of course we want to get on. But now we'd like to work things out on our own."

"Well . . . all right." The Wolf Queen didn't seem particularly irritated. She tilted her masked face sideways. "Take your time. I'll be back in a while."

She raised her arms as if she were going to float away, flapped them gently up and down, and then, in the blink of an eye, she vanished.

The seven were left speechless.

"Did you see that?"

"Yep. She disappeared."

"What the—?"

"Whoa."

Exclamations flew hard and fast between them.

As luck would have it, her absence meant Kokoro could speak up.

"I'LL START. I'M Aki," the ponytailed girl said.

They sat in a circle in the foyer between the double staircase, the grandfather clock looming over them.

The girl's tone was a little awkward, and Kokoro looked at her more closely.

She gave her first name. No last name.

"I'm in ninth grade. Nice to meet you."

"Very nice to meet you," Kokoro said, keeping it polite because she was slightly in awe of the older girl.

Kokoro had never experienced this before—a group of kids introducing themselves so formally.

Usually, when introductions were made there was a homeroom teacher or other adult present. This April, just after she'd started junior high, when students were introducing themselves and one of the boys near the beginning of the register announced his name before sitting back down in a hurry, their teacher, Mr. Ida, had teased him. "Come on," he said. "You can give us more than that, can't you? Tell us your name, the elementary school you've come from. And a few words about what you like to do in your spare time." After that the other kids mentioned baseball, basketball and other things they enjoyed. When Kokoro's turn came, she said, *Karaoke*. She thought if she'd said she liked reading, the others would label her an introvert, so when several girls ahead of her said they liked karaoke, she copied them.

Now with their so-called caretaker, the Wolf Queen, absent, no one urged anyone to add any extra detail. The only one who looked like she might do so was Aki, the girl who had already introduced herself, but since she merely said her first name and grade and nothing else, the others followed suit. It was enough.

"I'm Kokoro," Kokoro said boldly. She might not be able to

37

remember everybody's name immediately, she thought. Even introducing herself to such an intimate group was enough to get her stomach churning. "I'm in seventh grade. Nice to meet you all."

"I'm Rion," the handsome boy said next. "People tell me it sounds like a foreign name, but I'm Japanese. It's written with the *ri* in *rika*, science, and the *on* that means sound. I'm into football. And I'm in seventh grade. Nice to meet you."

Seventh grade. Like Kokoro.

Kokoro heard a smattering of *nice to meet you's*, and she could tell the situation felt awkward. Would they all have to explain which characters their names were written in, and their hobbies and things?

But Aki didn't seem to want to add anything to her introduction, and Kokoro wasn't about to take the lead either. Casually mentioning at this point that she was into karaoke would no doubt backfire.

"Hi, I'm Fuka. I'm in eighth grade."

This from the girl in glasses. Once you got used to her high voice, it wasn't so bad. Each word sounded bright and crisp. A couple of seconds of silence followed as she seemed to consider things, but then she broke it with a straightforward *nice to meet you all*.

"I'm Masamune. I'm in eighth grade."

This was the boy with the game console. He stumbled on, not meeting anyone's eye. "I'm tired of everybody always saying Masamune sounds like a samurai warlord's name, or the name of a famous sword, or a brand of sake or something. It's actually my real name."

He was the only one who didn't add a *nice to meet you*. The others lost their chance to respond, and the tall boy seated beside him took a breath, ready to speak. He was the one who looked like Ron in *Harry Potter*, and who'd earlier stood up and asked if he could go home.

"My name's Subaru, OK? Nice to meet you. I'm in ninth grade."

Kind of an oddball, was Kokoro's take on him. Otherworldly, you might say. She'd never heard any boy she knew end a sentence like that, with a challenging *OK?* But Subaru seemed the type who could say that and get away with it. He wasn't like any boy she'd met before.

"Ureshino," a small voice said.

This from the chubby boy who'd worried whether there was anything to eat.

"Eh?" the others responded.

He repeated himself. "Ureshino. It's my surname. It's a bit unusual. Nice to meet you."

His bashfulness struck a chord with Kokoro. She immediately found herself wanting to ask him which characters his name was written with, but she stopped herself.

"Really? So how's that written?" a casual voice asked, and Kokoro gulped. It was Rion.

Ureshino took a deep breath. He didn't seem to mind the question at all.

"The *ureshi* part is written with the character for *ureshii*—happy. And the *no* is the character in *nohara*—field."

"Whoa—lots of strokes in writing those characters. I don't even know how to write the first one. What year in school are you supposed to learn to write *ureshii?* Must be a pain during tests when you have to write your name at the top."

"Yeah, it takes so long to write it out that sometimes I've got less time to actually do the test."

Ureshino grinned, the very image of happiness. The mood lightened. "I'm in seventh grade," he added. "Nice to meet you."

"So we're all in middle school," Aki said, looking around and nodding. She seemed to be in charge. "I know the Wolf Queen might be listening in, but do you have any idea why we were brought here?"

Aki's voice was starting to sound a bit tense, and quivered slightly.

"Nope," Masamune said, not skipping a beat. "Not a clue."

"That's what I thought." Aki nodded. Kokoro felt a wave of relief herself.

Introductions over, they fell silent and looked awkwardly away.

They'd all spoken in different ways, but Kokoro was sure they had all come to the same realization. None of them was going to school.

None of them dared broach the topic.

But even if they didn't put it into words, it clearly weighed on everyone's minds.

The silence lingered until—

"Have you finished?"

The Wolf Queen, standing hands on hips at the top of the stairs. How long she'd been watching, no one knew. There were a couple of startled yelps as they turned to look at her.

"Come on, don't behave like you've just seen a monster."

It felt like that, though no one said it.

"So, are you all ready?" she asked.

Ready?

Did she mean ready to begin their search for the key, and make their wish come true? There was only one key. Only one person's wish could come true. Kokoro knew they were all thinking the same thing.

As if seeing through them all, the Wolf Queen said, "Well, that's it for today, then. You can do whatever you like now. Stay in the castle, take a stroll around, go home. It's up to you.

"Oh, and one other thing," she said. And the words that came next, so softly and gently, calmed Kokoro.

"You each have your own individual room here in the castle, so feel free to use it. You'll find your name plate outside, so check it out later."

June

MAY WAS OVER and June had arrived. Kokoro woke up to the sound of raindrops striking her window, the sort of weather she didn't mind at all.

When she was attending school, she'd go by bicycle, and on rainy days she would wear her school-approved raincoat. She liked its damp smell when she spread it out to dry in the evening. Some people might not like that smell—a mixture of water and dust, apparently—but Kokoro was fond of it.

On an afternoon back in April, she had been unlocking her bike at the end of the school day, and as she breathed in the rain, she turned to the students making their way home, and without thinking she said, "It smells like rain."

Later she saw Sanada and her little cohort lifting their raincoats theatrically to their noses and saying with a smirk, "Oh—it smells like rain." Kokoro froze in horror. They must have been spying on her.

And what was so wrong with liking the rain?

School wasn't a place where you could speak honestly.

SHE GOT OUT of bed, and made her way downstairs. Today when Kokoro again told her mother that she didn't want to go to the new School, she didn't get frustrated. Outwardly, at least, she kept her voice calm.

"Another stomachache, is it?" she asked. Kokoro's stomach really *did* hurt, and she couldn't understand why her mother had to use that tone of voice, as if she were faking illness.

"Um," she replied in a small voice, to which her mother said, "Well then, you'd better go back to bed."

Her mother couldn't bring herself to look at her.

Last month she had not managed to go to the School even once.

There were so many things she wanted to say to her mother—that she wasn't pretending to be ill, that she didn't hate the School at all. She felt she needed to open up about all her feelings, and explain them in detail, but she was afraid that if she stayed in her mother's company any longer, her mother would explode. She didn't want to hear her mother on the phone calling the School to explain yet another absence, and so, carrying her pain alone, she trudged back upstairs.

Curled up on her bed, she heard the sound of the front door slamming as her mother left for work.

She would always call out a cheery "See you later!" when she left, but today she walked out without a word. Kokoro slowly closed her eyes. In the silence of the empty house, she could hardly breathe.

After a while, she slid downstairs and peeked into the dining room. The usual bento and water bottle were waiting for her on the table.

When she went back upstairs, the rain still pounding on the window and filling the room with its wet smell, the mirror had begun to shine.

The entrance to the castle was open, inviting Kokoro inside. Kokoro found herself recalling the events of the day she'd last been in the castle.

* * *

AS SUGGESTED BY the Wolf Queen, they were all keen to check out their allocated room.

When Kokoro found hers, her jaw dropped.

42

It was so much more spacious than her own at home: thick plush carpeting, a rolltop desk with carved flower designs, and a wide bed. "Wow!" she squealed. She gave the bed a gentle pat, before perching on its edge. The mattress was soft and welcoming.

On one side was a bay window with velvet curtains and white latticework—a window like an empty birdcage she'd only ever seen in a Western fairy tale.

Up against the wall was a bookcase, a huge one.

Kokoro caught her breath. She thought she caught a whiff of old paper. The musty smell that hit your nostrils whenever you ventured into the far corner of a tiny bookstore, the place where few people ever went. A smell she loved.

The bookcase covered one entire wall and reached almost to the ceiling. As Kokoro sat on her bed contemplating her room, she felt a little dizzy.

Did everyone have a bookcase like hers?

Just then she thought she could hear the tinkle of a piano.

She perked up her ears.

Someone somewhere was hesitantly picking out a tune. It was a piece she recognized. *Someone must have a piano in their room.*

She heard a sudden bang, as if someone had struck the keys in frustration. Kokoro flinched. The performance was obviously over.

A teddy bear sat at the top of her bed, nestled among the oversized pillows. She picked it up and went over to the books; she ran her fingers along their spines, wondering if she would ever get to read them. She pulled out a couple. To her surprise, they were all in foreign languages. She might be able to read the ones in English a little, but the rest were in French, German or something else. Most of the books were fairy tales. She peered closely at the covers: *Cinderella, Sleeping Beauty, The Snow Queen,* and *The Wolf and the Seven Young Goats* by the Brothers Grimm. One cover showed an old man and a woman heaving up a huge turnip, which she figured must be the folk tale *The Enormous Turnip.* The Wolf Queen had called them all *Little Red*

Riding Hoods, and when Kokoro spied what looked like a German edition of the book, she felt a chill run through her.

She considered borrowing a book to take home. She might be able to get through an English one, with the help of a dictionary.

She carried on browsing.

She'd seen some of the more striking covers before. They might not be exactly the same, but they reminded her of the pictures on the wall, the warm feeling oozing within her, when she spent time at Tojo-san's house. She felt a stab of pain in her heart. *You can borrow any book you like*, her friend had said to her. Now Kokoro knew that would never happen.

She couldn't help feeling a touch disappointed that her room didn't have a piano. Even if they put one in here, Kokoro couldn't play it very well. The piano was no doubt for someone who could play it decently. Probably one of the two other girls—ponytailed Aki, or Fuka, the girl in glasses.

She sank back on to the bed and gazed up at the ceiling, tracing its intricate flower pattern. *This is so cool*, she thought. She took a deep breath and closed her eyes.

After a few moments, she felt impatient to see the rest of the castle, and jumped up to explore.

Along the walls of the hallway were the largest landscape paintings she'd ever seen, illuminated by candlelight. After wandering for a few minutes, she encountered a sort of parlor with a cold fireplace. There were numerous rooms beyond, and she seemed to be entirely alone. After a while, she decided to revisit the staircases in the foyer. There, leaning languidly against the wall, was the Wolf Queen, all by herself.

"Where is everyone?" Kokoro asked.

"They went home," replied the Wolf Queen.

Kokoro was taken aback. It hadn't been very long, yet they'd all left, without saying a word.

"All of them, together?"

"Everyone went home on their own. Though I imagine some might be back again later today."

When Kokoro heard she hadn't been left out, she breathed a sigh of relief. These were kids who did things on their own.

She should follow suit, she thought, and go back to her house, too. But there was nothing to do there. She considered starting a search for the key immediately, but didn't like how greedy that might look. She really had no idea how serious the others were about it.

After a while, Kokoro reached her hands into her shining mirror. Slipping through the membrane of light, she glanced back briefly. The staircases were still there, but the Wolf Queen had vanished.

*   *   *

KOKORO DIDN'T VENTURE back through the mirror for a while.

She'd stand in front of it and bite her lip.

"Should I?" she whispered, rooted to the spot, an arm's length away. Maybe she was being a coward, but after five o'clock, when the mirror stopped shining, a wave of relief swept through her. But she also realized she had a secret hope that someone—anyone—would invite her through.

Had the group got together again yet? If they had, then Kokoro would be an outsider. After the introductions, she thought she might make friends with a couple of them, but with each passing day, she felt less inclined to visit. *This is exactly like not being able to go to school,* she thought. And kind of like not feeling able to attend the alternative School her mother was so keen on.

But she couldn't get that beautiful, comfortable room out of her mind.

She also liked the fact that no one in the group had mentioned that they were all refusing to go to school. She'd never joined one of those internet off-line get-togethers, but she got the sense this was similar, how none of them had gone into detail about themselves.

They'd shared names, but that was it. No one had really said anything about who they were, or where they were from.

That made things easier, but the fact remained that she was feeling a slight hurt somewhere deep inside.

Only with kids who had gone through similar experiences could she really open up about what had happened, and how it made her feel. And now she'd gone and closed the door on that opportunity, and it was painful.

Even though they'd only met once, Kokoro felt an odd closeness to them all.

She stowed the bento and water bottle her mum had prepared for her into a tote bag, and took it upstairs. Then she changed into a clean set of clothes, gave her face a thorough wash, and stood before the shining mirror.

She began to feel a touch anxious. What if one of them had already found the key? She breathed a wish that no one had found it yet.

Because Kokoro had her own wish, and she desperately wanted it to come true.

That Miori Sanada would vanish from the face of the earth.

How wonderful it would be if this girl—who'd humiliated her for liking the smell of rain—had never been born. With the palms of her hands she gently touched the mirror's cool surface, and pushed through.

⁕　⁕　⁕

IT FELT LIKE being lifted up, bodily, into a pool of light. She held her breath.

She dared to open her eyes again and found the same tall grandfather clock, flanked by the staircases. In front, a bright stained-glass window.

She clutched her tote bag and scanned the room. There had been seven of them. Now there was no one. She found herself slightly relieved to be alone.

46

She turned around and looked at the mirror she'd just slipped through, now beaming out all the colors of the rainbow, like sunlight reflecting off an oily puddle. Two of the other six mirrors lined up in the castle foyer were likewise shining. The one on the far right, and the second one from the left. The remaining four appeared like ordinary mirrors, reflecting the staircases and, she realized with a start, herself.

Maybe the mirrors only shine when the kids are actually in the castle?

She sensed that the Wolf Queen might suddenly turn up to explain things, but when she spun around again, she was still alone.

She felt a little deflated, but suddenly a thought occurred to her. The mirror she'd emerged from was the one in the middle of the row of seven. There were no name plates to remind them whose mirror was whose. She thought she'd better remember which was hers, something she hadn't noticed before.

In the silence, she thought she heard a noise.

So somebody *was* coming.

She set off cautiously in the direction of the sound. It seemed to be coming from deeper in the heart of the castle, and it didn't seem to fit. It wasn't the tinkle of the piano from before, or the murmur of voices. It wasn't a sound that belonged.

If she wasn't mistaken, it sounded like the electronic beeping of a video game.

It led her to another room with a fireplace, sofa and table, the sort of space that in an ordinary house might be called the living room.

In a castle perhaps it was better to call it a drawing room, or the parlor. She wasn't exactly sure what the right word was, but it struck her as the sort of room you brought guests into, where people gathered.

The door was open so she walked straight in.

Her eyes alighted on two boys.

Boys she'd been introduced to before—Masamune, the abrupt one with glasses, and Subaru, the lean one with an unusual air about him. There was an old TV set, cumbersome and heavy, which she figured they must have carried in with them, and playing on the screen was a video game that Kokoro recognized. An action game based on the Three Kingdoms of China, where you sliced and diced your enemies.

"Whoa," she said in a small voice.

Since she spent so much time at home, she had had hours to search high and low for all the games her father had removed from her grasp—in his study, in her parents' bedroom, the kitchen, the patio, everywhere—but he'd done such a good job of hiding them.

I should have brought some of my stuff too, she thought, and as she stood there, tote bag in hand, gazing into the room, the two boys seemed to sense her presence. They glanced over in her direction, but Masamune quickly turned back to the TV screen. "Damn it!" he said, "my health bar went down. I'm gonna die," as if he was talking to himself. Kokoro realized he'd spotted her but had pretended he hadn't. She couldn't decide what to say to them, and no words came out.

It was Subaru who came to her rescue.

As before, he struck her as a little otherworldly, and as Masamune intoned he was *gonna die*, Subaru used the opportunity to put down his own game console, and turn to Kokoro.

"So you came, eh? Welcome!" Then he said, "It doesn't feel right to say that. This isn't actually my house, and all of us have the same right to it."

"He-hello," she said, a little unsteadily.

"Hey, Subaru!" Masamune called.

The way he called Subaru using just his first name—no *san* or *kun* attached—made her tense up. It was just as she suspected—in her absence they'd become friendly enough to address each other so casually.

Masamune ignored Kokoro. "Hey, don't give up halfway. What'm I supposed to do if I die because of you, eh?"

"Sorry, sorry." Subaru gave Masamune a look. "Do you want to sit down?" he asked Kokoro. "Will you play with us?"

"Did you bring those games with you?"

"Um. Masamune did."

Even hearing his own name wasn't enough to take Masamune away from his game. His eyes remained glued to the screen as he weighed up his controller. Then he spoke. "Talk about heavy.

"This old TV set was the one my dad had put away in the shed," he said. "He'd forgotten all about it, and I figured he wouldn't notice it's missing so I lugged it over here. But boy, you really want to kick the thing, it's so damn heavy. The console is also old; we weren't even using it anymore."

He got this out in a monotonic stream of words, and Kokoro wasn't sure who he was talking to. She managed a simple, "Oh, I see." Then: "Are you two the only ones here today?"

"For now, yes. Though someone might come later. We've been here every day, but the others sometimes come, and sometimes don't." Subaru smiled, a smile that to Kokoro seemed graceful. "You haven't been over for a while, have you, Kokoro-chan? I thought maybe you weren't interested."

"Well, I . . ."

She didn't know where to start. She felt some implied criticism for turning up all of a sudden, and was about to say something, but Subaru spoke first. "Sorry," he said. "I called you Kokoro-*chan*. It's a bit cheeky."

"No, it's OK."

She had only given them her first name so far, so it was understandable. He really *was* an unusual guy after all. Not that she liked Masamune's way of ignoring her, though that did seem like a more common reaction for a boy.

She took a closer look around the room.

On the wall hung a large painting of a light-blue lake and rugged forest—and a mighty set of knight's armor, which took her by

49

surprise. She was startled, too, by the stuffed deer's head and antlers, which reminded her for a second of the Wolf Queen's mask. She'd seen and read about these things in anime and fairy tales, but never seen them with her own eyes.

The two boys seemed settled on the thick patterned carpet, engrossed in their game.

Subaru picked up on her silence. "You OK?" he asked her.

Masamune had already restarted the game and was glued to the TV. "*Yes!*" he shouted at the screen. Then: "Are you *kidding* me?"

"Aren't you going to look for the key?" Kokoro asked.

"Hm?"

At this rate Masamune would never speak, no matter how long she waited. So she made up her mind to speak to him first.

"Masamune-kun, you sounded as though you wanted to find the key to the Wishing Room. So I thought maybe everyone had been looking for it while I wasn't here, and perhaps had found it already."

"But if I'd found it, we wouldn't be able to come back. Because then the castle would close up."

Masamune had become more talkative. He still wouldn't look at her, though.

"So that means no one's found it yet, right?" he went on. "I looked for it myself quite a bit, but nothing so far."

He spoke bluntly, but at least he had answered her question.

"I see."

"He looked pretty hard for it, did Masamune," Subaru chuckled.

"Shut up," Masamune muttered.

"I helped too, but we haven't found anything yet. So we decided to play video games instead. We started in Masamune's room, but then Aki-chan suggested we play where everybody can join in, instead of shutting ourselves away in a room."

"I see," Kokoro said again.

"They haven't come yet today, but Aki-chan and the others have been over now and then."

"Aren't you interested in the Wishing Room, Subaru-kun?" Kokoro was struck by what Subaru had said about *helping* Masamune.

"Me? Um, not really," he said. "To be honest, I'm not all that interested in having a wish come true. Looking for the key sounds fun, like solving a riddle, but actually I'm more interested in Masamune's games."

Subaru gestured at Masamune, dueling with the TV screen.

"I don't have any games myself," Subaru went on. "I've hardly ever played any, and when he let me try, I was surprised how much fun it is. Plus, don't you think this castle's wicked?"

"That's what I'm saying. We could just find the key and keep hold of it, and then we're good as long as we don't open the Wishing Room until next March."

Finally, Masamune was looking up—but he addressed Subaru.

"Then the castle won't close, and we can use it right up to the very end. That suits me, but others might want to have their wish come true straight away, and if they get hold of the key first, then it'll all be over. Which is why it'd be better if I find it, so I got Subaru to help me out. That way we can play video games here until March."

"So apart from you, Masamune-kun, are the others looking for the key, too?" Kokoro was confused. She'd never thought about it that way—to find the key but keep the castle open until the penultimate day in March. Masamune shot her an irritated look.

"It seems like it," Subaru said. "Nobody really says so out loud, but it seems as if everyone's after it. Nobody's found it, though. The two of us looked in all the obvious places—in the drawers, inside the candlesticks, under the rugs, behind the paintings, all over the place—but no sign of it so far. We've still to look in all our rooms.

"We checked with the Wolf Queen, didn't we? And she said she couldn't do anything to give anyone an advantage. Each room is a totally private space. There might be a clue somewhere though, and she said we should talk that over with each other."

"A clue?" Kokoro asked.

"There are hints placed all around the castle, and she said we should *do our best to find them.*"

Masamune imitated the Wolf Queen. Kokoro knew now that the Wolf Queen had spoken to the others again since her last time.

"Do you want to search for it too, Kokoro-chan? The key that'll make a wish come true?"

"Well, I . . ."

After Subaru had declared so calmly that he wasn't that interested, she hesitated to respond. She didn't want to be seen as a rival in the search for the key.

Which is why, when she answered, she was a bit vague. "I was just wondering."

Just then Masamune came out with something startling.

"So what I'm thinking is, she hasn't been into the castle for a while because she's one of those students who's still going into school. So why should she turn up today? Is she pretending to be sick? Has she taken a day off?"

"Eh?"

Her eyes widened in surprise. He seemed to be directing his words to her. By *she*, he must mean Kokoro.

Masamune looked at her properly for the first time. He'd paused the game, and the screen showed a Start display.

"School," Masamune repeated in a monotone. "I figured you must still be in school. So are you?"

Kokoro felt a wave of heat rush from her ankles up to her face.

Her first reaction was *why?* Hadn't they sort of promised not to mention school?

She'd found it comforting.

What if I show off a little? thought Kokoro.

Yes, I am going to school. But I'm sort of sickly so some days I can go, other days I can't, and I spend quite a bit of time at hospital having tests, etc. A nice idea, now that she thought of it. How great it would be if only that were true. Her parents wouldn't see it all as an emotional issue then. They would definitely prefer it that way.

"I . . . ah . . ." she began. If she let another ten seconds pass, she knew she would tell a lie.

But Masamune was still speaking, super casual.

"Nah, I just asked because I figured if you were going to school, we wouldn't have much in common. No worries."

"Eh?" Kokoro looked at Masamune. As usual, he didn't look back.

"Because, you know, it's normal. Compulsory education means going to school, letting the teachers tell you what to do without complaint. It's way beyond not cool. It's a nightmare."

"Masamune, that's going a little too far." Subaru smiled wryly, and glanced at Kokoro. "I think you startled her."

"But it's true," Masamune insisted. "My parents had a huge bust-up with my homeroom teacher in seventh grade. They figured a pathetic school like that was not worth going to, and gave up on it."

"So your parents said you don't have to go?" Kokoro found that hard to believe.

"Hm?" Masamune said, giving her a quick look. Then he nodded. "It's as if, even if I said I wanted to go, my parents would have stopped me. Because they despise that kind of school."

Kokoro's eyes widened. "But it's true, isn't it?" Masamune continued. "The teachers are so full of themselves, but they're humans after all. They might have teaching certificates, but most of the time they're not even as smart as we are. The whole thing makes me want to puke."

"That's the principle Masamune's family seems to follow," Subaru added, still with a wry smile on his face. "They figure what you study at school isn't all that helpful, so it's better to work on your own at home. They don't think it's Masamune's fault if he feels he can't fit in at school. Because some people do, and others just don't."

"It wasn't that I couldn't fit in or anything," Masamune said, giving Subaru a look. "Actually, my grades aren't so bad. I went to elementary school, but where I really studied was at *juku* after-school prep school, and online classes, and didn't pay much attention in lessons at school. But still, when I took those national mock tests, my grades and ranking were good."

"So even now you're just going to juku and doing online classes?"

"Just juku. But not the ones around here where the instructors suck. My parents found a place with a better reputation, and that's where I'm going."

The juku classes were in the evening, he explained, so during the day he was free.

"You know, schools, they're regimented systems for people who prefer to go along with the crowd, and because everybody else is going. I know the guy who developed this video game, and he hardly ever went to school, because he said it was boring. Said the teachers and the other kids were a bunch of lame morons."

"Wow! Imagine that—developing video games . . ."

Kokoro took a look at the game he was playing. It was a super popular game, a bestseller all over the world.

"Are you for real?" she said. "So—you know the man who created this?"

"Yeah."

"Wow!"

She remembered now that the small game console he'd had with him the very first day was a model she didn't recognize.

"And I was . . . wondering if maybe that game console you had before was something that hasn't gone on sale yet?"

"Eh? Oh . . . that one."

Masamune held Kokoro's eye for a second.

"You must mean the one he asked me to be a tester for."

"What do you mean by *tester*?" Kokoro asked.

"It's like a test drive. He gave me a new console to play the game on, even though it's still being developed. He wanted to see what

54

kids think of it, as well as adults, whether we notice any glitches or anything."

"Wow—you're so lucky!" she couldn't help saying. Masamune was a junior high student like her, yet he had adult acquaintances. It made him seem suddenly more sophisticated.

"That's wicked," Subaru said. "When Masamune told me, I was stunned."

"So, like, I think going to school is pretty pointless. I mean, I'm going to work in gaming myself someday, so I'm not using the ordinary path. My friend said he values my opinion, and even invited me to work for his company in the future."

"Invited you . . . ?"

In the future. That left Kokoro even more dumbfounded.

Masamune was on a roll. "This one I've brought today is version two. I have a version three, of course, back home. I was asked to be a tester for version four, but it doesn't work with this old TV. The terminal's different."

Kokoro didn't understand the technical side of it, but marveled all the same.

Masamune seemed quite satisfied with this over-reaction. "The *four* should blow you away," he laughed. "So you play games, even though you're a girl?"

"Yeah," Kokoro said, "loads of girls do."

A couple of her friends from elementary school came to mind.

"Really?" Masamune said.

Yeah, but wow, Kokoro thought. The whole thing was so astonishing she was speechless. Parents telling their child there's no need to go to school? Or rather, he didn't have to go, and that if he couldn't get on at school it was the teachers' fault. *Her* parents would never think that way.

I just asked because I figured if you were going to school, we wouldn't have much in common.

He was telling her it's *OK* not to go to school. A sort of roundabout, impolite way of saying it, sure, but this was the first time anyone was positive about her not going to school.

"Is it the same for you, Subaru-kun? The same as Masamune-kun?"

She hadn't meant to ask, but she did anyway. "Yeah, something like that," Subaru said, nodding. He didn't go any deeper, but his troubled expression told her he'd prefer her not to probe.

She was dying to hear more about these two. And about the other kids, who hadn't come over yet today, and what they were dealing with.

Kokoro realized she'd misunderstood.

She'd been sure they were all worried because they weren't going to school, and so they'd been avoiding the subject. But now that didn't seem to be the case. At least with Masamune and Subaru, they just hadn't brought it up because they didn't think it was all that important.

"Do you want to play with us?"

Subaru, controller in hand, turned to Kokoro. Masamune, sitting cross-legged, was looking over at her.

"Sure," she said, and she took the controller from Subaru.

NO ONE ELSE came to the castle that day.

Which, to be honest, was a relief. Kokoro had never experienced this before—having fun with two guys, with no other girls around. It made her anxious, wondering what the other girls, Aki and Fuka, would think if they ever turned up.

"You should come tomorrow, too," Subaru said.

Time had passed in a flash. Kokoro and the boys had played right up until the castle closed at five o'clock, taking an occasional break to go home to grab a snack, or to use the toilet—the castle had baths, but for some reason no toilets—but other than that they had spent the whole time immersed in the video game. Until the day her dad had confiscated her video games, Kokoro had played every day, and she was fairly skilled. Even snarky Masamune seemed to accept her as one of the gang.

"We'll probably be here, so if you're free, you should come," he echoed.

"Thank you," said Kokoro.

Honestly, she was so happy she wasn't sure how to respond.

Other than her parents, it was so long since she'd talked like this to anyone.

She didn't feel afraid to come here anymore.

Just then she heard a high-pitched howl, most likely the Wolf Queen's. But the Wolf Queen was nowhere to be seen.

"We always hear it at a quarter to five. The Wolf Queen howling," Subaru explained. "The signal for us to go home, I think."

"Isn't the Wolf Queen here every day?"

"Sometimes, but sometimes not. Like the young lady said that first day, if we call her, she'll appear. And sometimes even when we don't, she pops up out of nowhere. Do you want to call her?"

Kokoro shook her head quickly. She remembered the time she'd run away and the Wolf Queen had tackled her to the ground. The girl still scared her.

Kokoro was impressed, too, with how civilized Subaru sounded, referring to the Wolf Queen as *the young lady*, though she actually looked like a little girl.

When they were back in the grand foyer in front of the row of mirrors, Kokoro suddenly remembered something. "So where is the Wishing Room anyway? Have you seen it yet?"

This room, capable of granting one single wish, was somewhere in the castle. She was sure they'd already located it.

Masamune and Subaru exchanged a look. Behind his glasses Masamune screwed up his eyes. "Haven't found it yet."

"Then, you mean—"

"We don't only have to find the key, but also the location of the room," Subaru added, and Kokoro breathed out slightly.

"I see."

"Come on! She should have told us that at the start. That little Wolf Queen brat."

Masamune's words were so funny Kokoro couldn't stop herself laughing. "What?" he asked her.

"Nothing."

But it was funny all the same.

Cute, in a way, how this guy with his rough way of talking added the honorific *sama* to her title when talking about the Wolf Queen. If she'd pointed this out, it would probably irritate him, but still it was amusing.

I see, she thought.

Masamune's use of polite honorifics didn't exactly match the level of Subaru's *young lady*, but Kokoro was now sure of one thing: both these boys were real gentlemen.

"See ya."

Masamune stuffed the game console into his backpack, and gave a little wave as he stood in front of his shining mirror at the end of the row.

"Yep." Subaru nodded as he touched his own mirror, the second from the left. The surface seemed to melt under his fingers, drawing in his hand. It was like putting your hand into a rushing waterfall and stopping the flow of water. It still startled Kokoro, but the two boys were clearly used to it.

It was the first time she'd seen someone else enter a mirror.

It made her feel a bit strange.

These mirrors—with just a touch of the palm—would connect up with the other kids' rooms too, just like hers did. Could she visit their rooms, perhaps without them even knowing?

Not that she particularly wanted to.

That would be worse than sneaking a peek into someone else's diary. Kokoro shivered at the idea of an intruder in her room. But Masamune and Subaru, both standing with a hand inside their mirror as they waved goodbye, were people she could trust. And the same held true, she imagined, for the others.

"Bye."

After waving them off, Kokoro thrust out a hand towards her mirror and passed into a veil of light.

*　　*　　*

KOKORO VISITED THE castle the very next day.

She found she had no problem being with the others again, and wondered why she'd been so bothered about it before.

It was just after ten in the morning. She was playing video games with Masamune and Subaru in the living room, now transformed completely into their Game Room, when Aki breezed in with a "Hi, people." Kokoro hadn't seen her in quite some time, but Aki's lively "Hey, Kokoro-chan. How've you been?" made her forget.

Aki had said she was in ninth grade, the last year of junior high, and when she was with Aki, Kokoro definitely felt she was her *senpai*, her senior. Kokoro was happy that Aki addressed her in a familiar way—adding *chan* to her name—but she was unsure how to address her back.

"Hi, Aki-senpai," she said.

At which Masamune burst out laughing.

"Jeez! This isn't some school club, so what's with the *senpai*?"

"OK, OK—so what *should* I call her?"

Kokoro didn't think she deserved to be laughed at. But Aki said, "Hey, I don't mind. I like being called that!

"I don't mind what you call me—just plain Aki, or Aki-chan—it's all good. I find it kind of endearing that you're so polite, Kokoro."

Aki said this jokingly, but now that Kokoro heard herself being called, within moments, just plain Kokoro, it did catch her by surprise. Kokoro marveled at Aki's communication skills—the way she adroitly changed how she addressed people. It was clear there wasn't anything awkward in her relationship with the two boys either.

59

So how was it that someone like her couldn't cope with school? She'd easily be one of the popular girls.

"You're so sweet, Kokoro, and I imagine any senpai would treat you well."

"Ah . . . um. Actually I stopped going pretty early on, so I don't know any of the older students. And I'm not in any club or anything either."

Even if Masamune and the others insisted that it wasn't something to be embarrassed about, she'd still said *I stopped going*, leaving out the part about school. When she remembered how she hadn't even gone to the orientation for any of the clubs, it made her feel miserable.

Although she'd been joking, Aki's expression turned a bit chilly when Kokoro mentioned the clubs. Masamune and Subaru both opened their mouths in surprise, and by the time Kokoro had become aware of the atmosphere, Aki had turned to leave.

"I see. So you weren't in any clubs. The same as me, then," Aki said.

"Eh?"

"I'll be in my room today," she added. "Seems Fuka's here too, so why don't you invite her?"

She strode down the hallway towards their individual rooms. The hallway had red carpeting, lit up by the candles on either wall, and Kokoro watched through the glow, as the tall Aki faded into the distance.

Timing it with Aki's exit, Subaru sidled over to Kokoro. "One thing you should know," he whispered.

"Hm?"

Kokoro was confused—had she said something to upset Aki?

"That's a touchy subject. Aki-chan doesn't like to talk about school very much."

"Oh."

Kokoro could sympathize. She felt the same way. Problem was,

Masamune and Subaru talked about it in such an easy-going way she'd tuned in to that.

Masamune said, with an air of disdain, "I don't think it's something we need to worry about." But his eyes remained glued to the game monitor.

Kokoro remembered how when they'd first introduced themselves, they'd only said their names and year in school because that's what Aki, who'd gone first, had done.

She stared down the hallway after Aki.

As Subaru had said, it was definitely a touchy subject.

Kokoro murmured, "So, is Fuka-chan here, too?" She was just trying to recall what Fuka looked like. Fuka was in her second year of junior high, so she too was a senpai to Kokoro—one year ahead of her.

Masamune said, a little sarcastically, "What, aren't you gonna call her senpai, too?"

Kokoro was not used to being teased and began to feel a little flustered. She shook her head vigorously. "No, it's just—I used it with Aki-chan because, I don't know—she seems like such a senpai."

"Well, Subaru and me are your senpai too, for that matter."

Masamune was clowning around, kidding her. Kokoro was still trying to work out how to respond when he added, "Fuka comes here a lot. Almost every day. Though she doesn't hang out with us much."

"Does she stay in her room?"

"Yeah. I invited her once to play video games, but she said she doesn't play. I thought she was joking. I mean, she looks like such a loser."

"*Masamune.*" Subaru's tone was sharp.

"What?" Masamune protested. But when he saw the glare in Subaru's eye, he let out an exaggerated sigh. "She seems to stay shut up in her room a lot," he said, changing the subject. "I don't know what she does there, but she's basically a loner."

Changing the subject, Subaru said, "He wasn't here yesterday, but Ureshino usually turns up after one o'clock."

"I see." Kokoro nodded.

That made sense to her that he came in the afternoon. It seemed to suit him to have lunch at home first.

Like Kokoro, Ureshino was in his first year of junior high, and as she reflected, she remembered the other kid who was also in seventh grade.

"What about that other boy?" Kokoro asked.

Masamune turned his gaze lazily on her. "Who?"

"Rion-kun."

"Ah, the dish." His words sounded barbed.

It wasn't because he was handsome that she'd asked, but she had no idea how to explain that.

"What's a dish?" Subaru muttered. "Is it something bad?" When Masamune didn't respond, Subaru turned to Kokoro and raised his eyebrows.

"He always gets here in the late afternoon," Subaru replied in Masamune's place. "Always wearing a jersey, which makes me think maybe he's attending a juku or studying somewhere during the day. I often bump into him just as the castle's closing."

"He plays video games with us, too," Masamune added.

＊　＊　＊

THE HANDS OF the grandfather clock were pointing to twelve.

Kokoro went home, ate the curry her mother had prepared, brushed her teeth, and headed back to the castle. When it came to lunch, it seemed they each had different habits—some went home to eat, others brought in bentos.

For Kokoro, going home for lunch and then returning to the castle felt like her school timetable all over again.

Thinking they could all share it, she had taken an apple back with her—her mother had insisted that she peel apples herself—and put it in her tote bag, together with a small fruit knife, the blade wrapped in foil to keep it safe.

As she passed through the mirror and emerged into the castle, the mirror beside hers was also shining. It was Fuka. She was going in the opposite direction, on her way home.

"Oh," Kokoro said, and Fuka, her palm already inside the mirror, turned around, her face expressionless.

"Ah—he-hello there."

"Hi."

Her face was blank but her voice still had that smooth, sparkling quality to it. Within seconds, Fuka had turned to face the mirror, slipped inside, and vanished.

Back in the Game Room, Kokoro noticed that Ureshino had arrived, just as Subaru had said.

He was engrossed in a video game, and hunkered down just where Kokoro liked to sit. The TV had seemed pretty big, but with Ureshino now seated in front of it, it seemed to have shrunk.

He was that bulky.

Yesterday when she'd been in the Game Room with Masamune, he had more or less ignored her. But today, when Ureshino spotted her, he looked up immediately. "Ah . . . Let's see, so you are . . . Kokoro?"

"Yes, it's Kokoro-chan," said Subaru.

Ureshino had already fudged any *chan* or *san* suffix, so Subaru had stepped in to help.

"Kokoro—*chan*," Ureshino said, a little modestly, and gave her a look. "I didn't think you'd be coming."

"She started dropping in yesterday," Masamune said. "She's pretty smart at video games."

"Good to see you again, Ureshino-kun," Kokoro said.

Since there were only a handful of them, Kokoro found her words more easily than she ever had at school.

"Good to see you too. So now I have one more rival for the key," he said casually. Kokoro tensed up. *Not another pain in the neck* is what he seemed to be saying, in a roundabout manner.

The way he was so concerned about food that first day, she thought, *and there I was thinking he was so cute and cuddly.*

As Kokoro sat down in front of the TV, Ureshino, controller in hand, seemed nervous about whether anybody else was going to join them.

Picking up on it instantly, Subaru said, "If you're expecting Aki-chan, I doubt she's going to turn up."

Ureshino sat up straight, while Subaru continued. "She was here this morning, but she's probably in her room at the moment."

"Oh." Ureshino's shoulders slumped in disappointment.

"That's dumb," Masamune muttered. He let go of the controller, a rare move for him, and looked over at Kokoro with a grin.

"Do you know what Ureshino's wish is?"

Kokoro shrugged.

By *wish*, he must mean what Ureshino was hoping the Wishing Room would make come true. *But I just got here, so how would I know?* she thought.

Masamune shot a grimace at Ureshino. "He wants to take Aki out."

"Oh?" Kokoro managed to say, before Ureshino yelled out, "Hey! Why're you telling?" His face turned beetroot, and though he insisted Masamune hold his tongue, his tone of voice didn't seem that annoyed. Subaru said nothing.

"Ureshino-kun, you mean you like Aki-chan?" Kokoro asked.

Ureshino didn't reply. Kokoro was thinking she shouldn't push it, but after a while he said quietly, "Yeah, that's right. Is there a problem?"

"No, no problem."

"Love at first sight," Ureshino said. "I told Aki how I feel, but she shot me down. That was about a week after we started coming here. Pretty fast, no?"

"Aki-chan was confused by the whole thing too," Subaru said to

Kokoro, a knowing smile on his lips. He lowered his voice. "Aki felt a little awkward when Ureshino looked at her."

"Oh."

There were other kids Kokoro knew who were in thrall to a similar kind of crush, but these were almost always girls. It was pretty unusual for a boy to show his feelings so clearly. In fact, it was a first for her.

"Masamune, Kokoro-chan doesn't know what's going on, so why'd you have to tell her?"

Ureshino sounded angry, but he also seemed a little pleased. Kokoro felt she had to say something. "But she is pretty amazing, Aki-chan," she said. "She's smart, and fearless. I completely get how you'd fall for her."

Ureshino looked surprised. But then he broke into a smile.

"I know, right?" he said.

Still, she'd never expected love to blossom in the two weeks she'd been away from the castle. They'd said that Aki was not especially happy about it, but supposing Ureshino did locate the key to the Wishing Room, would Aki fancy him back? What did she really feel about it all? Kokoro's head was in a whirl.

Say a strange power did come into play and Aki fell in love with Ureshino. Would that be the original Aki who Ureshino had fallen for? If somebody manipulated your thoughts and feelings, would you still be the same person as before?

Kokoro took out the apple she'd brought and placed it on the table.

Instead of reaching for a controller, she sank into the sofa. "I brought an apple. Anyone want some?"

Ureshino's face lit up. "Can I?"

His over-enthusiasm left Kokoro a bit confused, but there was one thing she clocked about Ureshino: he was not a bad person. She smiled at the thought.

Masamune and Subaru looked uncertainly at the apple. "Aren't you gonna take it off?" It took her a beat to understand they meant the apple peel.

"Oh—sure."

"Hm," Masamune said, but didn't elaborate.

Kokoro didn't find his response unusual, and went to fetch her knife to peel the apple. She realized she'd forgotten to bring a cutting board or a plate, so she sliced it on top of the plastic bag.

"You're amazing, Kokoro-chan," Ureshino said, his eyes lingering on her hands. "You're really great at peeling apples. You're like my mum."

Masamune made no comment, but did munch happily on a couple of slices of apple while he continued his video game.

AS LATE AFTERNOON came, Kokoro decided to explore the castle.

The absence of a plate for the apple made her think she'd try to locate the kitchen, if there was one. The Wolf Queen had said there was nothing to eat here, but there could still be plates.

The castle was most definitely cavernous, yet not as absurdly vast as those with dungeons she'd seen in video games.

The grand foyer with the staircases and the seven mirrors was situated at one end of the castle. From there extended the long red-carpeted hallway towards their individual rooms. Beyond that was a common area, including the Game Room where they played their video games.

There was a dining room, too, which she had spotted earlier.

She stepped in gingerly and let out a yelp of surprise. Through this particular window she could see outside. The windows elsewhere in the castle were made of frosted glass.

The greenery was clearly visible. A closer look revealed an inner courtyard, and beyond that lay the wing with the staircases and mirrors, forming a U-shape around the courtyard.

Kokoro was dying to venture outside, but there was no handle on the French window to open it. Apparently, the courtyard was just there to be admired. Underneath a cedar tree was a bed of marigolds and salvia in full bloom.

Placed in the center of the dining room was an extravagantly long table. Kokoro often watched dramas where parents sat at either end of a long table. The dining room also boasted a fireplace, and above it hung an oil painting of a vase filled with flowers.

The room was still, and a cold chill lingered, as though no human presence had been felt in a long while. The table was draped neatly with a spotless tablecloth.

Kokoro spied a door at the opposite end of the dining room. It led directly into the kitchen, which turned out to be even grander than she'd been expecting.

She went over to the sink and tried lifting and lowering the handle on the tap, but no water came out. A mighty stainless-steel fridge stood in the corner, but it proved to be completely empty. She stuck a hand inside to check whether it was on. It was not. The shelves along one wall were filled with white ceramic plates, soup bowls and tea sets, none of which seemed to have ever been touched.

Why does this castle exist, if no one lives here? Kokoro wondered.

All the usual pots and pans were visible, but there was no gas or water. There were fancy bathtubs in the bathrooms, but no toilets. She wondered where the electricity came from to power their video games.

As she turned to continue her stroll through the castle, she thought how awkward it would be if she bumped into someone. Like a while ago, when she'd encountered Fuka near the mirrors.

Lost in thought, she gazed through the doorway at the brick fireplace in the dining room.

Suddenly she recalled the Wishing Room key.

Had someone already checked the inside of the fireplace? It must open up into a chimney. Or maybe, like the bathrooms and kitchen, the fireplace wasn't actually functional.

She peered into the fireplace, and let out a cry.

It wasn't the key. But she did find a faint *X*, about the size of her palm. It seemed to have been there for a while, since there was a light film of dust over it. Maybe it was just a flaw in the bricks? But no. On closer inspection, someone had clearly marked an *X*.

Just as she was about to stand up again, she heard a loud "Whoa!" from behind her. Kokoro yelped, and spun around.

A face with a wolf mask. The Wolf Queen herself, whom she hadn't seen for quite some time.

"Wolf Queen!"

"Are you looking for the key all by yourself? Impressive."

"Don't frighten me like that."

Kokoro's heart was pounding. She noticed the Wolf Queen was wearing a different outfit; a green dress, embroidered at the hem.

"Did you find the key?" asked the Wolf Queen, to which Kokoro replied, "Nope."

Announcing that she was going to join the others, she set off towards the Game Room before the Wolf Queen could comment.

Halfway down the hallway, she spotted someone coming towards her. Kokoro slowed down her steps until she could see who it was.

It was Rion—the *dish*, in Masamune's words. "Hey," he called.

He wasn't wearing a sweat suit today, just tracksuit bottoms and a T-shirt. The trousers, though, weren't the baggy style required by schools, but the smarter black Adidas version. On his T-shirt was a *Star Wars* villain. Kokoro had never seen any of the films, but she recognized the character.

Kokoro wondered whether she should try to explain why she had not visited earlier, but Rion beat her to it. "Long time no see," he said casually.

"Ah, I'm—Kokoro," she said.

Rion laughed. "Come on, I know that already." *So he knows my name.* The thought made her happy. Rion was wearing a watch, which he didn't seem to have when they'd met previously. She spotted the Nike swoosh mark on it.

"What?" Rion asked, when he saw how she was staring at his watch.

"Oh, I was just wondering what time it is."

Rion pointed down the hallway. "There's a clock over there, you know."

And of course there was—the tall grandfather clock, in the middle of the foyer with its staircases and mirrors. "Ah yes," said Kokoro, noticing how Rion's light brown hair hung loosely just above his smiling eyes.

So Subaru was right: Rion mainly came over in the late afternoon. He'd speculated that Rion probably spent the day at a juku or in lessons somewhere. Kokoro found it pretty strange that Rion, and Aki too, seemed so laidback, and able to go to juku and external lessons, yet had still dropped out of school. They both looked like they'd be really popular.

When they reached the Game Room, more of the group had gathered.

Fuka was sitting on the sofa in front of the table—the plastic bag Kokoro had brought the apple in was still there—and she was reading a book.

"Well, well, everyone's here today," the Wolf Queen said, appearing diminutively in the doorway. Fuka looked up from her book, and the boys from their video game. They greeted Rion with a quick "Hey" and "'Sup."

Fuka didn't say anything. She glanced at the Wolf Queen, and just as quickly dropped her eyes back down to her book.

"Hey, Kokoro-chan?" said Ureshino.

"Yes?"

"Do you have, like, a boyfriend or somebody you fancy?"

"Err?" Her eyes widened at this question out of the blue. Kokoro wondered if he was dying to talk to somebody about his infatuation with Aki. She looked around at the others and realized something was in the air.

Masamune had stopped playing the video game and was grinning. Subaru had an awkward smile on his face. Kokoro, stuck for a reply, stood stiffly, and Masamune said, teasingly, "My commiserations."

Even Kokoro understood in that moment what he was getting at.

"Tell me, Kokoro-chan. Will you be here tomorrow? What time, do you think?" Kokoro didn't respond and he asked again.

"I don't know," was the best she could manage.

She could see the Wolf Queen's teasing stare from the corner of her eye, as the Wolf Queen asked Masamune, "So, what's going on now? Has Ureshino switched his crush already?" She gave a small giggle.

Ureshino grimaced at the Wolf Queen. Then, his expression changed. He looked at Kokoro. "Did you hear what she said?" He sounded on the verge of tears.

Kokoro had no clue how to respond.

Rion shot her a quick look and changed the subject. "So what kind of games did you bring today, Kokoro?"

Then a high-pitched voice: "How dumb can you get?" Fuka, speaking to Ureshino. Her tone was piercing and caustic.

Kokoro bit her lip in confusion. Aki, Rion and the others all seemed so normal, and she still wondered why they wouldn't go to school. But when it came to Ureshino—she knew exactly why.

He was one of those boys in love with the idea of love—love for love's sake.

Everyone pitied him, and it was no wonder he didn't go to school.

July

BY JULY, KOKORO was feeling even more uncomfortable going to the castle.

And it was all because of Ureshino.

"I brought some cookies, Kokoro-chan, would you like some?"

"Kokoro-chan, when did you first fall in love? For me it was back in kindergarten . . ."

She enjoyed going to the Game Room, but in the afternoon Ureshino would appear and start pestering her with personal questions. Masamune would grin, which she hated, and Kokoro found herself spending more time alone in her room in the castle.

Even when she was holed up there, Ureshino would knock—"Kokoro-chan, are you in?"—and she realized there was no escape.

Whenever she decided to look for the Wishing Key, Ureshino would be right there, tagging along.

"Can I come with you, Kokoro-chan?"

He was the one who'd said they were rivals in the search, so how could it be OK?

Kokoro picked up, somehow, from the way the others behaved, that when she wasn't there, Ureshino took the liberty of referring to her by her first name alone, no doubt describing her as "not totally my type, but more the homey type . . ."

The guy's a little warped, she thought.

It wasn't that he really liked Kokoro, though. What he liked was to play up how much he enjoyed *being in love*.

Kokoro found she couldn't come right out and tell him she wanted him to stop. If she behaved coldly, he'd immediately start badmouthing her to the others.

"KOKORO-CHAN, WHAT sort of wish are you hoping will come true?"

When Ureshino asked her this so light-heartedly, she said, "I haven't decided yet." She knew if she told him what she really wanted, that a girl from her class would disappear forever, it could set him off with more questions.

"Oh, is that right?"

As they walked along the hallway, Ureshino kept giving her looks. He seemed to want to ask her something else.

In manga, often the heroes would use weird objects to get others to do what they wanted or to manipulate them. She realized they must be as ridiculous as what she was dealing with here.

When Ureshino let Aki know that he had switched his affections to Kokoro, Aki grimaced. "That's going to be rough on you," she said, openly sympathizing. After that, Aki started spending less time in her room.

Unlike Masamune, who teased her, Rion and Subaru never brought up any love-related conversation when Kokoro was around, which was a great relief.

She heard Ureshino hesitantly asking Rion, "Do you have a girlfriend? You're not thinking of making one of these girls here your girlfriend, are you?"

To which Rion replied, "Not really." Ureshino surely asked the other boys the same thing.

That meant she didn't need to worry about Aki or Rion.

And Masamune's teasing she could put up with.

But what really bothered her was Fuka's reaction.

There were only three girls here, and when they'd first introduced themselves, Kokoro thought she and Fuka might quickly become friends. But they'd never had a chance to open up to each other, and the words she'd spat out still stung.

How dumb can you get?

Fuka was referring to Ureshino's switch from one girl to another, and wasn't particularly commenting on Kokoro. Kokoro reassured herself of this whenever she passed through the mirror into the castle, and at night when she went to sleep, but somehow Fuka's words still bothered her. Whenever Fuka visited the castle, though, she either stayed holed up in her room or, on the rare occasions when she joined them, would sit silently reading a book.

Once, when Ureshino wasn't around and Kokoro was sitting with Masamune and the others in the Game Room, they grinned at her again and said, "What a mess, eh?" Fuka was with them.

Kokoro had no idea how to respond. "Mm." She nodded vaguely.

And Fuka, eyes still glued to her book, said what she'd said before: "How dumb can you get?"

Kokoro froze.

Fuka carried on. "Guys like that, who aren't popular, always falling for the pretty girl in class, or someone way out of their league, whenever I see that, it really annoys me."

"Whoa—that's pretty harsh. You're scaring me," Masamune said, and pretended to shrink back.

For Kokoro, it was hard to take Fuka avoiding her eye all the time. She bit her lip in frustration.

Was that *pretty girl* remark aimed at her? She had no idea.

She wanted to push back, but it seemed pointless.

She'd tried to be so careful.

She'd tried her best, when she was with the two boys, Masamune and Subaru, not to do anything that would make the other girls feel uncomfortable.

So why did things have to turn out the way they did?

UNABLE TO MAKE amends with Fuka, Kokoro grew despondent, and took a day off from visiting the castle.

A day off was an odd way of putting it, but since the beginning of July she'd felt as if the castle was like junior high, a complicated place she was compelled to go to.

The day after she'd skipped out, she went as always to check the Game Room, and what she heard made her gasp.

"Aki-chan, I know you think that, but the sequel of that film was way better."

"What? There's a sequel?"

"Are you kidding me? The sequel is fantastic!"

Fuka and Aki were seated side by side on the sofa.

Neither of them noticed Kokoro, standing at the door. She didn't know what they were talking about, but could see some flower-shaped cookies spread out on a tissue in front of them.

The kind that Kokoro loved—marigold-shaped cookies with chocolate cream in the center. The moment she spotted the pile, she was dying to have one.

But she couldn't tell them that.

She turned around before they noticed she was there, and hurried off to her own room. Hoping against hope that the two girls hadn't seen her.

When had the two of them become so friendly? Talking about things she didn't understand, chatting and having a good time. A painful, weary feeling came over her.

She focused on distancing herself from them, walking quickly down the hallway. When she got to the foyer, her mirror was shining. A rainbow-colored light leading to her home, where her parents were, and her real bedroom. Hoping for some respite, she gently touched the surface of the mirror.

This was the first time she had run back home from the castle.

She'd done her best, in the hope of being granted a wish, but maybe she'd reached her limit. *Maybe I'm just not cut out for it*, she thought.

* * *

KOKORO'S WISH.
To erase Miori Sanada.

MIORI SANADA HAD never spoken to her, not even once.

Her first impression was that Miori was an active, strong-willed girl, and when Miori announced she was running for class president, Kokoro said to herself, "So I was right. She's that type of girl."

It seemed predetermined that Miori would be on the volleyball team, and Kokoro overheard her friends discussing it. Her choice, without any hesitation, of a sports team as her after-school club, must mean she was athletic. Since elementary school, it was always the sporty students who were class president, not the ones with the best grades.

These were the things going through her mind in April, at the beginning of the new school year. She and Miori were in the same class, and after they'd all introduced themselves, Kokoro hadn't yet put all the names and faces together.

They were in Yukishina No. 5 Junior High School because they lived in the same school district, but children joined from six different elementary schools. It was a massive junior high. Even children from a neighboring district were given special permission to attend, and Kokoro found very few familiar faces in her new class. The class was a hodgepodge of children from all over.

There were only three boys and two girls from her elementary school.

Miori, who was from a relatively large elementary school, had plenty of friends from the start. She was also at after-school juku, and seemed to have made friends with other kids there who were from different elementary schools.

Miori had never been timid or hesitant, and even in this new classroom, she always spoke her mind. Kokoro, and the others who'd come from her elementary school, were more diffident. It felt as if Miori and her group owned the place, and Kokoro and her circle were merely tenants. Kokoro didn't understand why things turned out this way, but that's how it was from the very beginning.

They were all the same age, but it was as if Miori and the other girls in her group held all the power in their class.

They seemed to have first dibs on whatever club they wanted to join, and when other girls tried to join the same club, Miori and her gang had the power to spread rumors that these girls weren't up to it, and prevent them from joining—the power to decide who belonged, the power to decide what nicknames to use for their teachers, the freedom to choose which boys they liked, and which to fall in love with.

THE BOY THAT Miori Sanada *liked*, and started going out with, was Chuta Ikeda, a boy from the same class in Kokoro's elementary school.

Kokoro and Chuta had just been friends, nothing more. When they were preparing the traditional appreciation dinner for their teachers just before their graduation, Chuta complained it was all a stupid waste of time, but Kokoro was impressed how, despite his complaining, when things needed to be done, he stepped up. It wasn't as if she fancied him, or thought he was handsome or anything, just that she now reassessed her earlier impression of him as irresponsible.

"I always thought boys just couldn't do these things properly," she said, as a sort of throwaway comment.

"Eh?" Chuta said. "We just don't want to complicate things. But I reckon any boy would step up and do his part. We're not so lame, you know, and you've no right to say that." Their conversation petered out after this.

"YOU KNOW WHAT?"

This was in the middle of April, in the bicycle parking area at school. Kokoro turned around when she heard a voice. There was Chuta standing in front of her.

"Ugly girls like you are the pits."

"*What?*" The word rose up in her throat, but got stuck halfway.

Her field of vision, with Chuta at its center, seemed to quake and swim before her eyes.

Chuta's face was inscrutable.

Kokoro sensed the presence of other bodies, that someone was crouched down a short distance away, waiting with bated breath.

She stood frozen to the spot as Chuta proceeded to walk off, hands in his pockets. When he got near the hiding place where she knew her classmates were lurking, she heard laughter.

"Are you kidding?"

"Didn't it seem like she thought for a second that Chuta was actually going to tell her he fancied her?"

"Oh my god, she got that so wrong."

Girls' voices. A tall figure stood up. Miori Sanada.

"Was that OK, then?" Chuta asked her, curtly.

Kokoro felt Miori looking over at her, and she hurriedly looked away. Miori then declared: "Chuta, I really don't fancy you!"

She enunciated clearly, and it took Kokoro a moment to realize the words were meant for her to overhear. And then a voice said: "Don't pretend you didn't hear me, you stupid bitch!"

Kokoro was reeling. No one had ever spoken to her like that.

"You're so dumb," Miori said. "You can die for all I care."

BACK IN ELEMENTARY school, Chuta Ikeda had fancied Kokoro.

One of her friends had found out and told her. Kokoro was completely shocked, but apparently all the boys knew.

Once he became friends with Miori, Chuta had obviously filled her in about their *past*.

KOKORO AVOIDED THE castle for the next three days.

Because of the weekend, it meant she'd been away five days in a row.

She hadn't been able to go to junior high, or to the alternative School, and until now she'd found the castle a refuge, which meant her feelings about it were even more complicated. All the TV she'd enjoyed so much now seemed insipid and dull.

It was all so boring.

It upset her to see the mirror in her bedroom, turned towards the wall and shining.

Shining as if inviting her, beckoning her.

She had no idea if the rest of the group wanted her there. She decided, finally, that they didn't really care if she was there or not. But she wondered how they were all doing. There was no way at all of contacting them from this side of the mirror.

Even if, say, they wanted her to come back, she had no way of knowing.

ON SATURDAY HER parents invited her to go out shopping, but she said, "I'm OK. You two go," to which her parents didn't know what to say.

They looked at each other, and later her father asked her, "So, what're you planning to do? How are you going to manage if you never leave the house?"

Kokoro had no idea. She wished she had an answer.

But the thought of bumping into someone she knew paralyzed her.

What were the other kids who had also dropped out doing?

I've got to let Ureshino know his attitude is really unsettling me.

He hadn't yet confessed his feelings to her directly, but she hated to think the others might know. She needed to have a chat with Fuka, too.

*   *   *

ON MONDAY, SHE passed through the mirror and emerged into the castle for the first time in six days. As she came through, she noticed a light blue envelope stuck to the top of her mirror. It came fluttering down on to the carpet.

There was no addressee or sender's name on the envelope. She picked it up curiously. It was unsealed, and inside was a sheet of paper to match the envelope.

Dear Kokoro-chan,

Whenever you get here next, please drop by the room where we play video games. You might see something pretty wicked.

Subaru

Kokoro felt her heart pound.

She was elated that he'd been thinking of her. She thought of how she'd run away when she'd seen Aki and Fuka looking so cozy, and tears welled in her eyes.

She walked speedily over to the Game Room where the kids were all gathered, except for Rion. When she spotted Ureshino, she hesitated.

"Kokoro," Aki called.

"Hi, there." Ureshino's voice was low. She expected him to launch into his usual *Hey, Kokoro-chan* cloying self, but this time he didn't. For some reason he avoided her eye.

Kokoro struggled to explain her five-day absence and looked to Subaru to rescue her. But he just smiled broadly and said, "It's been a while, Kokoro-chan."

Masamune, game controller in hand, watched the proceedings with his usual smirk.

Something seemed off. "You know . . ." Ureshino began, and Kokoro braced herself.

But his eye was on—Fuka.

"Fuka-chan, what do your close mates call you? Do they ever call you Fuchan or anything?"

Fuka was reading her book. She spoke without lifting her eyes from the page.

"Nope. Even my mum usually calls me Fuka." She looked up and gave him a glare. "Why are you asking?"

"Nah. Just wondering what other people call you."

Fuka opened her book again, and her eyes met Kokoro's. She looked like she wanted to say something, but instead she pursed her lips and carried on reading.

Despite Fuka's chilly response, Ureshino continued staring.

Instinctively, Kokoro looked over at Subaru. He was the one, after all, who'd written the note telling her something *wicked* was afoot. But Subaru was simply observing, with a broad smile on his face.

Kokoro had no clue what had triggered it, but clearly Ureshino was now smitten with Fuka.

There were only three girls among them, and now he'd gone through each in turn.

"DO YOU WANT to get together for tea, just us girls?" It was Aki who was inviting her.

Kokoro was in her room. There had been a hesitant knock at the door, and Kokoro flinched for a second. But when she opened the door, it was Aki. With Fuka hovering behind her.

"Uh, well . . ."

Kokoro had yet to really chat with Fuka. And it still hurt when she recalled how the two of them had seemed to be getting on so well without her.

Honestly though, Kokoro was overjoyed to be invited. "Just a second," she said, and went to fetch some cookies she'd brought from home.

Aki led them to the dining room where Kokoro had been the previous week.

"I made tea," Aki said.

You couldn't boil water in the kitchen, so how had she managed? Kokoro saw her taking out a thermos from a denim shoulder bag decorated with heart-shaped badges, stars and lamé.

She unscrewed the top of the thermos and a thin curl of steam rose into the air.

Aki brought over three teacups and saucers from the kitchen, and poured out the tea.

"Thank you. Help yourself to these if you'd like." Kokoro placed her box of cookies on the table.

"Thanks," Aki said, smiling. "There's a kitchen here, but we can't use it since there's no running water or gas. Which is so strange, as the castle is lit up inside, and it never feels too hot or too cold. I wonder why."

Wow, you're right, thought Kokoro, and glanced up at the ceiling. A chandelier hung down with teardrop-shaped crystals, but it didn't look like any electricity was keeping it on.

"But there is electricity. The boys are playing video games, aren't they?" Fuka pointed out.

"You're so right." Kokoro was puzzled.

"I asked where they got the power, and they said they plugged into the wall socket like normal."

"So the Game Room has an electrical socket?"

There was no running water or gas, but there was definitely electricity.

Kokoro heard Aki chuckle.

"I like that," Aki said. "Your name for it—the Game Room."

"Oh."

"That really is all those guys do—play games. I'm going to call it that, too."

"The Game Room isn't the only room with electricity. What about this chandelier?"

Aki flicked the switch on the wall. An orange-tinted light filled the room.

The next time the Wolf Queen made an appearance, maybe they should ask her.

Fuka brought her hands together politely in thanks before the teacup. "Thank you," she said, and bowed her head a fraction.

How polite she is, thought Kokoro.

"Please, go right ahead," Aki said, and Kokoro followed suit, bowing her head and voicing her thanks. She lifted her cup and sniffed its fruity aroma.

"It's apple tea," said Aki. "It's also weird how the plates and cups I used were all washed up."

"*What?*" Kokoro said.

"The other day I used the crockery, and I couldn't wash up because there's no running water. When I came back later, they were all neatly back on the shelf. As if someone had washed them."

"Really?"

"I asked around, but no one had touched them. Maybe the Wolf Queen washes up after we've gone."

"Quite sweet, if you think about it."

"Right."

Kokoro pictured the Wolf Queen in her mask and dress, doing the washing up. It was quite funny. She had just lifted the cup to take another sip when Aki said, "That Ureshino is a bit irritating, though, isn't he," getting right to the heart of the situation Kokoro had been stressing about.

Kokoro gulped down her tea, its sweet-sour liquid warming the pit of her stomach so deliciously.

"It's a total pain," Fuka said.

"It's like they think any girl will do. Like they're making fun of us."

Then Fuka said, "He had a chat with me. Kokoro-chan, he came to ask whether he should check if you're all right after you didn't come to the castle for a while. He wondered if he went through your mirror in the foyer, he could get to your house. *You can't just turn up in her room*, I said, *and also, it's against the rules*. And after that, he just switched to me."

"Fuka really kicked off at him," Aki said.

The thought of Ureshino passing through the mirror and invading her bedroom gave Kokoro the creeps, but she never imagined that Fuka would stand up for her like that.

"Thank you," Kokoro said.

She tried to be sincere about it, and Fuka replied uncomfortably, "No problem.

"Anyhow," she went on, "you can't go through someone else's mirror. I tried to stop him, but Ureshino held his hand out to try it—"

"*What?*"

"But it wouldn't go through. He said it felt like a normal mirror, just a hard glass surface."

Kokoro had thought how awful it would be if one of them went through someone else's mirror by mistake, but now she knew she needn't worry. She breathed out, greatly relieved, and Aki chuckled.

"Fuka went a little too far when she spoke to Ureshino. She got all emotional and told him he's mad to think love is everything. *You can live without it*, she said, *so stop behaving like a sulky child*. But those words stuck in that guy's weird antenna."

"Antenna?"

"He said, *Fuka, when you say you can live without love it makes me think you've never been in love? That's so adorable!*"

"You are joking, aren't you?"

Aki's imitation of Ureshino's way of talking was spot on. Kokoro was beyond surprised—shocked, even. She couldn't work out at all what qualities Ureshino was looking for.

"He thought that you two, Aki-chan and Kokoro-chan, were out of his league, but me, he could win over. Ureshino—he just makes fools of us." Fuka said this to herself, and sighed deeply.

Kokoro felt secretly elated though, because Fuka had called her Kokoro-*chan* for the first time. *So she doesn't dislike me after all*, she thought, and she felt her legs about to buckle.

"I know I've already said this, but—thank you," Kokoro said.

"What?"

The two girls turned in unison towards her.

"Because I'm—no good when it comes to dating and stuff. I had an—awful experience."

As she said it, she realized how much she'd been hoping to tell someone what had happened. When she got caught up in Miori Sanada's crush on Chuta Ikeda.

The incident with Chuta at the bicycle parking area.

And the bullying in school that all started because of it.

As she told them her story, Kokoro felt the sweat trickle down from her armpits, and her ears burn.

She didn't really know these two girls, didn't even know where they lived, and it surprised her that she wanted to open up to them like this.

"Those guys came to my house. I was doing homework, waiting for my mum to come back . . ."

✳   ✳   ✳

THE DOORBELL RANG.

Who could it be this late? Probably a delivery. "Coming," Kokoro called.

"*Kokoro Anzai!*" a voice bellowed.

It wasn't Miori's voice.

It was a girl's voice Kokoro didn't recognize. She knew her face, and that she was a class president, but that was it. The girl was a friend of Miori's.

She suddenly found it odd that they knew she was at home. A chill rose upwards from her ankles. The front door was locked, as her mother always insisted when she was alone, and beyond it she sensed the presence not of one or two girls, but of a crowd.

Someone began pounding on the door.

"Come out! We know you're in there."

"Go around the back. We can see her through the window."

Kokoro's flesh began to crawl.

"Let's teach her a lesson," someone said.

Teach her a lesson. Kokoro didn't really know what it meant. But when they went into junior high, Kokoro and a friend had worried about it, and talked about what they should do to avoid getting *taught a lesson* by the older kids.

Lesson—like in school? Or more like *punishment?* The two ideas spun around in her head, painfully, absurdly—and she started trembling. And these weren't even older kids, but girls the same age as her.

Girls no different from her.

She raced back to the living room. She had to close the curtains in all the rooms as fast as she could. She had no clue if she'd do it in time. It was still light enough outside for her to see several silhouettes. And the shadows of their bikes.

Tojo-san. It must be her.

One awful scenario after another bubbled up in her mind.

She makes me totally sick. She's such an emo, let's teach her a lesson.

Moé-chan, you live near her, don't you? Show us where she lives.

Kokoro couldn't tell if Tojo-san was with them. A part of her wanted desperately to know, another part wanted to avoid knowing at all costs. Tojo-san was as cute as a doll, a girl she admired and wanted so much to be friends with, and just picturing her standing outside, and who knows what sort of look she had on her face, was enough to make Kokoro choke.

"Come out! You wuss!"

Miori Sanada's voice.

Kokoro held her breath and lay flat against the floor next to the sofa.

Outside the window was the lawn of their garden, lined by a low fence. Kokoro lay completely still.

Bang, bang, bang, bang, bang—they pounded at the back door.

So many voices; she figured there must be about ten of them, repeating each other's calls.

If the door weren't locked, she felt like Miori and her pals would march right into her house. And she actually felt that if that happened, they'd find her, drag her outside and—kill her.

She was so terrified she couldn't utter a sound.

In the low light, she could make out more shadows lurking beyond the curtains. They reached out their hands to the window. She heard several clicks as someone rattled it.

She realized with a flood of relief that the window was still shut. It was locked after all.

"It won't open," she heard someone say. One of her classmates' voices, sounding no different from when kids were talking in lessons.

She curled up, put her head between her knees and trembled, more like a turtle than a rabbit.

As she sat there, Kokoro silently asked her parents to forgive her. These kids she didn't know had trespassed into the grounds of their house while they were out. And had trampled over her mother's precious garden.

I'm so sorry, so sorry, so sorry.

"She's not coming out." Miori's voice sounded less savage. She started to sound tearful. "She's a total wuss, is what she is," she said in a faint, weepy tone, and one of the girls said, "Come on, Miori. Don't cry."

All the kids cared about was themselves.

"She flutters her eyes at someone else's boyfriend and she really loves it when they touch her," another girl said.

He never touched me, Kokoro thought, but her tongue was stuck to the roof of her mouth and she couldn't even whisper.

In the darkening room, the cold floor chilled Kokoro's legs. She was still in her school uniform.

"I can't forgive her," a voice said.

Kokoro couldn't tell any more if it was Miori speaking.

I don't care if you don't forgive me, she thought. *Because I'm never, ever going to forgive any of you.*

Kokoro had no idea how much time had passed. It seemed like forever.

Eventually, Miori and her gang seemed to grow tired of the game and she heard them call their goodbyes to each other. "See you tomorrow!"

Kokoro stayed glued to the spot, fearful it was a trap.

The sound of her mother's key in the front door quietly reverberated in the darkness.

"Kokoro?" she called out, sounding uncertain. Kokoro felt a slight pain in her jaw, and tears came to her eyes.

Mum, Mum, Mum.

She wanted to cry out, leap into her mother's arms and sob her heart out, but she didn't move. Her mother walked into the sitting room and switched on the light.

Kokoro looked up for the first time.

"Kokoro."

Her mother was standing there in her grey work suit.

"Mum," she said, her voice husky.

"Why is the light off?" her mother asked. "You startled me. I thought you hadn't come home yet, and I was worried."

"Um."

I was worried—the words struck a chord deep inside her.

Why, she didn't know.

"I just fell asleep," Kokoro said.

KOKORO TRIED TO convince herself she hadn't been at home that day.

Miori and the others had simply pounded on the door of an empty house, trampled over the patio, gone round and round the outside of the house.

But nothing actually happened.

Nothing at all.

She never was about to be killed.

And yet the next day, she said, "I have a stomachache."

And she really did. It was no lie.

And her mother chimed in: "You do look pale. Are you OK?"

And that's when Kokoro stopped going to school.

A LONG TIME later, Kokoro realized she was holding out a faint hope.

Wouldn't her parents notice that the garden had been trampled on?

Even if Kokoro didn't say anything, wouldn't some neighbor tell her parents about the Anzais' house being surrounded by a mob of unruly kids? And maybe they'd even reported it to the police?

But none of that happened.

It might have had more impact if she'd told her parents about the incident immediately, but if she brought it up now—this event that changed Kokoro's middle school life forever—they might not even listen.

And now she deeply regretted not having instantly leapt into her mother's arms, in tears.

Kokoro hopelessly realized now that if she put the incident into words, it would boil down to something so lame. They might have come all the way here to pick a fight with her, but in the end, they didn't. That's how adults would react. And with that, they'd put it out of their minds.

Those girls didn't wreck anything, or physically hurt her.

But Kokoro's experience of the incident went way beyond that; it was something far more decisive and intense. What if she went to school again, defenseless?

Would she be able to protect herself?

The only place she could now go to freely from her bedroom was the castle.

If I'm in the castle, she started to think, *then I'll be safe.*

Only the castle beyond the mirror could offer her complete protection.

* * *

AKI AND FUKA listened to Kokoro, their eyes fixed on her until the end.

She had trouble speaking at first. She spoke slowly, deliberately choosing her words, and halfway she found she couldn't look them in the eye anymore.

Her voice broke off at points, and she choked up.

Aki and Fuka didn't rush her, but patiently heard her out.

"Is this a problem that's still going on?" Aki asked after a while.

Kokoro didn't explain that this was why she'd stopped going to school. She was well aware that Aki didn't want her to go there. In fact, Kokoro really didn't know how Aki would react to her story. She might dismiss it as nothing very major.

"Yes, it's still going on," Kokoro said, and as soon as she did, Aki stood up from her dining chair and patted Kokoro on the head with her right hand, messing up her hair.

"What are you doing?" said Kokoro, her hair askew.

"I'm proud of you," Aki said, her eyes gentle and consoling. "I'm proud of you. That must have been so hard to take."

Fuka, who'd been silent, held out a handkerchief to Kokoro. Her eyes had the same soft glow as Aki's. Kokoro accepted Fuka's handkerchief, held her breath, then quietly inhaled, long and deep.

August

EVEN FROM INSIDE her bedroom, Kokoro could sense that the world was now on summer break.

She'd never expected to spend her first summer holiday in junior high like this, but August came to one and all.

During the day, when Kokoro didn't go out, she could overhear the school kids talking with each other as they rode by on their bikes. Their shadows cut across below her window, kids who attended the same elementary school she'd gone to.

Just after the summer holidays started, at the beginning of August, she was having dinner when her father said, "I'm glad for you."

For a second she didn't know who he was talking to. Since she'd dropped out of school, she thought nothing would ever get her father to say anything like that.

But he went on calmly. "So now you'll be like everyone else," he said. Kokoro's hand froze halfway to her food. Her father seemed in a light-hearted mood.

"It's the summer holiday so you can walk around anywhere you want, and not get picked up as a truant from school. So why not visit the library? It's got to be suffocating staying at home all the time."

"Darling," her mother interjected. "That's too much for her. You don't feel comfortable going out during the day and bumping into your friends from school, right? Isn't that so?"

"Um . . ."

Frown lines formed between her mother's eyebrows. "Kokoro,"

she said. "I've said this before, but if there's a reason you don't want to go to school, you can talk to me about it anytime."

"OK." Kokoro stared downwards, and lightly bit on the tips of her chopsticks.

At some point, her mother had stopped urging her to go to the alternative School. Kokoro sensed, though, that she and the teachers there were still keeping in touch. Kokoro didn't dare broach it with her mother, since she didn't want her to start urging her to go again.

But her mother's feelings had changed. Instead of hinting that her daughter was simply being apathetic, now she was more likely to ask, in a roundabout way, if something had happened to make her stop going to school.

Before the summer holidays started, her parents were trying to persuade her to attend a special summer session at a private juku.

Not one nearby, they said, but one some distance away. "You could commute from your grandma's place, maybe. A juku where nobody knows you. You could catch up on all you missed in the first semester. What do you think?" That night, Kokoro's stomach started to feel terribly heavy, and she couldn't sleep.

The junior high school textbooks she'd stuffed into a drawer had barely been cracked open. The other students had spent a whole semester ploughing through all that material, but Kokoro hadn't done a thing. She was convinced she'd never catch up.

She never wanted to go to school again, yet here she was, worried she'd never catch up.

She tried to imagine herself attending a juku summer session, but like the idea of going to the alternative School, it just didn't sit well with her.

"If you don't want to go, that's fine," her mother had said.

HER HOMEROOM TEACHER, Mr. Ida, had come so often to see her at the beginning of the school year. He didn't visit much anymore. Perhaps he'd given up on her, Kokoro thought.

Satsuki-chan, her friend from elementary school days, had regularly delivered school handouts to her house instead of Tojo-san, but now she too had stopped. There were times when Kokoro regretted not catching a glimpse of her when she came by, but her relief outweighed the regret.

What made her happiest, and most relieved, was if they all left her alone.

But she still wondered if it was going to be like this forever.

* * *

"I KNOW WHAT it's like to feel panicked when you can't keep up with schoolwork."

She was in the dining room at the castle the next day, and Fuka was speaking quietly.

It was now an unspoken rule that the boys would hang out in the Game Room, while the girls would get together in the dining room. When she arrived at the castle, Kokoro would drop off her belongings in her room and head straight to the dining room.

What Kokoro looked forward to most was seeing Aki and Fuka.

Even Ureshino was no longer the girl chaser he had been.

And slowly—ever so slowly—when Aki wasn't with them, Fuka began opening up about not going to school.

"You mean there're moments when you can't keep up with schoolwork, Fuka-chan? That's hard to believe."

Fuka looked like the perfect A student, what with her glasses and bowl haircut. But Fuka smiled and said, "You didn't see that coming, did you? I know I look a bit nerdy, but my grades are actually pretty bad. There's tons of schoolwork I just don't get. I often feel left behind."

"So maybe you could go to juku or—" Kokoro started to say, when a voice interrupted them.

"*Goood* morning, Fuka. Kokoro."

93

Aki walked in, sounding cheerful, and the two girls' conversation ended there.

Fuka was willing to open up more about school, but with Aki it still remained a sensitive subject.

"It's so cool in here, I feel revived," she murmured. She took out her thermos and got the tea ready.

Kokoro and Fuka took out the cookies they'd each brought, and today Aki had brought patterned paper napkins which she began to spread out. When she saw the napkins, with their border design of rose vines and birds, Fuka declared them "so sweet." Not the kind of comment she typically made. She fingered one delicately and asked, "Where do they sell these?"

"They are lovely, aren't they," Aki said, and smiled. "I went to a stationer's nearby at the weekend and they were selling them there. They had all kinds of other cool designs as well, and it was so hard to choose. Do you like these, Fuka? I'll give them to you."

"Do I like them? Yeah, I suppose so."

"They're so gorgeous," Kokoro piped up, and Fuka looked at her. "Aki-chan?"

"Hm?"

"Can I give Kokoro-chan one too?"

"Sure. Of course."

"Really?" Kokoro asked, and with a "Here you go," Fuka handed her the one she was holding. Aki poured the tea, the rising steam giving out its fragrant apple smell. The napkins and tea matched perfectly.

"Thank you," Kokoro said, and Fuka spread out another napkin and placed the cookies on top. Just then, as if waiting for this moment, who should turn up at the doorway to the dining room but Ureshino.

This was unusual, seeing as he normally never came to the castle until the afternoon.

He stood fidgeting, as if waiting for Kokoro and the girls to notice him.

"Hey, Ureshino," Aki called.

"Good morning," he said in a small voice, his eyes on Fuka, the present object of his affections.

Fuka shot him an indifferent glance, set down her cup, and stared at her hands.

"What's up?" Kokoro asked. It was pretty odd for him to turn up like this. She noticed he was hiding something behind his back.

Ureshino brought his right-hand round, and Kokoro gave a small gasp of surprise.

"It's your birthday today, isn't it, Fuka-chan? So I brought you some flowers."

There were two flowers, one pink, one white, with long stems. Kokoro didn't know what type they were. They were wrapped up, like a bouquet.

"*What?* It's your birthday?" Aki and Kokoro stared at Fuka.

Fuka looked up and murmured, "I'm surprised you remembered."

Ureshino looked pleased. "Because I happened to hear about it. I don't forget things like that."

"You should have told us," Aki said.

"It's not really worth mentioning," Fuka said, her voice as high-pitched as always, though maybe a bit embarrassed.

"Then let's celebrate. Cheers!"

Aki raised her teacup and clinked it against Fuka's. Fuka timidly accepted the bouquet, managed an awkward "Thanks," and Ureshino chuckled happily.

"Aki-chan, can I have some?" he asked, apparently planning to hang around.

Aki made her disgust clear. "Don't you understand? This is a girls-only party," she said. "So go away!"

"Don't you want me here?" Ureshino retorted, brazenly standing his ground. The scene was so comical that Kokoro couldn't help but laugh.

"Isn't it about twelve?" Aki asked, her signal that would send them all back home for lunch.

"Whoa, I gotta get home," Ureshino said, flying out of the door ahead of them.

Kokoro looked at the flowers on the table. They were blooming nicely, though they looked a little past their best.

"I bet he just picked them from his garden," Aki said. "And I bet he reused some old paper. Kind of tacky, if you ask me."

"Really?" said Fuka, looking uncertain. She quietly grabbed the bouquet and rose to her feet, about to leave the dining room.

"You know what?" Aki said awkwardly, aiming her remarks at the retreating Fuka. "If you'd like to display the flowers here, I'll look for something we could use as a vase."

"It's OK," Fuka said, without turning around. "There's no running water here anyway. I'll take them home."

"Oh—right."

After Fuka was gone, Aki and Kokoro didn't speak to each other. Finally, unable to stand the silence, Kokoro said, "OK, see you this afternoon."

"Yeah, see you."

Aki's expression looked as cheerful as always, but just as Kokoro was about to leave, she heard her mutter, "If she behaves like that, I bet she doesn't have any friends."

Kokoro heard these words on her way out the door, and they made her shudder.

She hadn't misheard.

It sounded as though Aki was just muttering to herself, but she probably didn't mind that Kokoro had overheard.

BACK HOME, KOKORO microwaved the frozen gratin her mother had made, and mulled over how much she disliked these new developments.

She liked both Fuka and Aki, and it bothered her that things could get so stiff and awkward even in the castle.

Aki and Fuka might both stay away from the castle this afternoon, she thought, but when she arrived back after one o'clock, both girls were already in the dining room.

They seemed to be waiting for her. "Ureshino came by again, but I sent him packing," Aki said, laughing. "Let's continue the birthday party. Here you go, a little something from me."

Aki held out her palm with three hairclips.

The clips were fancy ones, made of wood, with the ceramic shapes of a watermelon, lemon and strawberry on the front. They were in a small transparent bag, tied with a blue checked ribbon.

"I wrapped it with things we had at home, so it's a little makeshift," Aki said, but to Kokoro's eyes it didn't look that way at all. It looked as pretty as something you'd buy in a shop and get gift wrapped. Fuka held it in her hands, gazing at the present.

"Thank you," she said. "It's really lovely."

"I'm glad you like it," Aki smiled. "Happy birthday, Fuka," she said again.

* * *

THE NEXT MORNING, Kokoro felt excited.

Alone in the house, now that her parents had finished breakfast and set off for work, Kokoro took a few deep breaths.

The shops opened at ten.

She'd go out and buy a birthday present for Fuka.

In the hushed, silent house, no one else was aware of what Kokoro was planning to do.

All she had to do was secretly slip out and slip back in.

She looked at herself in the mirror—not the shining one that led to the castle but the one by the front door—and took a deep breath. She contemplated wearing a hat, but decided that while an elementary school kid could get away with that, it would be uncool for a junior high student to be seen wearing one.

She put on a T-shirt and skirt, scrubbed her face twice, and combed her long hair until it shone.

With a racing heart, she pushed open the front door.

The summer sun shone straight into the dark hallway, and she squinted at its dazzle. The sun was high in the sky. Birds were out. And heat radiated through her shoes as she stepped on to the asphalt.

She was outside.

In a world she hadn't set foot in for ages.

The air was fresh and invigorating, and she was relieved she didn't find it overpowering at all. Cicadas chirped in the distance; people walked their dogs while children played.

Kokoro slipped quietly out of the gate.

She had a good idea of what she wanted to buy Fuka as a present.

She'd go to Careo, a local shopping mall within walking distance. It had opened when she first started at elementary school, and had every type of shop, McDonald's and Mister Donut included.

It was exhilarating to go out, and she was filled with a fluttery expectation. She hadn't realized how good it felt to be out on her own.

Kokoro emerged on to the high street.

As she did, two bicycles whizzed past her. When she spotted them, she froze. From their tops, she knew these were boys attending the school she *had* attended—Yukishina No. 5 Junior High School. "No way! Hey!" they called out to each other in conversation. Each grade at school had different jersey colors, and these boys weren't wearing Kokoro's freshman blue, but a dark red, which meant they were in eighth grade.

She felt like she could actually hear her excitement being snuffed out.

She looked down, avoiding them as they cycled off into the distance. But she couldn't help looking up. She wanted to hear the boys' voices. Wouldn't they turn around and whisper about her?

Of course not.

Yukishina No. 5 was an enormous school, and they wouldn't recognize her.

But still she couldn't shake the awful feeling that swept over her.

What if they were friends with Miori? She suddenly wanted to crouch down and hide herself away. She turned to face the street again, and it felt like the heat of the asphalt was gripping her by the ankles. Far away, at the end of the long street, she saw the sign to the shopping mall. She couldn't believe it had seemed so close when her parents drove her there.

The thought of walking so far made her weak at the knees.

She'd been standing in one place for so long it felt like she was rooted to the spot. She willed her feet to move.

How far had she walked?

After a while, she began to feel ill, and stopped at a convenience store.

Inside, she felt blinded.

The lighting above the rows of bentos and drinks was far too glaring, and she couldn't keep her eyes open. She'd been here any number of times, and thought she was used to it, but now the colors seemed far more dazzling. And so much stuff! Row after row of sweets and juice she would apologetically ask her mother to buy for her, lined up like a mural covering the whole wall, and it all felt terribly wrong. So much choice made her head spin.

She reached out to grab a plastic water bottle, but dropped it clumsily. "Sorry," she muttered, picking it up from the floor, and as she held it against her chest, her face suddenly felt flushed and hot. There was no need to apologize. And her voice might have been too loud.

A man who looked like an office worker passed silently behind her, and though he didn't brush her back, she flinched all the same. She now only met people at home, or the other kids at the castle, and she found it hard to believe that someone she didn't know could come so close.

It all came down to one thing.

Fear.

She was absolutely terrified of the convenience store.

Clutching the water bottle, so pleasantly cool against her chest, Kokoro realized something.

This was impossible.

She would never make it to the shopping mall.

* * *

WHEN SHE WENT to the castle in the late afternoon, Fuka wasn't there.

Neither Aki nor Fuka was in the dining room, so she went to look in the Game Room. "Fuka was here this morning, but I think she might not come back for a while," Masamune informed her.

Kokoro had dashed out of the convenience store as if running for her life, randomly grabbing a box of chocolates, and now she stood here, sweets in hand, not knowing what to say.

"She said she has to go to a summer school her parents chose. For about a week. A short, intensive course. They want her to catch up at school."

Kokoro felt as if someone had slugged her in the head.

Summer school, to catch up at school. The same suggestion her parents had made, which had been weighing on her ever since.

She'd intended to ask Fuka and the others what they planned to do about their schoolwork. It felt like Fuka had suddenly stolen a march on her. Her stomach began to ache again, and she felt anxious.

"What about Aki-chan?"

"I dunno. Could be in her room?"

Today, unusually, Masamune was alone in the Game Room. Neither Ureshino nor Subaru had come over.

"Ureshino often doesn't turn up, and Subaru said something about going on a trip with his parents," Masamune explained. "Since it's the summer holidays and all."

"I see."

She remembered how sick she'd felt at the convenience store today. Subaru struck her as strangely mature, able to go on a trip.

"What are you doing about schoolwork, Masamune-kun?"

"What? You're asking this genius?" His tone was nonchalant.

"Didn't I tell you before about the juku? I still get good grades."

"Really?"

Kokoro left the room. As he watched her walk out, Masamune called, "Hey, you know what? FYI, all that stuff you study at school? None of it will help you in the real world."

"Guess not," Kokoro replied, and headed to the dining room.

SHE PLACED THE present for Fuka on the dining-room table.

She'd wrapped the box of chocolates in a page from an English-language newspaper her mother had happened to bring home, secured it with Sellotape, and covered it with mini character stickers. While wrapping it, she gathered as many things as she could to make the gift as attractive as possible, but now it struck her as pathetic.

Maybe it was a good thing she hadn't given Fuka the present.

With that thought, the events of this long day surged back to her in painful recall.

Despite all the months away from school, to her it felt like she'd only been off for a short while. And she'd already developed a fear of venturing outside.

Maybe she'd feel better if she sobbed it all out? But if somebody glimpsed her crying, they'd think she was annoying, and she didn't want that.

"Oh?"

She heard a voice. Kokoro turned to look at the door. She blinked a bit, for this was someone she hadn't seen in a long time. Rion.

"Are you by yourself today?" he asked. "Where are the girls?"

"I think Aki-chan's in her room. Fuka-chan's starting summer session today."

"Summer session? What's that?"

Rion strode into the dining room.

He had a nice nose, and large, sleepy-looking eyes with long lashes. Seeing him up close again reminded Kokoro how handsome he was. *He's so tanned*, she noted, *he probably has no problem going outside.*

"Don't you know about summer sessions? They do them at jukus—they go over a whole semester of classes."

"Ah, makes sense. Since it's the summer holiday. Must be tough though, studying."

Rion didn't seem to have any of Masamune's sarcasm. Kokoro stood, unaware she was staring at him.

"What?" he asked.

"You mean, you're not studying?"

"I don't like it, so I'm not doing much. But you seem like the studious type, Kokoro."

"I'm really not."

She really wasn't, and it choked her with anxiety, but here Rion had called her by her first name—with no *chan* attached—and it caught her by surprise.

"I see," Rion said, sounding uninterested. She noticed he was looking towards the top of the dining table.

"Is that a present?" he asked.

"Um."

"For Fuka?"

"Yes. Did you know it was her birthday?"

"Couldn't help it, with Ureshino all psyched up like that. He's quite a character. He had you in his sights too, up till recently."

"Don't."

She was embarrassed at the misshapen wrapping, and wished she could just disappear.

But Rion said, "That's a shame. You went to the trouble of bringing her a present, and now you can't give it to her."

He didn't mean anything by it, apparently. But Kokoro was feeling something warm pressing on her chest.

A not-so-great present, clumsily wrapped.

Something you could buy at any convenience store.

A box of chocolates she'd grabbed as she ran out.

"Yes," she said. "Yes, I really do want to give it to her."

When she'd heard that Subaru was away with his family on a trip, and Fuka was at a summer school juku, that one after another, the kids might all stop coming to the castle, she started to feel that coming here was a bit uncool.

Her parents had urged her to attend summer school, and she'd wasted the chance.

"I'm going to fall behind at school," she murmured.

"Hm?"

Rion glanced over and she quickly changed her expression. She laughed, so she wouldn't seem so down. "Nothing," she replied. But he had heard her.

"Are you worried about schoolwork?" he asked. "You said you're in the first year of junior high, aren't you, Kokoro? So am I."

"Yeah."

"Got it."

With that their conversation ended.

Rion might very well be in the same situation as her. That made her a little relieved, though she also felt sorry for him.

I'm afraid of not being able to keep up with schoolwork, she thought, *but I'm just as afraid of going to a juku.*

So what should I do?

There was only one answer.

She had to find the key to the Wishing Room.

＊　＊　＊

THE FOLLOWING WEEK, Aki didn't appear at the castle.

According to information from Ureshino and Masamune, she'd gone to her grandmother's house and had stopped coming to the castle.

Kokoro's parents were constantly busy with work and found it hard to get time off, and since Kokoro had refused to go to school or to the alternative School, it seemed like the idea that they might send her anywhere at all was now unlikely. And so she felt too awkward to ask them.

Masamune, like Kokoro, kept up his visits to the castle. At weekends Kokoro couldn't get there as her parents were home, but perhaps Masamune still turned up, when the rest of the world was off. Masamune's parents' ideas about school were so completely different from her own parents'—she wondered what sort of people they were, what kind of jobs they had.

Masamune was often all alone, and when she came into the Game Room he'd shoot her a glance and not even say hello.

When Subaru and the other boys weren't there, Masamune didn't play video games on the TV, but would spend most of his time absorbed in his portable game console.

"Oh, is that . . . ?" Kokoro asked one day.

"Hm?" Masamune looked up. Kokoro's eyes were fixed on his hands.

This was the portable game device Masamune had brought their very first day. He'd said his friend had asked him to be a *tester* for it. Kokoro was so envious, but as it seemed he had special permission to use it, it must be some sort of corporate secret, and so she wasn't at all sure if she could ask him to show it to her.

Masamune noticed where Kokoro was looking, and he glanced down at the device in his hands. Kokoro heard faint music. "Do you want to borrow it?" Masamune said, and Kokoro's eyes widened.

"Are you sure?"

"You said your parents hid all your games, right? No worries. I've got tons of brand-new games at home.

"Do you like RPGs?" Masamune asked, bending over to take out something from his backpack. When it came to games on portable devices, Masamune seemed to prefer role-playing games with storylines over the racing and action games he played with the others.

"I haven't played many RPGs," Kokoro said. "They seem so long." She said this without really thinking.

Rummaging through his backpack, Masamune shot her a *What the—?* sort of glare, and sighed loudly, deliberately.

"I thought, wow, she plays games, and girls aren't usually into that—but what d'you mean, *they're so long*?" Masamune looked contemptuous. "What you're saying is you've hardly ever played a game with a storyline? Do you think all video games are only primitive single-shot-and-it's-over ones?"

"It's because they seem so hard," she explained.

"Hard?" Masamune scowled. "Give me a break. You've got to play RPGs to really understand what's cool about video games. In my opinion. The first time I ever cried was over a story in a video game."

"What? You actually cried over a video game?" It was Kokoro's turn to be surprised. "Did you feel frustrated when it was game over?"

"No—I found it really moving. Don't make me say that, OK?"

Masamune sounded irritated. Kokoro was startled by his reaction. Sure, most of the video games she'd seen in commercials on TV played on your emotions, like in movies—but to cry over it?

"This is such a waste of time," Masamune grumbled. Kokoro didn't respond. "Have you ever cried over a novel, or a manga?" he asked. "What about an anime or a movie?"

"Yeah, of course."

"So how's that different from a video game? Maybe you lack imagination?"

Kokoro realized she'd upset him, and he really was exercised about it.

"Then you don't need to lend it to me," she said.

Masamune, clearly in a bad mood, narrowed his eyes. He was about to pass the device over to her, but said, "Oh, OK then," and pulled it back. "So you're not really into it, are you." She stayed silent, not wanting to argue any more.

Masamune was so tough he'd probably soon forget this little spat.

AT LEAST THAT'S what she thought, but when she came back to the castle after lunch, he was nowhere to be found.

Not only that, he didn't appear for the rest of the day. Kokoro sat alone in the Game Room, muttering about that "stupid *loser!*" She pounded one of the cushions on the sofa in frustration. "You stupid wuss," she yelled, punching the cushion three times and breathing out.

She looked at the video game console he'd left behind the TV. *Maybe I should break it while he's not here?* she thought. She'd never actually do that, of course, but the mere thought calmed her down a little.

Masamune must love those RPGs, the kind you could really get into on your own. But she realized that while he was over here, he always played the action-type games you could play with other people.

THE NEXT DAY SUBARU reappeared; the first time for a while.

Masamune still hadn't returned, and Subaru was alone by the window in the Game Room, listening to something on earphones. The cord was connected to a device inside his bag.

"Subaru-kun," Kokoro called, but he didn't hear. She tapped him lightly on the shoulder, and he finally looked up and slipped out the earphones.

"Oh, sorry," he said. "I didn't realize you were here."

"No, *I'm* sorry for bothering you. Is Masamune—?"

"Seems he's not here. It's a shame, because I was hoping to see him, too. It's been a while."

Subaru stowed away his earphones, and looked at her, his pale face full of freckles.

"Subaru-kun, has anyone told you that you look like Ron in *Harry Potter*? The first time I saw you, I thought there was this clear resemblance."

"*Harry Potter*?"

"The book."

As she said it, she realized the image was more of the character from the movie than the book. But Subaru shrugged. "That's the first time anyone's said that," he said, shaking his head. "You really like books, don't you?"

His gestures when he spoke struck her as so adult. *If only there was a boy like him in my class*, she thought.

"Subaru's the name of a constellation in the galaxy, isn't it?" Kokoro asked. "Sort of a fantastical name, I guess, which is maybe why I made that connection."

"Really? It's true, though—of all the things I've got from Father, my name's what I like best."

"Eh?"

What surprised her was less the origin of his name than how readily he used the formal word *father*. He smiled, and stared down at the earphones in his bag.

"Father gave me these, too. When I met him this month."

Met him this month? That struck Kokoro as odd. It's his dad, yet he said *met him this month?* Wait a sec—didn't he normally live with his father?

Subaru looked up at her, perhaps noticing how intently she was listening to him. She sensed he wanted her to ask him more questions.

"So, Subaru-kun, you—"

She suddenly felt someone's gaze from the doorway. Subaru had felt it sooner and was looking over. It was Fuka.

"Kokoro-chan, thank you for the present."

"Um."

Kokoro had leaned the present up against Fuka's mirror, so she'd see it whenever she decided to come. She'd put a card with it that said, *Sorry it's late, but Happy Birthday!*

Fuka was holding the present. She opened it on the table and stared fixedly at the box of sweets.

Kokoro had gone to such lengths to buy it, but now she couldn't help thinking it looked as if she'd just wrapped up something lying around the house.

Subaru stood up. "I'm going back for a bit."

"OK, sure," said Kokoro as she watched him leave.

Fuka continued to stare at the box of sweets. Kokoro thought maybe she should apologize for such a trivial gift. But then Fuka raised her eyes.

"Do you like this type of chocolate?" Fuka asked.

"What do you mean?"

"It's just, I've—never eaten this brand. I was thinking you must have chosen your ultimate favorite."

"Yeah. It's good."

It was true she liked it, but she wasn't sure she'd say it was her *ultimate favorite*. Fuka said she'd never eaten it, which might mean she didn't go to convenience stores very often. Fuka was a polite, well-brought-up girl, so perhaps her parents weren't the type to allow their daughter to eat such things.

Fuka smiled. "I'm so thrilled to have them. I want to try them."

She sounded genuinely excited.

Fuka, Kokoro thought, *is quite an amazing girl.*

Fuka didn't usually show her feelings openly, and so it was hard to tell what she was thinking.

"I'd like to eat them with you now, Kokoro-chan, but is it OK if I take them home and eat them there?"

Kokoro was surprised she felt she had to ask.

"I've never had them before, so I'd kind of like to have them all to myself."

"Of course. No problem."

That day Fuka apparently enjoyed the chocolates back home, for she faithfully reported to Kokoro that "they were delicious."

ATTENDANCE AT THE castle had dropped off, though there was one person she saw more often now that the summer holidays had started.

Rion.

Her first impression hadn't changed—he was an outgoing boy, definitely popular with girls. He'd steadily become more tanned, and taller too, it seemed. And she was startled when she saw the skin on his cheeks appear to be peeling off—maybe all he did was skip school and hang around outside? He didn't seem like the type to spend time with a gang of dropout friends.

"Where is everyone?" he asked.

"It's just the two of us today, Kokoro-chan and me," Fuka answered. "Subaru-kun was here this morning, but everyone else has something on over the summer."

Kokoro glanced at the clock. It was after four.

Rion cast a look around the Game Room, bereft of any boys, and murmured, "Hmm. So Masamune's not here either. That's odd. I was hoping he'd let me play his video games."

"I think I upset him," Kokoro said, and Rion looked at her.

"Really? How?"

Kokoro explained what had happened.

"I told him I thought RPGs were too long and complicated, and he got angry. He really put me down, and I felt pretty irritated too, to be honest."

But still . . .

"But he said I could still play his games."

Masamune had told her he'd be willing to lend her some of his games. It was Kokoro's stubbornness that had made her refuse his offer.

"I see—I don't know much about games myself. But I do think

you should apologize. I think Masamune must be worried about it, too—worried that he went too far with what he said."

He said it so casually Kokoro nodded in assent.

"I'll definitely apologize as soon as I see him."

*   *   *

AT DINNER THAT evening, Kokoro's father was still at work, so she ate alone with her mother.

Her mother had made it home just as the rice Kokoro had rinsed and poured into the rice cooker was ready. She changed her clothes and put on an apron.

Work kept her mother too busy to cook dinner, so she'd picked up some salad and gyoza at a shop in the Careo mall. "Sorry about this," she said, but Kokoro actually liked the food from that shop. The salad they made had nuts in it and was more interesting than the salad her mother usually threw together.

As she was getting the food ready, her mother said, "Kokoro?"

Her voice was calm, with a detectable hint of steeliness.

"What?" Kokoro said, bracing herself.

"Did you—go somewhere during the day?"

Kokoro's heart began to thump.

"What?" Kokoro said, a beat late. Her mother had been putting the plates down on the table, but she stopped and looked at her daughter. Kokoro was fetching the chopsticks.

"I'm not cross or anything. If you feel like going out, that's fine. And luckily, it's the summer holidays now."

Kokoro got caught on the word *luckily*, and so the rest of her mother's words didn't register.

Luckily, it's the summer holidays now.

If it was term time, her mother would never, ever want anyone to see her daughter missing school and wandering around town.

"I didn't plan to tell you, but the other day I came home from work at lunchtime."

Kokoro's senses faded, as if she'd received an invisible blow to the back of her head.

"And I found you weren't here."

"Why did you come home?" Kokoro shot back.

Kokoro knew it didn't make sense to get angry, but she couldn't help it. Daytime at home was *her* time, no one else's. *Doesn't Mum trust me?* she wondered. *Did she come back to check up on me?*

Kokoro was awkwardly aware of her facial muscles, the way her eyes moved.

"Understand I'm not angry, Kokoro," her mother said. "I really wasn't planning to say anything."

"Then why *did* you?"

"Why?" A knot of worry appeared in her brow, and her voice, calm until now, shot up a notch in pitch. "Because I was worried, that's why! Your shoes were still by the front door and at first I thought, *Oh my god, has she been kidnapped?*"

"My shoes."

She hadn't expected her mother to notice that sort of thing. Of course she'd gone into Kokoro's bedroom, too. The mirror wasn't shining, was it? She had no idea what the mirror was like when she wasn't there, though it might be set up not to shine once she'd gone through it.

Kokoro had no clue how her mother interpreted the shoes being there. She might very well think Kokoro had worn other shoes and gone out.

"Kokoro."

Her mother's eyes looked puzzled. Kokoro saw them and realized, with horror, that her mother no longer trusted her.

"I told you, didn't I? That I'm not blaming you? If you're able to go out, I think that's great. But where did you—"

"I just went out for a bit, that's all!"

Not true.

As she got this lie out, she felt she couldn't breathe.

She hadn't wanted to say it.

The truth was that Kokoro could no longer go outside.

On the high street, under the blazing sun, and where even the lighting in the convenience store was too glaring, just glimpsing the jerseys of the older boys from her school was enough to make her freeze. She really wished her mother could understand the distress she'd felt then. But all she could tell her was that she'd gone out. And this made her feel awful. Truly awful.

She was so terrified of going outside, and didn't want her mother to think she was like other kids, able to go out whenever they felt like it.

She'd said she wasn't angry, so why her mother's huge sigh?

"Do you want to try going to the alternative School one more time?"

That was all it took for Kokoro to feel a weight in the pit of her stomach. Registering her silence, her mother continued, "Do you remember Ms. Kitajima from the time we visited the School?"

The young teacher who'd shown Kokoro around. The one who'd remarked, *So Kokoro, I understand you're a student at Yukishina No. 5 Junior High School?* Kokoro recalled the name tag on her chest, with her name and a portrait of her drawn by one of her pupils.

I went there too, she'd said, and smiled kindly. Kokoro had been so jealous of her then, an adult who never had to go to that junior high ever again. The woman's short hair made her look so confident—and Kokoro had decided, *No, she's not at all like me.*

"Ms. Kitajima said she'd love to talk to you again."

Her mother gazed at Kokoro. Just as Kokoro had sensed, her mother seemed to be still in touch with the teacher, even though Kokoro wasn't going to the School. After a silence, her mother continued, "The teacher said it's not your fault at all that you can't go to school. She was worried that something must have happened."

Kokoro's eyes widened ever so slightly.

"She often reminds me, *It's not Kokoro-chan's fault. As her mother, you shouldn't ever get upset or blame her.* That's why, even though there are things I'd like to ask you, I've been holding back."

If she was holding back, then why reveal all this stuff now? Her mother looked seriously at her.

"The day after I found you weren't here, I slipped away from work and came home again. And you weren't here then, either, were you? I came home several times."

Kokoro remained silent. Her mother gave her a tired look.

"I was worried, wondering what I should do if you weren't home by evening. I went back to work, and when I came home you were here, weren't you? Looking as if nothing had happened. And I was thinking, *So she's going somewhere every day, and then calmly having supper with me.* And when I thought that—"

"OK, I get it. I won't go anywhere anymore. I'll stay put in the house." Kokoro almost spat these words out, and she heard her mother gasp.

"That's not what I'm saying," her mother said. "I'm fine with you going out. But I would like to know where you go. The park? The library? You're not going to Careo, are you? That game center there—"

"There's no way I can go that far!"

Which wasn't a lie. She really had no desire to go that far. But she still found it hard to stand her mother's ridiculous misunderstanding.

Kokoro slapped her chopsticks and bowl down on the dining table with a clatter. She leapt up and ran out of the room.

"Kokoro!" her mother called. But Kokoro was already upstairs in her bedroom. She fell face down on the bed.

The mirror wasn't shining at all now, and it made her resentful. She dreamed of going to the castle at night, going inside, and vanishing from her room.

Instead her mother was coming upstairs after her. "Listen, Kokoro." She heard footsteps on the landing. There was no escape.

She thought of the teacher at the alternative School, Ms. Kitajima. And what she'd said.

It's not Kokoro-chan's fault at all that she can't go to school.

"Kokoro." Her mother was outside the door. Kokoro got up.

The patterned paper napkin Aki had given her was lying on her desk. If her mother spotted it, she'd wonder where it came from.

She grabbed it and hid it under the bedclothes, crumpling it up.

She remembered the girls—Aki, and Fuka, how happy she'd been with the present. Regret welled up in Kokoro, and she felt like screaming.

Why couldn't they just stop interfering, and let her go where she wanted?

"Kokoro, I'm coming in," and her mother opened the door.

THE DAY AFTER she and her mother had argued, Kokoro didn't go to the castle.

Her mother apologized in an exaggeratedly gentle tone. "I'm really sorry about yesterday," she said. "I have no intention of criticizing how you spend your time. Coming home during the day wasn't supposed to be an unscheduled inspection. I'm sorry if it seemed that way."

Kokoro listened uneasily. "Um," she said.

"I won't be coming home during the day again," her mother said. "I won't do anything to test you."

Maybe she was acting on advice from Ms. Kitajima, or someone else at the School? She sounded so understanding, so motherly.

Thinking it might be a trap, Kokoro spent the day at home. Whatever her mother might say, she could still be monitoring her.

She closed the curtains to block out the sunshine, and turned on the AC. She read a book, watched TV to pass the time. Outside she heard children on summer break playing in the park behind their house.

She ate the lunch her mother had prepared for her, and peeked through the curtains. Evening came, but still no sign of her mother.

She'd gone to the trouble of staying at home, but there hadn't been any surprise visit.

She found that disappointing, and frustrating.

If she'd known, she would have gone to the castle.

THE NEXT DAY, she was still wavering—should she go to the castle or not? She waited until the afternoon and her mother still didn't come back, so at three o'clock she headed through to the castle.

Just for a short while, she told herself.

Just to see the rest of the gang briefly, and get home before her mother came back to check on her. Those were her thoughts as she slipped through the mirror.

What she found took her by surprise.

* * *

WHEN THEY HAD first visited the castle it had seemed sterile, but now, after three months, it was littered with the gadgets and snacks they'd brought with them, and it had begun to feel much more like home. Someone had set up name plates, written on cut-out drawing paper, in front of each of the mirrors that connected to their homes: *Kokoro*, *Aki*, *Masamune*, and so on.

Today, unusually, each mirror was shimmering with a rainbow glow. Kokoro was the last to arrive.

When she got to the Game Room, the scene inside took her aback.

"Oh—Kokoro-chan."

Masamune and Subaru, as ever absorbed in their video games, turned towards her.

The whole group was there. Fuka and Aki on the sofa, and the boys by the TV.

But it was one of them in particular who caught her eye.

Subaru.

The last time they'd met, he'd been talking about his father—he hadn't finished the story—but now his hair was dyed a light brown.

Not like Rion's, which was naturally bleached by the sun, but dyed artificially.

"Subaru-kun."

"Hey."

"Your hair."

The rest of the group were silent, clearly following the back and forth.

"Oh, this?" Subaru said, grabbing a strand of hair by his ear.

The gesture made Kokoro more puzzled, for Subaru had definitely changed. He seemed even more mature.

Underneath the lock of hair, she saw he had a small, round earring in his earlobe. "My older brother made me," Subaru said. "*It's the summer holiday, so you've got to do something new.* He almost forced me."

"Did you dye your hair?"

"No. Bleached it. When you dye it the first time the color doesn't take well, but if you bleach it, it does."

"I see."

Her heart thumped.

It was Masamune, playing video games with Subaru. He didn't have on his usual smirk.

"So you have an older brother," he said.

Kokoro was surprised. This was the first she'd heard about Subaru's older brother, but Subaru and Masamune were such good mates and even he didn't know?

"What about the piercing? Did your brother make you do that, too?"

"My brother and his girlfriend. The hole closed up at first, so he told me you've got to keep it in when you go to bed. And last night, there was blood all over the pillow where I'd slept on it."

"Really." Masamune nodded, but he kept his gaze down even more than usual.

Kokoro could not read how he was feeling.

The whole thing must have turned him off.

Dyeing your hair and getting a piercing clearly wasn't something people did in Masamune's world. But he seemed determined to pretend to be calm about it. Kokoro felt the same, and she was sure the others did too.

"Really now," a voice said. Kokoro turned and saw it was Aki.

There was an awkwardness in the air; Aki was the only one who confronted Subaru over what he'd done.

"But won't the teachers tell you off? They always get so stressed at the end of the semester, yelling at us not to come back from summer holiday with our hair dyed. Aren't you afraid they'll come down on you like a ton of bricks?"

"Sure, but I won't let it bother me."

"Lucky you. You know, maybe I should try that. With my hair."

"Wicked. You'd look so great, Aki-chan."

"Maybe I'll get Fuka and Kokoro to do it too. But—there's somebody who'd get all upset if I make Fuka do it."

Aki looked straight over at Ureshino and chuckled. Ureshino blinked his little eyes and stared at her in surprise. Fuka simply ignored it all.

Beneath the bleached hair, Subaru's cheeks looked transparent; all his facial features seemed to have altered. He was the same Subaru, and it surprised Kokoro that something as minor as this could make her so unsettled. Watching how Aki calmly talked with him, she sensed something she hadn't felt before.

Something that made it harder to approach him.

My brother and his girlfriend, Subaru had said.

Kokoro knew they were different from her, the sort of people she would not usually seek out. The kind of brash kids who dropped out of school and casually hung around instead at video arcades and shopping malls.

Just then, a loud voice: "Hey, listen!" It was Ureshino.

"I've got something to say."

"What is it?" Aki asked teasingly.

His face beetroot red, Ureshino scowled at her.

"Starting next semester, I'm going back to school."

Aki's eyes widened. Ureshino could not look any more serious, and his face had now turned an even darker crimson.

"I was worried about telling you, that's why I waited until now," he said. "None of you people are going to school. You *can't*, right?"

Kind of late in the day to bring that up, isn't it? Kokoro thought. Wasn't that pretty obvious?

But then she thought of something. Whenever Masamune and Subaru discussed how it wasn't worth going to school, and when Aki joined in and it all got a bit uncomfortable—it was usually in the morning, when Ureshino wasn't there. She hadn't really ever talked about school with him.

Probably because Ureshino was this gluttonous boy who believed in love above all, and reminded her of some anime character. And they hadn't actually checked with everyone to find out if it was true they weren't going to school.

The others were silent and Ureshino continued.

"It's stupid. You've all dropped out of school, yet here you act like *normal people*. But you're fooling yourselves. You people have no intention of ever going."

Kokoro nearly let out a shriek, but stifled it.

Aki was silent. It was her turn to go bright red, and she glared at Ureshino with a look that could kill. Her cheeks might be bright scarlet, but below the neck she was as white as a ghost.

"But *I* am going," declared Ureshino, pointing at his chest. He looked around at each of them. "I'll be back at school after the break. You guys can stay here forever, for all I care."

"That's a little strong, don't you think?" This was from Rion. He got to his feet and stood facing Ureshino. "It's really fun here!"

"Not for *me*, it isn't!" Ureshino suddenly raised his voice, his face twisted. Rion flinched, and Ureshino, seeing his opening, spoke hurriedly: "I mean, you guys are always making fun of me, aren't you? You always have. Always. I don't know why, but no one takes me seriously. And you think you can get away with anything because it's me."

"That's not true!" Kokoro interrupted.

But deep down, she was shocked. What he said *was* true.

Because it's only Ureshino, it's OK to make fun of him. Kokoro herself thought it was allowed. He switched his love interest so easily, jumping from one to the other, and the girls found this comical. And that had helped the girls to become close. They'd never taken Ureshino seriously.

I sort of knew, but couldn't admit it. And now all I can do is apologize.

"If we made you feel that way, I'm really sorry. But—"

"Ha, ha, ha—give me a break!" Ureshino exclaimed, and Kokoro took a step back.

"You too!" Ureshino glared at Aki, then turned to look at Subaru. "And you! And you! And you!"

He glared at each one in turn, and finally turned to Rion.

"You too, with your nothing-to-do-with-me look on your face! And yet all of you are the same as me—people hate you, they bully you, you have no friends."

"Ureshino, calm down, will you?" Rion said, and rested a hand on his shoulder.

Each of us has our own reasons, Kokoro thought.

Ureshino shook off Rion's hand. He looked ready to break down in tears. Despite his aggressive tone, he seemed to be pleading for help. It was hard to watch, yet Kokoro couldn't drag her eyes away.

"So who do you think *you* are, then?" Ureshino said, trying to provoke Rion. "What happened so *you* can't go to school, eh? Spit it out!"

Rion's eyes popped wide. Everyone was listening carefully for his response.

For an instant he seemed to hesitate. He pursed his lips and looked straight at Ureshino. "I *am* going to school."

"What?" The others all gasped. But Ureshino wasn't having it.

"You're *lying*! This late in the game, to lie like that—don't you think it's disgusting? I'm being serious here."

"I am *not* lying!" Rion said. He grimaced and shook his head a few times, as if shaking off his thoughts. "But it's not a Japanese school. I'm at a boarding school in Hawaii."

Ureshino stared at him blankly.

The same astonished look spread around the group.

Hawaii.

A far-off southern island, gentle breezes, sea, hula dancing and palm trees—these images fitted the tanned Rion perfectly. It made sense.

"In Hawaii, it's night now, not daytime. I come here when school is finished. I'm staying by myself in a dorm, away from my family."

She remembered that Rion always wore a watch. She hadn't noticed it recently, so she hadn't thought of it before, but he did always seem overly concerned about the time. And he was wearing a watch now, too.

Once Kokoro had asked him what the time was. He'd glanced at his watch, pointed to the grandfather clock in the grand foyer and said, *There's a clock over there, you know.*

He knew that the time shown on his watch wouldn't help her. Because it showed Hawaiian time.

"Hawaii?"

It was Masamune who voiced the surprise they all felt. A crooked smile came over his face.

"You mean—*that* Hawaii? You came here all the way from *there*?"

"The mirror in my dorm room was shining," Rion explained with a frown. "Probably as it did for all of you. And I passed through it. The distance is irrelevant."

"Now that you mention it . . ." A high-pitched, clear voice spoke up. Kokoro turned. It was Fuka. She looked intently at Rion. "When the Wolf Queen first explained things to us, she said the castle was open from nine to five, Japan time."

Ah, Kokoro thought. *She's right.*

"It struck me at the time—why did she say *Japan time*? She said it for your sake, didn't she?" asked Fuka.

"I don't think that's the only reason," countered Rion.

"Then why?"

"Because you're an elitist, that's why." Masamune didn't mince his words and it clearly made Rion uncomfortable. He fell silent. When he eventually looked up, in that flash of an instant, Kokoro couldn't help but notice the hurt lingering in his eyes.

He shook his head.

"No, I'm not elitist at all. The entrance exam for the school was easy. And the classes are probably not as advanced as in Japanese schools. It's like the school's motto is *Play football surrounded by the beauty of nature.*"

"So you went there to play football?" Even Subaru, whose thought process was always a mystery to Kokoro, leaned forward. "That's amazing. Your family must be really rich to send you to a school in Hawaii. As if you're a celebrity or something."

"That's not true. It's not like that."

No matter how much Rion denied it, Kokoro could tell the others had the same impression she did.

Rion isn't the kind of boy who can't go to school. He was probably just an ordinary boy who happened to be going to a school in Hawaii.

Still, Kokoro was shocked at the revelation.

Rion is not like us.

So why is a guy like that here?

He has somewhere to go back to.

"What the—?" Ureshino muttered. He threw an accusatory glare at Rion. "So why have you been hiding it?" he asked. "Are you making fun of us or something?"

"No way." Rion shook his head. But his awkward expression spoke volumes.

Maybe he wasn't making fun of them. But it was clear he did feel guilty. Maybe he hadn't intentionally hidden anything from them, though it seemed he wasn't going to tell them unless someone asked.

"I'm telling you—I didn't know what was going on at first. I thought you were all studying abroad somewhere too. I thought maybe you were all going to schools in Hawaii. But I noticed you all seemed to operate around Japan time, and when I heard that the castle was only open till next March, I finally understood."

Rion continued, "But even though I worked out this was daytime in Japan, I didn't notice you weren't going to school until someone mentioned it, and even then, I didn't really think much about it."

"Well, *excuse us*," Masamune said. Kokoro didn't think he meant it to sound so indignant, but Rion looked startled. Masamune sighed theatrically. "Excuse us for not being from schools in Hawaii. But don't worry about it."

"No offence intended," Rion said. "I'm sorry I kept quiet about it. But I really like it here. I don't have many Japanese friends." He lowered his eyes. "If you tell me not to come over anymore, I won't."

"No one's saying you can't come here," Kokoro said, finally snapping out of a stunned silence.

The thing with Rion was, indeed, a shock. Honestly, she felt even more intimidated around him now, knowing he was at school in Hawaii, than she did around ordinary students. And naturally she did feel betrayed to suddenly discover he wasn't like the rest of them.

Nevertheless, she didn't feel like Rion was making fun of them. He felt the same way she did—that it would be great if all of them could just get along.

So why had things turned out this way?

"Ureshino," Rion said emphatically.

Ureshino, silent till now, refused to look at Rion.

"What's wrong with going back to school?" a curt voice suddenly said. It was Aki. "You should go to school. Why not? No one here is that interested. Do whatever you like."

Ureshino didn't reply to Rion. Without a word, he slipped past Rion and left the Game Room. Nobody stopped him.

The room was suddenly quiet, until Fuka finally broke the silence. "Hey," she said to Rion, looking at his watch. "You're already living abroad alone, at your age? Does that mean you were scouted by your school, or by a coach or something?"

"Nah. The coach for my team in Japan wrote a recommendation letter, but that's about it. My parents picked the school."

"What's the time difference with Hawaii?"

"Nineteen hours." A tired smile finally appeared on Rion's face. The clock on the wall showed four.

"So it's nine now. Dinner's over and soon it'll be lights out."

"Is that yesterday? Or today?"

"Yesterday. Hawaii's nearly one whole day behind." With that, the room fell silent again. "I'm going back too," he said. "Sorry I didn't tell you."

He hadn't done anything, yet he still apologized.

FOR A WHILE, they all behaved as though the incident with Ureshino hadn't happened.

Yet Ureshino's anger had most definitely introduced a fissure in the normally tranquil castle.

A taboo had been broken. And this had brought a certain tension into the peaceful atmosphere.

A week passed, and Kokoro had grown used to Subaru's dyed hair and ear piercing, when another shock rocked the castle.

This time it was Aki who appeared with her hair dyed.

SECOND SEMESTER:
THINGS FALL INTO PLACE

September

SUMMER BREAK WAS over, and schools were reopening across the country.

Not that the incident with Ureshino was behind it, but since then, Aki had again stopped coming to the castle. And the day she did turn up, her hair was dark red.

Subaru had gone for more of a dark blond look, but Aki had chosen red.

"I did it!" Aki laughed when she noticed Kokoro staring. "Do you want to try it too, Kokoro? I found a really great hair dye. Shall I show you?"

"No. I'm good," Kokoro said.

As Aki approached, Kokoro picked up the scent of perfume from her, and that made her even more perplexed. It wasn't just the red hair; Aki had given up her trademark ponytail too, and her fingernails were all pink. Aki might not be used to painting her nails, for Kokoro spotted places where the color had spilled onto the skin. She felt as though she'd seen something she shouldn't, and quickly averted her eyes.

If I did that, Kokoro thought. *If I dyed my hair like that . . .*

My mother would faint. She'd blow her top, and force me to dye my hair back.

Were Subaru's and Aki's parents really fine with it?

After this, Ureshino stopped coming to the castle.

He said he was going to school, and that it would be good for him.

Maybe he wasn't at his original school anymore, but had transferred somewhere else.

Kokoro regretted not having spoken more often to him.

They needed to apologize. Ureshino surely must have felt they were making fun of him, with their teasing and jokes, and he must have hated it.

Ureshino's mirror in the grand foyer was right next to Kokoro's. His mirror didn't shine, and Kokoro was full of regret all over again.

We should have had a real heart-to-heart, she thought. *We shouldn't have parted like that, after arguing. We should have given him a proper send-off, now that he was going back to school.*

"Ureshino isn't coming, is he?" Rion asked her one day, as she was standing in front of his mirror. In spite of his awkward confession, Rion was still visiting the castle regularly. And Kokoro found this comforting.

"Yeah."

"I mean, no one cares, do they? Whether you go to school or not, you should simply come here and have fun. Like me," he murmured, sounding a little sad.

By mid-September, Kokoro and the others were still feeling the same.

Until Ureshino reappeared at the castle.

Gauze on his face, his arm bandaged, his face swollen.

He was back at the castle, covered in cuts and bruises.

THE BATTLE-SCARRED Ureshino turned up one day without a word in the Game Room.

He didn't seem to have broken anything, and he wasn't dragging a leg, or carrying his arm in a sling. All the same, he cut a pitiful figure.

He had slunk silently into the room.

That day everyone was present.

A video game was on, though no one was playing it, and the background music carried on cheerfully.

I'll be back at school after the break.

Ureshino's words came back to Kokoro.

The second semester had only begun two weeks earlier.

All eyes were fixed on Ureshino; no one uttered a word.

Ureshino himself seemed at a loss for what to say. He avoided their gaze, and was about to drop down into an empty sofa.

Kokoro had no clue if they should ask him what had happened.

Just then, someone spoke up.

"Ureshino."

It was Masamune.

He walked over to Ureshino and gave him a light push on the shoulder. The gesture looked awkward. But it was clear he was doing his best to seem casual.

"Do you want to play?" he asked.

Ureshino bit his lip, as if holding back something. There was a momentary hush in the room as they all watched.

"Yeah," Ureshino said. "I'd like to."

And with this, their short exchange was over.

There was one thing everyone here understood, without asking.

Kokoro didn't know the details of any of their situations. But she knew full well that whatever they'd experienced, it must have felt like jumping into a storm or tornado, one that would mangle and maim you.

Exactly like the feeling Kokoro had—that if she went back to school, Miori Sanada would murder her.

It must have taken a lot of courage for Ureshino to come back. And it upset her to think how much he wanted to be back, even after having jumped into the storm.

She knew exactly how he felt.

It was clear that even Masamune, forgoing his usual barrage of insults, quietly understood all this as well.

When Ureshino replied, "Yeah, I'd like to," his eyes had shone with a faint luminescence. A single tear, as if unable to bear its own weight, ran down his cheek, and he didn't wipe it away.

He settled down with them in front of the screen.

No one asked him about his wounds that day.

TWENTY-FOUR HOURS passed before Ureshino touched on the subject of how he'd been hurt.

He usually came over in the afternoon, but today he arrived in the morning, bento lunch in hand.

Rion, too, was there, though he was also rarely at the castle in the morning, and when asked about it he answered that he had a "temporary holiday." He didn't elaborate, but maybe, thought Kokoro, he'd come early as he was worried about Ureshino.

Around eleven o'clock, Ureshino already had his lunch spread out before him and was chomping away. The inside of his mouth seemed to hurt, and he muttered an "Ouch!" and grimaced, though his appetite seemed as healthy as ever.

"How come you've got the bento?" Masamune asked.

"I told Mum I was going to School and she made it for me. But I didn't want to go today so I skipped it." Ureshino kept on chewing.

Kokoro was taken aback a bit by the mention of School, and Subaru, looking doubtful, asked "*School?* Why use the English word?"

"He means the Free School," Masamune said.

Kokoro had become more used to Subaru's dyed brown hair, and though he and Masamune were back to playing video games together, things were still a bit awkward between them. The roots of Subaru's hair were growing out black again; this only added to the feeling that things weren't quite right, and Kokoro tended to avert her eyes.

"Isn't there one near where you live, too? For kids who've dropped out of school?"

"Yes, there's one near us." Kokoro's heart pounded as the conversation turned to her.

Masamune shot them a know-it-all look. "It's the type of place parents first turn to when their kids stop going to school and they're confused about what to do. There's one of those private support groups near the school I went to. But when I stopped going to junior high, my parents didn't really do anything. They just said, *Masamune probably wouldn't want to go there*, and that was it."

"I see," Aki said, sounding impressed. "We don't have one near us. I've never heard of them."

"Hmm," Fuka murmured. "I wonder if there's one near our school. I've never been aware of one."

"Didn't your parents ever try to get you to go to one?" Masamune asked.

"My mother's—sort of busy," Fuka said, lowering her eyes for some reason.

Kokoro couldn't bring up her own experience. She remembered the School was called *Kokoro no kyoshitsu*—Classroom for the Heart— with her own name in the title, and so she clammed up. It was just a coincidence that they shared a name, but she knew that if someone pointed it out, she'd die of embarrassment.

But she was impressed by Masamune—how he called it a Free School, and used the term *private support group*. She'd never given it any thought.

Masamune looked at Ureshino. "So you're missing School. Have you been going there all this time?"

"Yeah, but just in the mornings," Ureshino said, gulping down a mouthful of food. He looked up, hesitated a beat, and said, "No one's asked me anything so far, so I'll tell you."

He made it sound like a small thing.

"Boys in my class did this to me. It wasn't like I was being bullied or anything."

There was an audible gasp. He seemed not to notice.

"Whenever anyone gets beaten up, people instantly say it's bullying, and I don't like it."

"Why were you beaten up, then?" Rion asked.

Ureshino responded without looking up.

"It was guys I made friends with in junior high. We got on fine—they'd come to my house to play video games, we'd go to juku together. I thought we were friends, but then things got a little weird."

He said it casually, but the hard edge in his voice made it clear that Ureshino was far from calm about it. *If it's painful to discuss*, Kokoro thought, *he doesn't need to talk about it.* But Ureshino seemed to want to get it out.

She had no idea what kind of people these classmates were, but if she thought about her own classmates, she had a vague idea. She'd known boys like that since elementary school, who'd talk about you behind your back, tease you, and sometimes go too far.

But as Ureshino said, Kokoro had never thought of that as *bullying*.

Ureshino might feel the same way. *Things got a little weird*, he'd said, but he might not consider that a case of bullying either.

"When they'd come to my house, I'd give them drinks and ice cream and stuff, and I felt sorry for them since they didn't get any spending money from their parents, so when we went out, I paid for their food. And after a while they just started expecting it, for me to always pay, but the more I did it the more they respected me, the more they tried to please me. It wasn't as if they were making me do it, was it? But the teacher at our juku found out and told my parents, and my father blew his top."

Ureshino related all this matter-of-factly, and paused here for the first time. "*Aren't you ashamed, trying to buy friends like that?* my father asked me." The hurt showed in Ureshino's eyes.

He clutched the chopsticks into a fist. It seemed like he couldn't hold them properly.

"My mum got angry with my dad. *Why be angry with him*, she demanded, *when it's the other boys who are to blame for making him buy them drinks and suchlike?* I felt the same way, but I hated to see them fight. I was sick of it, and when they talked about it with the other parents it seems they got shouted at, and then things got super awkward and it was too stressful to go to school."

"Yeah, must have been." A clear, bell-like voice spoke up. It was Fuka. She asked him to carry on. "Then what?"

"And so Mother took me to the Free School and I enrolled. She took time off in the mornings. Honestly, it was so annoying. As though she was spying on me. It wasn't as if I was going to die or anything."

"Die?"

It was Subaru who looked doubtful. Ureshino gave a small laugh.

"What a joke, eh? According to my parents I was being bullied, and kids who are bullied blame themselves and often consider suicide. They read books on the subject and were really worried about me. It's so stupid, because I never thought I wanted to die. They'd cry and say, *Haruka-chan, you'll be OK.*"

"Haruka?" Masamune exclaimed at the revelation of Ureshino's first name, usually a girl's name. The half of Ureshino's face that wasn't covered in gauze flinched, as though he instantly regretted it.

"Who the hell is Haruka?" Masamune said.

"That's me." Ureshino looked up. "And so what?" he said cuttingly. "So my name's Haruka. Just forget it."

"What a sweet name. Like a girl," Aki said. She didn't seem to have any ulterior motive for saying this, but Ureshino's face turned beetroot.

"Anyway, it doesn't suit me at all," he said.

That must explain it, Kokoro thought.

When they had introduced themselves, everyone gave their first names, except for Ureshino, who only told them his last name. He seemed not to want to reveal it. He must have been mercilessly teased about it for years.

"So anyway, my parents were a real pain about it, my father saying I was pathetic for not going to school just because of that. The teachers at the School tried to convince them to give me a bit more time to sort things out, but Father said they had been too soft on me, so I'd have to go back to normal school in the second semester."

"What about your mum? Didn't she stand up for you?"

It was only when Fuka spoke that Ureshino looked up. But then he quickly hung his head again.

"She did, but in the end, she did what my father told her."

"Oh."

"But it wasn't what I expected. I heard our homeroom teacher say the boys were worried I'd stopped going to school because of them, but then when I came back, they weren't a bit sorry about what had happened. Which stressed me, so I tried to talk to them about it. My father must have said all kinds of things to their parents, I said, and I was sorry."

"I don't think you needed to apologize for anything," Masamune said bluntly. He sounded a little angry himself. Ureshino didn't respond.

He might say he and his classmates were still on good terms, but he'd had to apologize, and though he said they didn't actually do anything to him, he was still expecting them to show some remorse. Ureshino's story was riddled with contradictions, as if perfectly expressing his own confusion.

But he wasn't lying.

The emotions he felt at each moment were, no doubt, just as he described.

"One of the guys said to me, *Hey, if you're not going to treat us anymore when we go out, then I don't want to hang around with you.* The other guys smirked and laughed. And so I lost my temper and hit him, and they punched me back. And that's how I got hurt."

The group said nothing, and Ureshino went on with his story.

"I was the one who threw the first punch, according to them. Things have really escalated now. My parents are talking about suing them or something, and I have no idea how it's going to play out. Teachers at the School are worried about me, too. They're the only ones, you know, who've said anything to me, like, *Ureshino-kun, what do* you *want to do now?*

"So." Ureshino's voice became a little wobbly. He suddenly turned to face Masamune. "Don't get all high and mighty, and ridicule private support groups as though you're above it. The teachers there—they're the ones who really listened to me."

Masamune glanced awkwardly away. Fuka spoke up.

"What did you say to them?" she asked.

"When?"

"When they asked you what you want to do, what did you say?"

"I said I didn't want to do anything," Ureshino said. "I told them I wanted to stay at home by myself. I didn't even want my mother to be there. I'm OK with going to the School sometimes, I said, but mainly I just want to chill out at home. And with my injuries, they let me do that."

"But you did want to come to the castle?" said Fuka.

"Is that wrong?" he asked.

"No—it isn't," Masamune answered in Fuka's place.

Everyone turned to look at him.

"You had it tough, didn't you," he said curtly, an unusually serious look on his face.

After they'd heard Ureshino's story, it was nearly time for the castle to close for the day. They stood in front of their mirrors in the grand foyer and said goodbye.

"Well, see you tomorrow," Aki said.

"Yeah, bye now," they said to each other. As if it were the natural thing to do.

NOT EVERYONE WAS there every day. After they'd dyed their hair, Aki and Subaru were often absent. She wasn't sure how to put it, but to Kokoro the two of them seemed to talk about more superficial subjects these days.

Kokoro was especially surprised when Aki told her she had a boyfriend.

Fuka and Kokoro weren't used to the subject of boyfriends, and Aki seemed to enjoy watching them squirm. "He's not my first," Aki added, and the two younger girls recoiled even more.

Kokoro felt she had to ask something, so she said, "What's he like?" to which Aki simply replied, "He's older. Twenty-three. He's going to take me out on his motorcycle next time."

"How did you meet?"

"Well, it's kind of a long story."

She deflected the question, probably intentionally.

Aki didn't keep her story for the girls only, but hinted at it with the boys as well.

"That's weird," Masamune said once, when Aki wasn't there. "A girl who's a senior in junior high and a twenty-three-year-old man? What the hell's that guy thinking?"

"I know," Subaru said, "but my brother's friend Mitsuo, who's nineteen, has a girlfriend who's in second year in junior high."

Masamune clammed up in a huff.

Unlike Aki, Subaru didn't say things because he enjoyed making them feel uncomfortable, and Kokoro felt just as awkward as he did.

After Subaru had bleached his hair, there was a distinct distance between him and Masamune that hadn't been there before.

Subaru didn't come over to the castle as often as before, and even when he did, he'd often just sit by himself on the sofa in the Game Room and listen to music on his earphones.

"What are you listening to?" Kokoro asked him once.

"When I'm at home, most of the time I listen to the radio," he said, "but I can't get any reception here."

That's how Kokoro found out there was no radio signal at the castle. Come to think of it, except when they used the TV for video games, they couldn't watch TV either.

"This player was broken once, and I went to Akihabara to see if I could get it fixed, but they told me it'd be better to just get it replaced. I didn't know what to do, so I searched the back alleys and found a shop that could fix it for me."

The music player his father had given him was clearly a prized possession. "I see." Kokoro nodded, and Masamune looked up from his video game and murmured, "So you've been to Akihabara?"

Kokoro was curious.

She had no idea where Subaru and Masamune lived. But since Subaru had gone to Akihabara, it must mean he lived in Tokyo. So he must live close enough to go there alone? Or did someone else take him?

Other than Rion talking about Hawaii, this was the first time any place names had come up in their conversations. Kokoro prepared herself for more details about where each of them lived, but Subaru just nodded. "Yeah," he said.

An unnatural silence descended and their chat died away.

IT WASN'T JUST Subaru who had begun to mention things outside the castle. Aki did too, and often.

Aki dressed differently now. After summer she often arrived in tiny hot pants, in white or a dazzling neon. Even Kokoro was a bit uncomfortable at the display of her long slim legs.

"Last Saturday," Aki announced, "my boyfriend and I were almost picked up for hanging around on the street. Christ, I freaked out. The guy caught up with us and my boyfriend told him, *Oh, she's seventeen. She's already graduated from junior high.*

"So what do you think?" she asked Fuka and Kokoro. "Could I pass for seventeen? Maybe a bit too easily?"

With her dyed hair and glitzy clothes, Aki did indeed look more grown-up, a fact that Kokoro found daunting.

"Sorry," Aki said. "You girls are quite sensible, so you probably find all this boring."

"No, I wouldn't say that."

The word "sensible" made it sound like she was making fun of them, and neither Kokoro nor Fuka knew how to respond. It wasn't that Kokoro felt jealous, but the whole thing left her uneasy.

So what sort of relationship did Aki and this man have now? The fact that Aki had a life in the world outside weighed on her, and made her anxious.

EVERYONE'S CIRCUMSTANCES WERE different.

She'd thought this before, but after hearing Ureshino's story, it hit home even more clearly.

And she started to wonder what Rion, this ordinary boy who was studying in Hawaii, thought about the rest of them.

"Rion-kun, what do your parents do?" Kokoro ventured one day.

"Hm?"

"I was thinking, since they had the idea of sending you to Hawaii, maybe they worked in something related to that."

"Oh." Rion nodded. He took a breath and said, "Well, my dad works for a large company, and my mother doesn't work. I heard she used to work in the same company as my dad, but she gave it up when I was born."

"Oh."

"What about your family, Kokoro?"

"Both my dad and mum work."

"Really?"

"Do you have any brothers or sisters? I'm an only child."

"I have one older sister."

"Is she in Hawaii too?"

For some reason, Rion's face looked a bit troubled. "Japan," he replied. "She's in Japan." He suddenly became serious. "I wanted to ask you—have you dropped out of school too?"

Her chest ached at the question. Even though she herself had brought up the subject, this was the first time someone had asked her so directly. And of all people it was Rion, who *was* going to school.

"Yeah," she managed to say.

"So did something happen, like with Ureshino?" he asked.

"Um—sort of."

She was struck by a sudden desire to tell Rion all about it. About Miori Sanada, and all they'd done to her.

But Rion didn't ask. "Oh," he said. "Must be tough." And with that their conversation ended.

* * *

AFTER SHE'D GOT home from the castle, she checked it was dark outside and went to look in the mailbox.

The best thing about going to the castle was that she could avoid hearing the clang of the mailbox, and the rustling sound when the school handouts were slid inside.

That said, she couldn't exactly wait until after her mother came home to check the mailbox. If her mother saw the papers, it would remind her all over again that her daughter wasn't going to school. So as a rule, Kokoro emptied the mailbox herself before her mother got home.

And she was just about to do that when it happened.

The front doorbell, which rarely rang, sounded through the house.

Kokoro peeked outside from her bedroom window. She was pretty sure it wasn't them, but it would be awkward if it were Tojo-san, or another classmate. Maybe Miori and the others were barging in all over again.

Time had passed since then, but the fear was still a part of her. She froze instinctively at the sound, and her stomach ached. But it wasn't a classmate. There were no bikes around. Instead, a woman was standing there.

The woman turned her head slightly, and Kokoro caught a glimpse of her profile. She realized who it was.

"Coming!" she called, and skipped downstairs.

She opened the door to find Ms. Kitajima from the Classroom for the Heart School. She looked kindly as always. She beamed at Kokoro.

"Hello," Kokoro said.

Kokoro had just returned from the castle, and she wasn't in her PJs or casual indoor clothes, so she shouldn't have felt awkward, yet she found it hard to meet her eyes. "I'm so happy to see you," Ms. Kitajima said. Kokoro stood there with bated breath.

This was the first time Ms. Kitajima had come to her house.

AFTER THEIR RECENT argument, Kokoro's mother didn't question her any more about her whereabouts during the day. Maybe Ms. Kitajima had advised her that it wasn't good to pressurize her, or something along those lines. Her mother still seemed to be in touch with her.

Ms. Kitajima's tone was friendly and light-hearted. "It's been a while," she said. "How have you been? It's still so hot, isn't it, even though it's September."

"Yes."

Kokoro didn't think her face revealed what she was really thinking, but Ms. Kitajima laughed and said, "I didn't come for any particular reason. I just thought if I visited during the day, I might catch you. I really wanted to see you again, Kokoro-chan."

"Yes."

Kokoro could manage nothing but to repeat herself. She was also relieved Ms. Kitajima had picked a moment when Kokoro was back home. Otherwise she might inform on her. She'd said she hadn't seen Kokoro in a while, but the fact was they'd only met once, when Kokoro visited the School. Still, this visit must be part of her job as well.

Kokoro stood in the doorway, silently steeling herself, yet inside she felt the warm, tingling sensation of the words Ms. Kitajima had said to her mother. Words that Kokoro wanted to cling to.

It's not Kokoro-chan's fault at all that she can't go to school.

Kokoro didn't think Ms. Kitajima had looked into what had

happened to her, but the teacher did know that she wasn't missing school simply because she was lazy.

She understood.

"Ms. Kitajima?"

These thoughts finally let her speak.

"Yes?" Ms. Kitajima asked, and gazed at her.

"What you said to my mum—is that really true?"

Ms. Kitajima's eyes wavered a bit, and Kokoro, unable to hold her gaze, looked away.

"You said it wasn't my fault I can't go to school."

"That's right."

Ms. Kitajima nodded. A clear, emphatic nod. Her certainty made Kokoro's eyes widen, and she looked back more intently.

"I did say that."

"But how . . . ?"

A hundred thoughts whirled in her brain as she looked up at Ms. Kitajima, and then, in an instant, she understood. *I didn't really want to ask her how she knew I wasn't to blame—but rather that was my* wish.

The wish that Ms. Kitajima would realize all this.

But Kokoro couldn't say it.

These people are adults and they're bound by rules. She knew that Ms. Kitajima's kindness would no doubt extend equally to everyone. If Miori Sanada were in trouble, and claimed she couldn't go to school, Ms. Kitajima would surely be equally kind to her.

She knew if Ms. Kitajima were to ask her anything more, she might end up telling her everything. In her heart, Kokoro was hoping that Ms. Kitajima would ask her, *What happened at school? There's got to be a reason you're not going, no?* Kokoro was impatiently waiting for those very questions.

But what Ms. Kitajima said next was completely different.

"I mean, you're battling every single day, aren't you?" she said.

Kokoro breathed in silently.

Battling. Kokoro had no idea what she meant by this. But the

141

instant she heard it, the most vulnerable part inside her chest grew hot and constricted. Not because it hurt. But because she was happy.

"Battling?"

"Um. It seems to me like you've struggled so hard up till now. And are battling even now."

She must think that Kokoro was spending all day napping or watching TV, and misinterpret her absence from the house as her going out to have fun—and if she hadn't been going to the castle, that might actually be true—but despite all that, Ms. Kitajima still said she was *battling*?

She found herself trembling.

This idea of kids battling to get by might just be a generalization. This was Ms. Kitajima's job, after all. So perhaps she was simply saying what applied to everyone.

But her words shot straight to the very core of Kokoro's heart. She hadn't thought of it that way before, but now that she did, she realized that yes, she *had* been trying to battle through each day. Even now, not going to school in order not to be killed.

"Is it OK if I stop by again?"

Ureshino's words suddenly came back to her.

The teachers there really listened to me.

"Of course."

It was all Kokoro could do to get this reply out.

"Thank you," Ms. Kitajima said. "Here's a little something for you," and she held out a small package.

What could it be? Kokoro wondered, eyeing it without taking it.

"It's tea. Teabags," Ms. Kitajima said.

It was in a pretty light blue envelope with a drawing of wild strawberries on it.

"It's a kind of flavored black tea I like. Please try it if you'd like to. Will you take it?"

"Of course." Kokoro managed to thank her.

"You're very welcome. I'll see you soon, then."

Their conversation had died away, but Kokoro found herself wanting more, wanting to somehow keep her from leaving.

After seeing her off, Kokoro realized she felt a strange sense of closeness with Ms. Kitajima.

She reminded her of someone. Even though she hardly knew anyone Ms. Kitajima's age.

Or was that exactly why she was a teacher at the School, because she was good at winning over children?

Kokoro opened the envelope with the tea. It wasn't sealed. Inside were two teabag sachets that matched the color of the envelope. At home her parents drank black tea, but she'd never been asked if she'd like some. It made her happy finally to be treated like a grown-up.

October

IT HAPPENED SOMETIME at the beginning of the month.

Kokoro was preparing as always to leave the castle just before it closed at five o'clock, when Aki asked, "Are you planning to come over tomorrow?"

It was unusual for Aki to ask. "Sure, but what's up?" Kokoro replied.

Aki said meaningfully, "I have something I want to say. Something I want to tell everyone. If I do it when one of us is missing, it won't be fair."

Her manner left Kokoro uneasy. *Is it about me?* she wondered. *Did I do something?* Worrying would only make her feel ill, but Aki said, "OK then, see you tomorrow," and slipped through the mirror for home.

THE NEXT AFTERNOON, with Rion the last to arrive, all seven of them were together.

It transpired that Aki had already warned them all she had something to tell them. Kokoro was surprised to see it wasn't only Aki who had something to say, but Masamune as well.

Kokoro wondered about this unlikely pairing. Masamune was the first to speak.

"Hey, so I wanted to know—how seriously are you people looking for the Wishing Key?"

The group looked startled. Since only one person's wish would come true, they all saw each other, as far as this was concerned, as rivals.

Which might explain why they'd hardly ever talked about it. The Wolf Queen had made it clear that if someone located the key, found the Wishing Room, and had their wish granted, then the castle would close down permanently, even before the 30 March deadline.

As the castle was still open, it meant no one had yet had their wish granted, but Kokoro could sense that everyone was still conscious the key was yet to be found.

"I have looked for it, but not recently. I haven't had time, plus it's fun here."

This was from Ureshino, whose bandages were off now. The gauze on his cheek had been replaced by a plaster, and he seemed to be in much less pain.

Masamune glanced over at him and continued.

"Same for me. But we've all searched for it a bit, am I right? No matter what your own wish might be."

"I suppose," Subaru said. When the subject had come up before, he'd said he didn't have any particular wish and would help Masamune look. But it seemed even he had done some looking on his own. "After the Wolf Queen explained it all, of course I wondered about it. Like—who knows, maybe it'll just turn up. But it hasn't."

Aki nodded. "Masamune and I have a proposal. We think it's entirely possible that someone has already found the key and perhaps has a plan to hide it until the last possible moment in March, or else is struggling to locate the Wishing Room. So we thought we'd ask you all."

"A proposal?"

Masamune and Aki exchanged a look.

"The other day, the two of us just happened to be alone in the castle and we started talking about it. I'll fess up—Masamune and I searched very hard for the key. We looked everywhere."

"We were told it would be in some public area, not in any of our individual rooms, and though it's a big space there are only so many places to look. And believe me, I scoured the place."

"So did I," Aki said. She sighed and looked round. "But we couldn't find it. Honestly, I can't think of a single spot I didn't look. I was getting pretty exasperated, and Masamune, who was desperately looking too, happened to bump into me in the dining room."

"What're you talking about—*desperately*?" Masamune interrupted, sounding a bit frustrated. "How can you say that about me—you who pretends not to give a toss about it when we're all here, and yet who, more desperately than me, I can tell you, is out there licking every single plate, one by one, in search of it."

"How about you? Don't you sit there all the time, pretending to spend every minute in the Game Room, but as soon as no one's around you leap into action? I think *you're* the desperate one."

Masamune and Aki glared at each other until Subaru intervened. "Hey, you guys—come on! So, what are you proposing?"

"That we all work together," Aki said.

"It's already October," Masamune added. "It's been a while since we were first summoned here last May, and we still haven't found it. I think the Wishing Room, too, must have some kind of hidden entrance to it. We've only got half a year left, remember."

"It might turn out that the final day will arrive and no one's wish has come true," Aki said. "I'm thinking we shouldn't see each other as rivals, but search for it together, then discuss whose wish gets to be granted. Or else cast lots, or decide by rock-paper-scissors." She paused for a reaction.

"Because we just couldn't find it," Aki lamented. "We really bust a gut. It'd be a total waste if we finish here without finding it. We just need to get it done, and not worry about how desperate we might look."

"Makes sense." Fuka, who'd been silent till now, nodded. "I had no idea, Aki," she said, "that you had a wish that you wanted so badly to come true. It's hard to believe Masamune was so keen, too."

Aki seemed upset, perhaps taken aback to be confronted so directly by Fuka. She looked away.

"If you're told it'll definitely come true," Masamune said, "then everyone will have a wish or two."

But Fuka's next words startled them all even more.

"Have a wish or two? *I* don't."

Kokoro couldn't tell if she was being serious. Then Fuka said, "It's OK. I'll help out. I'm on board with the idea of us all looking together for the key. By the way, I haven't found it. Not that I searched much."

It was true that when Fuka was over in the castle she spent more time shut up in her room than anyone else. She really might not be that interested in looking for the key.

Kokoro had no idea what to say.

Of course she, too, had a wish she wanted to come true. But it was kind of a questionable wish she was unsure she wanted to reveal. Especially to the boys, who would probably start to avoid her if she told them. OK—so if they did locate the key, how would they decide whose wish to make come true?

Deciding by rock-paper-scissors would work, but if, one by one, they were to explain their wish in front of everyone, like an election speech, trying to convince the others of the intensity of their desire, then Kokoro, who wasn't much of a speaker, would be at a disadvantage. Aki or Masamune would certainly run away with it.

But the key was yet to be found. And there was no guarantee it ever would be.

Kokoro herself, when she was in the mood, had secretly looked around, but had come up empty-handed. Like Aki said, it would be a real shame if it all ended with no one's wish coming true.

"I'm OK looking with you all," Rion said.

Ureshino nodded his assent. "Me too. Sure."

Ever since Ureshino had left the castle to go back to school, and had returned beaten up, the atmosphere in the castle had definitely changed. Everyone was more comfortable about opening up to the rest.

We two still haven't replied, she thought, and her eyes and Subaru's met. Kokoro was the first to nod.

If her wish came true, that would make her happiest, certainly, but enjoying her time in the castle until March was equally important. It was only now, when she heard that they had just six months left, that the reality sank in. She'd been so oblivious. What would happen if, after the castle disappeared, she was still not able to go to school?

She'd been thinking the next school year was way off, but it was inexorably coming nearer. When she thought of herself as a sophomore in junior high, she felt the blood drain from her and her stomach started to ache.

For Kokoro, too, there was no other option—they *had* to find the key.

"I agree. Let's look for it together." Kokoro nodded, and Subaru, beside her, broke into a smile.

"OK," he said. "We're now going to start searching for it properly. So let's do things systematically. What if we draw a map of the castle and cross off the areas we've already covered?"

"I think I did a complete search of the dining room," Aki said, quickly raising her hand. "I looked everywhere—from the empty fridge to right at the back of the curtains. Of course, I'd like all of you to check, too."

"I looked five or six times in here," Masamune said, casting his eye around the Game Room. He pointed at the mounted stag's head and the fireplace.

Subaru nodded, too.

"I checked in the kitchen and bathrooms. I wondered about them, since there's no running water. So I checked over the taps and drains, but found nothing. I couldn't find the entrance to the Wishing Room either."

"Really?" Masamune gave Subaru a knowing smile.

"Got a problem with that?" Subaru shot back.

"Nah, I just hadn't thought that you would look so keenly. But now I see you were actually really into it. You're bad, y'know that?"

"And you aren't?"

This back and forth made Kokoro a little anxious, but the two boys were smiling. They seemed pleased they could finally banter like this, freely open up to each other.

"I have one request." It was Rion's turn to raise a hand. He waited until he had everyone's attention. "The Wolf Queen said the castle was open until March, but she also said that if we find the key and a wish comes true then it will close down instantly."

"She did," Aki agreed.

"Then," Rion said, "I'll join in, but since we're all doing it together, could you promise one thing? Even if we find the key, we don't use it till March? And keep the castle for us to spend time in until the very end?"

Kokoro caught her breath and looked at him.

She'd been wanting the exact same thing. Next April was the new school year, and even if she was able to move classes at junior high, the thought of going back made her so depressed she wanted to hide.

She'd been absent from school a long while now, and not even the prospect of a new class was enough to persuade her to go back. And Sanada would still be in the same school year.

She didn't think she could make it till March, holed up alone in her bedroom. She was too frightened. She wanted the castle to stay just the way it was. She and Rion were on the same wavelength.

Rion said, "No matter whose wish comes true, could we all stick to our agreement? No one goes off on their own?"

"Of course," Masamune said. He looked at the others, trying to read them. "We all want to stay here as long as we can."

No one opposed that.

Not Subaru, with his bleached hair and civilized manner of speech; not Aki, with her older boyfriend; not Fuka, who had no wish;

and not Ureshino, who'd come back beaten up, and still didn't believe he'd been bullied.

They were silent.

"Good," Rion said. He smiled brightly. "I'm relieved to hear it."

"SO, YOU'RE JOINING forces. How completely wonderful that you've worked out a strategy."

It was then that they heard the voice.

It was right behind Kokoro, who let out a scream. She jumped away and looked round. It was indeed the Wolf Queen—making her first appearance in quite some time.

"Wolf Queen!"

They had been caught off guard. They stared, wide-eyed. She was wearing a dress they'd never seen before, but the mask was as bewildering as ever.

"Well, well, nice to see you all, my Little Red Riding Hoods," she said, strutting into the center of the group.

"What're you doing—scaring us like that?" Masamune and Rion said.

"My apologies," the Wolf Queen said, fluttering her hand, her expression as always unseen behind the mask. "You Red Riding Hoods seemed to be having such a good time. So I just popped away for a bit. But I realized I hadn't told you one important thing."

"Important thing?" Aki asked, head tilted. "It isn't against the rules, is it, for us to all work together to look for the key?"

"No problem at all," the Wolf Queen said. "In fact, that's excellent. It's splendid to see you cooperating so efficiently. Helping each other is beautiful, so give it your all."

"Good."

"But there is one thing I forgot to say, and I came here today to tell you."

She perched awkwardly on the table in front of the sofa.

"Having a wish fulfilled is all very well, of course. Just understand, though, that the moment you use the key and enter the Wishing Room to realize your wish, you'll lose all memory of this castle."

"*What?!*" It was a collective response.

The Wolf Queen chose to ignore it.

"The instant your wish is granted, you will forget everything—the castle, and all that has unfolded within its walls. You'll forget each other. And of course, you will forget me.

"A bit sad, no?" she added, looking intently into their eyes. "If no one's wish is granted before the thirtieth of March, then your memory will remain intact. The castle will close down, but you'll remember all that happened. That's how it works."

The Wolf Queen gave a little shrug and slid off the table. Kokoro couldn't imagine what sort of expression she wore underneath the mask.

"I'm so sorry I forgot to tell you," the Wolf Queen said airily.

THE GROUP WAS dumbfounded.

Kokoro, too, needed time to digest things. They would forget *all that has unfolded within its walls*—the words were a shock.

"Are you . . . joking?" a voice finally piped up. Rion, sounding puzzled. "It's not as if I don't believe you, but are you serious?"

Kokoro could fully understand Rion's confusion. He could understand her meaning, but his emotions rejected it. And he wanted to make sure. Kokoro—and probably the rest—felt the same.

"I'm utterly serious," the Wolf Queen said serenely. "Do you have any other questions?"

"So what happens to our memory of our time here?" It was Masamune who asked this. There was a hint of aggression in his tone. "Several months are passing, so what will we have been doing all that time?"

"Your memories will be filled in as needed," said the Wolf Queen. "They'll be filled in with a repeat of the things you were doing before. Sleeping, watching TV, reading manga and books, going out shopping occasionally, playing in video arcades. Memories of those sorts of things, I imagine."

"So you're saying that memories of reading any books or playing video games here will be replaced with something else? So something new I've read here, a manga story for instance, won't stay with me at all? What a waste of time."

"Maybe, but is that such a problem?" The Wolf Queen's tone was brusque. "Is it that important to you to store up new manga stories?"

"Of course it is. Don't be stupid."

Masamune pouted, his irritation finally showing. For her part, Kokoro was reflecting how, in her bedroom with its light orange curtains, she enjoyed watching, day after day, the reruns of her favorite TV soap. And how, by the end of the day, the storyline would have half faded in her memory anyway. It wasn't just dramas. Talk shows and variety shows, too—the content was quickly forgotten.

But for Masamune, who was moved to tears by video games just as he was by manga and movies, not being able to build up new knowledge from their content might truly be a colossal loss. The Wolf Queen just shook her head.

"Then give them up. They might be important to you, but that's how much energy needs to be expended to make a wish come true. If you don't like it, then, if you find the key, don't use it."

The Wolf Queen had a stern look in her eye, as she stared into each of their faces.

"But what you Little Red Riding Hoods have done on the other side of the mirror will remain. Playing football, finding a boyfriend, dyeing your hair. Going back to school and getting beaten up."

Kokoro could sense Ureshino tense up. "You mean me?" he asked in a tight voice. "Are you making fun of me, Wolf Queen?"

Ever since the incident, Ureshino had become calmer, never once raising his voice or even falling in love with any of them, and Kokoro was at pains to avoid the subject coming up again.

Unexpectedly, the Wolf Queen replied, "No, I am not. I find

your courage in going back commendable. I just mentioned it as an example, and if it has bothered you, I'm sorry. My apologies."

Her uncompromising reply left Ureshino deflated. "Eh?" he said. He turned to Fuka, next to him, and asked, "Commendable? What does that mean?"

"It means she respects you."

Ureshino's eyes opened wide in astonishment.

"Any more questions?" the Wolf Queen asked.

What Kokoro wanted to say wasn't a question but more of an opinion. Or to put a finer point on it, something that dissatisfied her.

Their memories would vanish. They'd forget the castle, and naturally that meant they'd forget each other as well.

Kokoro had no idea how the Wolf Queen interpreted their silence.

"If there's nothing else, I'll be going," she said. And with that, she was gone.

They hadn't seen her disappear like that in a while, but no one dared comment. When she'd first performed her vanishing act, it had caused quite a stir, but now the atmosphere had changed. Kokoro missed those earlier days.

"So our memories vanish—so what?" a voice said, breaking the silence.

It was Aki. The group gave her a look. Kokoro wasn't sure if she was doing it intentionally or not, but she met their eyes with a cool response.

"That doesn't bother me one bit," she said. "I mean, we can only be here in the castle until March anyway, and after that we won't be able to see each other anymore. The key will grant any wish, and not to use it would be a huge waste. Right?" Aki looked at each of them in turn, as if seeking agreement.

"All of this didn't exist before, so it will just mean going back to our earlier lives. What's wrong with that?"

"Everything."

They all turned in surprise at the voice. It was Ureshino. He tended to get emotional, but his voice seemed unusually quiet.

Aki, uncharacteristically, didn't respond, and Ureshino continued, "I hate the thought of it. I don't want to forget how you've all heard me out. Or how the Wolf Queen said she respected me."

"She didn't say she respected you; she said she found your action *commendable*," Masamune said.

"So?" Ureshino looked serious. "If it means forgetting you all, then I don't need to have my wish granted." His eyes looked straight ahead and shone, for once, without any hint of spite. He turned to Aki, tilting his head. "Don't you feel like that too, Aki-chan? Would you really prefer your wish to come true?"

Kokoro listened in surprise. Ureshino had admitted to hunting for the key, but now declared he'd rather keep his memories than have his wish granted. She was part of these memories. So were Masamune and Aki, with all their bickering and arguing. Every one of them.

Kokoro felt something warm seeping out of her, from deep inside. And she realized it was a feeling of happiness.

Aki might have been experiencing the same sort of elation. Despite her tough words, she seemed thrown off her stride.

"No . . . it's not like I—" she said.

Maybe Aki was just putting up a brave front. Could she really say that as long as she had her wish, she didn't care?

Ureshino piped up. "In fact, I might really go for it and get hold of the key first. Then I'd break it, or hide it. I might actually try to block you, Aki-chan."

Aki turned a bright red, and glared.

"Sorry." Ureshino looked down, and no one spoke.

A silence descended on them, even more stifling than if someone had been angrily shouting. Finally Aki spoke up.

"Fine. Do whatever you want."

And with that she departed from the room.

The group were left to look at each other blankly. The unspoken message: it was time to go.

"I wonder what Aki's wish is." This from Subaru, who'd not spoken up till now. It didn't sound like he was seeking anyone's opinion, merely voicing his own thoughts. "Well, I suppose it's each to their own," he murmured, and smiled. "But still, the Wolf Queen's so mischievous. I mean—why tell us that *now*, at this late stage? Or perhaps she was waiting for this to happen?"

"Waiting?" Kokoro asked. *He's always got such an unusual take on things*, she thought.

"Yeah," Subaru replied. "Maybe she was waiting for us to get to know each other first. Waiting until the moment when we don't care about our wish anymore. Maybe she never intended to grant anyone's wish anyway. Perhaps there isn't even a key at all."

"I can see that," Masamune muttered.

"True, no?" Subaru said.

"Nah." Rion shook his head. "I think the Wolf Queen does mean to grant one of us a wish. I don't think she's doing all this out of spite. She could be testing us, though. To see if we'll go for the wish in full knowledge of the consequences. No matter what we decide, I think she'll go along with it. I have the feeling she wasn't lying when she said she'd simply forgotten to tell us earlier."

Kokoro got the faint sense the Wolf Queen was still listening in on their conversation.

"What do you think, Fuka?"

"Me?"

Fuka turned around to face them. She had an odd expression. "I'd been thinking that even when we return to the real world, I'd still keep in touch with you all."

"Eh?"

"Till now, I'd always thought if we tell each other who we are and where we live, we could carry on seeing each other. So I didn't find it all that upsetting."

"Oh."

Kokoro understood what Fuka meant, since she'd sort of been thinking the same way. She couldn't imagine never seeing them again.

Fuka's *real world* took on an even heavier weight.

This *was* real, being here in the castle, she thought, but their *reality* lay outside, the kind of place she didn't want to go back to if she could avoid it.

"But if we forget everything, isn't that impossible? We might exchange addresses, but won't we forget that we've even done it?"

"But if a wish isn't granted, then it might be a good idea to exchange our contact info, just in case," said Masamune.

"Addresses and phone numbers?" Subaru asked, and Masamune nodded.

At the beginning, the two of them had played video games together all the time and they'd seemed quite similar, in part, but after the summer break, when Subaru had bleached his hair, they began to seem a bit mismatched. Kokoro just couldn't picture them—Masamune and the flashy yet so polite Subaru—together in, say, a classroom.

Our contact info—the words pierced her.

The real world, our outside contact info.

It hit home for Kokoro that so many things here in the castle were the exception.

They really knew nothing about each other.

Rion apparently was living in Hawaii, she knew that much, but she'd always felt she couldn't ask the others where they were from, and so she hadn't. Certainly she was dying to know, but she resisted the notion of anyone knowing anything about her.

I wonder why, she thought.

Because I want to forget it all myself.

While she was here, she wanted to be free from it all—from being a student at Yukishina No. 5 Junior High, from that class with Miori Sanada in it, from Tojo-san who lived two houses down the road.

The others may have felt the same way. They might at some point start to show some interest in Fuka's idea of exchanging personal information, but none of them seemed ready to take that step today.

SO OUR MEMORIES *vanish—so what?*

Aki's parting words, and since then she hadn't been back to the castle. Maybe she was being stubborn. It was possible she didn't really feel that way, but had said it to make herself look tougher.

Those who still came to the castle had become conscious of Aki's absence. Masamune said jokingly, "Doesn't she wonder what'll happen if someone finds the key when she's not here?" But they had until March, and so they didn't feel in any rush.

It was, after all, still only October.

Hunting for the key, making a wish and losing their memories—it was still too soon for all that.

IT WAS EARLY November before Aki came back to the castle.

Kokoro was the first to find out she'd reappeared. Aki was in the Game Room, on the sofa, crouched in the corner and hugging her knees.

"Aki-chan."

She said it hesitantly, and Aki looked up from where her head had been buried between her knees.

She seemed about to weep. The room was brightly lit, but somehow the area around Aki lay in shadow, as if she had sucked away all the light. Her face was pale, imprinted with a crease from her skirt.

"Kokoro," Aki said. Her voice was thin. It caught in her throat, hoarse and dry, sounding almost as if she was asking for help.

Kokoro gave an audible gasp.

Aki was wearing school uniform. Kokoro realized no one had ever come to the castle dressed in uniform.

She had a bluish-green sailor-type collar, and a dark red scarf.

As she looked up, Kokoro saw the school badge on the right breast pocket of her blouse. The name of the school was embroidered beside it.

Yukishina No. 5.

She stared again at Aki's uniform.

She recognized it. There was no mistaking it.

"Aki-chan." Her voice was stiff. "Aki-chan, do you go to Yukishina No. 5 Junior High?"

Aki followed Kokoro's eyes and looked down at her uniform. "Yeah." She nodded, her movement sluggish, as if only now realizing what she was wearing.

"Yes," she said again, and looked at Kokoro doubtfully. "Yukishina No. 5."

November

KOKORO WAS THUNDERSTRUCK.

"What's wrong?" Aki asked, standing up.

Her eyes still looked cloudy, though in Kokoro's company, a clear spark of life had returned. The red crease from the skirt still showed on her cheek; Kokoro thought that she may have been crying. Perhaps because of the tears, a few stray strands of hair were stuck to her cheek.

"Oh!"

They heard voices, and turned to find Subaru and Masamune standing in the doorway. They could have come through the mirrors around the same time. They stood fixed to the spot, eyes wide, and looked incredulously at Aki.

Kokoro had no idea what to say. She saw the two boys' gaze slide quickly from Aki's face to the school badge on her chest.

"What?" Masamune said. "Why the uniform? I mean—is that actually your school uniform?"

"What do you mean?"

Her eyes narrowed as she realized something was up.

"Because—it's exactly the *same*."

Aki frowned.

"It's exactly the same uniform worn by the girls at my school!"

Subaru, restless beside him, began to wrinkle his brow.

"At yours too?" Subaru asked.

Aki looked at Kokoro, astonished. "Wha-what? What're you . . . ?"

And then at the faces of the boys, pale with shock.

"Yukishina No. 5 Junior High," Aki said, as if piecing together the syllables one by one. "You are joking, of course. It's not just that the uniform's familiar," she added. "You're actually telling me you both go to Yukishina No. 5 Junior High? In Minami Tokyo?"

"And me," Kokoro managed to say. Now it was Subaru, Masamune and Aki's turn to stare at her in utter astonishment.

What could this all mean?

Why was the Wolf Queen doing this? Kokoro couldn't fathom it.

We are all kids going to the same junior high.

Or more precisely, who should *be going.*

They'd always avoided the subject of school. She'd never imagined they were even living so close.

"Oh!"

Fuka, the next to come into the Game Room, let out a little yelp. She had also caught sight of Aki's uniform.

By now they were no longer surprised.

THEY WAITED FOR late afternoon, when Rion would appear.

Fuka and Ureshino had displayed the same reaction: *What the—?*

When Rion arrived, they understood he would be the one exception, but that riddle, too, was soon solved.

When they told him that they should all be attending the same junior high, Rion looked taken aback. "That's . . ." he began.

"That's in Minami Tokyo City."

"Yep!" they said in near unison.

He took a deep breath. "I was due to go there, too."

They stared, speechless.

"The plan was for me to go there, if I hadn't gone abroad."

"So then, is this what it means?" Aki asked, arms folded. "That we're all kids who were supposed to go to Yukishina, but actually aren't going? Is that the common factor that's brought us together?"

"I guess so. But . . ." Fuka wrinkled her nose in puzzlement. "Aren't we quite a big group?" she asked, to no one in particular. "Are there really this many kids who've dropped out of the same school? I always thought it was just me."

And I thought it was just me, thought Kokoro.

Kokoro, Rion and Ureshino were in the first year of junior high.

Fuka and Masamune were in their second year.

Subaru and Aki were in their third.

Kokoro hadn't been aware Rion and Ureshino were from the same school as her, let alone in the same grade. Rion's situation was different, but the incident with Ureshino must have taken place in a classroom very near her own.

Kokoro remembered overhearing her mother talking to the head of the alternative School.

Elementary school is such a pleasant, comfortable place for most children, so it's not at all unusual for many to have trouble fitting in when they make the transition to junior high. Especially with a junior high like Yukishina No. 5, which has grown so large, what with other schools merging.

She remembered how repelled she had felt when she'd heard this, turned off by the thought that she was being so easily classified as one of those who had *trouble fitting in.*

"Isn't it because Yukishina No. 5 has so many students? We can't be expected to know everyone," she said.

Fuka inclined her head. "I wonder. I mean, each grade has about four classes, doesn't it? That's not so many."

"Really? Is that true of second year?"

"Yeah." Fuka nodded.

"But third year has eight classes?"

"That many?" Fuka was surprised.

"There're six classes in second year," Masamune corrected her. "Fuka, how long's it been since you stopped going to school? Maybe your memory's a little hazy."

"I don't think so." Fuka seemed unconvinced, but Kokoro, too, thought that what Fuka said didn't sound right. There were about the same number of students in the second year as in the first. As Masamune had pointed out, Fuka may not have attended school much in her first year either. Maybe she'd never gone at all.

"Which elementary school did you go to?"

Yukishina No. 5 Junior High was in a district made up of many elementary schools. Compared to junior high, these schools were relatively small, and if they'd come from the same elementary school, they were bound to be aware of each other. "Elementary School No. 2," Masamune said sulkily.

"I was at No. 1," Fuka said.

"Oh!" Kokoro said.

Fuka caught her eye. "You were in—the same school?"

"I was."

Yukishina Elementary School No. 1 had two classes in each grade. But probably because they were in different grades, Kokoro had no recollection of Fuka.

On top of which, Fuka wasn't exactly the type who stood out. She didn't seem about to star at track or swimming meets. Nor did Kokoro, so it wasn't strange that Fuka had no memory of her either.

Nevertheless, she still felt there was something odd.

To think that she went to the same school as me!

"So you two don't remember each other?" Subaru asked. Kokoro shook her head. "I bet, if I tell you where I went to elementary school," he said, "none of you will have ever heard of it." All eyes were on him now. "I went to Nagura Elementary. It's in Ibaraki prefecture, but when I went into third year at junior high I moved to my grandparents' house in Tokyo. The two of us, my older brother and I."

"The two of you?" Masamune asked, and Subaru nodded.

"What about your parents?" Masamune asked. He and Subaru seemed to get on fine, but it wasn't until the summer break, when Subaru dyed his hair, that he told Masamune he had a brother. Subaru insisted he hadn't been hiding anything.

"My parents aren't around. When we were still in Ibaraki my mum left us, and my dad remarried and is living with his second wife. That's why my brother and I went to our grandparents'."

Masamune's face dropped. The rest of them gasped.

"My older brother and me," Subaru went on. "At first I didn't really want to go to school. I didn't know anyone there. If you wanted to fit in, April was the month to go, when the school year started. It's not that I was pushed out, or that anything serious happened, so unlike all of you I just dropped out because I'm lazy, and it makes me feel guilty."

Hearing him say this made Kokoro feel contrite.

Maybe it was true nothing serious had happened to Subaru at school, but she imagined his troubles had started earlier in life. He could put on a brave face when he talked about living with his grandparents, but was he really smiling inside?

Summer break. Subaru said he went on a trip with his parents. He was given a music player by his father. These things now took on a significance.

"Aokusa Elementary." Rion's voice rang out in the silence.

Aokusa Elementary lay in the opposite direction from Kokoro's Yukishina No. 1 school, with the junior high situated in between. So Rion hadn't gone abroad at that stage, but had been living very near Kokoro.

Ureshino suddenly shook his head. "You've got to be joking," he said.

"About what?" Rion said.

"I went to Aokusa Elementary too!" Ureshino said, looking shocked. Rion, too, looked back at him in astonishment.

"You're in the first grade of junior high, aren't you, Rion? So we were in the same grade in elementary? Are you *kidding* me? You weren't there, were you? I used to be at school every day. Were you really there? *Really?*"

"I went every day too . . ."

Rion looked confused.

"You didn't know Ureshino either?" asked Subaru.

"I don't remember him. He might have been there, but I don't think I ever played with him."

"How many classes per year were there? Is Aokusa Elementary big?"

"Three classes."

Kokoro felt a little pained listening to their back and forth.

Unlike she and Fuka, who had been in different years at school, to be in a school that small, and in the same grade, and not remember each other, they must have lived in very different worlds.

"I went to Shimizudai Elementary."

The last to pipe up was Aki. Her school district was the furthest away from Kokoro's house, but still within walking distance. They all lived really close.

All of them were now at Yukishina No. 5 Junior High, and each had passed through the mirror in their own bedroom to come here.

"So you live near Careo?"

Aki must live near Careo and the shopping district by the station. Careo was where Kokoro was heading the day she had her panic attack. This was the most happening area around, so it somehow made sense that Aki, with her dyed hair and outlandish outfits, went to the elementary school there. Had Aki gone to the video arcade in Careo as well?

Aki looked puzzled, so Kokoro went on.

"I'm thinking maybe you bought Fuka's birthday napkins from one of the shops there?"

She was about to tell her how she'd thought of looking for the same napkins when Aki shook her head.

"I bought those napkins at Marumido in the shopping center," she said. "The hairclips, too."

Kokoro had never heard of that shop. But Subaru exclaimed, "Marumido! Wow, now that's a real local shop. You must really live in the neighborhood to know it. Weird, but I'm so glad to hear that. So where do you usually hang out, Aki-chan? The McDonald's near the station?"

"I go there sometimes, yeah."

Kokoro lived nearby, but it had been a while since she'd been to the shops near the station. They'd built a McDonald's?

"So there's a McDonald's there now," murmured Fuka.

Kokoro was a little relieved. She wasn't the only one who hadn't cottoned on.

HANG OUT MEANT something different when Subaru, with his wild hair and forced laid-back air, said it. It meant being up to no good.

"So what do you want to do?" Masamune asked, glancing at the wall clock in the Game Room. "It's almost five. If we're going to call the Wolf Queen, we'd better do it now. Shall we?"

"Call her." They spoke virtually in unison.

Masamune raised his face to the ceiling. "Wolf Queen!"

"Did you call?"

As ever, she casually flickered into being.

THE WOLF QUEEN wore a different dress today, with a puffy hem, like an antique doll. How many outfits did she actually have?

"Why didn't you tell us?" It was Fuka who asked. Aki, looking uncomfortable in her uniform, hugged her arms to her chest.

"Tell you *what*?" the Wolf Queen said.

"Why didn't you tell us we're all students at the same junior high?" Masamune said.

"You didn't ask," said the Wolf Queen icily. "All you Little Red Riding Hoods had to do was start talking to each other. And then you'd know immediately you were all from the same school. It took you far too long to find out." She let out a long breath.

"Perhaps you people are all too self-conscious."

"Don't be stupid!" Masamune grimaced, and was getting to his feet with a hard look on his face when Ureshino called, "Don't do it!" and stood in his way. "She's just a little girl," he said. "Don't do it."

"What? A little girl? She might be small, but she's extremely powerful and will come back even stronger in a *New Game*. She'll be reborn and start all over again. This is the afterlife for her. She's a ghost, I'm telling you."

"Enough!"

A loud voice halted his tirade. It was Rion. Normally calm and collected, he was now red-faced and clearly angry.

When calm had returned, Rion said quietly, "I have a question."

"What is it?"

"You've done this before, bringing other Little Red Riding Hoods here and telling them they could have a wish granted, haven't you? Were those Little Red Riding Hoods also students at Yukishina No. 5 Junior High? Every few years you bring a group of them here, don't you?"

"Every few years—I think it's more consistent than that, but if you want to think of it that way, I won't mind." The Wolf Queen spoke petulantly.

"So every time, you choose kids from this school district who've dropped out? Or maybe . . ." Rion took a shallow breath. "Maybe you select from all the kids at Yukishina? You make their mirrors glow and you open up the castle here. But most of the kids are at school, so they never catch their mirror when it shines. The only students who do are the ones at home."

Kokoro's heart beat faster. It seemed entirely plausible.

"So, really, every student at the school has had the same opportunity to come here. And we haven't actually been hand-picked?"

Kokoro's chest tightened, and she found it hard to breathe.

"Not true," the Wolf Queen said emphatically. "I selected the seven of you from the start."

"Well then, what about me?" Rion narrowed his eyes. "My school isn't Yukishina No. 5, and yet here I am. Why did you summon someone like me?"

He was trying to meet the Wolf Queen's eyes.

Kokoro was sure she'd deflect the question, along the lines of *How would I know?* or *You'll find out soon enough.*

But she didn't. She turned her wolf-masked face to Rion.

"But you badly wanted to go, didn't you? To the public junior high in your area?"

Rion looked like he'd been struck by lightning. His back straightened, as if in that very moment he'd been pierced by an arrow.

The Wolf Queen ignored his reaction. She stepped closer in to the group.

"Do you have anything else to ask? I'll answer as best I can."

"Yes, I do. Where exactly are we?" Aki said.

Kokoro still wasn't used to seeing her in the uniform. The uniform she knew all too well.

"This is the castle in the mirror," the Wolf Queen replied, a little grandly. "Your own castle, open for you until March. Use it in whatever way you like."

"What do you want us to do?"

Aki's voice sounded tearful, as if she were tired. She always put on a bold front, but even she was clearly feeling brittle. Her voice was pleading, but the Wolf Queen answered curtly.

"Nothing really," she said. "I expect nothing. As I explained at the beginning, I've merely given you the castle and the right to search for the key that will grant you a wish. That's all. Now, if you'll excuse me," she added, her voice rising into the air.

And with that, she vanished. At that instant they heard a far-off howl.

It was a quarter to five. The howl was their signal to go home.

Kokoro remembered with a shiver, and for the first time in quite a while, the Wolf Queen's warning that they would be eaten alive if they stayed after the curfew. She couldn't believe it was true, yet she still felt a chill run up her spine.

DESPITE THE CURFEW, Kokoro and the others wanted to stay on and talk. They all lived so close to each other. And they all were at the same school, knew the same school buildings and grounds and gym and bicycle parking area. How incredible that they were all so familiar with it!

Kokoro suddenly felt much closer to them. They probably all went to the same convenience store, shopped at the same supermarket, even at Careo. They were almost neighbors.

The clock was ticking towards five.

They wanted to say more, but instead they obediently trooped back to the line of mirrors. One thing in particular had been on Kokoro's mind, and she turned to Ureshino as he was about to pass through his mirror.

"Tell me," she began, "was the teacher who listened to you at the School called Ms. Kitajima?"

Ureshino halted and blinked his eyes so slowly, she felt she could hear them moving.

"The Free School. I was thinking you'd gone to the same place as me."

"Oh, yeah. Her name was Ms. Kitajima."

Ureshino looked as if a great tension in him had been released.

I thought so, Kokoro said to herself.

"Was it the same teacher?" Fuka asked. She must have overheard them. "That's amazing. You really do live close."

"Yeah. She's so pretty, Ms. Kitajima."

Kokoro said this casually, but Ureshino tilted his head.

"Pretty?"

Kokoro had been vaguely thinking that Ureshino, with his inclination to fall in love, would have been aware of Ms. Kitajima's looks, but she found his reply a little unexpected.

She remembered the teacher's hands when she'd offered Kokoro the teabags; slender fingers and neat nails. She'd worn a wonderful perfume, as well.

Did anyone else know Ms. Kitajima and the Classroom for the Heart? Masamune had referred to it as a *private support group*, as if keeping his distance from it, so he might never have actually visited it.

How about Aki and Subaru? Kokoro looked over at Subaru, just as he turned to face Aki.

"Aki-chan, can I ask you something?"

"What?"

Kokoro was certain he was going to ask something about the School, but he didn't.

"Why are you in your uniform today?" he continued. "Did something happen?"

Aki seemed to freeze.

"I went to a funeral." There was an audible intake of breath. Aki's cheeks were pale and drawn. "It was my grandmother, who I lived with. My cousins and I were told to wear our school uniforms."

"Didn't you need to go home afterwards?" Fuka asked. "Is it OK that you were here with us?"

"Well, that's . . ." Aki said, her voice cracking. She seemed about to launch into her usual bold front and say something like *It's none of your business* or *It doesn't matter.*

But Fuka had no ulterior motive in asking; she was simply concerned about her. "It's fine," Aki answered. "It's better being here with all of you."

When Kokoro had arrived at the castle that day, Aki had been crouching on the sofa, alone. She had her own room in the castle and could have shut herself away. Instead, she was in the Game Room, face pressed into her knees. Kokoro remembered Aki's face and the look in her eyes, and felt a stab in her chest.

"I see," Subaru said lightly, finally breaking the silence. "Were you close to your grandmother?" He asked this quietly, as if it wasn't important.

Subaru said he's living with his grandmother and grandfather, Kokoro thought. Without his parents, just his older brother. Only he could have asked that question.

A surprised look surfaced in Aki's eyes. Her lips tightened, and she didn't respond immediately.

"Um," she said finally, her voice small and husky. "She could be strict sometimes, and I never really thought about whether I loved her or not. But now I realize I really did."

"I'm so glad you wore your uniform," Subaru said. "Thanks to that, now we know we all go to the same school. If not, March would have arrived without anyone saying anything."

Aki's eyes seemed to tear up. Kokoro spoke up quickly. "Yes. Thank you, Aki-chan."

"It just happened," Aki said, and turned away.

That's when they heard it.

Aooooooooooooooooooo.

Aooooooooooooooooooo.

The noise rang through the castle. It was the warning howl they'd heard earlier, but much, much louder.

"Whoa!" they shouted. The air shook, the floor began to sway, and they were rocked off their feet. They knew exactly what was in store.

It was five o'clock.

"Let's get out of here!" shouted Rion.

Kokoro stumbled and grabbed at her mirror. She saw the others doing the same. But as a huge tremor struck, she couldn't keep her eyes open. The quaking was so vigorous, she'd lost control of her facial muscles.

She grabbed the mirror's frame tightly, trying to crawl inside. The rainbow-colored light beyond it was wavering. "Wait! Don't go away!"

With all her strength she heaved herself through.

*　*　*

WHEN THE SHAKING stopped, Kokoro found herself back in her own room.

The same bed, her familiar desk, the usual curtains.

Even though they were closed, she could sense how the atmosphere of the city had changed, now that it was November and winter was coming.

Her back and forehead were bathed in sweat; her heart was still pounding. She knew she was lucky. She'd only just escaped being eaten.

She looked over at her mirror—it was no longer glowing. Her knees shook as she remembered that deafening howl. Her bones were still reverberating.

She wondered whether the others had made it through.

She parted the curtains and spied a graceful crescent moon in the evening sky. For the first time in forever, she slid open the window, and leaned out for a better view of the city.

Houses just like the one she lived in; tall condos, apartment buildings that looked, from where she stood, like matchboxes. In the distance, she could catch the lights flickering in the supermarket.

They are all out there somewhere.

Every one of them, in the same district as her.

December

THE CITY TWINKLED with Christmas lights.

She could feel it, even from inside her house. Kokoro's family wasn't the type to put up Christmas decorations, though the neighbors always festooned their house from top to bottom. She didn't have to go outside to see them. She could pick up the flashing of their lights reflecting on the walls and windows of her house.

*　*　*

"DON'T YOU THINK we should do something for Christmas?" Rion asked.

It was December and they were gathered in the castle.

On the sofa, Fuka raised her head from her book, and Masamune glanced up from his video game. They all looked at Rion.

"I mean, we've got this space all to ourselves, so shouldn't we get a cake or something to celebrate?"

"Do they have Christmas in Hawaii too?" asked Fuka. Christmas was about chubby old Santa Claus in his red outfit flying across the snowy sky. It was hard to picture this character on a tropical island.

Rion laughed. "Yes. Of course. Though they don't have the image of a white Christmas like in Japan. There's tons of posters with pictures of Santa surfing and stuff."

"Surfing?" Kokoro didn't mean to raise her voice, but Rion chuckled even more.

"The holiday's so big in America, much more than in Japan. It's more like *Very* Christmas than Merry Christmas over there. You can't get away from it."

"I see."

"Yeah. So why don't we do something on Christmas Eve? We don't need to give presents, just bring some sweets and things. I'll bring a cake—and let's invite the Wolf Queen," he added. "It's December already. The castle will close at the end of March, so shouldn't we do something fun before it's all over?"

The Wishing Key still hadn't turned up. Or at least no one seemed to have found it. And they still weren't sure if after March they would even have any memory of each other at all.

"I like it." When Aki voiced her assent, there was a scattering of nods.

"OK, but," Masamune began. "When shall we do it? The twenty-fourth—are you free on Christmas Eve? Don't you have other plans?"

"Works for me," Rion said. "Because of the time difference, it won't overlap with the dorm party for students staying over the holidays."

"Christmas Eve suits," Fuka said in her bright voice. "But I can't make it on the twenty-third. I have a piano recital."

Oh, Kokoro thought when she heard this.

"Do you play the piano?" she asked.

"Um," Fuka said. "I don't go to school, but I still have private piano lessons."

On Kokoro's first day at the castle, she'd heard the sound of a piano. It must have been Fuka. So there was a piano in her room.

Kokoro had taken piano lessons up till elementary school but had given up. She envied Fuka having something going on outside school.

"I heard a piano being played in one of the rooms before," Kokoro said, and Fuka gave a little gasp of surprise.

"Was it too loud?" she asked, and Kokoro shook her head.

"Really? I'm relieved," Fuka said. "Isn't there a piano in your room, Kokoro? Am I the only one?"

"As you're a pianist, perhaps the Wolf Queen put it there especially for you."

"What do you have in your room, Kokoro?" Fuka asked.

"Bookshelves. But there're hardly any books I can read. They're all in foreign languages—English, Danish and others."

"Danish? Wow. How do you know it's Danish?"

"Hans Christian Andersen is a Danish author, and there are lots of his books."

She remembered Tojo-san showing her. Kokoro's room in the castle had many of the same books.

"That's cool. So your room is filled with books. I had no idea."

I wonder what the other rooms are like, Kokoro thought. If there was a piano for Fuka, then there must be something in each room to suit them.

"OK, the twenty-third is out. So what about the twenty-fourth?"

"That doesn't work for me," Aki said. "I might have a date with my boyfriend." No one seemed to know what to say.

Aki appeared ready to elaborate, but Rion simply said, "Sure, got it."

So they settled on having their Christmas party on the twenty-fifth.

NOW THAT THEY knew they were all from the same school, the atmosphere in the castle shifted a little.

Not that there was anything specific, but Kokoro sensed they'd grown more relaxed around each other.

For instance, when Masamune told Kokoro and the others, "That Free School teacher came to visit me too."

They looked at Masamune, bewildered. "Weren't you two talking about it? The Classroom for the Heart?" he expanded, and an affirmative "Ah!" arose from Ureshino and Kokoro.

"You mean Ms. Kitajima?"

"Think so. It was a woman teacher."

"So you've met her too, Masamune!"

Masamune seemed, for some reason, a bit self-conscious. Kokoro wondered why, but then it hit her.

He was feeling anxious because he'd never discussed things outside the castle.

"So did you visit the Classroom for the Heart?" Kokoro asked, still a little uneasy that the name of the School was the same as hers, but she knew that this group, unlike the kids at her school, would never tease her about it. And sure enough, Masamune shook his head, without dwelling on the coincidence over names.

"No, I haven't," he said. "My parents seemed to know about it, but they said it's for getting kids to go back to their school. They weren't thinking of sending me there."

"So your parents still think if you don't want to go to school, you don't have to?"

This was so different from her parents. Masamune only shrugged.

"I mean, my parents know all about the hideous things that go on in schools these days. There's news all the time, isn't there, about bullying and all kinds of underhand things and how kids commit suicide? My dad said, *There's no way we're going to make him go if it means school will kill him.*"

Masamune imitated his father's voice. *School will kill him* was a gruesome way to put it, but she was astounded to hear there were parents like his.

"The thing is," Masamune continued, his eyes glazing over, "they're really into looking for a school where I can feel safe. My dad said the Free Schools are nothing more than private NPOs. But then Ms. Kitajima came to our house, and said she'd like to talk."

Masamune drew in a small breath.

"My mum stood at the front door and argued with her—*Why are you here? We didn't ask you to come. Did his junior high say something?* Ms.

Kitajima said no, the school didn't ask her to come, she just happened to hear about me from one of my friends and thought she would come over for a chat."

Kokoro had never met her, but she could picture Masamune's mother scowling. *Did his junior high say something?* Masamune's parents really must have an intense distrust of public schools. She remembered Masamune had said, months ago, that teachers were just *humans after all.* And that *most of the time they're not even as smart as we are.*

Masamune must have sensed what Kokoro was thinking, because he said, in a small voice, "When I first stopped going to school, my parents got into a heated debate with my homeroom teacher. They said public school teachers aren't any good."

"I see."

"But I realized that the Free School teacher you two were talking about was the same one, so I agreed to meet her the other day."

Kokoro and Ureshino exchanged a glance. Kokoro felt something warm inside.

Masamune's decision to meet Ms. Kitajima was down to them.

Maybe it was an exaggeration, but Kokoro was thrilled he trusted her.

Masamune still looked uncharacteristically shy about discussing outside things. His nervousness made him speed up his words.

"We didn't really talk about anything much, but she said she'd come again."

"She's a good person," Kokoro said.

"Yeah," Masamune agreed. "I could kind of pick up on that."

"Hm . . . I wonder if she's going to come over to my house soon," Aki murmured. She'd been listening quietly beside them. "I was sure there was no Free School near us, but we're talking about the same junior high, aren't we?"

"Maybe she will."

If Ms. Kitajima did visit Aki, Kokoro hoped she'd agree to meet her, like Masamune had.

They had worked out that they lived near each other, but that didn't mean they ever considered meeting up away from the castle.

Picturing Ms. Kitajima's face, Kokoro discovered a fresh joy in realizing that they had real connections in the outside world. It seemed now that even Masamune, for all his sarcasm, and Aki, who absolutely refused to talk about school, were less resistant to discussing their real lives.

Though she never turned up wearing her school uniform again, Aki seemed to visit the castle more often.

And as a group, all seven seemed to hang out together in the castle more than ever before.

* * *

KOKORO HAD NEVER imagined herself celebrating Christmas with a party of her own peers again. She was overjoyed. Last year, she and her friends had met up at her classmate Satsuki's house.

She wondered how Satsuki was. A bolt of pain shot through her.

They had been in different classes at Yukishina No. 5 Junior High. Kokoro remembered how Satsuki said she'd joined the softball team. It was tough going, the practice grueling, but she was doing her best. And Kokoro could picture her giving it her all.

They'd been friends for such a long time, living parallel lives, but now Satsuki must view Kokoro as one of the *special* students who didn't go to school. Kokoro was used to it now, but it still hurt to have these thoughts.

The second semester was almost over.

Winter break was around the corner.

The year was nearly over.

IN THE MIDST of all this, as Christmas drew near, Kokoro's mother came up to her bedroom one evening and asked, "Can I talk to you?"

Her voice was tense, and Kokoro was filled with dread. Something was waiting to bring an ache to her chest and a heaviness to the pit of her stomach.

A part of her wanted to know what was coming, another part not so much.

Her mother said, "Mr. Ida mentioned he wanted to drop by tomorrow during the day. Is that OK?"

Her mother had probably stayed in touch with him. Just like she'd done with Ms. Kitajima.

But there was a fundamental difference between Ms. Kitajima and Mr. Ida.

Whenever Mr. Ida dropped by, Kokoro became incredibly anxious. She would begin to sweat, feeling as if she were about to suffocate.

He's coming by now because the second semester's finished, she suddenly thought.

At this point, he had to take note of anyone not attending—that was his job, after all.

Her mother's voice was still strained, or at least it seemed that way.

"He said he has something he wants to tell you about another girl from your class."

Kokoro wasn't at all sure that she could maintain her composure. The words pierced straight to her heart.

"A girl—in my class?"

"A girl called Sanada, who's the class president."

A siren began to wail somewhere deep inside her ears. Then it faded. Her mother looked at her, suddenly stern, and Kokoro found it hard to breathe.

"So something *did* happen? What was it?"

"What did he say?"

"He said he thinks you and that girl had an argument."

A chill shot up her spine.

An argument.

She made it sound so innocuous. Anger started to boil up inside her, so intense that she thought she was going to pass out.

In an argument, two people can communicate their point to each other. They are on an equal footing.

What had happened to Kokoro was by no means an *argument*.

Kokoro stood, lips pursed and silent. Her mother sensed something.

"Let's meet him," she said. "Let's meet him, you and I. Did something happen?" her mother asked again.

Kokoro bit her lip, and after a pause said, "They came to our house."

She'd finally come out with it. Her mother's eyes widened.

Kokoro raised her head slowly. "I—"

You should never say you hate anyone.

Her mother had always said this. That no matter how disgusted you might be with a friend, you should never speak ill of them. Kokoro thought she'd annoy her mother if she said anything.

"Mum, I . . . I hate Sanada-san."

Her mother's eyes narrowed.

"And we never argued."

MR. IDA DROPPED by the next morning.

It was a Tuesday and school was still in progress, but he apparently arrived between lessons. Kokoro's mother had taken the day off work.

His hair was a little longer than the last time she'd seen him. He took off his well-worn sneakers at the door and turned to Kokoro. "Good morning, Kokoro. How are you?"

From the beginning, Mr. Ida had called her simply Kokoro—with none of the usual suffixes. She'd only spent a month in his class, yet he used the same casual form of address as he did with anyone he liked. And it certainly had made her happy to be spoken to this way, since it made her ordinary, just like the others. But after this initial happy feeling, she got the sense that Mr. Ida had intentionally used that form of address in order to make her feel relaxed.

It was his job. Showing concern was part of it. She knew it was immature and stupid to worry about something so petty, but she couldn't help it.

He was, anyway, at the beck and call of Miori Sanada and her little gang. Even if she tried, Kokoro couldn't forget a scene in the classroom back in April.

Mr. Ida, do you have a girlfriend? one of the girls had asked him.

Even if I did, I wouldn't tell you! he said.

But I want to know! What a liar you are, Ida-sen! she said, contracting the word *sensei*.

Wait, that's not the way to speak to me, you know. He was laughing. *You guys . . .* he said. He wasn't really angry with them.

He was completely *Ida-sen* to Miori and her little gang.

And these were Kokoro's thoughts whenever he'd said to her, *Don't push yourself too hard.*

Don't push yourself too hard. But everyone will be glad if you come back to school.

He may have said it with kind intentions, but it seemed to her he didn't really care one way or the other.

Why don't you like going to school?

Did something happen?

When he'd first asked her, and she hadn't responded, she got the sense he'd labeled her a slacker, and his impression hadn't changed.

But she didn't mind. *What do you expect?*

Teachers were invariably on the side of students like Miori Sanada, who stood out. The ones who spoke confidently in class, who played with their friends at break, the lively straightforward ones.

She desperately wanted to tell him what they'd done, and see him look dumbstruck, but she was pretty sure even after he heard the whole story, he'd still take their side. In fact, she *knew* it.

She knew he would go straight to Miori to ask if it was all true. And she'd never admit it.

She would only mention whatever made her look good.

When Miori and her friends had surrounded Kokoro's house, and Kokoro had lain on the floor, trembling, Miori had started to cry. And her friends had tried to comfort her, saying, *Don't cry, Miori.*

In that world, Kokoro was the villain. Unbelievable, but true.

THE THREE OF them sat in the living room: Mr. Ida, Kokoro and her mother.

Compared to his earlier visits, her mother was clearly anxious.

The previous night, Kokoro had told her mother the story of what had happened with Miori back in April. She'd never talked about it in all these months, but she wanted her mother to hear it directly from her. Especially as Mr. Ida would have explained it as some kind of *argument.*

When Mr. Ida arrived, Kokoro was told to wait upstairs in her bedroom. *Your teacher and I will talk first, just the two of us*, her mother had said.

Her mother's expression was so cold and angry, she did as she was told.

ENOUGH TIME HAD passed since the events of April that when Kokoro told her mother the full story of what had happened, she could do it without breaking down in tears. She thought it would actually be fine to cry, to show her mother how much she'd suffered, but somehow no tears would come.

It was tough for her to explain it was all as petty as boyfriend-girlfriend stuff, who liked who, but she managed.

She wanted her mother to get emotional and upset. For her to say, *What awful people*, and protect her daughter.

Mum'll be so angry, was her first thought, but in the end she wasn't.

As she told the story, her mother's eyes welled up. When Kokoro saw the tears, she was shaken and even less able to cry herself.

"I'm so sorry, Kokoro," her mother said. "I never realized any of this was going on. I'm so, so sorry."

She hugged Kokoro close, and clasped her fingers. Her mother's tears plopped down on to the back of Kokoro's hand.

"We'll fight this," her mother said, her voice trembling. "It might be a long battle, but let's fight it. Let's do it, Kokoro."

BACK IN HER bedroom, she saw the mirror was glowing again.

Today everyone would be getting together beyond the mirror.

And she badly wanted to be with them.

But instead she quietly left her bedroom, walked down to the bottom of the stairs, and pricked up her ears. It was a small house, so even though the door to the living room was closed, she could still just make out what they were saying.

"There seems to be some trouble among the girls," she heard her teacher say.

"*It's not an argument*, is how Kokoro put it," her mother said. Kokoro felt a stab of pain in her heart. The voices grew louder, then quieter, like waves ebbing and flowing.

"Wasn't Ms. Kitajima supposed to come with you today?" she heard her mother say.

"Um, no," Mr. Ida said. "I came alone. Since this is an issue in our school." Kokoro remembered Ms. Kitajima, and the teabags she'd brought her.

We can use those teabags at our castle Christmas party, she thought, *and everyone can taste them.*

Ms. Kitajima might have told Mr. Ida something. Wanting to cooperate with the school, she might have looked into what had happened in April.

You're battling every single day, aren't you?

Remembering her voice, Kokoro longed to see her again. She

185

gently closed her eyes. Then she heard her teacher's voice; it sounded as if he were making excuses: "You see, Sanada has her own . . . She's a cheerful, very responsible student."

"*What* did you say?" Her mother's voice grew sharper, and emotional for the first time. Kokoro wanted to plug her ears.

She slipped back upstairs to her bedroom. The mirror was shining.

The rainbow light that opened the entrance to the castle was so gentle. Kokoro touched the glowing surface softly with her fingers.

Help, she thought.

Help me.

Someone—help me.

A WHILE PASSED before she was called downstairs.

The faces of both her mother and Mr. Ida had reddened since earlier, and when Kokoro joined them, they tensed up even more. The atmosphere was so heavy it was as if the very color of the air had changed.

"Kokoro," her teacher said. "Would you be willing to meet Sanada to talk through what happened?"

When she heard his words, she felt she couldn't breathe. Her heart began to pound in its cage.

She stared mutely at her teacher.

"She's the kind of girl that people often misunderstand, and I'm sure there were things that hurt you, Kokoro. But I talked to Sanada and she's concerned about you. She regrets it."

"I totally doubt that," a voice said. It was Kokoro's heightened voice, trembling.

Mr. Ida stared at her in astonishment. Kokoro shook her head.

"If she regrets anything, it's that you might have been annoyed with her. There's no way she's worried about me. She's just afraid no one will like what she's done."

Kokoro got this all out in a rush. She never imagined she'd say so much. She could tell how it unsettled Mr. Ida.

"Kokoro, the thing is—" he began.

"Mr. Ida."

Her mother stepped in between them. She held his eye, her voice calm.

"Shouldn't we first hear, directly from Kokoro, what happened? Just as you've heard Miss Sanada's account."

Mr. Ida looked on silently. He was about to say something, but her mother spoke first. "That's enough for today," she said. "Next time I'd like you to bring the teacher in charge of the whole year, or even the head, with you."

Mr. Ida said nothing, his lips drawn tight. He looked down, avoiding her mother's eyes, and Kokoro's.

"I'll come again soon," he said, and got to his feet.

After she'd seen him off at the front door, her mother called her. "Kokoro."

She was about to ask her something but stopped, changed her mind. She looked tired, but calmer, more collected.

"How about coming shopping with me?" her mother asked. "We don't have to go to the mall. If there's somewhere else you'd prefer, let's go."

IT WAS A weekday, around midday, so she could get away with not seeing any other junior high school students.

She was seated in the food court at Careo with her mother, eating an ice cream.

Inside Careo were the McDonald's, Mister Donut, and even Misudo that Kokoro liked, but she avoided them, since students from school were often there.

It had been so long since she'd been outside her house, since the day she'd bought the chocolates for Fuka at the convenience store.

The light outside seemed dazzling, and she was consumed with awkwardness around anyone other than her family or the castle group, but her mother was with her today so she felt less frightened.

As these thoughts ran through her head, she realized she was searching for someone.

Whenever she saw a young person with dyed hair pass by, she'd look carefully, hoping it was Aki or Subaru. Would Ureshino or Fuka turn up on the walkway over there, arm in arm with their parents, like her? Would Masamune pass right in front of her, carrying a bag with the latest video game he'd just bought? She hoped it would come true. She even hoped that Rion, away in Hawaii, might suddenly make an appearance.

How awesome it would be if one of them spotted her, and she could introduce them to her mother as *my friend*.

But no one appeared.

As it was a weekday, the food court was almost deserted. The others must be in the castle.

"In the days when you were younger, Kokoro"—her mother, sitting opposite, was likewise scanning the passersby—"the mall wasn't as colorfully decorated as it is now." These days, the stores were decked out with vibrant red, green and white decorations, and "Jingle Bells" rang out relentlessly from speakers above them.

Her mother carried on voicing her thoughts. "Do you remember when you were little and we went to eat in a restaurant at Christmas? A French restaurant. You had just started elementary school, or maybe it was a little before."

"Sort of."

She definitely remembered going with her parents to a fancy restaurant that was quite unlike the places they usually went to. And she remembered the lively end-of-year atmosphere in the shops. She remembered how they brought out so many varied dishes, each on a separate plate, different from the usual rice-omelet lunch she was used to at ordinary family restaurants, and she recalled thinking, even as a child, how this was the real thing when it came to food.

"I remember how they brought out one little dish after another for you and Dad, and I thought it was odd. You finished one and they brought out another. I was wondering if it would ever end."

"That's because we rarely eat a set meal like that," her mother said. "I remember too. You asked, *Can't we go home now? How much more are you going to eat?*" Her mother laughed. "Let's go somewhere this year, too. That restaurant is closed now, but your dad and I can look for another one."

Kokoro thought maybe she knew why her mother seemed to be avoiding the subject of Mr. Ida or Miori. She hadn't felt like discussing anything either. Not so soon.

But there was one thing she did want to say.

She turned to her mother, whose gaze was far away.

"Mum?"

"Hm?"

"Thank you."

Her mother looked intently at Kokoro but her face was expressionless. Kokoro had needed to get that out.

"Thank you for saying that to Mr. Ida. For telling him what I said."

Truthfully, she was worried whether her story had been properly conveyed. Her teacher must really have a negative impression of Kokoro now. He'd suggested she meet with Miori Sanada, but Kokoro had refused, and now he must certainly view her as a problem child, with none of the honesty or integrity he expected to see in his pupils.

"You believed me, Mum."

"Of course I did." Her mother's voice sounded a bit husky, and she looked down at her hands. "Of course I did," she repeated, her voice now clearly trembling.

She dabbed at her eyes with her fingers, and when she looked up, Kokoro saw they were red.

"You must have been so frightened," her mother said. "When I heard the story, *I* was frightened too."

Kokoro blinked in surprise.

"And I just really wish you'd told me sooner. When I was talking to your teacher, I felt I could understand how you must be feeling."

Her mother lifted the corners of her mouth into a tired, listless smile.

"When I told him it wasn't your fault, I was convinced of it, but I was still worried whether he'd believe me or not. I wasn't sure I'd properly explained how frightened you really were, that maybe he hadn't understood, but it took courage to say that."

Her mother reached across the table and took Kokoro's small hands in hers. "Do you want to change schools?" she asked.

"Change schools?" At first the meaning didn't hit her. She felt her mother's cool palm holding hers and then it came to her—she was actually talking about transferring to a different school.

Kokoro's eyes widened.

The idea had occurred to her before. Sometimes it seemed like a great idea; at other moments, like a backward way of thinking, as if she was running away. There were students from elementary school days that she really liked. It frustrated her to think the likes of Miori would force her to leave. Miori and her gang would never regret what they did, and the anger and embarrassment made her sick to her stomach, picturing them laughing over how they were the ones who had got rid of her.

Until now, though, it hadn't seemed a realistic option. Even if she'd wanted to transfer, she hadn't thought her mother would allow it.

But now, her mother explained it. "If you want to transfer to a different school, Kokoro, I'll look into it. It might mean going further away, but let's research it together—whether there are junior highs in the next school district, or private junior highs, that you could attend."

But Kokoro was still anxious that even in a new school, she might still fail to manage. Transfer students stood out, and her new classmates might soon discover that she'd run away from her old school.

Still, the possibility remained that she might actually fit in to a new school, as if nothing had ever happened.

It was certainly a sweet-sounding prospect. More than anything, her mother seemed on board with the idea, which gave her a warm, soft feeling inside. Her mother recognized her daughter wasn't going to be hopeless forever.

"Jingle Bells" continued to peal out from the sound system, interrupted by cheerful announcements of Christmas sales.

"Can I . . . think about it?" Kokoro asked, thinking of her friends in the castle.

Going to a new school was a tempting idea, but it did mean losing her status as a student at Yukishina No. 5 Junior High. She may well lose the right to visit the castle, and not be able to see anyone there ever again. She could not bear the thought.

"Of course," her mother said. "We'll think about it together."

Afterwards, Kokoro went food shopping with her mother.

She spotted a box of assorted chocolates. "Can we get this?" she asked. She wanted to take it to the Christmas party.

She was thinking her mother might find it suspicious, for she surely couldn't eat them all herself, but she readily agreed and dropped it into her shopping basket.

They were on their way to the car park, when Kokoro stopped suddenly to gaze at the array of shops that lined the mall.

"Is something wrong?" her mother asked.

"It's just been such a long time since I've been outside."

The gleam of the lights still made her dizzy. But she found herself getting used to them.

"Mum, thank you for bringing me."

For a moment, her mother looked at her as if struck by some unseen shock. She took Kokoro's hand and pulled it closer to her. "I'm so happy we could come together."

They hadn't walked like this, fingers interlocked, since the lower years in elementary school. Hand in hand, they returned to their car.

* * *

AT THE CASTLE Christmas party, Rion arrived with a cake. The group gave a "Wow!" when they saw it.

"It looks so delicious!" Kokoro chimed in.

It was a chiffon cake, with a hole in the middle. The icing was uneven. It didn't look as though it had been bought in a shop. The fruit decorations on the top were a little irregular too, but that gave the cake its charm.

"Is it homemade?" Masamune asked.

"By a girlfriend?" Aki asked, and Kokoro's heart beat fast for an instant. All eyes were on Rion.

Boys who played football were always popular with the girls. Maybe that was why he was studying abroad. They hadn't talked about it, but it certainly would make sense if he had a girlfriend.

But Rion shook his head.

"Nope. It's my mum's," he said. "She bakes one every year. She came over for Christmas, stayed in my dorm and gave it to me, so I brought it."

"Can she stay in your dorm?"

"Yeah. Parents can stay for a few days. They have rooms with kitchens for them."

Kokoro glanced at the clock on the wall and vaguely considered the time difference.

It was midday in Japan. So in Hawaii it would be the late afternoon of the previous day. It was Christmas Day in Japan, but for Rion it probably still felt like Christmas Eve.

Kokoro had the impression that it was more usual for people from other countries to spend Christmas as a family than in Japan. Kokoro's family was the same—they'd gone out for a meal the night before, but today, Christmas Day, her parents had, unusually, gone out together, which allowed her to come here.

"Rion," she asked, "are you—coming back to Japan for the break?"

It wasn't as if she was asking to meet him outside the castle, but his living so far away in Hawaii made it impossible for them ever to meet outside, and just the idea that he might come back to Japan, and be somewhere nearby, made her happy. But Rion shook his head. "No, *I'm* not going back," he said. "My mum was only in Hawaii for two days, and then said she had to go home. She said she was busy."

"Oh, I see."

"Um. Let's eat," Rion said. He'd brought a cake knife to cut it into slices. As he unpacked it, Kokoro considered something.

Rion's mother had brought the cake, but hadn't stayed to actually eat it with her son.

Maybe she thought he'd share it with his friends. But it was Christmas, and the other kids in the dorm would have gone back home to their families. That must be what Rion meant when he'd said so emphatically, *I'm not going back.*

Kokoro remembered that it was Rion who'd come up with the suggestion to have a Christmas party in the castle, saying that he'd bring a cake.

What was he feeling when he made that suggestion?

She recalled his voice. The words Rion had spoken to the Wolf Queen. *My school isn't Yukishina No. 5, and yet here I am. Why did you summon someone like me?*

And the Wolf Queen's response: *But you badly wanted to go, didn't you? To the public junior high in your area?*

What did *that* mean? Going to school in Hawaii—just the sound of it made them single him out as wealthy. *It's not that great,* he'd told them.

"Hey, let's invite the Wolf Queen, too. Wolf Queeeeen," he called, slicing into the cake. He put the knife down. "I can't cut even slices. One of the girls have a go."

Ureshino said, "Kokoro should do it. She peeled an apple for me once. She'll be good at it."

"Eh? I've no idea if I can do it properly." Kokoro smiled wryly as she remembered what trouble peeling an apple had led to. But she was happy to be asked to be in charge of the cake.

"You called?" a light voice spoke, and the Wolf Queen materialized.

"We have cake," Rion said. "But can you even eat it with that mask on? Do you ever actually eat?"

The Wolf Queen moved her head slowly to the side and studied the homemade cake, chiffon with ripples of icing on the top. The tableau was surreal, but the combination of her dreamlike dress and mask, and the sugary cake, seemed to work together somehow. She finally answered.

"I won't eat it here." She lifted her head slowly at Rion. "If you cut me a slice, I'll take it back with me."

The group looked on with bemused smiles. They'd never imagined that the Wolf Queen, whom they'd taken to be a completely fantastical character, would show such appetite, like some little girl.

But all Rion said was, "OK. And this is for you, too." He reached around to take a small package out from his backpack, and handed it to her. "We had this at home, but if you don't mind, I'd like you to have it."

They'd talked about not exchanging presents, but he'd apparently brought something anyway. The Wolf Queen stared for a time at the package in his hands, before finally accepting it.

"OK," she said, placing it behind her back.

Kokoro had expected the Wolf Queen to unwrap it immediately. Rion made no comment.

"So, let's have some cake," he said.

DESPITE THE DECISION not to bring gifts to their Christmas party, Aki, too, had brought something: pretty patterned paper napkins like the ones she'd brought before. She handed one out to each of them. These were part of the same series as those she'd given Fuka on her birthday, though in a different pattern.

"Jeez, I should have brought something, too!" Ureshino said loudly.

What surprised Kokoro most was the moment when Masamune laid out a pile of manga products for boys and told them they were presents.

"Take as many of them as you want," he said.

Kokoro was stunned. A lot of them were freebies found in the back of manga, but there were some gift tokens for books, too.

"Wow! Tokens for the *One Piece* series!"

Kokoro loved manga, too. She turned the gift token over and noticed there was the maximum amount of 500 yen on it. Masamune always brought in lots of video games, and seemed to own so many things. But he didn't seem to consider money and possessions as particularly important.

"These are all manga for boys. So I don't know what they are, and I don't need any," Aki said, making a face.

But Subaru said, "Hey! Are these new? In that case, I'll take one." He reached out for one of the gift tokens.

"Which ones do you prefer?" Aki asked him.

"If you're not bothered about them"—Masamune was irritated— "then don't get involved."

"It's such a surprise," Aki shot back. "Whether I'm interested or not is beside the point. I'm just so astonished that you'd even think of bringing us presents, Masamune."

"You're so annoying. If you're going to diss them, then give them back. It took time to get all this stuff together, you know."

"No, I'll have one, actually."

Kokoro moved in to thank him.

"No problem," Masamune said, looking away and blowing out his cheeks.

Rion's mother's cake was deliciously spongy, rich with egg and light as air.

Rion was thrilled with the assorted chocolates Kokoro had brought. "I haven't seen these in a long time," he said. "I used to eat them a lot when I was back in Japan."

Kokoro had made tea from the teabags Ms. Kitajima had given her, and she poured out a cup for each of them from her thermos. Aki and Fuka oohed and ahhed at the strawberry tea flavor and its delicious aroma.

"It's so good," they said, which made her glad.

"I'd like to have it again one day," Fuka added.

When Kokoro told her she'd got the tea from Ms. Kitajima, Fuka said, "Perhaps I should go there, too. To that Free School you went to, Kokoro. I'd like to meet Ms. Kitajima."

Fuka had, at some point, also dropped the *chan* when she addressed Kokoro.

"OK," said Kokoro. "I'm sure she'd love to meet you."

"ACTUALLY—I'D LIKE your advice on something."

Masamune had begun a serious conversation around four o'clock, an hour before the castle was due to close.

He was speaking to all of them while they relaxed, chatting. The Wolf Queen had departed at some point, taking her slice of cake and the unopened present from Rion.

Advice on something—that sounded a touch formal from Masamune.

"What?" said Aki.

Masamune stood up in the center of the group. The rest were sitting on the floor or lying down, hands behind their head.

He held his right elbow tightly with his other hand. Kokoro noticed how hard he was gripping it. Masamune didn't usually do tension.

"Advice?"

They seemed doubtful.

"I was wondering . . . if you all . . . just one day . . . if you could, during the third semester . . . school . . ." Masamune went on.

His voice sounded painfully husky, and he was avoiding their eyes. He broke off and looked up at them.

"Could you come to school? Just for one day. One day would be enough."

A chorus of gasps.

Masamune gripped his elbow harder.

"My . . . parents told me . . . to think about . . . going to a different school . . . starting in the third semester."

A pain shot through Kokoro. She remembered her mother, in the food court at Careo, asking her, *Do you want to change schools?*

It was because the second semester had finished, Kokoro thought.

Kokoro's situation was a bit different. But this might not be the first time the idea had been discussed in Masamune's house, as his parents had been criticizing public school teachers for quite a while.

"I've always dodged the idea, but now things are getting real. My dad said that during the winter break he was going to put my name down for a private junior high."

"So you'd start in a different school for the third semester?" Fuka asked. Masamune nodded.

"But maybe that's a good idea, don't you think?" Ureshino said, sounding solemn. "I've been thinking about it too. That it'd be easier to just move somewhere else and start again in a new class."

"I was thinking about it, too. But you know, if you're going to change schools wouldn't it be better to do it later, when the new school year starts? I would never consider moving so soon, in the third semester of *this* school year."

Masamune usually had quite a condescending manner, and Kokoro couldn't believe how mild and feeble he had become. She knew he was describing real feelings—that he'd been driven to the point where he *had* to leave.

Kokoro knew how he felt.

But being a transfer student at a new school in the middle of the academic year—that was a different story altogether.

"And also—I hate the thought."

Masamune seemed to be making himself angry.

"If I start at a different school then it's likely I won't be able to—come here anymore." The others chewed their lips in silence.

They knew exactly what he was trying to say.

They'd only be able to keep visiting the castle till the end of March. But if they were to lose even that precious diminishing time . . .

"So I told my father I didn't want to switch to a private school yet. I said instead I'd try going back to Yukishina No. 5 Junior High."

Masamune had started speaking more quickly, as if trying to justify himself.

"I'd go on the first day only. That would be enough. I'll tell them I gave it a try, but couldn't take it, and that'll delay them sending me to a new school until April, when the new school year starts."

"And you want all of us to go into school then because . . . ?" Aki asked.

Masamune's face tensed up, eyes darting between them. "I was just hoping . . . that all of you could . . . come into school on the same day as me." Masamune hung his head. This wasn't like him at all. "You don't actually need to go to your classroom. You could just go to the nurse's office, or the library. They'll think it's progress that you've even made it in."

"There's even an expression, *going straight to the nurse's office*, isn't there?" Subaru said, and Masamune looked up.

"I've been wondering this for a while," Masamune said. "Why were we all summoned here from the same school—Yukishina No. 5 Junior High? I was thinking there must be some reason. I don't know if the Wolf Queen intended it that way, but I was thinking we could all help each other."

All help each other.

Masamune's eyes looked super serious, on the verge of tears.

Kokoro gazed at his expression and felt the weight of his words. And she remembered how at the food court with her mother she'd scanned the walkway, hoping to catch a glimpse of one of them. How she was waiting for someone to round a corner and she'd be able to wave to them. How she was fantasizing about it—how great that would be.

"So it wasn't *advice* you wanted, but our *help*," Subaru said. He gave an exaggerated shrug and waved the voucher card Masamune had given him. "Is this Christmas present a bribe, then? To convince all of us to help you?"

Masamune looked at Subaru stiffly. "I know I have a lot of nerve asking this," he said curtly, "but . . ."

"OK. I'll go," Subaru said. "I'll be waiting in the classroom on the appointed day."

Masamune's eyes widened hopefully.

"I'm in Classroom 3 in Third Year. If you go to your classroom and you feel you can't take it, you can come to mine. I haven't been at school for a while, but I might score some points if a younger student starts to suck up to me."

"I might not be able to stand going back into a classroom," Aki said. Her tone was sharp as usual, though it didn't sound like she was angry. "Though if it's only to the nurse's office . . ."

"I think it'll be fine if you hide out there. The teachers should allow it."

"Me too," Kokoro burst out.

Mum and Dad will be so happy if I tell them I'm going to school, she thought. *They'll warn me not to overdo it, but I know they'll be relieved. With Sanada-san around, I'll skip the classroom and go straight to the nurse's office. Actually, my parents might feel better if I do that.*

Above all, the thought of meeting the others outside the castle made her jump with joy.

She knew how Masamune was feeling. *I feel so sorry for those loners!* Sanada-san had said about her. The words still smoldered inside her. She wanted to show them she was no loner. *I too have friends. And in other years. These kids are all my friends!*

And Masamune must feel the same way.

I might not have any friends in my class, Kokoro thought, *but because all of us are supporting each other, I can go into school.*

"Then I'll go to the nurse's office too," Fuka said, as if completing Kokoro's thoughts. "When is the opening ceremony at school? What day should we go?"

"January the tenth," Masamune said quickly, as if half afraid of the date and half anticipating it. His eyes looked even more tearful.

"Gotcha," Fuka said. "During the holiday break I'm going to go to juku again from my grandma's house, so I won't be at the castle for a while, but I'm on board. The tenth—I'll be there, I promise."

"Can I—think about it?" Ureshino's beady eyes flitted around. And then he quickly added, "I'm not saying I don't like the idea of being there for each other. That's not it. It's because at the beginning of the second semester, the day of the opening ceremony, I went into school and had that terrible experience."

Kokoro thought of the day Ureshino had turned up covered in bandages.

"So my mum might not let me. Sorry," he muttered, and looked over at Masamune. "If I'm allowed to go though, I will. Is that OK?"

"Yeah." Masamune nodded. He gazed down, as if unsure where to look. "Thank you, guys," he said. His voice cut out at the end. He bowed his head one more time, just slightly. "Thank you. I mean it."

"I envy you people. I can't join you." Rion's eyes reflected his words, and he looked a little sad. "I'm envious you're going to meet up outside the castle."

Kokoro's heart leapt, as if taking wing, at those words. Her chest still felt shackled by the fear, but her heart beat fast at the thought of seeing all of them waiting together in the nurse's office, dressed in their school uniforms.

It'll be fine, she thought.

We're going to support each other.

We'll fight—together.

THIRD
SEMESTER:
GOODBYE

January

KOKORO: 7TH GRADE CLASSROOM 4
Ureshino: 7th grade Classroom 1
Fuka: 8th grade Classroom 3
Masamune: 8th grade Classroom 6
Subaru: 9th grade Classroom 3
Aki: 9th grade Classroom 5

THEY EXCHANGED ESSENTIAL information about their classrooms, except for Rion, who of course lived abroad.

They promised if anything happened, they'd escape to the nurse's office.

If the nurse's office didn't work out, then they'd go to the library.

If the library wasn't looking good, then the music room.

And if none of those worked, they'd make a run for it.

Run out of the building, back home, and escape through the mirror to the castle.

They worked this all out in time for 10 January.

THE DAY BEFORE they were due to meet was a holiday, Coming-of-Age Day, when twenty-year-olds across the country celebrated reaching adulthood.

Kokoro's parents stayed at home that day, but Kokoro chose a moment when they wouldn't come up to her room and slipped through the mirror into the castle. She wanted to confirm with

Masamune and the others their promise to meet up at school. The others seemed to be doing the same, for most of them were also there, escaping their parents' watchful eyes.

Just before saying their goodbyes, Kokoro caught up with Masamune. They were standing in the grand foyer, about to exit the castle through their mirrors.

It was almost five o'clock.

"Tomorrow's the day," she said to him.

At that moment, the Wolf Queen's howl rang out like a siren, signaling the closing of the castle. They'd been hit by such powerful tremors recently when they were about to exit at five o'clock that it scared them, and so they usually made sure to leave before they heard the curfew howl, fifteen minutes before the hour.

"Yeah," Masamune murmured, ignoring the howl. He seemed self-conscious and reluctant to engage.

His cheeks looked pale. Kokoro didn't know the details of what had made him drop out of school. She knew his parents were pretty progressive, and respected their son's decision not to go, but there had to be some reason behind it all.

Just like with her.

"Masamune," she said, "there's a girl in my class I don't get on with at all."

Don't get on with was a convenient expression. It helped her avoid all the other possible nuances—*I hate her, I can't stand her, she bullied me*. What happened to Kokoro wasn't a fight, or bullying. It was neither, she thought, but *something* she couldn't put a name to. When adults and friends put it down to bullying, it made her so irritated she wanted to cry.

"I don't want to go to school because I know she'll be there, but if you and the others are with me, Masamune, then I'll be fine."

"What?" Masamune said, almost inaudibly, and looked at Kokoro. "What the hell? Are you trying to show me how heroic you are by saying you'll go in with me, even with all that crap that happened to you? Are you trying to show me how hard it will be for you?"

"Not at all."

Kokoro was relieved to hear Masamune back to his usual cynical self. Not long ago that tone might have frustrated her, but now she knew she shouldn't take him literally. All the time they'd spent together had taught her that.

She knew that Masamune was actually grateful to her for being willing to ignore past events and meet up with him. He'd just twisted it around to sound like the opposite.

"What I'm saying is, despite what's going on for me," she said, "I feel safe knowing all of us will be together. You're not the only one who's uneasy about it. You feel you'll be safe knowing we'll be there. Well, we feel the same, knowing *you'll* be there."

Masamune heard her out, and was reaching for the mirror when his fingers clenched and he grabbed hold of the frame.

"Yeah," he murmured.

"See you tomorrow," Kokoro said, emphasizing the words more than usual.

"Yeah. See you tomorrow. *At school.*"

∗   ∗   ∗

"MUM, I'M GOING to go to school tomorrow."

Kokoro's mother looked momentarily blank, as if time had stopped. But it was only an instant. "Oh, is that so?" she said.

Kokoro knew she was deliberately showing a lack of concern. Kokoro had bided her time, avoiding saying anything until the day before she was due to go in. The evening of the ninth.

They were doing the washing up together when Kokoro gave her the news.

"Are you sure you're OK with that?" Her mother avoided her eye. Kokoro followed suit, keeping her gaze on her hands as she dried the plates.

"I'm fine with it. I'd actually like to try going in, even for one day."

She planned to arrive after lessons had started at nine-thirty.

And go straight to the nurse's office instead of her classroom.

And straight back home if she couldn't manage it.

She explained the plan to her mother. "So don't worry about me," she pleaded.

"Do you want me to go with you?"

"No, I'll be fine," Kokoro said.

In all honesty, though, she would have loved for her to come.

Her heart was pounding. Just the image of the hallways and the front entrance was enough to make her freeze up.

But the rest of the group would no doubt come in alone, without a parent.

Masamune's parents, so down on the state school system, would definitely not accompany him. And Subaru wasn't even living with his parents.

Ureshino, Fuka and Aki might bring their mothers along, but if even one of them arrived on their own, Kokoro wanted to do the same.

Her mother said she'd contact the school—Mr. Ida—to tell them in advance that Kokoro would be going in the next day.

"This is so sudden. Why don't you go a little later? Like next week."

"But it's the opening ceremony."

"What?" her mother said. She put down a wet plate, and wiped her hands on her apron. "The opening ceremony was the end of last week. On the sixth of January."

"*What?*"

Her mother brought out a piece of paper which had been lying in the small rack for letters in the living room: a note from school that Tojo-san had delivered. Kokoro usually just handed these to her mother without looking at them.

On the school events calendar, sure enough the opening ceremony was on January the sixth.

"You're right."

As the opening ceremony had already happened at the end of last week, lessons would begin the next day. A three-day weekend, including the Coming-of-Age holiday, fell in between, but the first day of class was tomorrow.

Had Masamune misunderstood? She suddenly wanted to dash back into the castle to check, but that night, her mirror didn't shine. She regretted not exchanging phone numbers.

Ah—but maybe that's right, she thought.

Masamune had said he was going back to school at the start of the third semester. It was Fuka who'd asked, *When is the opening ceremony at school? What day should we go?*

Kokoro had naively concluded that Masamune was going to school on the day of the opening ceremony, but he'd never actually said that he would go to it. With students trooping to and from the gym, it could get chaotic. If they were going to meet in the nurse's office, an ordinary school day would surely be preferable.

See you tomorrow. At school.

The promise Masamune and Kokoro had made to each other.

"Thank you for worrying about me. But I'd still like to go," she said.

THE NEXT MORNING, her mother set off for work as usual. Kokoro had told her she wanted her to.

Even so, her mother fussed about at the front door, checking on Kokoro several times, and though her usual time to leave came and went, she still lingered.

"Don't overdo it, OK? If you feel you can't handle things, come home early," she said. "I'll call you in the afternoon."

"OK."

Her mother finally stepped through the front door.

"I'll be off in a minute then, Mum," Kokoro said, seeing her off with a wave. When she reached the gate, her mother turned around.

"Your bicycle," she said. "Last night your father cleaned the seat for you. It was really quite dusty."

"Oh?"

"He said he'd come home early today. He said to tell you not to overdo it."

"Um."

Last night he'd said the same thing directly to her. He seemed quite anxious. But also a little relieved. "You're an amazing kid," he told her. "To decide on your own to go back—I think you're incredible."

It hurt to think that she was only going in for a day, but hearing him praise her did make her happy.

And maybe . . .

Maybe seeing everyone today, she wouldn't be so scared of going in the next day. She might be able to attend school properly, together with all of them.

She left home at nine, avoiding the window when other students usually arrived. She hadn't ridden her bike for so long, and as she climbed on, the seat felt cold under her skirt. She breathed in the chilly air.

As she started to pedal, a thought struck her.

I'm not going into my class, she thought. *I'm not going to school.*

I'm going to see my friends.

It just happens that the place we're meeting at is school.

THE ENTRANCE TO the school was deserted.

When she reached the bicycle parking area, she hesitated to leave her bike in the space reserved for her class, and instead parked it in the eighth graders' area.

It still hurt to remember what Miori and her boyfriend had done to her here last spring.

But today, no one was around. And it was another season.

She could hear the sound of lessons taking place inside the school. The sound of teachers lecturing. Not many students speaking, though.

She slipped off her shoes in front of the cubbyholes at the entrance where students stored their outside shoes.

The action was so familiar, but as she located her cubbyhole, an invisible force made her chest tighten.

She felt a gaze from the side, and when she glanced over, her eyes widened.

The other girl's eyes widened, too. It was Moé Tojo. The girl who lived two doors away on her street.

They were both speechless.

Tojo-san was wearing a jersey and carried a school-approved satchel. She seemed to have just arrived too. She was as pretty as ever—with her perfect nose and her round eyes with a touch of light brown, an almost European look.

If there had been plenty of students around them, Kokoro could have looked away, but it was just the two of them.

A physical pain ran across her shoulders, down her back, through her entire body.

And she was reminded, *Ah—this is how it feels.*

She had intended never to forget the pain, but now she realized she had actually begun to forget. Until last May, she'd had this sensation every single day. Her stomach heavy and aching.

I don't want to go in, she shouted inside. But then Tojo-san made a move.

She suddenly reached out to retrieve her slippers from her cubbyhole. She put them on, averting her eyes from Kokoro, and without a word started walking briskly down the corridor. Heading towards the stairs that led to her classroom.

Moé had left her behind, completely ignoring her.

Her figure grew smaller before she disappeared up the stairs. She'd definitely given Kokoro a good look. Those mesmerizing, doll-like eyes, which Kokoro once felt so compelled to stare at, had swiftly blanked her.

So you're back, eh?

She'd been expecting some remark, even if it was sarcastic.

Just a word or two.

Things around her started spinning.

Her breathing grew shallow. As if she were in water, drowning. *Moé had once delivered handouts every day from school*, she thought, *but now she can't even say a word to me?*

Why would she be here at the school entrance at this time of morning? *This is the only time I could bear to come in. But you—you can just march in any time you want.*

She'd been so looking forward to seeing Masamune and the rest, but that happy anticipation now began to wither. *Someone, help me!* She felt weak as she leaned against the cubbyholes.

Kokoro had been picturing her slippers, and her desk, covered in graffiti. The depictions of bullying on TV always showed such things happening. The kid who wouldn't come to school always found her chair and desk with vicious messages like *Die!* scrawled all over them.

No matter how often she told herself that what was between Miori Sanada and her wasn't bullying, she was still terrified of it happening to her.

But nobody had written graffiti on her slippers, or filled them with thumbtacks. Instead, she spotted a letter.

An envelope with a small bunny sticker on it.

Hand trembling, she picked it up.

The sender's name was on the back of the envelope.

It was from Miori Sanada.

A deafening noise rang through her ears, a smashing of glass as if the world was splintering. She ripped open the envelope.

Dear Kokoro Anzai,

I heard from Mr. Ida that you would be coming to school and he advised me to write a letter to you, so I have.

I know you hate me. But I'd still like to meet you and talk.

You must think I'm horrible for suggesting it.

I know you're upset by what happened with you-know-who (but don't worry, I didn't tell Mr. Ida about him. Actually, I broke up with him in the summer. I thought if you still like him, I'd cheer you on).

Miori :)

Her hand shook even harder.

What the hell is this?

She recalled the laughing, playful banter: *Mr. Ida, do you have a girlfriend? Even if I did, I wouldn't tell you!* She remembered Tojo-san's cold eyes, and how she'd blanked her, and then she began to hear her own blood boiling in the veins of her temples.

She screwed the letter up tightly and put on her slippers. She pushed her toes right inside, squashing down the backs with her heels, and headed off to the nurse's office.

If she could get there quickly, she'd be able to breathe again.

She shut her eyes and took a gulp of air, but no matter how many breaths she took her chest still hurt, and she felt herself drowning all the more.

If only she could get to the nurse's office, Masamune would be there.

Her friends would be waiting.

All of them.

She wanted to show Masamune the letter, and hear him say, "What a load of crap. What a moron she is."

My thoughts exactly, Kokoro thought.

Tojo-san had spotted her, so the news that she was at school would surely reach Miori's ears, and quickly too. Lessons had begun, but Kokoro could picture Tojo-san scuttling over to Miori's desk the moment the bell went.

"Hey, you know what? *She's* here."

Kokoro felt faint.

I know you hate me. But I'd still like to meet you and talk.

Her body literally shook.

She turned the door handle to the nurse's office.

If some of her friends hadn't turned up, that would be OK. To see just one of their faces would be such a relief she might break down in tears.

She pushed open the door.

The nurse was sitting at her desk. Alone.

There was a space heater emitting a red glow. The nurse was seated in front of it. Kokoro knew the school nurse by sight but had never talked to her. She seemed to be expecting Kokoro. Mr. Ida must have let her know.

"Anzai-san?" the nurse asked, looking at her in surprise.

"Is Masamune . . ."

She was gasping, her voice reedy and trembling.

She looked over to check if anyone was lying on the bed. But no one was.

"Hm?" the nurse said, inclining her head. "Masa—*who?*"

"Masamune . . . kun. In eighth grade. Did he come here today?"

Which class in eighth grade was he in?

He'd told her, but her mind was so jumbled she couldn't recall. Fuka was, she was sure, in Classroom 3. Kokoro's speech sped up.

"Did Fuka-chan in eighth grade, Classroom 3 come too? And Subaru-kun, and Aki-chan, both in ninth grade?"

As she got the words out, she realized that without their last names the nurse would have no idea who she was talking about. Unless you were particularly close to someone, students didn't call each other by their first name. Kokoro suddenly reddened at having called Masamune by his first name to the nurse.

Still lingering in the doorway, she decided that if no one appeared, she'd go to Subaru's classroom, where he said he'd be waiting. She could see him, easy-going, cool. "Hey, so what's up?" he'd say.

"Anzai-san, please don't stress, come in and sit down," the nurse was saying.

"Then what about Ureshino-kun, from seventh grade?"

Kokoro suddenly remembered that she knew Ureshino's full name. After his incident last semester, the teachers must surely remember him.

"Haruka Ureshino. Did he come by to see you today?"

As she spoke, an uneasiness came over her.

Masamune, Aki, Subaru, Kokoro—weren't the teachers surprised all these kids who'd been absent so long suddenly turned up on the same day? Wouldn't their parents contact their homeroom teachers, as Kokoro's mother had done with Mr. Ida?

The school nurse gazed patiently at Kokoro, a look of confusion in her eyes.

"Ureshino-kun?" she said. "I'm sure there's no seventh-grader with that name."

Kokoro felt like a huge gust of wind had struck her. The nurse looked genuinely perplexed.

Haruka Ureshino. An unusual first and last name. She had to know him.

A sudden thought hit her—what if Ureshino had lied? What if he was the only one who wasn't at Yukishina No. 5 Junior High but had lied about it to go along with the others?

The school nurse frowned doubtfully.

"And I don't think there's anyone with the first name Masamune in eighth grade, either. Aki-chan, Fuka-chan—I'm trying to think if I know them. What are their last names?"

"Their last names . . ."

215

Instinctively, she knew. She knew it for certain. Not in her mind, but in her gut. *They're not here.*

Why she knew this, she wasn't sure. She became convinced she would never be able to see Masamune and the others in their world outside the castle.

"Masamune," she said quietly. "What am I supposed to do?" And she felt that she was about to cry.

What the hell? Are you trying to show me how heroic you are by saying you'll go in with me, even with all that crap that happened to you? Are you trying to show me how hard it will be for you?

She remembered Masamune's snarky reaction.

Masamune had agreed to come because he thought they'd all be there too.

This means we've betrayed him.

A picture came to her, clear as a bell, of Masamune alone, dazed, in the nurse's office. She felt like making a run for it in search of help. And then someone said her name:

"Kokoro-chan."

It was a soft voice. She turned around. In the doorway stood Ms. Kitajima.

She reached out a warm hand and touched her shoulder, and all Kokoro's tension drained away.

"Ms. Kitajima . . ."

A faint sound came out of her, as if air from deep in her throat were being expelled, and then Kokoro collapsed to the floor. With a crack, everything went black.

WHEN SHE WOKE up, Ms. Kitajima was still there, sitting next to her.

Kokoro felt the scratch of the starched bedcover over her as she lay on a bed in the nurse's office. The warmth of the space heater was not far away.

She looked around to see if maybe another student was in the other bed. But she didn't sense anyone else beyond the partition.

"Are you OK?"

Ms. Kitajima looked into her eyes.

"I'm—OK," Kokoro said, less to report her condition than because she was embarrassed to find someone gazing at her as she lay there defenseless on her back.

She'd never fainted before. She had no idea how long she'd been out. Her throat was parched, her voice hoarse.

"Ms. Kitajima?"

"Yes?"

"Why are you here?"

Ms. Kitajima's smiling eyes met Kokoro's.

"I came over because your mother told me you'd be at school today."

"I see."

She came because she was worried.

Kokoro and Ms. Kitajima were alone in the office.

Ms. Kitajima must have been keeping in touch with the teachers at the school, *coordinating* things.

Kokoro had already resigned herself to the fact that she would not be seeing the others. But pinning her last hopes on one final question, she asked, "Was I the only dropout student that you heard about today?"

Ureshino and Masamune had both said they'd met Ms. Kitajima.

Ms. Kitajima brushed away the hair that had fallen over Kokoro's eyes.

"That's right," she said.

She was simply answering the question she was asked, and didn't seem to find it at all significant.

"So you didn't hear anything from Ureshino-kun or Masamune-kun's families?"

"Hm?" was all Ms. Kitajima said in response. Kokoro shut her eyes tight. It was just like the nurse had said—there was no one by those names in the school. Kokoro couldn't believe it, but there it was.

"Nothing," Kokoro said.

So it's true, she thought, as her mind reeled.

What had it all meant—all these days up till now?

Was the world of the castle in the mirror not real?

Now that she thought about it, it seemed like an all-too-convenient miracle.

How could her bedroom connect up so efficiently with a different world?

Meeting these kids, thinking they were her friends—wasn't it all just wish fulfillment?

And then she thought: *Is there something seriously wrong with me?*

Masamune and Ureshino and Aki and Fuka and Subaru and Rion.

Had she been living since May, without realizing it, in this delusion of being with them, when in reality she'd been alone the entire time?

The thought that she'd gone crazy chilled her, but another thought frightened her even more. *From tomorrow I may not be able to go to the castle, ever again.*

"Kokoro-chan, I'm sorry," Ms. Kitajima said. "When you fainted a while ago you dropped a note, and I'm afraid I saw what it said."

Kokoro slowly bit her lip. The contents of that letter came rushing back. The rounded handwriting on the envelope. Miori calling herself *horrible*. The boy she'd referred to obliquely as *you-know-who* was, of course, Chuta Ikeda. Kokoro didn't care that he might have been Miori's boyfriend, or that they'd broken up.

They didn't understand each other at all, Kokoro realized despairingly.

What Kokoro had been through, and the way Miori Sanada saw things, didn't mesh at all. Had they even happened in the same world?

She'd agonized over whether to come today, thinking she might be killed, and here was Miori settling the whole matter by saying, in a throwaway fashion—of a boy that Kokoro had nothing to do with—*I thought if you still like him, I'd cheer you on.* Kokoro couldn't put into words how frustrated it made her feel. It was so humiliating her insides felt like they were on fire.

I want to kill her, she thought.

She shut her eyes as tears of frustration welled up.

"I spoke to Mr. Ida a few minutes ago," Ms. Kitajima was saying. "The letter doesn't really address what went on." Her tone sounded unusually stern.

Kokoro kept her face covered with her forearm. The tears felt hot on her sleeve. "I'm sorry," Ms. Kitajima said.

Kokoro had never expected a teacher to apologize.

"Ms. Kitajima . . . Moé Tojo . . . was there . . . a little while ago." Her convulsive breathing made the words come out in fits and starts. "She was . . . at the school entrance . . . and saw me . . . and she . . . blanked me. She didn't say a thing. She used to bring letters from school to my house every day, but when she actually sees me, she ignores me."

Kokoro wasn't sure what she was trying to say.

But she was sad. So terribly, terribly sad, and her chest felt like it was going to burst apart.

Kokoro almost shouted: "Ms. Kitajima, if it was Moé who put that letter in my cubbyhole, what should I do? If Miori asked her to, and Moé did as she was told?"

As she spoke, she understood what she was really afraid of, what she hated here.

Last April, when the kids had surrounded her house, Kokoro hadn't been able to verify if Moé had been among them. She might have been. But the very thought was too painful, and she wanted to cling to the possibility that Moé had not been there.

She couldn't bear the thought that Moé had turned into an enemy. She hadn't been willing to think Moé hated her. Until today.

"Kokoro-chan . . ."

Ms. Kitajima clutched Kokoro's arm so hard she let out a little cry. Then she brought her face right up close.

"It's OK."

Ms. Kitajima's grip on her arm was so firm, Kokoro felt encouraged.

"It's OK. Mr. Ida told Sanada-san to put the note in your cubbyhole. Tojo-san had nothing to do with it. I mean, Tojo-san was the one who explained to me what's been going on."

Kokoro had been sure that none of the kids who hung out with Miori would ever dare betray their ringleader.

But if it was Tojo-san, then—

"She bumped into you so suddenly, so perhaps she was too surprised to speak. But believe me. Tojo-san is worried about you. Truly worried about you."

But why? Kokoro couldn't help still wondering.

If she was that worried, then why look the other way?

But at the same time, a part of her felt like she already knew the reason.

Because she felt guilty.

Tojo-san must have been among the kids who'd surrounded her house, after all. She was there, yet she didn't try to stop them. And now she felt extremely bad about it. The possibility made Kokoro feel she could breathe, a little.

"Kokoro-chan," Ms. Kitajima said. Kokoro had stopped crying.

"There's no need for you to fight."

The words sounded like a foreign language.

Eyes shut tight, she didn't know how to respond, and just gave a firm nod.

The very idea that she didn't need to fight made her whole body feel enveloped in peace.

When she next opened her eyes, she felt more in control of herself. Ms. Kitajima was gazing at her, and Kokoro gazed back.

"What I want to do—is go home."

Ms. Kitajima nodded.

KOKORO'S MOTHER CAME from work to pick her up. The nurse had apparently contacted her just after Kokoro fainted.

Kokoro lay down slowly on the sofa, while her mother sat silently beside her.

Half an hour later, Ms. Kitajima came by.

She had wheeled Kokoro's bike back.

Then she explained that the reason Tojo-san was at the school entrance later than usual was because she had felt a cold coming on, and had stopped at the pharmacy on her way to school.

That's all Ms. Kitajima told her, nothing more.

Kokoro suddenly remembered.

Mr. Ida had wanted Miori and Kokoro to speak to each other, and didn't Ms. Kitajima want Kokoro and Tojo-san to see each other, too?

Kokoro's mother asked her to go upstairs while she and Ms. Kitajima talked over things alone for a while.

Kokoro took a deep breath, and looked hesitantly up the stairs. After the events of the morning, she was now afraid of going into her room.

There's no seventh-grader with that name.

The nurse hadn't looked like she was lying.

Did it mean that everything that had happened in the castle was in Kokoro's head? If the illusion was undone, then wouldn't the mirror stop shining?

Kokoro climbed the stairs and boldly pushed open the door.

She gasped.

The mirror was shining.

She remembered how they'd all promised each other what they'd do.

If the nurse's office didn't work, then they'd go to the library.

If the library was out, then the music room.

And if none of those worked, they'd make a run for it.

They promised to run away from school, and come back through the mirrors to the castle.

And her mirror was calling out that promise to Kokoro.

DOWNSTAIRS, HER MOTHER and Ms. Kitajima were still talking.

Kokoro didn't know how long they would take. And they might suddenly ask her to join them.

It was entirely possible, if she didn't answer, that they'd think it odd and come upstairs to look. But still, her desire to go through the mirror was even stronger.

She placed her hands on the mirror and, as ever, her palms fitted perfectly, as if being sucked through the surface of water. She splayed out her fingers and sank into the glow.

Everyone will be there, she told herself.

* * *

ON THE OTHER side of the mirror, the castle was silent.

None of the other mirrors was shining.

Oh. No one is here yet, she thought.

She looked over at Masamune's mirror, reflecting the grand staircases.

Please—come.

I'm begging you.

I went into school. I really did go to see Masamune. I didn't betray him.

She set off for the Game Room.

The castle really does *exist*, she thought.

She stroked the walls and fingered the candlesticks, tested the soft red carpeting with her toes. *This is no illusion.*

But what is *this place?*

Kokoro looked around her again.

A fireplace no one could use. A kitchen and a bathroom, also unusable. All the facilities were here, but with no gas or water, it was more like a toy she'd played with as a child.

After wandering a while, she came to the dining room.

She reached out to touch the brick fireplace in the middle of the far wall. Cool to the touch, it felt real.

She suddenly thought of the Wishing Key.

She remembered finding an *X* marked inside the fireplace. Did it carry some special meaning?

She peered inside. The *X*, about the size of her palm, was still there.

"Kokoro," a voice said behind her, and Kokoro's shoulders leapt. She spun around.

"Rion!"

"You surprised me. I saw your mirror shining but you weren't in the Game Room. So how did it go? Were you able to meet up with Masamune and the rest?"

Rion's tone was cheerful. Kokoro gazed steadily at him.

He really exists, she thought.

He's here, alive, moving, talking.

"I . . . didn't see them."

In her own mind, she sounded like a ghost talking. Rion was clearly puzzled. And she had no idea how to explain it.

"I don't know why, but they weren't there. But it wasn't just that they didn't turn up. I was told there weren't any students called Masamune or Ureshino."

"What?" Rion frowned. "What do you mean?" It helped that his tone was light. "What's the story? Were they making it all up? Claiming they were at the same junior high?"

"No."

The same thought had occurred to her. But there were a lot of things this fact wouldn't explain. First of all, there was no reason for them to do that.

"I don't know," Kokoro said, breathing hard.

She needed to get back soon. There was no telling when her mother and Ms. Kitajima might finish their conversation and come upstairs looking for her.

Rion might have picked up on her impatience. He was silent. Kokoro found it hard to wrench herself away, but she had to.

"I have to go," she said. "My mum's at home today and if I don't go back, she'll think something's up." She looked intently at Rion. "I'm glad I've seen you. I was thinking perhaps everything is a delusion. I'm glad I can see you really exist, Rion."

"What are you talking about?"

He was clearly confused. Her hasty explanation wasn't enough; it only served to bewilder him. She regretted it.

"Where are we? This castle, the Wolf Queen. What *is* it all?"

She had to leave quickly, but what she really wanted to do was call the Wolf Queen. Get her to give them some answers.

Rion murmured, "I was thinking, too, the whole thing feels a bit fake."

"What do you mean?"

"The way the Wolf Queen calls us all Little Red Riding Hoods." He paused. "I gotta go, too. I snuck out during a time-out from football practice. I thought today was going to be an important battle for you all, and I had to find out how it went."

"What time is it in Hawaii?"

"About five-thirty in the afternoon." Rion had his own tight daily schedule, but was concerned enough about all of them to come over. Kokoro began to feel less tense.

A question suddenly occurred to her that she just had to ask. She and Rion seldom got a chance to talk on their own. So this was her one opportunity.

"What would *you* do, Rion, if it was you?"

"Do?"

"If you found the Wishing Key."

Rion's eyes looked clear, as if gazing off into the distance.

"My wish is—"

Kokoro didn't want to hear what his wish was. Having a wish come true meant everyone here would lose their memory. So she was expecting him to say that he didn't care about the key if it meant he would lose his memory.

But instead, he carried on.

"Please bring my older sister back home."

Their eyes met. Rion's lips trembled, as if he had surprised himself by saying it aloud.

Kokoro had no clue what to say, and Rion gave a resigned smile.

"The year I started elementary school, my sister died. She was sick."

Kokoro was suddenly filled with pity. She looked patiently at Rion, willing him to continue.

"Sorry. I'm sure you don't want to hear this. I'm not expecting you to respond or anything."

"No, it's OK."

Did Rion want to talk about his dead sister? Or not? She couldn't tell.

She didn't think he'd picked up on her thoughts, but he gave a relieved smile, and went on. "If there really is a Wishing Key, and my sister can come back, then I might use it. If any wish can come true."

"Oh . . . I see what you mean."

"I haven't talked about this for a long time. I've never told it to any of my friends at school over there."

Seeing how uncomfortable he was, Kokoro stayed stock still.

She felt a lump in her throat, and thought: *I am so terribly small.*

In the face of Rion's wish, her problems with Miori Sanada faded. *What a pathetically small thing I've been wishing for*, she thought. She felt her heart beating audibly within her.

If his wish can come true, I'm willing to give up my own.

"Will you be here tomorrow?" Rion asked.

"I will."

She realized she had to dash back in case her mother's conversation with Ms. Kitajima had finished.

But all she could think about now was that they really existed. And when she saw the others the next day, she could be completely sure of it.

HER MOTHER DIDN'T bring up her conversation with Ms. Kitajima, and so Kokoro waited patiently for the next day when they could all see each other again.

When she passed through the mirror the next morning, they were indeed there. All except Masamune and Rion.

Rion's timetable was such that he couldn't spend all day in the castle like the others. But Masamune's absence was significant.

"Kokoro." When she arrived at the Game Room, it was Aki who first spoke to her. She looked a little angry.

As did Ureshino, Fuka and Subaru.

They must already have been discussing something, Kokoro thought. She came in, silent, and they stared at her.

"Why weren't you there?" Aki said.

She'd known the question was coming. But now that she actually heard it, the shock was greater than she'd imagined.

"I was!" she said. She looked directly at Aki. "I *was* there! I went to school just like we promised."

And right then, a possibility crossed her mind.

Maybe all the others *did* meet up?

All of them except Kokoro had met in the nurse's office, everyone but her. Was that all it was? If so, to them that meant Kokoro had betrayed them.

Aki's eyes narrowed. She looked over at Fuka.

"Are you telling me the same thing?"

"What?"

"The same thing as Kokoro—and Subaru."

Kokoro gasped and looked at Fuka and Subaru for confirmation. They nodded. Ureshino's face turned bright red.

"I was there too," he chimed in.

Kokoro felt her shoulders go limp.

Ureshino had made the trek back to school. That must have taken some courage.

"Me too."

"And me."

"But I didn't see any of you," Fuka said.

So that was it. It had happened to every single one of them.

They had definitely been to school yesterday, but for some reason they couldn't meet up.

"They told me there's no seventh-grader called Kokoro," Ureshino said. "Kokoro's an unusual name, and I asked a teacher who was passing by. But he said there was no one called Kokoro at the school."

"I asked too, but they said there was no one in seventh grade called Haruka Ureshino."

Ureshino's face clouded over.

"I'm real, you know."

"Me too. I'm in seventh grade at Yukishina No. 5 Junior High."

Subaru, standing there with arms folded, said, "Me too. I went to my ninth-grade classroom. I waited and waited but Masamune never appeared, so I went over to his classroom. But he wasn't there either."

A hush came over them.

"What's going on?" Aki asked, to no one in particular. She ran her fingers roughly through her hair in frustration. Kokoro noticed her hair color had changed again.

Her reddish dyed hair had gone back to black.

So she could go to school. She'd probably dyed it black the night before, after she'd got home from the castle.

Aki wasn't making it up. Like Kokoro, she'd set her mind on going to school, and indeed she had.

"Even though I didn't want to see the girls from the volleyball club." Aki seemed to murmur this unintentionally. She spoke so faintly, so weakly, that it was painful to hear.

So Aki was a member of the volleyball club? This was news to Kokoro. These past eight months she'd never mentioned it.

Her frail tone sent a sharp pain racing through Kokoro.

The volleyball club. Miori Sanada's volleyball club.

227

Had Aki still been going to school when Miori started at the club? Could Aki, so close to her now, be that girl's senpai?

"Shall we ask the Wolf Queen?" Fuka suggested. All eyes turned to her. "She might be able to explain what's going on. Then again, she might not, just to be tricksy."

"We could, but shouldn't we ask Masamune first?" Subaru said.

Kokoro agreed. They all looked over at Masamune's game controller, lying idle.

"Masamune may not be here today . . . but the same thing must have happened to him—he couldn't meet us. Right?"

Actually—I'd like your advice on something.

I was wondering . . . if you all . . . could you come to school? Just for one day. One day would be enough.

Kokoro recalled how timidly Masamune had broached the topic. Her chest ached as she remembered how he'd prepared Christmas presents for them, and how hard it must have been for him, with all his pride, to ask this favor.

He was so desperate for them to be there, and yet—they weren't.

How had Masamune taken it?

"Do you think he misunderstood what happened?" Fuka said. Her eyes were sad. "Thinking none of us turned up?"

"I think so. And if that's why he isn't here today, that totally sucks."

"Maybe it's just coincidence he's not here. Perhaps he'll appear this afternoon."

Ureshino shook his head.

"Maybe when he went, they beat him up . . . I'm just thinking of what happened to me."

They were holding out hope that Masamune would slip through his mirror in the grand foyer and show up any minute now.

But that didn't seem about to happen.

It felt like his unspoken anger lingered, and it pained Kokoro.

Please come, Masamune. This was everyone's silent wish.

They stayed around in the castle, waiting.

After a while, they heard someone come in and glanced up. But it was Rion, looking in on them from the hallway.

"Where's Masamune?" It hurt to hear how casually he asked.

"He hasn't come," Subaru said.

They all attempted to explain the events of the previous day.

"What do we do if he doesn't come back?" Kokoro asked. It was approaching the end of the day.

"It'll be OK," Subaru said. "Video games are his life. At least he'll come back to pick up his game console." He looked over at Masamune's device, lying untouched on the floor.

BUT MASAMUNE DIDN'T appear.

Not that day, or the next, or the next, or the next.

February

MASAMUNE DID NOT turn up at all in January, but finally, early in February, he walked in.

His hair was neatly cut, and at first Kokoro thought it was some new kid.

He'd got in before anyone else, and sat in the Game Room, blithely playing video games.

"Masamune."

Kokoro stood frozen to the spot.

"Hey," he said. His gaze was fixed on the TV screen as he played a racing car game. "Oh, no way . . . whoa!" he said to himself.

Kokoro hovered in the doorway, unsure what to say. One by one, the rest of the group appeared.

"Masamune, we've been dying to talk to you."

"Masamune, we didn't break our promise!"

"That's right. Why didn't you come over earlier? We all kept our word." Aki said this in an unsteady voice, and Masamune put down the game controller for the first time. His car crashed spectacularly on the screen. The "game over" music played.

"I know," Masamune said, and looked over at them. His short hair made his eyes seem more piercing than before. "I know that all of you came into school that day. The day I asked you to, the tenth of January."

Everyone gasped.

"I never thought you didn't come. I knew there was no way you wouldn't."

Kokoro was so relieved she felt about to cry.

Masamune believed them all.

"Then why didn't you come to the castle?" Fuka asked.

Masamune switched off the TV.

"I needed some time to think. I knew you wouldn't let me down, yet we still couldn't meet up. I wanted to think why. I thought about it, over and over. And . . ." Masamune took a short breath.

"I came to a conclusion. I think we're all living in parallel worlds."

"Parallel worlds?"

"Yep."

Kokoro's eyes widened.

The term was unfamiliar, and she couldn't quite grasp it. She looked around and saw them all gazing at Masamune with equally vacant expressions.

"Each of us is attending a different Yukishina No. 5 Junior High. None of you are in my world, and I'm not in any of yours. The world's divided into seven different branches, one for each of us."

THE WORLD'S DIVIDED.

Kokoro couldn't grasp what this meant. They all looked at each other in puzzlement, and Masamune, in a slightly irritated tone, said, "You people hardly ever watch anime, or read science fiction, do you?

"You need to read more," he went on. "In the world of science fiction, it's a totally obvious concept, the idea of parallel worlds."

"I don't exactly follow, but are you saying that something unreal's happening, like in science fiction?" asked Kokoro.

"If you want to talk about what's unreal, this whole castle is completely unreal. You lot really need to get used to the idea—that we're already in a situation that's supernatural, or if not fantasy then something we can't explain.

"Listen up," he said, facing them all. "The world we live in—the world beyond the seven mirrors in the foyer—seems the same for all of us, but it isn't. Even if there's a Yukishina No. 5 Junior High in

Minami, in Tokyo City, Japan, in all our worlds, the people there and the details all deviate slightly from each other. All seven of us are living in our own individual worlds."

"So," Aki said, arms folded, head tilted, "what does that mean?"

"It's easier to understand if you think of it like a video game." Masamune looked over at the game controller he'd tossed aside.

"Each of us is the hero in a game called *Yukishina No. 5 Junior High in South Tokyo*. And there are seven versions of the game. The data depends on the software of whoever's playing, get it? Each character has their own saved data, and there can't be two heroes simultaneously. My data is mine, Subaru's data is his, Aki's is hers."

Masamune looked around at each of them in turn.

"In the world where I'm playing, naturally I'm the hero, and nobody else is there, and in Aki and Subaru's software I don't appear. The same is true for everyone. There's only one hero for each set of data. On the game screen it's set up so you have to choose one from the seven of us."

Masamune crossed his arms.

"It's the same software so it looks like the same world, but since the hero is different, it subtly adjusts events and small details. Even if the software we're given is the same, it makes sense to think that there are separate routes designed to take us down different storylines."

"I still don't get it." Fuka slowly shook her head. "But I have heard the term *parallel worlds*." They'd been using the English words, and now she gave the Japanese equivalent.

Kokoro repeated the Japanese characters to herself, and now she could picture it better.

She pictured the grand foyer of the castle. And parallel light radiating out from the seven mirrors side by side. The lights of each of the worlds beyond the mirrors never intersected.

Fuka said: "That idea was in a manga I read once. In the story there were as many parallel worlds as there were choices, and the main character had a kind of reunion of all his possible selves from

233

those worlds. There were a lot of selves in all kinds of worlds, as many as the choices in his life—like what life would be like if he'd married his girlfriend, or if he'd stayed true to his dreams when he was young, and so on."

"Exactly! The number of choices is what I mean by the branches." Masamune nodded enthusiastically.

Fuka's example made it a little easier for Kokoro to follow.

If only I'd done that, then reality would have turned out differently—that was something Kokoro thought about a lot. If only she hadn't stayed away from school. If only she'd been in a different class from Miori Sanada. If only she hadn't ever been a student at Yukishina No. 5 Junior High.

A hypothetical reality seemed preferable to present reality, and the more she fantasized about how great it would be if certain things could come true, the more reality that world seemed to take on.

"And the branches of our parallel worlds are each of our stories. If you go by that example you gave, it's as if I chose A, but if I'd chosen B it'd be a different world. In our worlds we each have a world where we exist, but each one's slightly different."

"OK, but then—what about Ms. Kitajima?" Kokoro asked. "Aki said she'd never met her, but didn't Masamune, Ureshino and I each meet Ms. Kitajima? Doesn't that mean Ms. Kitajima exists in all our worlds?"

A doubt crept into her mind.

On that day, the only student Ms. Kitajima had been told would be going into school was Kokoro. She didn't seem to have been waiting for Masamune or Ureshino.

"I guess the different worlds have some characters in common."

Characters—the word made Kokoro bite her lip. Masamune was just continuing with the video game analogy, but the reality she was living started to feel to her as if it was all made up, like a miniature garden or something.

"For instance, Aki and Subaru have never actually heard of the Free School, have they? So of course they've never met Ms. Kitajima."

"Right."

"Yeah."

Masamune waited for the two of them to agree. "So in their two worlds there *is* no Free School. It doesn't exist. The possibility is that the person called Ms. Kitajima herself doesn't exist there. Or else she does but is somewhere else, doing a totally different job."

Masamune had clearly been spending his time thinking deeply about this, trying to tie up his ideas. He had no doubt been digging around in books and other resources, researching the subject of parallel worlds.

"And the geography around Yukishina No. 5 Junior High as we've talked about it seems a bit vague. Like . . . Kokoro. What's the main shopping center near your house?"

"That would be . . . Careo."

When she saw their reactions, she was shocked. Fuka's eyes widened. "Don't you go to Careo, Fuka?" Kokoro asked.

"We go to a shopping mall called Arco. Where they have a cinema."

"What?"

Arco? Kokoro had never heard of it.

Masamune nodded in agreement with Fuka. "Same as me, it's called Arco. When you first mentioned Careo, Kokoro, I thought you'd made a mistake and meant Arco. But that's not true, right?"

"Yeah."

Kokoro nodded vacantly. She couldn't remember when she'd talked about Careo.

Aki's face clouded over. "I don't know either of them—Arco or Careo," she said. "Now that you mention it, you asked me where I went to elementary school and you said, *Oh, that's near Careo.* I had no clue then what you were talking about."

"No way."

"And McDonald's, too," Fuka said in a low voice. "I often go to McDonald's inside Arco, but is there really one in front of the station? Didn't you and Subaru say there was, Aki?"

"Yeah, in front of the station."

Aki and Subaru shared a confused look.

"When you guys said that, Aki, I thought they'd just opened it and I didn't know about it, but when I went to check it out, there wasn't one. I thought it was strange. Do you know it, Kokoro?"

"I know the McDonald's inside Careo."

Kokoro had tried to avoid that McDonald's since kids from her school would probably be hanging out there.

"What about the truck selling things from Mikawa Market? It's been coming to the park near my house a couple of times a week ever since I was little," Kokoro asked.

"It's A Small World" swirled around in her head.

The little truck blasting out the song from her favorite ride at Disneyland.

It seemed like ages since she'd heard that tune. It had always made her feel low when she heard it sitting alone at home, during the day. Since she'd started coming to the castle, she hadn't heard it.

"I don't know. Maybe it doesn't stop by our neighborhood."

"But Fuka, didn't we go to the same elementary school? Elementary School No. 1? I thought the truck drove around that area."

She'd been convinced that Fuka lived nearby. They'd never actually met, but she'd always found this encouraging.

"It comes near me. It plays 'Small World,' doesn't it?" Aki said.

"Yes!" said Kokoro.

"My grandmother used to do her shopping there," Aki said. "She said it was so helpful."

"I think it comes around our area too," Ureshino said. "But it doesn't play music. And it's not really a truck, more of a van, isn't it? The one that sells vegetables and things? A lot of elderly people can't make it to the supermarket. My mother always times it so she can do her shopping there. She can't drive, and so it's awkward for her to go to the supermarket."

Ureshino seemed to be describing something a little different from what Kokoro and Aki knew.

"And then there's the date," Masamune said.

Kokoro and the others looked puzzled. Ureshino chimed in. "Listen, Masamune, the date you gave us to go into school, the tenth of January, that wasn't actually the day of the opening ceremony."

That's true, thought Kokoro.

Then Ureshino said something startling.

"It was a Sunday, wasn't it?"

"*What?*" The word got stuck halfway up her throat. She gave Ureshino a surprised look and he looked back, confused.

"I haven't been going into school so I've sort of lost any sense of what day of the week it is, so I made a mistake. When I told my mother I was going to school the next day, she laughed and told me it was a Sunday. I thought you'd all made a mistake, but I went in anyway, and the entrance was shut, so I waited half the day in front of the gate."

"No way!" Kokoro said, but Ureshino was looking dazed.

"It's true," he said.

When she saw his look, Kokoro was convinced.

Ureshino, having been beaten up a few months previously, risked it happening all over again, and Kokoro had admired his courage in going back. But if it had been a Sunday, well, that changed things.

She was suddenly feeling very confused.

Even if he had waited outside the gate, there would have been students in clubs coming in and out, and so that really took guts to hang around there.

"I figured Masamune had made a mistake about the date, so I thought I'd better come back on Monday, but my mother told me

Monday was Coming-of-Age Day and school was out. Two days off in a row. So then I really couldn't work out what was going on."

"Eh? Coming-of-Age Day is the fifteenth, isn't it? I didn't think it was a two-day holiday," Subaru said.

"The days of the week are a little out, for all of us," said Masamune. They blinked in surprise.

"In my world the opening ceremony was the tenth of January, but for some of you it wasn't, right?"

"The opening ceremony's one thing, but I thought Coming-of-Age Day would be the same for everyone," Aki said, and looked to the others for confirmation.

Subaru nodded. "In my world, the opening ceremony was the tenth of January. The same as Masamune."

Masamune and Subaru's eyes met.

"Everyone was really surprised since I hadn't been to school for so long. Though no one actually spoke to me."

"You turn up all of a sudden with that hair color—maybe you scared 'em?"

"I went over to your class, Masamune. Eighth grade, Classroom 6. But the kids there said there wasn't any student with your name in their class."

Masamune was taken aback. After a moment he said, "Thank you. So you came over to my class . . ."

"Yeah."

"Thanks."

"You're welcome."

"About that . . ." Fuka ventured, raising her hand hesitantly. She was addressing Masamune. "You said you were in Class 6 of eighth grade, no? I'm in Class 3, and once when I said there were only four classes in eighth grade you got a bit cross, remember? But this time when I checked it was true—there are only *four* classes in eighth grade. There's no such thing as the sixth class you said you're in."

We're in different worlds—Masamune's words now seemed all the more believable. There was no other way to explain it.

"Listen." Above the chat, someone raised their voice.

It was Rion, who'd kept quiet till now. Rion's world was in Hawaii, in Honolulu.

Kokoro suddenly remembered that Rion and Ureshino were in the same grade, in the same elementary school, but didn't recall each other.

That in itself was pretty strange. Back when the subject came up, she should have thought how odd it was. She'd explained it away by telling herself that Rion and Ureshino moved in totally different circles.

Thinking about it now, she felt disappointed in herself. *If that's how stupid I can be, I might very well not be able to get on properly like ordinary kids.*

"I can be a bit slow, and don't exactly understand all that stuff about parallel worlds," Rion said, "but what you're saying is we can never meet up in the outside world?" The others were silent, their faces solemn.

"Yep." Masamune nodded after a while.

We could all help each other.

Kokoro remembered Masamune's words, his eyes tearful and pleading.

"You mean we *can't* help each other?" Rion asked.

Masamune was silent for a time. Everyone turned their gaze on him. "That's right," he said. "We can't help each other."

FOR A WHILE, no one said a word.

Ureshino's eyes had popped wide open, like those of a startled cat. Aki looked down, pouting grouchily.

"So why were we all brought here anyway?" Fuka asked, breaking the silence. The others looked at her mutely. Fuka was staring into space. She seemed to be thinking aloud, trying to gather her thoughts.

"So each of us is in a different parallel world at Yukishina No. 5 Junior High, none of us are actually going to school, and we can only meet in this castle through the mirrors. That's the scenario, right?"

"That's about the size of it," Masamune said.

"That does make sense," Kokoro said. She looked at the others. "When I realized we were all students at Yukishina No. 5 Junior High, I had my doubts about whether there could be so many kids from one school who had dropped out. Yukishina's huge, but still, I was thinking, that's a lot. But if our worlds are different, then I can understand it. If there's one of us per year."

"But we don't know if it's one per year," Masamune said, letting out a big breath, still a little disgusted. He glared at Kokoro. "Wouldn't surprise me if there're other kids besides me who aren't going.

"It's like, if there's a lot of absenteeism, teachers will leap in, and try to assess what's going wrong in a certain year or class. But really, a couple of kids might have their own issues and decide they want to take time off. I hate that trend—when teachers study school refusal and bullying, and put things into categories like generation and social background."

"I agree. If you and I *were* in the same class, Masamune, we'd have had our own personal reasons for not going to school," said Subaru.

He spoke lightly, and shot a pleasant smile at Kokoro. She felt she'd irritated Masamune, who was standing silently now, shoulders hunched.

"But doesn't that make sense? Each of us is from the same school, we're representative school dropouts from different years."

"And the only place we can all come together is in this castle. It's like there are seven people's worlds—with this castle at its center. Something like that." Aki's words spurred on an image in Kokoro's head.

"But then why is it we can only meet here? What's the point?" Aki asked.

Masamune's expression changed. "It's just that," he began, looking serious, "in most sci-fi and anime about parallel worlds, some of these worlds branch off, then vanish."

"Vanish?"

"It's easier if you think of it as a thick tree," Masamune said. "Actually, in lots of manga that's how it's illustrated. Anybody got a pencil?"

Fuka took out a notebook and pencil from her bag. Masamune started drawing on a blank sheet of paper.

"OK, so you start off with the world as one big tree."

Masamune drew a large trunk, and labeled it *The World*.

"And our worlds now branch off."

He drew branches coming out of either side of the trunk. Seven in all.

"Each of these is one of our worlds—the world I'm in, in Minami Tokyo City, the world Rion's in, the one Ureshino's in. And if there're too many of these worlds, it's better that some disappear."

"But why?" Ureshino and Kokoro said in unison. *Disappear— vanish*—neither one sounded good.

"If it disappears, then what happens to the people in it? Do they die?"

"It might be a little different from—dying. But they do disappear. It's as if they were never there to begin with."

"But who decides if one is going to disappear? Whose choice is it?"

"It's different, depending on the set-up of the novel or manga. Most of the time it's like the will of the world. Or the will of God."

Masamune pointed his pencil at the drawing.

"The trunk part decides that the branches are too heavy, and needs to get rid of some. Most of the time they use the term *weed out*. It's like in nature, where those who adapt to the environment survive, and the others die out."

Masamune looked up. "Anyhow, most fictional parallel worlds

have that set-up, with worlds being weeded out and selected. *Gate W*'s like that too, no?"

"Gate *what?*"

"You know it, don't you? I mean *Gateworld*. Nagahisa's mega bestselling game at the moment? You seriously haven't heard of it? No way."

"*Nagahisa . . . ?*" Subaru asked dubiously. Masamune looked irritated.

"Laughlin Nagahisa, guys! The genius director of that video game development company." As he spoke, he seemed to give up. "Jeez—do I have to start from scratch?" He scratched his head. "Do you actually need me to explain the famous parallel world story? You people don't even know the most basic things."

"I know it. They made it into a movie too, didn't they?" Ureshino said.

"No, they didn't. Forget it. If you don't know, then just keep quiet." Masamune shook his head as if they were getting nowhere.

"In *Gateworld*," he went on, "the representatives from each of the parallel worlds get together to fight it out. The ones who lose, their worlds vanish, so it's a story about which world survives. The winning world becomes the sole *trunk* left. So they all fight to the death so their world can continue. That's the kind of game it is."

"Are you saying that's what's happening to us?" Subaru asked.

Masamune shrugged. "I thought it was a possibility. It's pretty unique, don't you think, for us to gather here? If we're representatives of seven worlds, then this is like a world summit or something. There's gotta be something they want us representatives to do. And then I remembered—the quest for the key."

Masamune waited a moment. "I feel like the Wishing Key that grants wishes is suggestive of something. Only the world of the person who finds the key survives, and the rest all vanish. I was thinking maybe this is how our game plays out."

"All worlds except one disappear?"

Disappear—the idea didn't seem quite real, and Kokoro had her doubts.

Kokoro's home, waiting for her when she went back through the mirror. Her parents, her school; like it or not, the real class with Miori Sanada and Tojo-san.

How could they all vanish?

I can't bear to think about it. And then another emotion welled up inside her, which felt unexpected. *Actually—it might be OK after all. It might be OK if they all somehow disappear.* She wasn't planning on going back to school. And she couldn't picture herself starting at some other school.

A hope had always burned inside her: the possibility that she could meet these kids outside the castle. Thinking that the others existed somewhere out there had been like the beam from a lighthouse, shining in the dark sea of her heart.

How had the others understood it? She didn't know. The one thing they did seem to share, though, was a sense of bewilderment. Kokoro hadn't thought about it in ages—this Wishing Key they'd once falteringly searched for but never found. Masamune's story seemed even more believable.

Apart from the world of the person who located the key, everyone else's worlds would vanish.

"The Wolf Queen told us, didn't she?" Masamune said. "That if a wish is granted then all of our memories will disappear. But if the key isn't found, and a wish isn't granted, our memories remain. Even when the castle has closed for good, we will never forget what happened here."

"Right."

"The Wolf Queen's told us that many times. We're here in order to weed out people's worlds other than our own."

"That sounds right," Subaru said.

"If that's true, then isn't it better not to find the Wishing Key?"

Fuka asked. A trace of sadness—and terror at the alternative outcome Masamune was suggesting—showed in her eyes.

Hearing this stated so baldly left them all stunned. Fuka stared fixedly downwards. "And it's already February," she said. "We have less than two months. All we'll have left is the memory of having been here, right? If that's true, then I want to hold on to that memory." Fuka's voice seemed to resonate within their silent circle.

Whenever they'd discussed the vanishing of their memories, Aki had said she didn't really care, but now she was silent. Kokoro herself felt close to tears.

All we'll have left are these memories.

We won't be able to help each other.

"It would be ideal if none of our worlds vanished," Subaru said, "but if, like Masamune said, *all* our worlds disappear, what does that actually mean?"

Kokoro gasped, and she heard Fuka—and the rest of them—do the same.

"If no one finds the key, all our worlds will disappear. And the castle won't be here anymore for any of us to escape to. So it would be better to look for the key and let at least one person's world survive."

"Shouldn't we be putting all this directly to the Wolf Queen? I mean, so she can explain the logic of it?" Rion asked. "You're listening, aren't you, Wolf Queen?" He raised his voice towards the ceiling. Then he looked towards the empty hall through the doorway. "You heard everything we said, didn't you? So come on out, Wolf Queen!"

The air suddenly seemed to be stirred by an unseen force, and Kokoro sensed a gust of wind like a tiny tornado graze her face.

"What a dismal racket you make!"

From an opening in that soft twist of air, a little girl in a wolf mask finally materialized.

AS EVER, SHE was wearing a frilly dress. The red patent shoes on her small feet looked shiny and new; the expressionless face on her mask seemed distinctly colder.

"You heard it, didn't you? What Masamune has just been saying?"

"Can't say that I didn't," the Wolf Queen said in her usual evasive way.

"I'm right, aren't I?" Masamune said. "We're in parallel worlds, so you brought us together to weed them out. You're the gatekeeper."

The Wolf Queen turned to face him. Behind the mask, she seemed to be staring very intently.

Could Masamune have found her out? They watched, with bated breath, for her to reveal the truth.

"You're totally wrong," she said, shaking her head.

The tension in Masamune's face ebbed away, as if he'd been completely mistaken. "*What?*" he croaked.

The Wolf Queen flicked her hair flippantly upwards.

"I listened to you going on and on about your grandiose theory. It must have taken a lot of effort to come up with that, but unfortunately, I have to tell you it's all in your imagination. I told you from the beginning. This is the castle in the mirror. The place you come to look for the key to grant your wish. That is all. It has nothing to do with weeding out worlds, an outcome which sounds completely terrifying."

"You're lying. If that's true, then why can't we meet up outside?" Masamune looked stern. "That's how it is with parallel worlds, isn't it? If each of our realities is different and we can't meet in the outside world, then what reason is there to gather us here other than to weed out our worlds?"

"You can't meet outside? I don't remember ever saying that," the Wolf Queen said casually, stifling a yawn.

"You mean—we *can* meet?" Ureshino asked.

The Wolf Queen gave a small giggle. "Um. I'm not saying you can't."

"You are such a liar!" Masamune was enraged. "We can*not* see each other!" His cheeks and ears turned bright red. "I'm telling you,

I asked them as a favor to meet me, and they did, but we still couldn't see each other. How do you explain *that*?"

Masamune clenched his fists. Kokoro shut her eyes. Watching a boy cry was just too much to take. "Masamune!" *Enough already*, she thought.

"That's right, Wolf Queen. We couldn't see each other."

"But I never said you can't meet up, or can't help each other. It's time you people worked things out. Don't start barking up the wrong tree. *Think* about it, and don't expect me to tell you everything. I've been giving you clues all along to help you find the key."

The group fell silent. Masamune was still breathing heavily.

"What do you mean, *clues*?" Aki asked. The Wolf Queen turned to face her, and the group felt a force and tension in Aki's words that hadn't been there before. "You said you gave us clues, but what does that mean?"

"Just what I said."

The Wolf Queen's voice sounded neither fed up nor irritated, just even-toned and unflappable.

"I don't get it. You always skirt around things. I mean, for one, you're the biggest mystery in this whole place. With that mask over your face the whole time, and calling us lost Little Red Riding Hoods. You're just making fun of us."

"Well, you're right, I call you all Little Red Riding Hoods, but sometimes you all seem to me more like the wolf. Is it really that hard to find it?" The Wolf Queen seemed to suppress a smile.

"That's what I said—the way you talk to us is so tricksy."

"I'll say it again: this is the castle in the mirror, where you look for the key that grants your wish."

"Then I have a question." Rion raised a hand. He waited for the Wolf Queen's full attention before he spoke. "This search for the key. I've sort of been looking for it all along. Under the bed in my room I found an *X*, so what does that mean?"

"What?" The others all looked at him in surprise.

"At first, I thought it was just a stain or something, but it's a clear *X*. You said you wouldn't hide the key in any of our rooms, so what's the story?"

"So you have one in your room too, Rion?" Fuka asked. The group turned to look at her, eyes wide. "I'm pretty sure there's one under the desk in my room. I thought it was just my imagination. It looks like an *X*, but maybe it isn't . . ."

"There's one in the bathroom, too," Subaru said. "The bathroom next to the dining room. I thought it was weird that there were taps but no water, and I found the *X* when I was investigating. There was a laundry basket lying in the bathtub, and when I moved it I found an *X*. I thought maybe it was just a scratch."

"There's one inside the dining room fireplace," said Kokoro.

Like Subaru, she'd been curious to know why there was a fireplace, if there was no fuel.

"Dining room?" Masamune sounded on edge. "That means I found one too. In the summer. There's one in the kitchen, isn't there? Behind the pantry shelves."

"Really?"

"Yeah." He frowned. "I thought perhaps the key was somewhere there, so I banged and scraped around, but nothing ever came out. So I thought the same, that it was just a stain."

They exchanged a look, then silently turned to the Wolf Queen.

"Were these clues too?" asked Aki.

"You can decide that for yourselves," said the Wolf Queen primly. "Like I said, you've had plenty of hints. I leave the rest up to you. Including whether the wish is to be granted or not."

She took a breath. "But I do make one promise," she said quietly. "Even if someone has their wish granted, no one's world is going to disappear. As I said before, once the wish is granted, this castle will vanish from your memories. And you will all simply return to your own realities. These will never disappear.

"For better or for worse," she added.

"So, can I ask one more thing?" Rion said.

The Wolf Queen pointed her muzzle in his direction. Rion waited until they were face to face.

"What is your favorite fairy tale, Wolf Queen?"

The question came from left field, and the Wolf Queen had clearly not expected it. She was for an instant speechless. "Do you really need to ask me?" she said. "Just look at my face. It's *Little Red Riding Hood*."

Kokoro wasn't sure at all why Rion had asked this. Maybe he just wanted to take her by surprise.

"Anything else?" the Wolf Queen asked.

Kokoro felt like she had a million things she needed to ask, but no idea how to ask them. That evasive answer still didn't make it totally clear whether they could—or could not—meet up outside.

"Hold on a sec!" Masamune said.

Too late.

"When you have anything else to ask, you know where I am," the Wolf Queen said. And then she vanished.

The group were left staring at each other.

"That girl said, *You will all simply return to your own realities*, didn't she?"

"What?"

They looked at Subaru. He was always so mature, so easy-going. If anyone could get away with calling her *that girl*, it was him.

Subaru looked at Masamune.

"Our worlds won't vanish, won't be weeded out. She sort of dodged the question of parallel worlds, but at least the Wolf Queen said, *your own realities*. That must mean something. She seemed to be saying we could see each other, yet the worlds we all live in seem to be different."

"And no one can reach anyone else's world."

Wouldn't it be awesome if the others could join my world, thought Kokoro. She could take them to her school. If only she could do that . . .

I SOMETIMES FIND MYSELF DREAMING.

A new transfer student has started at our school, and everyone wants to be friends with them. The most cheerful, kind and athletic person in our class. And smart, too.

Out of all my classmates this new student picks me out with a generous smile, as dazzling as the sun, and says, "Kokoro-chan, it's been such a long time."

The other students can't believe it. "What?" they say, looking at me meaningfully. "Do you two already know each other?"

In another world, we were already friends.

There's nothing special about me. I'm not athletic, and I'm not smart. There's nothing about me anyone would envy.

It's only that we had the chance to meet before, and form a special bond.

We go everywhere together: when we move to a different classroom, when we go for break, and when we walk through the school gates at the end of the day.

Sanada's gang may be dying to be friends with them, but all the student says is, "I'm with Kokoro-chan."

So I am no longer alone.

I've been hoping something like this will happen for such a long time.

Though I know it never will.

And it didn't this time, either.

"SHOULDN'T WE MAKE that our wish?" Fuka said, startling Kokoro out of her reverie. "We should use the Wishing Key to ask that all our worlds become one."

"Um," said Aki.

I'm not saying you can't. Kokoro remembered the Wolf Queen's words.

"Aha . . . so we probably can use the Wishing Key to make all our worlds one," said Kokoro.

"Yeah. Then we can all meet up in the outside world. Isn't that what the Wolf Queen meant when she said, *I'm not saying you can't?*"

"But that means making a wish come true, and then won't all our memories vanish? If we don't recognize each other, then being in the same world is meaningless, isn't it?"

"Yeah, so that's why our wish should be, *Please put all of us in the same world, and let us keep our memories* . . . Let's ask about it the next time we see her." Fuka seemed determined.

Maybe her cryptic way of telling them *I'm not saying you can't* was based on the underlying assumption that they would have lost their memories. Once Kokoro had thought this through, it felt more and more likely.

"But so long as we don't find the key, it's only a possibility."

Fuka looked at Masamune. He'd been so enthusiastic, explaining his theory, but now that the Wolf Queen had shot down his idea he seemed to have visibly shrunk.

"Masamune," Ureshino said, and Masamune raised his head.

"What?"

"I'm glad you're back."

Masamune blinked in surprise. Rapid blinks, like the beating of a bumblebee's wings.

Ureshino smiled. "I was so sure you would never come back. And I didn't want things to end like that, so I'm really happy you're here." He laughed. "See, right at the beginning of the second semester when I felt awkward about coming here, you were so glad I had made it. So I thought the next time you came here, I'd feel the same thing. Masamune—I'm glad you made it."

Masamune's cheeks and ears reddened, as if he was trying to hold something back.

"So, what happened? Did things work out?" Subaru asked. "Do you have to transfer schools?"

"I'm OK for the third semester at least. Because I made it to the opening ceremony." Masamune's voice was monotonic, and he was still looking down. "I couldn't find any of you, and then I bumped into someone I didn't want to see, but things are OK."

"Cool."

A lengthy silence fell.

Masamune raised his head. But his eyes below his short fringe were still looking down. "Lying Masa . . . is what they called me."

"What?"

"Lying Masa. Masamune the Liar."

Kokoro couldn't imagine why he'd suddenly brought this up. But seeing how serious he was, his voice trembling, she couldn't look away.

"I told you all that the guy who made this game was a friend of mine. Well, that's not true. I'm sorry."

Masamune looked at the video games lying scattered on the floor. Kokoro had no idea which one he was looking at.

Yet somehow she understood why he had felt the need to reveal this to them. It might not mean much to any of them, but it certainly did to him. In Masamune's world, that lie was a big deal.

It might have had something to do with why he'd stopped going to school in the first place.

"I get it," Aki said. She usually had a sarcastic comeback for him, but now she seemed to be speaking for the others.

"Sorry," Masamune said again. "I'm really sorry."

ONCE THEY HAD accepted that they all lived in parallel worlds, it made it easier to spend time together.

Because they'd all given up.

The end of next month—March—would truly be the final farewell.

Time weighed more heavily on them, and Kokoro felt determined to make the most of each remaining day at the castle.

None of them seemed very interested in finding the key anymore. Fuka's wish, that their worlds could all become one, was all very well, but they were still resistant to the idea that their castle memories would be wiped completely.

And as ever, there was no sign of the key.

Still, they could not forget that it was somewhere in the castle.

IT WAS THE last day of February.

They were hanging out in the Game Room when Aki came in.

"That reminds me. Those *X* marks we talked about, I found one in my room too. In the wardrobe."

"Really?" Kokoro said. "So, there's a wardrobe in your room, Aki-chan?"

"Don't you have one in yours, Kokoro?"

"No. Only the desk, bed and bookshelves."

Fuka only had a piano in her room.

"Having a wardrobe suits you, Aki, because you're such a fashion queen," Kokoro said.

"I am?" Aki said coolly. She didn't seem especially happy about it.

"So anyway, what is that *X*? Does it mean anything? We were told that the key isn't in one of our rooms, to keep things fair, but I wonder if there are *X*'s in all the other rooms, too."

"I bet we'll find more if we look. How many have we found now? The one in the fireplace, one under Rion's bed, one under Fuka's desk, one in your wardrobe."

They'd also mentioned one in the kitchen, and one in the bathroom. Kokoro was running through the list when Aki said, "You know, it's OK, isn't it, if a wish comes true? If someone finds the key, I mean."

"What do you mean?"

"I know we talked about not wanting to lose our memories, but if and when the key is found, we could think about what to do then. But in the end, it's OK for a wish to come true, isn't it?"

"Do you mean you found the key?"

Kokoro creased her brow. Had Aki already found it?

Aki laughed. "No. I'm just saying. Everyone's memory might be wiped, but we each still have the right to look for the key. Nobody will blame anyone, right?"

No one knew how to respond to this. "Listen," Aki said, and gave an exaggerated sigh. "If we can't see each other in the outside world, all we'll have left at the end is our memories, no? Isn't that a bit of a waste? Our memories won't help us. Isn't it better if at least one of us has their wish come true?"

"I really don't want to forget any of this," Fuka said.

Aki's smile suddenly dropped.

"I'm just saying—*if* we found it."

They'd talked this through together already, so why was Aki suddenly saying this?

"Well, let me know if you find any more *X*'s," said Aki, and left to go back to her room.

The group watched blankly as she walked off.

"She's got issues. A lot of issues," Subaru said when she'd gone. His cool tone gave Kokoro goosebumps. She sensed something was wrong.

"You shouldn't say that," Kokoro said without thinking. Subaru looked at her flatly. "Don't say that. I don't like it."

Subaru's words, *a lot of issues*, bothered her. Time was running out. And it hurt to be reminded she might also be in the same bracket as Aki.

She headed off to her own room. It had been quite some time since she'd been in it.

She lay on her bed and stared up at the ceiling.

What about me? she wondered.

As Aki said, if the key was found, what would she wish for? To erase Miori Sanada from her life—that had long been her wish. But would that be enough for her to return to her own reality? To a time before Miori had ruined her life?

There was a knock on her door.

"Yes?"

"It's me."

Subaru's voice. She opened the door and stepped into the hallway. Subaru was alone.

He stood there, slim and tall, and she noticed how the roots of his hair had grown out black again. He was beginning to look like a weirdo, and now she thought of it, she probably wouldn't have gone near him if she hadn't got to know him before.

"I'm sorry I said that," he said. "I forgot how much I used to hate it when people said that about me."

"Oh." Hearing his gentle tone, she felt suddenly deflated.

"And I'm glad you called me out on it. I've just been to apologize to Aki-chan."

"Oh! You didn't have to do that. She didn't hear what you said."

"I know. But the fact remains that I said it."

This kind of slightly misjudged behavior was just like him.

Honest to a fault, but a little too by-the-book.

"What did she say?"

"She was pretty disgusted. Just like you were. She said she didn't hear me say it, so I shouldn't have told her. She said I always overthink things."

"That sounds exactly like you, Subaru."

Kokoro might have called him out on it, but the fact remained that Aki *did* have issues. Something Aki herself must be well aware of.

"Thank you, Kokoro-chan. Today's the last day of February, and I'm annoyed with myself for making us all feel bad." Subaru gave her a smile.

Maybe he was a little too by-the-book, a boy who never did himself any favors, but that's what she liked about him.

Only one month to go.

The time had finally come when they had to say goodbye.

March

When Kokoro got to the castle, she found Aki and Fuka already there. Surprisingly, they were playing one of Masamune's video games in the Game Room.

"You're too good at this, Fuka. Go easy on me, will you?"

"Come on, this *is* a competition, you know."

Yesterday things had become uncomfortable as the two of them argued over whether one person's wish should be granted or not, and whether it was a waste or not for their memories to be the only thing left, but now they were obviously getting on fine.

"Fuka, about yesterday," Aki said, her voice sounding upbeat, and Kokoro found it hard to interrupt them. They must have found time to make up yesterday. And there was Subaru's apology to Aki, which might also have contributed to her good mood.

This was how the month began, the month of their farewell.

＊　＊　＊

AT SCHOOL THE third semester would be coming to an end, and the spring holiday would be starting soon.

As they'd be going into a new school year, her homeroom teacher, Mr. Ida, brought her slippers and seat cushion round to her house.

Kokoro caught up with him for a bit. She had just got back from the castle and her mother hadn't come home from work yet.

She wasn't very keen to see him, but was relieved he hadn't tried to visit while she was in the castle. She imagined him questioning her about where she was, and the last thing she would have wanted to do was talk to him, even if just to give him some excuse.

She was still angry about Miori Sanada's note. Ms. Kitajima must have told Mr. Ida how upset it had made her. So Kokoro had been expecting him to bring it up, but when she came to the front door he only greeted her with a simple "Hey."

Then he went back to behaving like a model teacher again.

"Kokoro, how are you?" he asked.

Kokoro nodded a greeting—not angry or sad, just a bit down.

Mr. Ida seemed uncomfortable, and she was pretty sure she wasn't imagining it.

"Everyone'll be waiting for you at school in April, when the new academic year begins," he said. He put down the slippers and cushion he'd brought her.

She didn't think he really thought that. He just wanted to be able to say he'd visited her. If she came back, it would mean one less problem for him, and if she didn't, he didn't really care. That was the vibe she picked up from him.

They were changing classes anyway, and he wouldn't be her homeroom teacher anymore.

It seemed possible she could repeat a year, if she wanted to. But that was the one thing she wanted to avoid. So she would just be moved up, along with Miori Sanada and Tojo-san.

"Well, see you later, Kokoro."

"Um, OK." She nodded.

Mr. Ida seemed as if he had more to say. And Kokoro, too, felt like she should say something—but she had no idea what.

"If you feel up to it, do you want to write a reply?"

"A reply?"

"To the letter from Sanada-san."

The moment she heard her name, she felt faint. She held a hand to her stomach and patiently waited for the feeling to pass.

Mr. Ida sighed. A huge, over-the-top sigh.

"It bothered Sanada," he said. "She felt you were making fun of her."

Kokoro took a short breath, and held it in.

"When she wrote it, in her own way, Sanada was trying her best. So think about it, OK?"

As she listened to the sound of the front door closing, Mr. Ida's steps becoming fainter, she stood on the other side, stupefied.

Some people would never understand each other.

In their world, Kokoro was the one at fault.

The stronger ones could boldly attack her because they felt nothing they did was questionable.

She felt you were making fun of her. The words whirled in Kokoro's head.

She was on the verge of tears. But it was galling to fall victim to their logic, and the tears wouldn't come. She beat the wall in frustration and the more she did, the more her palms throbbed with pain.

That girl robbed me of time.

She breathed out and gritted her teeth. How could people like that remain at the heart of school life, as if the world revolved around them? The thought made her want to tear her hair out.

How long she was standing there, she didn't know.

She suddenly heard a clatter outside.

Kokoro held her breath. Mr. Ida was long gone. So it wasn't him. And she hadn't heard the postman's motorcycle. So it must be Tojo-san. Perhaps bringing over the last school notice of the third semester.

After several minutes she ventured outside, but there was no one near the front gate or by the mailbox. Relieved, Kokoro opened it. And there, along with the folded school newsletter and some other printouts, was something else. A sealed envelope.

It was addressed to her: *Kokoro Anzai-sama.*

On the back, *Moé Tojo.*

Gripping the letter, Kokoro looked up and gazed at Moé's home, two doors down from hers. The house looked quiet.

Leaning against the front door, she quickly slid her fingers under the envelope flap and opened it.

The letter contained a single line.

To Kokoro-chan. I'm sorry. From Moé.

Her eyes scanned the line over and over, struck by the way she was addressed.

To Kokoro-chan.

She recalled the moment when they'd just become friends, and Moé's voice when she said, Kokoro-*chan*. She missed hearing it.

She had no idea what Tojo-san was apologizing for, or why she'd written the note. But she knew she'd done it on her own. She could sense this from its brevity.

Kokoro slid the note back into the envelope, bit her lip, and closed her eyes.

*   *   *

"LISTEN, EVERYONE."

When she was back in the castle the next day, Masamune wanted their attention. "I'm going to a new school."

They stared at him. "I went to look at it," he said. "It's about a one-hour commute away, but my dad's friend has a son going there, too. It's a private junior high. I took the entrance exam for transfer students and they announced the results yesterday. I passed."

"Really?" they all said—casually, but tension was ratcheting up. Starting in April—that was next month.

If Masamune decides to go to a new school, Kokoro thought, *then that's a good thing.*

But the thought of someone among them beginning somewhere

new made her chest tighten in panic. It wasn't Masamune's fault, but the news hurt.

"How do you feel about it?" Subaru asked.

Masamune turned slowly, and a little stiffly, to face him.

"I mean, you originally said you didn't want to transfer. But now you're agreeing to it?" Subaru pressed.

"Yeah. Because it's the beginning of a new school year."

"I see."

"Actually, I might switch schools too," Ureshino piped up. All eyes were now on him. "I might go abroad with my mother . . . Not straight away, though."

Ureshino looked uneasily over at Rion.

"I told her someone I know goes to school abroad, but she said she didn't want me to go alone like you, Rion."

Ureshino's family sounded wealthy enough to change plans quickly.

"My mother said it must have been hard for your parents to send you away like that. She said she wouldn't have been able to."

"It might not have been such a big decision for my parents, really . . ." Rion said. "Are you coming to Hawaii? Or somewhere else? Like Europe or something? I'd like it if you came to Hawaii, though we couldn't hang out together or anything, could we."

"Yeah, I had the same idea for a second, that if I go to Hawaii I can see you. But that's not going to happen."

"No, it's not. But I was thinking, about Hawaii—" Rion started to say.

"What?" Ureshino asked. Rion took a deep breath, as if thinking it over, then slowly shook his head.

"Nothing. Ureshino, if you really do want to go abroad, you'd better study English, or whatever language they speak where you're going." He gave a wry smile. "I didn't really prepare, so it's been tough."

"If you were there, I'd go to the same school as you. Though don't

259

count on me to play football. But most of the schools abroad start in September, don't they? That's sort of the world standard. In that sense Japan's not in line with the rest."

Masamune replied, "Could be, but so what? The rest of the world might do it one way, but we have to do things the way they're done in Japan."

"Yeah . . . I see what you mean."

As Kokoro watched this back and forth among the boys, someone tapped her shoulder from behind.

"Wow, that's really something—parents considering your future and stuff. Not like our parents, right, Kokoro?" Aki said this out of the blue.

Aki seeking her agreement like this made her feel sort of gritty inside.

Mum is surely considering the next step, she thought. She'd spoken with Ms. Kitajima, and had asked Kokoro whether she wanted to switch schools. If she hadn't mentioned a plan yet, it was out of sensitivity towards Kokoro.

But Kokoro didn't know how things were at Aki's home, and so was reluctant to share her thoughts.

Aki and Subaru were in ninth grade, the last year of junior high, on the cusp of high school.

Had neither of them taken the entrance exams to high school? Kokoro couldn't bring herself to ask.

When Kokoro didn't respond, Aki said with a hint of annoyance, "Kokoro?" and gazed directly at her. When Kokoro still didn't react, she let out an exaggerated sigh.

"From next month I'm going to repeat ninth grade." This time Aki addressed Subaru.

Kokoro was startled. "Repeat a grade?"

"Yeah. I could graduate, but this strange woman who was a friend of my grandmother's went to the school and insisted I repeat a year. I don't really care one way or the other, and I haven't given any thought to high school."

"You're going to repeat the year at the same school? Not in another school nearby?"

"You mean, go to the next nearest school, like No. 4 Junior High or something?" Aki asked. "That's impossible, isn't it? I'll be staying put."

Kokoro was mulling this over—the fact that such possibilities existed—when a voice said, "I'm going on to high school."

It was Subaru.

Aki and Kokoro—and the rest—stared at him, eyes wide.

"Wait—didn't I tell you people already?" Subaru asked, sounding very much like he always did. "I took the entrance exam last month. It's for Minami Tokyo Technical High School, their part-time program."

The news took Kokoro by surprise. She'd never got the sense that Subaru was studying for entrance exams.

"Have you been studying?" she asked.

"Sort of, just before I took the exam. I met this man in Akihabara who repairs electronic goods, and I asked him about his work. He told me if I was interested, that's all they teach at the technical high school."

Subaru looked over at Aki. Her face had turned red.

Kokoro knew exactly how she felt.

She understood the fear. Not knowing what the future would be for her, not knowing how long she'd be like this. Seeing people who were moving on was enough to make her feel an excruciating pain in her chest.

Even Kokoro, who was just a spectator, felt Subaru's revelation was a sort of betrayal. If he'd been studying for an exam, why hadn't he said anything to Aki? The two of them were both in ninth grade, the most crucial time to be making a decision about their future.

He never seemed to be studying in the castle, so he must have done it at home. Was he trying to get ahead of them?

Kokoro thought Aki would feel bitter about it.

"I see," was all she said, flatly.

"I wonder if we can all meet on the last day?" Fuka changed the subject. "The thirtieth of March. Not the thirty-first, right? Didn't the Wolf Queen tell us that the last day of March was a maintenance day for the castle?"

"Yeah."

The day was fast approaching, the key was still not found, and no wish had been granted.

But Kokoro was fine about it.

Memories were not the only thing she'd take away from here.

The not-quite one year she'd spent here would remain. And making friends like these would be what sustained her. *I do have friends*, she told herself. *Even if I never make any more, I'll know I did have friends. Right here. Right now. And I'll have that for the rest of my life.*

This made her feel immeasurably more confident.

"Let's have a party on the last day," Fuka said. "Like we did at Christmas. And all of us bring notebooks to write messages to each other. I'm sure we'd be allowed to take them back to our own world."

"I'm up for it," Kokoro said.

As long as proof remained somewhere that they'd all once existed, they should be able to make it through.

*   *   *

"KOKORO, WE HAVE something we need to talk about," her mother said one day, as the end of March approached.

Here we go, Kokoro thought.

As they were to talk about Kokoro's academic future, her mother had asked Ms. Kitajima to join them.

"Actually, Mr. Ida also said he wanted to talk to us," Ms. Kitajima said, prefacing their conversation, choosing her words carefully.

Ms. Kitajima said she'd consulted with people at city hall and had special permission for Kokoro to transfer to another school nearby.

Of course, she could also stay at Yukishina No. 5 and she would be placed in a different class from Miori Sanada.

This all came as a surprise to Kokoro. "I'll make sure they keep their promise," Ms. Kitajima added, an earnest look on her face.

Kokoro nodded silently. "What about Moé Tojo?" she asked.

She didn't dislike the idea of being in the same class as her.

Especially if, as Ms. Kitajima had told her, Tojo-san was the one who'd informed her about the problems between Kokoro and Sanada-san.

The note she'd received flitted through a corner of her mind.

That note with the single line. *I'm sorry.*

"Well, as for Tojo-san," Ms. Kitajima responded, her voice striking Kokoro as somewhat brusque, "she'll be transferring again. This time to Nagoya."

"What?"

"Did you not know that her father is a university professor?" Kokoro was so taken aback she couldn't even nod.

Last April when they were still traveling to school together, Kokoro remembered seeing all the picture books inside her house, all the unusual foreign books which Tojo-san had shown her. She'd even told Kokoro she'd lend her some.

"Her father will be teaching at a university in Nagoya starting in April. So Tojo-san will be going to a school there."

"Even though she's only been here for a year?"

"That's right. Tojo-san's changed schools a number of times in the past."

Kokoro wasn't sure how to feel about this. She'd no longer be living in the house two doors down.

I'm sorry. The line came back to her. When Moé wrote it, the transfer might already have been confirmed. What was she feeling when she wrote her note?

"Tell me anytime if you'd like to visit No. 1 and No. 3 junior highs," Ms. Kitajima said. Her face suddenly showed concern again. "There's one more thing I'd like you to remember."

"What's that?"

"Neither your mother nor I are trying to force you to return to school."

Kokoro's eyes widened and Ms. Kitajima went on. "If you don't want to go back to your current school, or either of the other junior highs, we'd like to consider all the alternatives, what's best for you. Coming to our School is certainly one choice, and we can even consider whether homeschooling is possible. You have many options, Kokoro-chan."

Kokoro looked silently at her mother, sitting quietly beside Ms. Kitajima. When their eyes met, her mother nodded at her.

Kokoro choked up.

Her mother took her hand and squeezed it.

"We'll work this out together," she said.

Kokoro struggled to keep back the tears. She was happy, yet a part of her felt suddenly pained. What about Aki and Fuka?

"Ms. Kitajima?"

"Yes?"

"If I end up staying at Yukishina No. 5, Mr. Ida won't still be my homeroom teacher, will he?"

She knew it wasn't right to hate him, or even dislike him. Since he was trying to do what he thought was right.

"Mr. Ida told me that I needed to respond to Sanada-san's note. He said Sanada-san felt I was making fun of her, and it upset her. But that's not my fault."

The words came pouring out of her. She wasn't sure if she was angry or upset, but either way she didn't like the way her voice trembled uncontrollably.

Ms. Kitajima looked at Kokoro. "I think Sanada-san has her own troubles. And when she sees how you're different from her, maybe she really does feel like you're making fun of her."

Kokoro was silent.

"It's not something you need to understand right now. Sanada-san needs to sort out her own issues."

Ms. Kitajima looked intently at Kokoro's mother.

"Mr. Ida won't be your teacher next year," she said.

In her voice Kokoro thought she could hear echoes of her earlier words, *you're battling every single day, aren't you?*

It was as if a jolt of electricity had run straight through her. The desire within her was so intense to say to Ms. Kitajima right there:

Could you please help my friends in another world, too?

To stand up for Aki, and Fuka, and Ureshino, in each of their own worlds.

But she knew it would never work.

KOKORO COULDN'T PICTURE at all what Sanada-san's *troubles* were, but she knew that Ms. Kitajima would help sort them out. This seemed absurd and painful, but that was the kind of person Ms. Kitajima was—which was exactly why she could trust her.

At the end of March when the castle closed, and the seven friends had returned to their worlds, what would happen to them? She would never know the sequel to their lives, no matter how much she worried about them now, in this moment.

And this hurt.

Please be well, all of you.

IT WAS 29 March, the day before their farewell party.

Kokoro had already been to visit two other junior highs.

The No. 1 and No. 3 junior highs were, compared to Yukishina No. 5, small schools, and the teachers who showed her around emphasized how *cozy* they were.

Kokoro had mixed feelings. She could sense they thought she was one of those students who *didn't fit in at a large-scale school.*

Judging by the cold wind that whistled down the hallways in the schools, the heating wasn't on this late in March. She could hear the school brass bands practicing, and the cries of the athletics teams, urging on their teammates. Underneath, she caught the sound of students her own age happily chatting and laughing. It made her tense. She knew it wasn't possible, but still she felt like they might be laughing at her.

She hadn't worn school slippers in a while, and her toes, sticking out at the top, were feeling chilly.

Her mind wavered.

She still felt some reluctance about leaving Yukishina No. 5.

Fear that she wouldn't fit in, that the others would soon find out what had happened.

There was still a little time left before she had to decide.

She thought how nice it would be to see the others on the last day, the thirtieth, and share her decision.

TODAY SHE FELT like making a trip to Careo.

She was keen to buy some cakes for tomorrow's party. It might be good, too, to take some of those cool paper napkins like the ones Aki had once given her. It was the spring holiday now, and even if she failed to make it all the way, she could at least get to the convenience store.

Once she'd got back from her shopping excursion, she also wanted to make it to the castle. She had a feeling the others, too, wanted to be there as much as they could.

From the day after tomorrow, she'd never be able to go to the castle ever again.

It was hard to grasp.

Kokoro smiled wryly to herself. When she'd first arrived at the castle, she questioned its very existence. How times had changed.

As the final day loomed, she began to consider things more carefully: perhaps all the kids in the world who'd dropped out of school were, like Kokoro, invited over to the castle?

Kokoro was in junior high, but perhaps any school kid who wasn't going to school had spent time with the Wolf Queen. The reason it remained a mystery was because they'd found the key and their wish had come true, and their memories were then wiped clean.

They'd simply forgotten about it.

If that were the case, then it made all the more sense for them to cede the castle to the next group. Since they hadn't managed to find the key, in the Wolf Queen's eyes they were probably a bunch of failures. But that meant they were allowed to keep their memories of the castle. *Someday*, she thought, *we and other kids might be able to share our knowledge that the castle really existed—that we'd all been there together once.*

BUT TODAY OF all days, her mother asked her to stay at home as she was expecting a delivery.

"I ordered a large houseplant to be delivered this morning, and I need you to sign for it," her mother said. Kokoro was worried.

Having to sit tight at home this morning meant she couldn't go to the castle. And there were only two days left. On top of that, she wanted to get to Careo.

"I think they'll deliver fairly early this morning."

"OK," Kokoro said cheerily. The last thing she needed was for her mum to feel suspicious.

But the delivery was not at all early; the delivery man arrived, apologizing for the delay, at three minutes to twelve, so technically still the morning but just under the wire.

Kokoro was despairing. She signed for it with a surly thank you. But she knew showing any irritation was pointless.

She placed the plant carefully in the hallway, grabbed her purse, ran out of the house, jumped on her bike, and raced down the road.

It was going to be hit or miss whether she still had time to get to the castle after all this.

Whenever she passed other junior high-schoolers on the road, she felt herself shrinking, and gripped the handlebars tighter.

I should have worn gloves, she thought.

She'd forgotten how sharp the air could be in March.

When she reached the shopping center, she was a little confused about where to go. Cakes, napkins—she wasn't totally sure where she'd find them, and by the time she had, it was getting close to three o'clock.

Just below the entrance to Careo were advertising banners exhorting shoppers to buy stationery for the new school year. Kokoro couldn't bear to look.

Whenever her eye caught anything with an April date on it, she looked away. By then the castle would no longer exist.

Her mind was filled with these thoughts as she pedaled furiously home. Somehow she made it back. She climbed off the bike, and was about to go inside—

"Oh."

She thought she could hear a small voice nearby. She looked up from her bike.

The small figure of Tojo-san.

She was standing on the pavement in front of the house, gazing across at her.

She was wearing a cool duffel coat and checked muffler, and looked a thousand times smarter than when she was in her uniform. She was holding a bag from a convenience store, as if she too were just back from shopping.

"Tojo-san," Kokoro called, worried she might ignore her as before.

"Kokoro-chan," Tojo-san said.

Kokoro's chest tightened. It had been a long time since she'd even heard her voice, let alone when she called her name.

"Thank you for your note," Kokoro said quickly, to preempt her walking away. "Is it true that you're going to transfer?"

"Yeah." Tojo-san nodded, coming closer. Suddenly, Tojo-san broke into a smile. "Would you like to come over to my house?"

Kokoro's eyes widened, and Tojo-san held up the plastic bag in her hand. "I bought some ice cream, and it'd be a waste if it melts. Let's go home and eat it."

IT WAS NEARLY a year since she'd last been at Tojo-san's.

She was reminded how the layout was almost the same as her own house, though furnished entirely differently; the ornaments, paintings and rugs could not be more contrasting.

The floor was now covered with cardboard boxes. White boxes with *Moving Centre* printed on them. Kokoro realized, with a twinge, that it was true. She really *was* moving away.

The walls were still lined with the European prints collected by her father. Kokoro's eye was drawn to the illustration from *Little Red Riding Hood*, the scene where the wolf, having swallowed Little Red Riding Hood and her grandmother, is lying in bed as the hunter arrives.

Naturally this reminded her of her own Wolf Queen.

"Oh, about that drawing . . ." Tojo-san said, noting Kokoro's interest. "It's from *Little Red Riding Hood*, but she's not actually in it. I told my dad I thought it was strange to hang a picture from a fairy tale when the main character isn't shown there, but he said it was the only one he could buy. He said drawings with Little Red Riding Hood in them were way more expensive and he couldn't afford them."

"Now that you mention it, you wouldn't be able to work out from this single illustration that this is about Little Red Riding Hood. But I remember you telling me before, Moé-chan, so I already knew."

The single clue was the wolf showing a swollen belly and the basket of wine lying on the floor.

Kokoro suddenly realized she'd called Tojo-san by the more

familiar *Moé-chan*. Tojo-san didn't seem to notice. "Right?" was all she said, smiling in agreement. It made Kokoro feel happy.

"Come over here," Tojo-san said, showing her into the sitting room. She took out two small tubs of ice cream from the bag. "Take whichever you like."

Kokoro chose strawberry, Tojo-san took macadamia nut, and they sat opposite each other in companionable silence.

After a few minutes, Tojo-san suddenly said, "I'm sorry."

She said it casually, and Kokoro knew she was trying to make it sound as light as she could. Tojo-san had been chipping away at the same spot in her ice cream, apparently carefully choosing the right moment. That's how it struck Kokoro.

Kokoro bit her lip. She was painfully moved by Tojo-san's apology, but she responded in the same tone. "It's OK," she said.

Kokoro thought she knew why she was apologizing. Jabbing at the ice cream with her spoon, Tojo-san carried on speaking, though she avoided Kokoro's eyes.

"At the beginning of the third semester when I saw you by the slipper cubbies, I really wanted to say something. But I couldn't. I'm sorry. Things were a little sensitive then."

"Sensitive?"

She steeled herself, certain of something hurtful coming her way, when Tojo-san looked up and said, "Things were sensitive between me and Miori and her group."

A yelp of surprise stuck in Kokoro's throat.

Kokoro could well imagine what had happened. She sat mutely on the sofa, and Tojo-san smiled.

"Miori and her group were starting to blank me. I was being left out. So if they found out you'd talked to me, I was worried Miori's gang would find a reason to be mean to you."

"But why . . ."

Why had things turned out like that? At the start of the first semester Tojo-san was a new transfer student, cheerful and outgoing, a popular girl everyone wanted to be friends with.

She thought about it for a moment, and turned pale.

"Was it—because of me?" She could feel the blood drain from her face. "I heard from Ms. Kitajima that it was you who'd told her what happened between me and Sanada-san. Is it because of that?"

Why hadn't she thought of this? Whether he had any idea of what Miori Sanada had done or not, even Mr. Ida knew something was going on. And Miori must have wanted to know who had told him. Kokoro could well imagine what sort of awful things Miori would do to anyone who betrayed her.

"No, that's not it," Tojo-san said, scraping at the ice cream again. She gave a faint smile. "That might have . . . been a small part of it, but I don't think that was the real reason. They said I was stuck up, that I was making fun of them, and they wouldn't put up with it."

"Making fun of them . . ."

A phrase Kokoro had heard quite recently. Being made fun of, making fun of.

"A while before, Nakayama-san in their group accused me of stealing away her boyfriend, called me a man-stealer, and after that, I just didn't care anymore. Dad had told me he might be moving to a different university in April, and as I was going to leave, the whole thing just irritated me, and I gave up trying to make excuses for them."

Gave up—she made it sound light, but there was also a hint of sadness in it. Tojo-san took a spoonful of ice cream. Kokoro did likewise. The sweetness slowly melted in her mouth.

"I probably did . . . make fun of her." Kokoro understood. "And our teachers probably think that's not a good thing to do. Ida called me in and said so. *You're pretty mature*, he said, *and perhaps you look down on the others a bit, but the other girls are trying their best to be friends with you*, yada yada yada."

"Yada yada?" Kokoro said in surprise, and Tojo-san's eyes sparkled mischievously.

"I couldn't care less," she explained. Compared to the last time they'd caught up with each other, Kokoro found her way of speaking now more direct and cool.

"Of course I look down on them. All those girls think about is love and what's right in front of their eyes. They might be strong personalities in our class, but their marks are lousy. Ten years from now, who's going to end up on top, I was thinking."

Tojo-san sounded tough, even caustic. Kokoro's eyes widened. She'd had no idea that Tojo-san had the same negative view of Miori Sanada as she had.

"Wow . . ."

"What?"

"Moé-chan, I've never heard you speak like that before."

"Well, it's true!" Tojo-san sighed, and leaned back into the sofa. "Have I put you off?" she asked, a look of worry in her eyes, and Kokoro shook her head.

"Not at all. I've been thinking the exact same thing. I could never talk to them either."

"And the way Mr. Ida said, *You're pretty mature,* as if he's analyzing everything, makes me sick. He's wrong anyway—it's not that I'm so mature, those girls are just childish. That's why I was thinking that if you ever came back into school, Miori and her group would have tried to be friends with you."

"No way! Why do you think that? After they did those hideous things to me."

"Doesn't matter. Right now the person they want to cast out is *me,*" Tojo-san declared. "Since they've now done that, if you came back you might be friends with me again. So they'd probably get all chummy with you to freeze me out even more."

"No way . . ." Kokoro was speechless.

She remembered the note inside her slipper cubbyhole at school.

Wasn't that a sign Miori Sanada was trying to get back in with Kokoro? Was it a way of ensuring Kokoro and Tojo-san would not be friends again?

She'd been in agony all those months, certain she was going to be killed—and those same kids would forgive her just for that?

She was stunned.

"Forgive"—what is *that, anyway?*

I did nothing wrong, and it's me *who's not going to forgive. But there I was unconsciously expecting to be* forgiven *by them, which is so stupid.*

Tojo-san looked at Kokoro. "It's only school, after all."

"Only school?"

"Yes."

The phrase whirled in her head. She'd never, ever thought of it that way.

School was everything to her, and both going and not going had been excruciating. She couldn't consider it *only school.*

Mr. Ida's words, that she was so *mature,* had irritated Tojo-san, yet Kokoro did find her a little different from the others. Maybe because she'd changed schools so many times. She didn't consider she belonged in any one place.

"To be honest, I always thought you'd turn up at school again, Kokoro-chan. But the only time you did was that one day, wasn't it?"

"Eh?"

Tojo-san looked intently at Kokoro. "I'm sorry," she said again.

"I didn't help you when it was all going on. I'm sorry."

"No—it's OK."

At least Tojo-san had kept going to school, which Kokoro found amazing.

"Moé-chan, are you really changing schools?"

"Yes."

"Are you worried about going to a new school?"

"I am, but after all the stuff that went on here, I feel less worried than free, and I'm looking forward to it. It's as if I can reset things."

"I see."

Kokoro couldn't bring herself to tell her that she was mulling over whether to switch to another junior high in another area. But Tojo-san might have picked up on it. "If you ever transfer to another school," she said, "and no one talks to you the first day, it's OK to cry."

"Cry?"

"Yeah. In front of everybody. Do that, and a couple of people will come over and ask, *Are you OK?* or *Please don't cry.* Make friends with them. Cry, and you'll stand out and at least some people will pay attention to you."

"*Seriously?* Doesn't that only work because it's *you*? You have to be pretty or they won't let you get away with it."

"You think?"

Tojo-san was really being straightforward today, and deliberately provocative. She didn't even deny she was pretty. Kokoro hadn't thought she'd believe in a game plan like crying on purpose.

"But you didn't cry like that at junior high, did you?" Kokoro asked.

"No, I didn't. Everyone was kind to me, so I could get by without crying." She winked.

"But isn't crying a bit childish? I mean, wouldn't it just draw the wrong kind of attention?"

Tojo-san frowned.

"Really?" she said. "Hm. Maybe you're right. But it worked whenever I changed to a new elementary school. Guess I won't be trying it at my next junior high."

"I'm sure there'll be students who want to be friends with you."

Kokoro knew she had been made privy to her friend's true feelings and it made her happy.

Kokoro and Tojo-san resumed eating their ice cream. The topic of conversation switched to their favorite TV series and celebrities.

When they'd finished their ice cream, Tojo-san's expression turned serious.

"Don't let them get to you," she said, her voice stern. "There are bullies like them everywhere, and there always will be."

It sounded less like Tojo-san was talking to Kokoro than that she was convincing herself. There was a tremor of regret in her voice.

There are bullies like them everywhere—this statement sounded as if it was based on Tojo-san's own experience. *There always will be.* Not just Miori Sanada, but probably everywhere.

"Yeah," Kokoro said, nodding.

She had no idea what she wanted to do in April.

And it was 29 March.

The castle would close tomorrow.

She didn't know what the future would bring, but she wanted to pledge this to Tojo-san.

"We don't want to lose," she said.

"I'M SO GLAD we could talk," said Moé, as Kokoro was going through the door.

"That teacher, Ms. Kitajima, told me," Moé went on, "as we're neighbors and it's the spring holiday, that I should see you and catch up. I wasn't brave enough to go over to your house, but I told myself the next time I bumped into you I'd try to talk to you."

Tojo-san's face looked more relieved and cheerful than before.

"I'm glad we could talk, too."

BEFORE SHE REACHED home, disaster struck.

She glanced casually up at her bedroom window. It was past five now, too late to go to the castle. She didn't regret not going any more.

Tomorrow was their farewell party, so everyone would be there. She looked up at her window again.

There was no mistaking it. The mirror was shining, but not with the usual rainbow-colored light. It was now completely dazzling, a blinding white ball of fire swelling up into a huge mass just beyond the window.

Kokoro stood dead still in shock, until she heard a huge *bang!*

She remembered a scene in a TV drama where a fire had made a window shatter. This was the exact same sound, with shards of glass flying in all directions.

As if on cue, after the bang, the blinding ball of light suddenly vanished, leaving its image still imprinted on her eyes.

In three strides, she reached the front door, fumbled with the key before unlocking it, then leapt over the front step and raced upstairs to her bedroom.

She pushed the door open, her breathing ragged. Then she screamed.

The mirror was cracked.

At the center of her portal to the castle was a huge fissure. The glass around it was smashed to pieces. This mirror had always coolly reflected Kokoro's room, but now that it was in pieces it looked cheap, like thin aluminum foil.

"*Why?*" Kokoro shrieked. She reached out to touch the mirror. She didn't care about cutting herself. Tears rolled down her cheeks.

"*Why? Why? Wolf Queen, answer me! Wolf Queen!*"

She shook the mirror violently, her face reflected over and over in the tiny shards. Every one of them showed her bawling her eyes out.

"*Wolf Queen!*" she screamed. "*Wolf Queeeeeeeeeeen!*"

A dull light began to shine from the mirror's cracked middle.

It was different from the usual array of rainbow colors.

The light now resembled the pattern on the skin of a giant snake.

A mottled black and inky-grey pattern wriggled around, glistening like scales.

As when oil falls on a puddle and spreads; as if stirring the surface of the mirror, the dull light moved around like something alive.

"KOKORO."

She heard a voice.

A faint voice coming from beyond the mirror.

In the dim light of evening, she peered hard into the inky glow. Looking for the figure of the Wolf Queen.

In a tiny fragment of glass, a face came into view.

"Rion!"

"Kokoro."

In her confused vision, she noticed more movement in another fragment of glass.

Masamune and Fuka's faces.

"Kokoro."

"Guys!"

She heard their voices calling her name. In another shard of glass she saw Subaru and Ureshino. They all seemed to be there.

Distorted faces, as if being compressed by the haze of dull light.

Kokoro went into a panic. Had everyone gone to the castle today? And were all the mirrors in their homes like this? She heard another voice.

"Help us, Kokoro."

She could hear this voice more clearly, bell-like.

"What's going on? What in the world is happening?"

"Aki. She broke the rules."

It was Rion.

Kokoro held her breath.

"She didn't go home, it was after five o'clock. And she was—eaten by the wolf."

The fingers of her right hand tightly gripping the pink stone frame of the mirror, Kokoro covered her mouth with her left, in shock. Her eyes stared unblinking.

Rion's voice continued.

Among all the friends' faces reflected in the shattered mirror, she realized Aki wasn't there.

"I think we're *all* going to get eaten!" Subaru said this.

Before Kokoro could respond, she heard Masamune: "Collective responsibility."

The faces in the mirror wavered.

"Everyone in the castle is going to be punished."

"We were on our way home when we got pulled back through the mirrors. Aki had apparently hidden in the castle until closing time."

From beyond the mirror, Kokoro could see that Fuka was crying.

"We're all trying to get away now, but the howling—" Ureshino said.

And just then, two loud howls.

Aooooooooooooo!

Aooooooooooo!

From the other side of the mirror, they struck Kokoro with force. Like being hit by a powerful wind, the sound made her heart quail.

"It's here!" she heard Fuka scream. They covered their ears, wrapped their arms around their heads, and closed their eyes.

Kokoro pictured them all running for their lives, dashing to the double stairs in the grand foyer, staring into the mirror that led to Kokoro's house.

"Kokoro, *please!*"

Their voices were fading. She couldn't tell who had called. Fear and shock had clouded her vision.

"Guys!" she shouted back. "*Guys!*"

"The Wishing Key—"

Among the cacophony of voices she heard the words.

"Find it and make the wish—"

"And help Aki—"

This last from Rion.

"It's not *Little Red Riding Hood*. The Wolf Queen is—"

"Guys!" Kokoro shouted, shaking the mirror. "You guys, *please*— answer me!"

Aooooooooooooo!

Aooooooooooo!

This howling was the only response she got.

The faces had disappeared. Something passed in front of the mirror she was clutching. Long, like a tail.

Still clutching the frame of the mirror with her fingers, she screeched and pulled away. When she looked into the mirror again, she saw nothing.

No faces, not the shape that looked like a beast's tail.

Only a dark patch lingering on the surface, proof that the mirror and the castle were still connected.

HER FINGERS WERE shaking so much she couldn't feel them. She let go of the mirror and sank down on the floor. She felt a stab of pain, and when she looked at her right palm, she saw it was cut, blood oozing out. She cringed at the brightness of it.

But her mind was clear and sharp.

She had to get back up—there was not a second to lose.

She reached her hand into the largest area of uncracked glass. The dark patch wavered, avoided her hand—and her arm was sucked into the world beyond.

She pulled it back and looked at the clock in her room. It was five-twenty.

Kokoro's mother always came home between six-thirty and seven. She had to do something before then. When her mother came back, she would no doubt try to get rid of the broken mirror straight away. Today was the only time she could get to the castle.

She had to get the others back home.

Think! Think! she told herself. And along with this inner voice, a second thought intruded.

Aki was eaten.

She's got issues. A lot of issues.

What Subaru had said came back to her.

But *why?* The shock and confusion of it all still overwhelmed her. How could Aki have stayed on in the castle? It was just like committing suicide. Why would she—?

There was suddenly no need to think any more. It was obvious, wasn't it? she thought, on the verge of crying.

Aki didn't want to go back home.

She had preferred to stay on in the castle than return to the reality of her life.

Even if it was suicidal, even if it meant dragging down the rest.

It's utterly selfish. But I know just how she feels, Kokoro thought. *Because I felt exactly the same.*

Wow, that's really something—parents considering your future and stuff. Not like our parents, right, Kokoro?

Aki had been pretending to be tough, and when she was in that mood, what sort of decision had she arrived at in her heart? What sort of reality did this girl face that made her feel it was preferable to be eaten, for it all to be over?

Kokoro couldn't bear to think about it, and a fierce anger welled up inside her.

She should have told us. Aki was an idiot to come to this all by herself, bringing everything to an end. *If it made her depressed to hear what the others were planning to do in the future, she should have said so. If she hated saying goodbye to everyone that much, she should have told us!*

Kokoro, please!

The Wishing Key!

Find it and make the wish.

And help Aki.

Kokoro knew what they were asking her to do.

She felt crushed by the pressure all of a sudden. Would she be able to do it?

She would go into the castle and look for the key.

The key they'd all been searching for unsuccessfully for almost a year, she would have to find by herself in just one hour.

Please save Aki, save all of them.

"Please forget that Aki broke the rules. Bring her back."

280

DING-DONG! THE front doorbell rang suddenly, the banality of its tone out of place. Kokoro looked down from the upstairs window to the front gate. For a second she felt desperate, thinking her parents were back—but it wasn't them.

It was Tojo-san, to whom she'd only just said goodbye, standing at the front gate. She was gazing up at the window of Kokoro's room, a worried look on her face. Kokoro was afraid they'd lock eyes through the gap in the curtain and she hurriedly dropped back.

She was in a rush to get to the castle, but she went downstairs anyway, opened the front door and walked over to the gate, where Tojo-san was standing.

"Oh, I'm glad you're in, Kokoro-chan."

"What's up? Do you need something?"

"I heard this loud noise, and it sounded like it might be coming from your house."

"Oh, it was nothing . . ." Kokoro said, and then she noticed that Tojo-san was holding something. A cell phone.

Tojo-san followed Kokoro's eyes.

"It's my mum's," she explained. "She usually leaves it at home, but I brought it since I thought if Miori and the others were over again or something, I could call the school and get our teacher to come."

Kokoro was touched.

She felt a lump in her throat. "Thank you," she managed to say. "Thank you . . . so very much. It wasn't that. It's just that the mirror in our house . . . fell off the wall and broke."

"Seriously? Are you OK?"

Tojo-san's gaze fell on Kokoro's injured right hand. "You're— you're hurt."

"Yeah, it's OK."

"All right then, if you're sure." Tojo-san started walking back to her house. After a few steps, she looked back and waved.

BUT IT REALLY wasn't OK. Her hand throbbed terribly.

And her heart was racing. She was going to set off, on her own, to the castle. How far did the Wolf Queen's penalty extend? She'd heard that everyone would be eaten soon, but would she be excluded from this *collective responsibility* since she'd been absent from the castle? She suddenly thought about the burden of finding the Wishing Key, and wanted to throw herself on the bed and weep.

Just then, she heard Rion's final words through the mirror.

It's not Little Red Riding Hood. The Wolf Queen is . . .

Suddenly her vision cleared.

She raised her head and stared at Tojo-san, still walking along the pavement.

"Moé-chan, could you do something for me?" she called through the gate.

"Yes, what?"

"Could you show me the drawing in your house? The one in the hallway?"

"The original illustration from *Little Red Riding Hood?*"

"No, the other one."

Kokoro shook her head. Why hadn't she seen it?

I've been giving you clues all along to help you find the key.

I call you all Little Red Riding Hoods, but sometimes you all seem to me more like the wolf. Is it really that hard to find it?

Don't be tempted to do anything you've read in a story, such as calling your mum to come and rip open the wolf's stomach and stuff it with rocks.

I was thinking, too, the whole thing feels a bit fake.

The way the Wolf Queen calls us all Little Red Riding Hoods.

Rion had noted this.

That's why he asked the Wolf Queen what her favorite fairy tale was.

There are seven of us.

We'd talked about it—seven different realities, seven parallel worlds.

Little Red Riding Hood wasn't the only fairy tale to feature a wolf. The Wolf Queen had left them clues all along the way.

"Could you show me the illustration for *The Wolf and the Seven Young Goats?*" Kokoro asked Tojo-san.

Tojo-san seemed caught off guard for a second. Which was only natural. Kokoro knew she'd react the same way if a girl she'd just been talking to had an injured hand and was now making a strange request out of the blue.

Tojo-san opened her mouth to say something, but then shut it. "OK." They walked side by side in silence to her house.

Standing in front of the illustration on the wall, Kokoro's whole body let out a deep *ah*.

"I have the picture book too," Tojo-san said, and brought it over. "It's my father's."

When Kokoro saw the cover, she gasped. On the bookshelf in her room in the castle was the same German book: *Der Wolf und die sieben jungen Geißlein.*

The Wolf Queen had given this hint as well, and Kokoro regretted that she'd never even opened the book.

"Thanks."

"You can borrow it anytime. The same illustration's inside too."

Kokoro respected Tojo-san for not asking why she was suddenly so interested. *I wish we'd been good friends much earlier,* she thought.

"Take this, too," Tojo-san said. She handed a Band-Aid to Kokoro.

"When your mother comes home, you should ask her to dress it properly for you. OK?"

"OK."

Accepting it with her good hand, Kokoro suddenly choked up. She felt so grateful for the worlds she had—the extraordinary world of the castle, and the ordinary world that contained her mother and Tojo-san. *I really want to come back here,* she thought.

"When are you moving?"

"The first of April."

"Very soon then."

"Can't help it. Dad wanted to move in March, but the first of April is a Saturday this year so he has the day off."

"Thank you, Moé-chan."

Kokoro clutched the book tightly and bobbed her head. She wanted to talk more but she'd run out of time.

"I'm really happy I could be friends with you, Moé-chan."

"You don't need to say that. It's making me embarrassed." Tojo-san smiled.

Kokoro remembered what she'd said about a reset in life. How she was looking forward to making a fresh start with people in her new school.

But Kokoro hesitated to say the other thing she was thinking about.

"Just don't push the reset button on *me*," she murmured.

It's OK to forget me, she added to herself. *Because* I'll *remember it all. What happened today, and you, Moé-chan. And how we were friends.*

✳   ✳   ✳

SHE HAD MADE up her mind, and placed her hand inside the mirror.

Slowly, as if stirring up muddy water.

The bottom, unshattered half of the mirror was just big enough for her to squeeze through. Taking care that the shards didn't cut her or rip her clothes, she slipped through. *This might be the very last time*, she thought.

With the mirror so badly broken, she expected her mother to get rid of it the next day. She clutched the picture book tightly, like a good-luck charm, desperately hoping that while she was in the castle the mirror wouldn't crack any more, and that she'd be able to get home safely.

She came out on the other side of the mirror, and was shocked at the scene in front of her.

The castle was almost pitch dark inside, not lit with its usual dim glow. The walls and the flooring looked unfamiliar, as if she were somewhere else completely. The silhouette of the castle outside had faded, making it seem amorphous and twisted.

The mirror she emerged from was also broken, cracked in exactly the same pattern as the one in her bedroom.

She was sure she'd come through into the grand foyer, but if so, it appeared utterly transformed. The other mirrors were lying on the floor, shattered in the same way. Shards of ornaments and urns were scattered across the floor, as if after a terrible storm.

It took a while for her to understand that she'd emerged into the dining room. So had her mirror been moved?

Nothing about the dark and ruined room reminded her of the noble old space she remembered. Kokoro took slow quiet breaths, and gripped the book tightly to her chest, trying to avoid attracting attention from the wolf, who might still be nearby.

A far-off howl rang deep in her ears—or was she merely imagining it? She crouched on all fours and slowly crawled her way around, using the overturned dining table as a shield. Gradually, she moved through to the kitchen where she took a close look at the shelves.

Masamune had said he'd discovered an *X* nearby. She looked around. It was still there.

The fourth young goat hid inside the kitchen shelves.

She gently placed a fingertip on the *X*, and felt a terrible shock strike the middle of her forehead.

"LYING MASA!"

The force of the voice smashed into her head as if she'd been hit with a heavy, blunt instrument. Her consciousness faded.

Kokoro was sitting at a desk in a classroom reading aloud some words scratched into the wood.

Masa is a liar.

Always bragging about my friend this *and* my friend that.

Die, why don't you.

The words became distorted. The scene faded. She saw the face—of a boy she didn't know.

"I—hate that."

The boy looked as if he was about to cry, and Kokoro felt her heart being squeezed. Then she realized. *This is Masamune's memory.* The memory of a time that traumatized him.

"Maybe you thought that lie was no big deal, but to me it felt like you'd totally betrayed me. Especially because I always admired you, and envied you."

That's not true! Masamune's thoughts ran right through her.

But it was true. He knew better than anyone that he had lied. So he had no way of defending himself.

What he wanted to say was, "No, I never meant to hurt anyone," but he wasn't even sure of that.

"He doesn't need to go. I never thought public schools were any good anyway."

Masamune's father was in his bedroom, tying his necktie. Masamune was listening outside the door at the top of the stairs.

"I mean, I heard from colleagues at my office who work in TV that the conditions for the teachers are often appalling."

The voice made Masamune's chest ache.

"But—they are doing their best, and there *are* some very good teachers doing really good work," said his mother.

Perhaps I'm the one who invented excuses for not fitting in. Masamune swallowed back these words.

Instead, he murmured to himself, "That's right, Dad. The teachers are to blame. Every one."

He got up and went back to his room. It was spacious, overflowing with toys and books. And tons of video games.

There was a mirror in the room and it was glowing.

Entranced, Masamune stood in front of the rainbow light. He placed his palm flat and splayed his fingers on to the surface of the mirror. And his body was sucked into the light.

"Hey there."

The Wolf Queen was standing on the other side of the mirror.

"Whoa!"

"Congratulations! Aasu Masamune-kun, you have, happily enough, been invited to the castle!"

The next thing she saw was the nurse's office, in winter.

Kokoro recognized the room. She felt the warmth of the space heater on her bare legs.

"They're not gonna bail on me. I know it."

Masamune was sitting on a hard chair in the nurse's office.

Someone was rubbing his back. His shoulders were heaving, as if he'd just been crying his eyes out; he had bawled so much that he was having trouble breathing.

"They're gonna come. I know it."

He was talking to himself.

The hand kept rubbing his back.

"Something must have prevented your friends from coming."

She could see now the face of the person standing beside Masamune.

It was Ms. Kitajima.

SHE FELT ANOTHER shocking pain travel through her forehead, a bolt of pain, like eating cold ice cream.

Disorientated, she focused her vision. She was in front of the kitchen pantry. Her finger still resting on the X.

Down at her feet she noticed a pair of glasses. Hands trembling, she picked them up and fingered them carefully. The bottom of the right lens was cracked, the frame twisted. These were Masamune's. She shivered in horror.

When they said "eaten," did that mean literally *eaten*?

You'll be swallowed up whole.

A huge wolf will appear. A powerful force will punish you. And once it's triggered, there's nothing anyone can do to stop it. Not even me.

The first day they'd all gathered together, the Wolf Queen had explained the rules. But they hadn't paid much attention.

Kokoro's breathing grew ragged. She shook her head vigorously to drive away the growing terror, and put the glasses down as carefully as she could. She gripped her arms to keep herself from fainting.

She peered up close at the *X* inside the pantry.

She must have just experienced Masamune's own memories.

He must have run away from the wolf, and hidden right here in this pantry and dropped his glasses. She was curious about the spot he had chosen to hide in. Why here?

She opened the book she'd borrowed from Tojo-san.

She had to confirm each location. She had to make absolutely sure.

Bang, bang, bang! Open up. It's me, your mother.

The young goats hid from the wolf. As Rion had said, when the Wolf Queen called them Little Red Riding Hoods, she was hoodwinking them all.

The first goat hid under the table.

(*I'm pretty sure there's one under the desk in my room.*)

The second hid under the bed.

(*Under the bed in my room I found an X, so what does that mean?*)

The third goat hid inside the unlit stove.

(*What's this?* Kokoro thought when she found the mark inside the fireplace.)

The fourth hid in the kitchen pantry.

(*I found one too. In the summer. There's one in the kitchen, isn't there? Behind the pantry shelves.*)

The fifth one hid inside the wardrobe.

(*I found one in my room too. In the wardrobe.*)

The sixth one hid inside a laundry basket.

(*There's one in the bathroom, too. There was a laundry basket in the bathtub, and when I moved it I found an X.*)

All these *X*'s marked where the young goats were hiding before the wolf gobbled them up.

She felt like they'd all been cleverly blindsided.

The feeling that they'd been hypnotized into believing they'd never, ever find it.

The Wolf Queen's voice came back to her.

I call you all Little Red Riding Hoods, but sometimes you all seem to me to be more like the wolf. Is it really that hard to find?

In the fairy tale *The Wolf and the Seven Young Goats*, there was one spot which the wolf never checked. Where the seventh little goat hid, and was saved.

There was just one place where you'd never be found.

The Wishing Key was inside the large clock in the grand foyer.

The first thing you saw when you emerged from the mirror.

It was the one place no one had ever looked.

AOOOOOOOOOOOOOOOOO!

For a moment, Kokoro's whole body shivered, as if every single pore had opened. She felt the air and the floor move around her. She lay down on the floor, cheek pressed hard against the prickly rug.

Then she got up into a crouch, avoiding the shards of smashed cups and plates. In the castle, the dining room and kitchen were the furthest away from the grand foyer. She didn't know if she could make it all the way to the clock.

She glanced around the dining room. It looked like it had been trashed by a monster. But the glass door leading out to the courtyard was strangely intact.

Her heart banged loudly in her chest, almost painfully.

Aooooooooooooooooo!

A cry squeaked up her throat. The vibration of the howl made her knees weak, and she collapsed back on to the floor. She spied the fireplace in the middle of the back wall. If only she could get there. She started to crawl.

She could see the *X* inside the fireplace.

Without thinking, she reached out a finger and touched it.

She felt another shock in the middle of her forehead. It grew hot and feverish.

THE VERY FIRST thing that slammed into her head were memories of 10 January, when Ureshino thought he had been stood up.

He was hanging around waiting for Masamune and the others. Feeling hunger pangs, he took the rice balls his mother had made out of their aluminum foil wrapping, and started shoving them into his mouth.

"Guys, it's him."

"You're right—why has he come? So weird."

"He's stuffing something into his mouth. Ugh. Look!"

Malicious voices. Kids at a school club, even though it was a Sunday, were staring like he was some bizarre creature.

Ureshino knew very well they were saying nasty things about him. Kokoro could hear it all now, in her own ears. But Ureshino just stared at his rice ball, and carried on chewing.

A large bird flapped its wings as it crossed the cloudless sky.

"I wonder if that's a migratory bird. Hope he can make it over to his friends," Ureshino said. Not so anyone else could hear, but just to himself.

Speaking aloud gave him courage.

"Masamune and the others sure are taking their sweet time," he murmured, glancing through the school gate.

Just then a warm feeling spread through his chest.

The warmth and strength that surged through him were pure and clear, unwavering. Ureshino knew that, at this moment, he was happy.

Whether Masamune and the others came or not.

The rice balls were delicious, the winter sky was clear, and he could see a bird flying.

This was a happy day, Ureshino thought to himself. Even if he had been stood up, he wanted to tell the others all about it in the castle tomorrow.

"Haruka-chan," he heard a voice call.

"Mama," he said and looked up.

Kokoro could also see who it was. Ureshino's mother, wearing an apron, had a kind, round face. Very different from the person Kokoro had been imagining. Ureshino's mother wore hardly a trace of make-up and her coat was covered in bits of fluff. She seemed modest, yet she had a big-hearted smile.

This was the woman who'd said she would accompany her son if he chose to go to school abroad.

Someone was with her.

"Kitajima-sensei—so you've come too!" Ureshino said happily. "I saw a beautiful bird flying, and I was wondering if it was migratory," he said, pointing up at the sky.

"AKI-CHAN!" URESHINO called. "Aki-chan, where are you? It'll be time soon and we need to go home. The howling has started . . ."

"It's OK, Ureshino. There's nothing we can do," Fuka said. Her face was pale. They were gathered in the grand foyer, standing in front of the line of seven mirrors. Only Kokoro's wasn't shining.

Aki wasn't with them and they were beginning to get impatient.

"Why don't we go home now, just us. Time's running out."

The Wolf Queen's howls grew more shrill.

"Let's go!" Fuka shouted, and grabbed Ureshino by the arm.

"But Aki's not—"

Ureshino's body started to pass through the mirror—but when he was halfway through, he was violently dragged all the way back.

Gyaaaaaaaaaaaaaaaa!

A piercing scream.

Ureshino was back in the grand foyer. With all the others.

The scream was Aki's.

The five looked at each other in horror and were suddenly bathed in a violent blinding light, like a ball of fire, which swelled up, splitting open the mirrors with a deafening bang that echoed through the castle.

DAZZLED BY THE light, Kokoro found her consciousness returning.

The pitch-black interior of the castle was now completely quiet. She was crying. Why, she wasn't sure. "Guys," she said, wiping away tears with the back of her hand.

She reflected on what she'd seen. Reflected and reflected.

There was something she had to be sure of.

If what she'd seen just now by touching the *X* in the fireplace was Ureshino's memory. And if what she saw in the kitchen pantry was Masamune's . . .

If she could follow their memories to the point when they were eaten . . .

It wasn't as if she was some voyeur or anything, but she wanted to make sure. She slowly got to her feet.

She remembered her conversation with Tojo-san a little while ago. In her reality that existed beyond the castle.

Kokoro had expressed how sad she was that Moé was moving away in April. To which Moé had replied, "Dad wanted to move in March, but the first of April is a Saturday this year so he has the day off."

This year.

Kokoro squeezed the hardback book to her chest, pressing it into her with her palms.

I'm going back, she thought. *To return this book and say a proper goodbye to her.*

The earlier howling had come from the grand foyer, where the clock was.

That meant she still couldn't go there.

Without further thought, she dashed quickly in the opposite direction, towards the bathroom.

The Wolf Queen's words really were clues for them, weren't

they? Kokoro's chest was ready to burst. But not out of fear, like a moment ago.

I never said you can't meet up, or can't help each other. It's time you people worked things out. Don't start barking up the wrong tree. Think about it, and don't expect me to tell you everything. I've been giving you clues all along.

The small laundry basket was still inside the bathtub.

She moved the basket to one side. There it was. She reached out a finger and touched the *X*.

SHE FELT THE scalding hot air of a hairdryer on the top of her head. In her vision, she could see . . . a bathroom. In the bathroom mirror Subaru was reflected, with his unmissable dyed hair.

Beside him was a bottle labeled "hydrogen peroxide."

I'll tell them my older brother made me do it, he thought.

Actually, his brother hadn't been home in several days. *And he thinks I'm a total loser, but even so I'll tell them it's because of him.*

"Suba-chan, how much longer are you going to be in the bathroom? It's time to eat."

"Hurry up, Subaru. What kind of dumbo has a bath in the morning, eh?"

"OK. I'm coming!"

He grimaced at his grandmother's slow drawl, and his grandfather's grumpy tone, and turned off the dryer.

The house was in need of renovation, and the sliding glass door rattled. He picked up a thin towel, a cheap freebie printed with the name of a construction company. There were a few stains on it.

"Looks like blood," Subaru muttered.

As he emerged from the bathroom, his grandfather, in T-shirt and long johns, frowned at him.

"What's happened to your hair?"

He didn't comment any further, probably because his older brother already had blond, spiky hair. Subaru's brother had roared up in front of the house on a motorcycle which he said he'd borrowed from *an older friend*; their grandmother had yelled at him about the ugly roar it made, but what concerned Subaru was his suspicion that the motorcycle was stolen. His brother had some pretty expensive embroidery on his school uniform, and Subaru wondered where he'd got the money to do that.

"You two don't go to school, don't work—you're hopeless, just like your father."

"I'm sorry, Grandpa. Really."

"These days you've got to graduate from high school or you won't amount to anything."

"Yes, yes, darling. It's time for breakfast, so let Subaru have something to eat."

They started the day early in Subaru's grandparents' house. Until the moment his grandfather went out to play *go* with his buddies or to work in the fields, Subaru had to endure all his sarcastic remarks. He'd vaguely laugh it off, silently eat the meal his grandmother made for him, and then, in the same room, open his school textbooks. And study until the time came when the castle opened, all the while enjoying listening to music on the player his dad had given him.

"My marks are good and I do well in most subjects, so I don't have to go to school," he lied to his grandmother, and she believed him. But his grandfather wouldn't buy it.

"You gotta go to school. It's important," he insisted. He might say that, but his grandfather never actually communicated with his teachers about his situation. He confined himself to directing snide comments at Subaru.

For their part, the only contact the teachers made to urge the brothers back to school was through their father, who lived far away. Their parents had labeled both brothers as *kids with issues*, and had washed their hands of them. All they did was get angry, tell them they had their own lives to lead and that the brothers, too, should get a grip and take responsibility for their own lives. All of which led Subaru to one conclusion: no one really cared all that much what happened to him.

That makes things easier, he told himself, *but it's dull, too.*

The Walkman he'd been using clicked off. The sixty-minute A-side of the tape had finished. Subaru put his pencil down on the table and flicked the tape over to its B-side. He usually preferred the radio, but it was harder to work to.

The thing his father had given him which he most appreciated was his name—Subaru, which meant the constellation of stars called the Pleiades.

Kokoro told him the association with the stars gave his name a fantastical feel, but most people told him it reminded them of the pop song sung by Tanimura. But that was fine, he thought, since the song itself was inspired by the constellation, also known as the Seven Sisters.

The second thing he liked that his father had given him was the Walkman. A new model had become available that year, but his father had given him the old model. Subaru had thought it was cool to listen to music while walking around the castle, but the others hadn't really noticed.

Subaru much preferred thinking about these new ways of listening to music than about schoolwork. His father said he'd pay whatever fees were needed, so he thought he'd take whatever exams necessary to get into high school, as long as he could study something he actually enjoyed.

He wondered what everyone else was going to do.

He wanted to talk it over with them, but it felt against the rules to do so in the castle.

"Well, I'm off to help out with the Ladies' Group," his grandmother announced.

"OK."

After she left, the mirror started glowing.

The other kids all have mirrors in their own bedrooms, he thought, *but I have a grandma's mirror.* He rested a palm on the old-fashioned mirror, draped with a purple cloth.

I'll go to the castle.

Everyone will be there.

In Subaru's world there was no Free School, no Ms. Kitajima.

They all seem pretty happy, he thought, *with their own bedrooms, their own parents at home.*

They have people who really care about them.

Subaru didn't feel angry or jealous, or like making fun of them. He simply made the observation. *They don't know how good they have it.*

And here I am, not really caring what happens to me.

Today I'll probably stop by the castle, but tomorrow I should hang out with my brother's friends, he thought. He didn't care one way or the other, but his brother had told him one of the guys wouldn't give him back his manga, so he was going to knock him around a bit to show him he shouldn't mess with him. *So you come with me,* his brother had said.

Whatever.

I mean, in ten years or so the world might end anyway.

The other day, he'd tried using a gift token Masamune had given him as a Christmas present to call his father, but the code didn't work. He gazed at it. The card had drawings of manga characters on it which he didn't recognize.

He was going to tell him about it, but he forgot.

I'll tell him next time we meet.

Before the end of March, when we have to say goodbye.

At least that was the plan.

HE HEARD THE Wolf Queen's howl.

"Aki-chan, where are you? It'll be time soon and we need to go home," called Ureshino.

"It's OK, Ureshino. There's nothing we can do."

"Why don't we go home now, just us. Time's running out."

Halfway through the mirror on his way back home, he thought of Aki.

I bet Aki actually wanted to find the Wishing Key.

She must have a wish she really wants to come true.

She chose to stay in the castle, rather than go home to her reality. Subaru found her courage amazing. He knew he could never do that.

But as soon as he got home, he was pulled back through the mirror.

Back to Aki's screams and the wolf's piercing howls.

"Subaru. Over here! We've got to get Kokoro in!" Rion shouted. "Kokoro's the only one of us who didn't come today, so she won't be forced back and eaten. We've got to get Kokoro to help—"

As he watched them all fleeing for their lives, a feeling came over him for the first time ever.

I don't want to die.

I don't want to die—not yet.

I haven't done anything with my life. He suddenly realized: he wanted to do *something*.

The wolf howled again. Louder this time.

"Eeee!" Fuka screamed, eyes shut tight.

"Fuka-chaaaan!" Subaru called out to her.

I don't want to die, not yet, he thought again.

And I don't want the others to die either.

THE PAIN THAT had struck her in the forehead began to recede.

Kokoro found herself crying again. She wiped away the tears with her fingers.

I have to save them, she said to herself.

I have to save them all.

The castle fell quiet.

She thought about where she should go.

The grand foyer was at the end of the long corridor with their rooms off it.

She normally strolled nonchalantly down this hallway, passing the landscape paintings and the candlesticks without a thought, but today, stepping through the rubble on the floor, it seemed endless.

But she had to go.

She took a deep breath and started to run.

I'm the only one who can do it.

But what if the wolf hears me running? In tears, she changed her mind and headed towards the Game Room.

It was a complete shambles.

Masamune's game device was nowhere to be seen, lying somewhere in the wreckage of the overturned sofa, table, shattered ornaments, stag's head and flower vases.

Kokoro turned away, unable to look, and when she started to run in the direction of their individual rooms, another loud howl rang out.

Aooooooooooooooooooooo!

The howl was so loud she couldn't tell where it was coming from. She grabbed the door handle to the nearest room. The shock of the howl hit her cheeks like a gale.

Once inside the room the aftershocks of the howl seemed to fade, and the wind died away.

Her eyes traced the shapes in the darkened room. It had been wrecked, just like the rest of the castle.

The lid to the piano was propped open. The keyboard, like a mouth with missing teeth, had been destroyed, and it looked pitiful.

Fuka's room.

She'd never been in here before. The room was smaller than Kokoro's. Aside from the piano, there was no bed or bookcase like in her own room.

On top of the broken desk were textbooks, reference books, pens and notebooks.

I'm pretty sure there's one under the desk in my room.

An *X*.

She waited a few moments before reaching underneath the desk. She placed her finger firmly on top of it.

She needed to know, to access all their memories, to hear everyone's full story.

FUKA WAS PRACTICING in the piano room in her house.

Fuka enjoyed having quiet time alone to practice.

A calendar hung on the wall: 23 December, a national holiday, was marked in red. Underneath, it said: *Piano competition*.

It was coming up very soon.

"FUKA-CHAN IS quite the genius, ma'am," the piano teacher had said to her mother.

Fuka had not yet started elementary school.

Fuka's mother, busy with work, had taken her daughter to free introductory lessons at the piano school, at the invitation of Mima-chan's mother, who lived nearby. The three free lessons had run out when the teacher spoke to Fuka's mother.

"She has a real gift," the teacher said.

Fuka's mother was both astonished and pleased. "Really? My little Fuka?"

"She absorbs things so much more quickly than other children. I've been teaching for many years but have never seen such potential. You really should consider her future, perhaps send her to study abroad at some point."

Fuka listened in while they were talking.

"You're . . . not just saying this because you want us to continue lessons with you now that they're no longer free?"

Her mother seemed suspicious. Her cell phone started buzzing inside the bag she always took to work, the one with the worn handles. Normally she would have answered it but she chose not to.

"Not at all," the teacher went on. "I am honestly amazed by her playing. I don't say this to all the children."

What he said was true.

The teacher hadn't said the same thing to Mima-chan, who'd gone with Fuka, or to Mima-chan's mother.

I am gifted. I am gifted.

I'm different from other kids.

AT PE AT school, Fuka sat on the sidelines and watched.

The others had formed a circle, and were tossing the ball to each other.

She was sitting on the gymnasium floor, hugging her knees, her back up against a corner, when Mima-chan came over with a group of girls.

"Don't you want to play?"

"Um . . . no."

Fuka always sat out during PE. It would be a disaster if she hurt a finger playing volleyball.

Back when she was a freshman, they'd been practicing vaulting when Fuka missed her landing and twisted an ankle, and her mother had come into school to complain and the whole thing had escalated. *This is a critical time for her,* her mother had shouted, *she has a competition soon! So she's hurt her foot, but what if it had been her hand?*

Mima-chan and the others exchanged a look. "It's because Fuka-chan has piano."

"Oh."

The girls walked off. She heard them giggling.

"My fingers are so important and it just wouldn't do to injure them."

"I just have to play the piano, you know?"

Their voices were shrill, as if they intentionally wanted her to overhear.

PIANO, PIANO, PIANO.

Fuka's days in elementary school were clearly divided into

boxes—school and piano. Gradually, she spent more and more time at the piano than on schoolwork, and as far as she was concerned that was fine.

She was told to take time off from school to have lessons in Kyoto with a famous piano teacher. She would attend lessons from her grandparents' house, who lived in the area.

She was often told to practice more, but not once did an adult ever caution her to study harder.

Her mother said to the teachers at school, "You're concerned about her school attendance, but would you have a look at her record in piano competitions? Couldn't you consider this as equivalent to her school record?"

She didn't attend school much, and she thought that was OK.

Until the final piano competition of her elementary school days when, aiming at the top prize, she came nineteenth.

IT WASN'T THAT she wasn't feeling well, or was out of sorts.

She'd thought she'd played as well as always, and hadn't made any mistakes, at least none she was aware of.

And yet look what happened—she ended up in nineteenth place.

This was a national competition, her grandmother said, so to come nineteenth was amazing, but her mother's face expressed only shock. Later when she saw how she was marked, the difference between her and the top ten highest scores filled her with dismay.

"Things aren't easy, are they," she heard her grandfather say to her grandmother. "How much longer is Fuka planning to play?"

Fuka didn't have a father.

"You're a single parent, so you shouldn't overdo it," her grandparents said.

"I'm not!" her mother snapped.

They hadn't made any decisions about studying abroad, in which country or school, or with which teacher, so Fuka stayed in Japan.

Fuka secretly thought it was a question of money. Her mother

301

worked all day long, and when Fuka got home from her piano lesson, she still wasn't back. Cold rice balls awaited her in the twilit room, and once when she tried to heat them up in the microwave, the electricity had been cut off.

When her elementary teacher paid them the standard home visit, he was more than a little astonished to find a quality piano and soundproofed walls all around the practice room in their tiny apartment. The only items in the fridge, though, were bentos and bread brought back from her mother's job. Fuka hardly ever saw her mother cooking or cleaning. Since all she did was work, work, work.

Even so, the gas had been cut off. Gas, electricity, water—all shut off in that order, and Fuka was strangely impressed at how the one most essential to life was the last to go off. Her mother had given her a cell phone to take with her, since she went to her piano lessons alone, but the previous day when she tried to call her mother the service had been discontinued.

As she continued to have longer and longer piano lessons, it hit her forcibly: *I'm doing something that's beyond our means.*

And she didn't just mean money.

It's a matter of talent, too. It's not just lack of money that's stopping me from traveling abroad.

HOW MUCH LONGER *is Fuka planning to play?*

When she heard her grandfather's words, Fuka realized a few things.

That she wasn't able to keep up with junior high schoolwork.

That if she continued to practice the piano as much as she did, she would never have enough time for schoolwork.

"I don't believe it!" her mother had said, and wept loudly when she heard what Fuka's grandfather had said. "Why are you saying this, Dad?" she asked. "I'm never bringing Fuka here again. I won't let you see her." Then her grandmother stepped in with a suggestion.

"Why don't you live with us in Kyoto?" Her grandparents had

proposed this many times before, but her mother had always rejected the idea. "I'm a full-time employee at my company now," she said, "and if I leave, I won't be able to get another full-time job. Then we won't be able to manage, Fuka and me. And she'll have to drop the piano."

When she started at junior high, Fuka's mother encouraged her piano playing even more.

Fuka adored her mother.

She raised her lovingly, making up for the loss of Fuka's father, who'd died in a car accident when she was five. She worked at two jobs: all day in the office of a delivery company, and at night in a part-time job making bentos.

"I never had any particular talent," her mother told her. "And if you have talent, Fuka, I'll do everything in my power to help you."

The thing was, her mother's face was becoming more and more gaunt and exhausted. Fuka often thought she shouldn't be playing the piano but rather helping her mother out.

Instead of going to a lesson, she wanted to make her mother a home-cooked meal, some rice and hot miso soup. She was always eating bentos from her part-time job, and it'd be nice to make her something else to eat.

And not performing well at the piano competition made her truly sad.

Which is why she thought that to give up now would be a waste.

All the time and money they'd invested in piano lessons for her would be for nothing.

When she started at junior high, she went to school even less often. Even then, she didn't have much to talk about with the other girls. She didn't do PE and wasn't in any clubs. She felt left out.

But that was OK. She didn't need friends.

ONE DAY, WHILE she was practicing, the mirror near the front door of their flat started to shine.

And she landed up at the castle, and met everyone . . .

When she went to her own room, it too had a piano. She pressed a couple of keys to test the sound; the next moment she banged the keys down hard with both palms.

I don't need a piano here, she thought.

"Summer school starts tomorrow so I won't be able to come over to the castle for a while."

That's the line Fuka gave them, but actually she was having piano lessons in Kyoto in preparation for a summer competition.

The student who had a lesson before Fuka sounded so much better than she did, she thought, and it made her want to plug her ears. She'd practiced way too much to even know if she herself was any good anymore.

In the competition, Fuka's mark in the first round placed her out of the running. Anyone ranked thirty or below was automatically eliminated.

Even though she'd been told the competition was on a much smaller scale than the previous one she'd played in.

When Fuka saw the results posted on a noticeboard in the hallway, she went weak at the knees, as though her whole body, along with the piano, were sinking fast into an icy sea.

The summer competition over, she returned to Tokyo, and when she went over to the castle, she was given a box of sweets by Kokoro.

"A birthday present," she said.

Eating a whole box of sweets wasn't something that anyone did very often in her house. She relished them, savoring the taste, one by one.

Before the competition, Aki had also given her a birthday present. And Ureshino had told her he *really liked* her.

His romantic focus flitted from one girl to the next and Fuka had reacted with a predictable shriek when he said this, but the thought that a boy who'd fancied girls like Aki and Kokoro now said he liked her honestly made her happy, even though she had looked grumpy about it.

Masamune had let her play some of his video games.

She'd always thought that boys only let the pretty girls touch any of their gadgets.

Subaru added the intimate *chan*, calling her *Fuka-chan*. She liked how gentlemanly he was.

Even Rion, the sort of boy who stood out in a crowd, treated her as one of his friends, and called her simply *Fuka*.

Whenever he did so, she was happy to be her, to be just "Fuka."

Whether I have any talent or not—none of that makes any difference here. They're all happy to know me.

"HELLO. HAVE WE . . . met before?"

"Hello."

As they exchanged greetings, Fuka thought: *So this is Ms. Kitajima. I'm finally able to meet her.*

The others had apparently all gone to the Classroom for the Heart alternative School with their mothers, but Fuka went alone; it was her secret.

The others had talked often about this Ms. Kitajima, how she was someone they relied on for support. She found herself wanting to meet her as well.

Ms. Kitajima often stopped by Yukishina No. 5 Junior High, and had already heard about Fuka, an eighth grader who had had several absences from school. "I'm so happy you've come," she said.

Little by little, in a broken, rambling way, Fuka opened up to her.

After the results of the competition were announced and Fuka had been eliminated, Fuka's mother began to lose heart. She no longer urged Fuka to practice like she used to. It didn't seem to matter to her whether Fuka went to her piano lessons or to school. Fuka pretended she was going to school, but actually she was spending her time at the alternative School and at the castle.

She knew she wasn't about to go back to school. And she wondered what her mother really wanted her to do.

How much longer is Fuka planning to play? Her grandfather's words were like a curse she heard ringing out from the depths of her being.

As she talked over things with Ms. Kitajima, she realized how very depressed and anxious she'd been.

"I can't go back now," she said. "I can't keep up with schoolwork. I don't know if I should go on playing the piano."

"OK, then—let's start to study," Ms. Kitajima said cheerfully. "I'll help you. It sounds to me," she went on, "as if you feel you've become involved in a high-stakes activity."

"High stakes?"

"You've been working towards a single goal for years, and worried about what might happen if you can't win competitions or become a pianist. With that in mind, studying—schoolwork—might be a much lower-risk activity for you. If you try hard, you'll always see results, and it will never be wasted, no matter what you end up doing in life."

"So let's do both," Ms. Kitajima said with a smile. "I totally understand how much the piano means to you, Fuka-chan. But let's do our schoolwork too, not just agonize over the piano."

"Will you . . . be my teacher?"

"Um," Ms. Kitajima responded, tilting her head. Her eyes looked pleased. "Of course. This is a school, after all. I'll help you with your schoolwork."

HOLED UP IN her room in the castle, Fuka opened a textbook, and got down to the homework Ms. Kitajima had set her. She was sure she could catch up with the next grade's level of work pretty soon.

Without her mother or anyone else around, she could concentrate on her studies in peace and quiet.

Not once did she touch the piano in her room in the castle again.

Until February—the last day of the month.

When she got to the castle, no one else was there. Hers was the only mirror shining, and Fuka suddenly wondered, *Was it today that the castle was going to close forever?*

"Wolf Queen!" she called out, uneasy, but the Wolf Queen didn't appear. This was a first.

She walked along the hallway to her room, where she had a sudden urge to play the piano.

She opened the lid, rested her fingers on the keys, and began to play. The notes rang out beautifully, and she knew the piano had been perfectly tuned.

Feeling the keys under her fingers, she became totally immersed.

She could concentrate and listen to the sounds she was making.

She loved the stillness. *This feels so good*, she thought.

She didn't notice, until she had stopped, that someone was standing in the doorway listening.

The door was open, and there stood Aki.

"You startled me."

Aki's eyes were wide. "Sorry to come in without asking. But Fuka—you're so good!"

"Um. Yeah. Well—"

"You're a musical genius, aren't you?"

"Not exactly."

The term should have stabbed at her, but when Aki said it, she gave a wry smile.

"Hey!" Aki said. "What's this? A textbook? I thought you were staying cooped up in your room a lot. Have you been studying?"

"Yeah . . ." Fuka glanced at the pens lined up on her desk.

"Studying is low-risk."

Why's that?"

"Instead of investing everything in one talent, this is a slow and steady way to grow, the most certain way." She hoped it didn't sound false. "Someone told me if I do it, it will never turn out to be a waste."

Aki was usually irritable, edgy, but with just the two of them in the castle today, Fuka felt strangely more relaxed with her.

She told her the whole story—about the competitions, about schoolwork, about her mother and about Ms. Kitajima. And how they all led her to pick up her studies again.

"Maybe I'll try that, too . . . studying," Aki murmured.

Fuka nodded. "You should. Let's do it together."

I NEVER WANT *to forget what happened here.*

I never want to forget the time I spent with everyone.

I made my own decision. I stopped feeling anxious.

I'm so happy to have met them all: Kokoro, Aki, Subaru, Ureshino, Masamune and Rion.

"AKI!"

Fuka was standing in front of the glowing mirror, calling out for Aki.

"Let's go home now, Aki-chan!"

But Aki didn't appear.

She stood in front of Kokoro's mirror, and pleaded. *I don't want to forget any of it. If someone's wish comes true, I'll forget everything.*

She was so angry at Aki's selfishness she could hardly speak.

"Please, Kokoro, the wish . . ."

Aki, whom she'd spent so much time with—she couldn't just vanish forever.

Not now, when we've promised to do our studying together—I just can't bear it.

Make a wish come true.

Find the key.

She begged this, from the bottom of her heart.

THE STABBING PAIN faded from Kokoro's forehead. She wiped away her tears, and laid her palm on the broken piano keys.

"Just hold on," she called, looking over at the desk, at Fuka's neatly arranged pens lying idle.

"I *will* help you. And then I'll say to you: I'm so happy I met you too, Fuka."

The room next to Fuka's belonged to Rion.

She hesitated for a moment, before turning the handle and pushing the door open.

It was definitely a boy's room. A burlap bag and football lay on the floor, things he must have brought with him at some point. Just like the other rooms, the Wolf Queen had trashed it. Even so, Kokoro thought: *This is clearly Rion's room.*

Just as Rion had said, there was an *X* underneath his bed. She scraped it lightly with her fingernail.

Rion had noticed that the Wolf Queen was not the wolf from *Little Red Riding Hood*, but from *The Wolf and the Seven Young Goats*.

How did he even know? And why didn't he tell anyone?

She was thinking this when she heard a singsong voice.

"KNOCK, KNOCK, KNOCK. It's your mother! No, it isn't! It's the wolf!"

A young girl—of elementary school age perhaps—had a book open on her lap and was reading aloud from it.

It was Rion's older sister, Mio-chan.

She was wearing a hospital gown and a cap. Kokoro saw she had no hair.

Rion was only five years old, and loved to come to the hospital to visit his sister.

Mio may have been bald, but her eyes were large, her skin creamy. Whenever Rion was asked in kindergarten who he would marry, he always answered, "Mio-chan!"

Mio-chan was so good at reading aloud, and she'd brought alive the same scene many times—"It's your mother! No, it isn't! It's the wolf!"—with all the appropriate facial expressions.

"OK, so who do *you* think it is?" she asked him. "The mother? Or the wolf?"

And Rion cried out, "It's the wolf!" as if he were inside the story himself.

"Well, then . . . we shall see, won't we . . ." said Mio-chan, turning the page.

She was skilled at making up her own stories as well. Rion thought she should write her own: of robots from the future, or the search for a spy in a locked house. She came up with so many amazing ideas, all of them far more fun than anything to be found in a book.

"All right, Rion. It's time to go home," their mother cut in, and they each nodded a reluctant "*Okaay.*"

They got up to leave the hospital ward, with its faint odor of disinfectant, and Rion took his parents' hands. "See you later, Rion," Mio-chan said, with a small wave.

"We'll come again tomorrow, Mio."

As they were walking home along the tree-lined road, the autumn leaves a burnished gold, Rion's mother suddenly turned to him and said, "Rion, I don't think it's such a good idea for Mio-chan to read that story."

"Why not?"

His mother's hand, grasping his own so tightly, was trembling.

"*The Wolf and the Seven Young Goats,*" she replied, sounding irritated, "was the play that Mio was supposed to be in at kindergarten. I'm sure she hasn't forgotten."

"Come now," Rion's father said. "That's a long time ago, and I don't think Mio remembers. She likes that book, and they both seem to enjoy it."

"*Oh, be quiet!*" Rion's mother shouted. She sank down on to the ground. "Why?" A tiny whisper escaped her lips. "Why Mio? Why did it have to be her?"

Rion stared in shock at his hand, which his mother had shaken off. His father was rubbing her back. He helped her to her feet.

Rion stared at his parents, confused. "I'm sorry," he said.

He thought they were angry at him. But his mother didn't reply, just silently bit her lip. "It's OK," his father said instead, and ruffled his hair with his fingers.

"RION?" HIS SISTER said to him, another day when he was visiting the hospital. "You stay well, OK, and be with Mum and Dad always."

"Uh—OK."

Rion really didn't know what she was getting at, but nodded anyway. Mio smiled.

A new decoration had arrived in her ward that day. A miniature Christmas tree had been placed by the window, and Rion realized what season it was.

On her bed lay a large toy which she had been playing with: an exquisite doll's house, each perfectly formed room brightly lit with tiny bulbs. It was foreign made and an English instruction book lay open beside it.

"If I'm not here anymore," Mio said, "I'll hope for one single wish for you, Rion. I'm sorry you've had to put up with so much. You missed that trip, and then Mum couldn't go to your dance recital either, could she?"

Rion couldn't understand why she was bringing these things up, and he stared at her blankly.

Mio-chan was stuck in a bed, and so not being able to go on a trip, or Mum not attending whatever—it was only to be expected. What was she talking about?

"I'll hope for one wish for you," Mio-chan said again.

"I want to be able to walk with you to school," he said. Rion would soon be going into elementary school.

His sister was silent. Rion wondered why she'd suddenly gone quiet.

After a while, she looked up and shook her head.

"Next year when you start elementary school, Rion, I'll be in junior high. We won't be going to the same school." She paused. "But if I do go back to that school, then I want the same as you—to walk to school together, Rion, and to play with you."

Her junior high uniform was hanging on the wall.

HE WAS SURE she would never die. But then she did.

The last time he spoke to her was only a few hours earlier.

She reached out a hand to his and, in a barely audible whisper, said, "Rion . . . I'm sorry I scared you. But I had a good time."

Rion remembered thinking that even up till the moment she died, she was always thinking about others.

Like she said, seeing her suffer was indeed very scary. Rion couldn't stop crying; from fear, but also from not wanting to say goodbye.

Her funeral was at the beginning of April; a spring rain was falling as Rion sat beside his father. His mother was a pale shell of her former self, and when a guest came up to her she merely bowed, her eyes vacant.

You stay well, OK, and be with Mum and Dad always.

Rion finally understood what his sister's words meant.

Her junior high uniform hung in her hospital room for a year. They'd hung it there in the hope that she would one day start, but she never wore it, not even once.

"YOU'RE REALLY LUCKY, to be so healthy."

The first time his mother said this was when Rion was in first grade in elementary school, the same age Mio had been when she fell sick.

Rion had joined a local football team and was beginning to enjoy learning a new sport. And then, as Rion was about to go out to play, ball in hand, his mother said, "If only she'd had half the energy you have."

Rion was caught off guard.

He couldn't think what to say. "Uh . . ." he managed.

"*Uh* . . . you say," his mother mocked, and lowered her eyes.

They had been told of Mio's condition while his mother was pregnant with Rion. Simultaneously monitoring Mio's treatment and taking care of baby Rion overwhelmed her for several years, and Rion knew she resented having to manage both of them at the same time.

Photos of his sister were on display on the far wall of the living room.

There was a photo of her last piano recital before she went into the hospital, a photo of the whole family, a photo of Mio and her mother in the hospital just before she passed away. And over by the window, they kept the exquisite doll's house her parents had bought for her, and which she had loved so much.

Even if I'm healthy, and living with them . . .

That wouldn't comfort his parents. Rion wasn't sure when he'd realized this, but he had become certain of it.

He was more sporty than his peers. But even that made his mother wonder why. "Why is the younger brother so much stronger than his older sister?

"If only a little bit of that good health could have rubbed off on Mio . . ."

"Rion-kun is quite amazing, isn't he? I heard a scout's coming from a club team to check him out," one of the other mothers had said to Rion's mother.

But Rion's mother downplayed it. "He's not that good . . ." she said, shaking her head. "He does it because he enjoys it, but it's not as if that's what his father and I want for him."

RION WAS SURE he'd continue to play football in a club team with his friends, and go to the same junior high together.

But when he was in sixth grade, his mother handed him a brochure. "Have a look at this," she said.

The brochure was for a school in Hawaii.

When he saw it was a boarding school, Rion's heart froze.

He despised the very thought of it.

"I thought it would be a huge opportunity for you," his mother said.

She stared at him solemnly, and he suddenly realized. His mother wanted him far away.

"WOW, A SCHOOL in Hawaii?"

"Some professional players went to that school, right?"

"Rion, you're amazing."

The more his friends commented, the harder it got for him to back down. And he himself started to think maybe this was all for the best.

"I'm sure it's a good school, but what did Rion say about it?"

"He said he'd like to go."

He overheard his parents talking one evening. His father had just got home from work. "Are you sure?" he asked. "Kids still in elementary school don't know what they want. They just do what their parents tell them. Are you sure that's what he said?"

"He did. He said he'd like to go."

Listening to his father, Rion thought, *No, Dad, you're wrong.*

Elementary school kids do know what they want.

Even I can see that if I stay here a moment longer, it'll only cause you both more pain.

And I feel the same way—I want to get away from you.

I don't know what to do, Mio. I'm sorry.

I kept well, but I wasn't any use.

HIS MOTHER HAD come to visit him at Christmas, and baked him a cake—then she'd gone home.

She hadn't said a word about taking him back with her for the New Year holiday.

It was late afternoon, and he was lying on his bed in his dorm. He stared at the dead mirror, hoping it would start to shine. He gave it a stroke—"Come on, shine, mirror, shine."

When it finally did begin to glisten with its rainbow colors, he broke into a wide smile. He put on his watch and ever so slowly thrust his hand inside.

AOOOOOOOOOOOOOOOOOOOOO!

"Aki-chan, where are you? It'll be time soon and we need to go home. The howling has started."

"It's OK, Ureshino. There's nothing we can do."

"Why don't we go home now, just us. Time's running out."

He tried to go into the mirror, but was pulled back.

This is bad, he told himself, *this is really bad.*

"Subaru. Over here! We've got to get Kokoro in!" He turned to face Kokoro's mirror. "Kokoro's the only one of us who didn't come today, so she won't be forced back and eaten. We've got to get Kokoro to help—"

Honestly, he'd known all along.

That the Wolf Queen's insistence on calling them "Little Red Riding Hoods" was completely fake.

There are seven of us.

According to the fairy tale, the key had to be inside the grandfather clock.

The piece of knowledge that Rion had kept to himself, thinking it was he who would be granted a wish.

KOKORO'S FOREHEAD ACHED.

She felt a massive blow to her face.

As if she were practicing on a horizontal bar and accidentally smacked her face against it.

At that moment, Rion's shape started to break up. She heard a voice.

"Your wish—"

Whose voice, she didn't know. She wasn't sure if she'd actually heard it, or imagined it. And then she heard another voice. A child's. A girl's.

"I—"

"I'm all right. So take her and—"

"Can you see it?"

A voice had intruded while she was experiencing someone else's memories.

Kokoro's eyes widened in astonishment. She pulled her hand out from under the bed and turned around. She screamed.

"WOLF QUEEN!"

The Wolf Queen had pushed open the door and was standing outside in the hallway.

Looking the same as ever.

A pinafore dress with frills, and the wolf mask.

Yet in the darkness of the castle, now engulfed by some weird force, she seemed different. Kokoro's immediate instinct was to move away, but from the small room there was no other exit. The Wolf Queen stood, as if blocking the door.

Kokoro got to her feet and was about to push past when the Wolf Queen said, "Wait!" She let out an exaggerated sigh and folded her arms.

"This is the second time you've tried to run away, isn't it. I remember you on that very first day."

"Well, what do you expect . . ."

What do you expect when there's a wolf lurking about who is known to have gobbled up six living creatures?

Kokoro had the feeling this little Wolf Queen had created herself in the image of that wolf. And all the while, Kokoro had been trying her best to avoid any attention from her, but now . . .

I never expected we'd actually be having a conversation, Kokoro thought.

Just moments earlier, she'd been terrified out of her wits, yet now she was feeling so much calmer.

When she looked closely at the Wolf Queen's dress, she had to reconsider her theory. The hem was ragged and torn. The frills were ripped and frayed. Her entire outfit including the wolf mask was damaged and dirty.

"Even I can't do anything about it. Once the rules are broken it can't be stopped," said the Wolf Queen. "That was the condition when I created it. There's always a price to pay."

The Wolf Queen pointed the muzzle of her wolf mask towards Kokoro.

"You, however, will not be eaten. You've had a narrow escape."

"But the others—"

"They're buried. You saw them, didn't you? Underneath those *X* marks."

Ah, Kokoro thought, and shut her eyes.

The *X*'s did remind her of grave markers.

"You noticed?" the Wolf Queen asked with a drawl.

Kokoro thought she knew what she was asking. "Um," she replied. "I think I did."

"I see."

"Could you tell me something, Wolf Queen?"

"Now what?"

"We're able to 'meet,' aren't we?"

The Wolf Queen fell silent for a moment.

As ever, Kokoro couldn't see her expression behind the mask: maybe she didn't actually have a face? The lonely keeper of the castle in the mirror. *This wolf mask might be the only face this girl's ever had.*

Was she an enemy, or an ally? Kokoro wasn't at all sure.

Kokoro pushed her line of questioning a little further.

"I don't mean immediately, but at some point in the future, we'll probably be able to meet. Won't we?"

"Only if you get home safely now," the Wolf Queen said.

Kokoro took this as a yes. *So it's true*, she thought, mulling it over.

"It's not my intention for you all to be eaten." The Wolf Queen aimed her muzzle petulantly at the ceiling. She turned back to Kokoro. "The rest depends on you," she said. "Oh, and by the way, Aki is currently in the Wishing Room." Then, she vanished.

You've had a narrow escape.

The Wolf Queen's words rang inside her head.

AKI'S ROOM WAS closest to the grand foyer along the hallway.

Kokoro took a deep breath.

"No hesitating this time," she said quietly.

She was going to save Aki.

She was going to bring that tricky girl back.

To stay in the castle past the agreed curfew was an act of suicide. And yet she'd done it anyway.

Aki's words always seemed to have a spiteful edge.

So our memories vanish. So what?

It's OK, isn't it, if a wish comes true? If someone finds the key, I mean.

If we can't see each other in the outside world, all we'll have left at the end is our memories, no? Isn't that a bit of a waste?

Wow, that's really something—parents considering your future and stuff. Not like our parents, right, Kokoro?

Gently, she turned the handle to Aki's room and pushed open the door.

The wardrobe was open. She looked around quickly for the X inside it. There it was.

She placed the tip of her forefinger over the mark.

And Aki's memories came flooding in.

THE SMELL OF incense.

Aki was sitting in front of the commemorative photograph of her recently deceased grandmother.

She was wearing her school uniform and sitting beside her mother and cousins.

The man seated beside her mother was her stepfather.

Her mother always said her father had been totally self-absorbed. He had left them when she was still very young. "If I hadn't got pregnant with you," she said, "we would probably never have got married. In the end we broke up, so there we are."

This was how she explained things to her daughter.

Despite this, whenever their relatives got together, she'd go on about how his sports business in Chiba provided all the equipment for the local teams that went on to play in the national baseball tournament in Koshien Stadium.

The commemorative photograph showed her grandmother when she was much younger. Her uncles complained that the last time she'd had a decent portrait taken was a long time ago, and so the only photos they had of her were out of date.

When Aki dyed her hair, her grandmother had let out a shriek.

Aki was sure she was going to shout at her, but actually her reaction was joyful. "What a lovely color!" she said, and Aki was both deflated and happy.

Her grandmother had been a lively character who loved a joke, the total opposite of Aki's mother. So different that it made Aki wonder how she could possibly have given birth to her. "Don't let your mother find out," her grandmother said whenever she gave her any money. "If she finds it, she'll spend it. This is our little secret, Akiko, just you and me," she added, with a clumsy wink.

When Aki introduced her to Atsushi, a college student she'd met through telephone dating, her grandmother's only reaction was to exclaim "Goodness gracious," before presenting him with *senbei* crackers, green tea and pickled vegetables. Aki was embarrassed by her old folks' hospitality, but Atsushi enjoyed it.

"I didn't expect you'd introduce me to your family so quickly," Atsushi said.

"Sorry," Aki said. "Is it a bit depressing?"

"Not at all," he said.

Atsushi was twenty-three, but had never had a girlfriend. "You're my first," he said, "and I want to look after you. I don't have much money, but I do want to get married."

But Atsushi didn't come to her grandmother's funeral.

They hardly communicated these days. She'd send him a message on his pager, and get no reply.

"Atsushi-kun's the only person I really wanted to be there."

"You poor child."

This was from an old woman who said she was a friend of her grandmother. She turned to Aki's mother and scowled. "You've never paid her any attention."

Aki wanted her to mind her own business.

But my mother's house is the only place for me to go, thought Aki, *so what's going to become of me?*

AKI WAS BACK from the funeral, and alone in her bedroom, when she heard a familiar voice.

"Maiko, Maiko. Where are you?"

He'd come looking for her mother, even though Aki's mother had said she was extremely busy and would be back home late.

Aki hoped he'd give up and leave, but it only made him keener: "Maiko! Maiko! Hey, Maiko!"

"She's not here!"

He barged suddenly into her room, and Aki drew up her legs on the bed and screamed, "SHE'S NOT HERE. She's not home yet."

"Oh, Akiko, you're here."

Aki's stepfather had forced open the sliding door to her Japanese-style room, and was now staring at her. His necktie was askew, the buttons on his shirt undone.

His face looked flushed and his breath stank of alcohol. Aki shrank back further.

Oh God, she thought. Usually she hid in her mother's wardrobe, staying totally quiet while he was around.

She made a sudden dash to get out of the room.

"Wait! Where are you going?"

He tried to catch her by the shirt and cajole her into staying.

When she ignored him, he grabbed her bare arm, his sweaty palm finding a firm grip. Her legs began to tremble.

"NO!" she shrieked.

Her stepfather pulled her towards him, clamping down her arms.

"ATSUSHI-KUN!" screamed Aki.

He slipped his hand inside the neck of her school shirt. With his other hand he covered her mouth.

"Help me!" breathed Aki.

She began to kick and kick. She turned and managed to knee him between the legs, broke free and fled into the living room, propping the sliding door shut with a broom handle. She grabbed the telephone sitting on a small table in the corner, knocking over the memo pad, calendar and pen stand. She struggled to recall the correct numbers she needed to send a message, frantically converting the letters of her message into the appropriate numbers.

Four-one—*Ta* . . . three-three—*Su* . . . two-four—*Ke* . . . four-four—*Te*. Each set of numbers standing for a Japanese syllable. *Ta-su-ke-te* . . . *Help!*

"Akiko! Akiko!" shouted her stepfather from beyond the sliding door, shaking it so violently she thought it might break.

She threw the phone on the floor and let out a long scream.

At that moment, a small but distinct light caught her eye.

A small mirror lying on the floor had begun to shine.

Usually it was the mirror in her bedroom that shone, but this light came from her mother's small hand mirror. The Wolf Queen had told them she wouldn't allow any mirror to shine if adults were around.

"Akiko!"

A roar came from behind the sliding door which her stepfather was vigorously rattling. It wouldn't take much before it came crashing to the floor. She placed her hand on the small round face of the shining mirror and let herself slip inside.

It was a small mirror, but strangely enough her whole body passed smoothly through it.

She looked around and realized she was back in the grand foyer of the castle.

Her heart was pounding, her arms and legs still covered in goosebumps. The top buttons on her shirt were ripped open.

The Wolf Queen was standing in front of her.

She was holding a small hand mirror, the size of the one Aki had just passed through. And it was shining, in rainbow colors.

"Wolf Queen!"

Aki's breathing was still ragged. Why had she made her mother's mirror shine? She'd allowed her to come here, even when an adult had been around.

"I had to step in. Because you were in a tight spot," the Wolf Queen said.

Aki knew the Wolf Queen had seen everything. The Wolf Queen cocked her head—not in her usual sneering way, but in the manner of a small girl.

"You mean, you'd rather I didn't help you?"

"No." Aki shook her head. Over and over. "Not at all. Thank you, thank you, thank you."

Now the tears came, flowing down her cheeks. Her body started to tremble. She reached out to hold the Wolf Queen's hand. The Wolf Queen didn't refuse it.

It was warm, and smooth, and tiny. Holding it made Aki feel as if she too could be pure and beautiful.

"Can't I . . . live here properly?" Aki asked, shoulders heaving.

Her grandmother's face misted over in the distance.

"That's completely impossible."

The Wolf Queen had resumed her customary arrogance.

Aki gritted her teeth.

"But I don't want to go back . . ."

Spending every moment trying to avoid her stepfather, her friends, her school—she hated all of it.

I was always the best player on the volleyball team, she thought, *and it*

322

irritated me to see the other girls just standing there. "Stop being so spaced out!" I used to shout. Perhaps I overdid it a bit. We'd gather the younger, less experienced girls, and we older ones would surround them and demand they tell us exactly what the hell they thought they were doing.

Every club used to do it, and it wasn't as if I was the only one, yet before I knew it those kids, and everyone else, were telling me they wouldn't put up with my attitude.

My presence was destroying the volleyball team.

They told me I was a bully.

That wasn't what I intended, and yet it turned out I was the one they wanted out. There was nothing for it but to leave the team.

"That's completely impossible," the Wolf Queen said again.

But she seemed to be keeping something back. She didn't shake off Aki's hand, but instead held it tightly. Which made Aki very happy.

AKI WAS CROUCHED on the sofa in the Game Room.

And then—Kokoro walked in. She gazed at Aki as if she couldn't believe what she was seeing. She was staring at Aki's school uniform.

"Aki-chan, do you go to Yukishina No. 5 Junior High?"

Aki slowly followed Kokoro's eyeline and looked down at her own uniform.

"Yes," Aki said. "Yukishina No. 5."

Kokoro's eyes had widened with astonishment.

A few moments later, Masamune and Subaru came through the door, one behind the other. "It's exactly the same uniform worn by the girls at my school!" Masamune said, joining in the conversation.

We are all—all of us—at the same school.

Which means—

"We could all help each other."

Aki took Masamune's words the most seriously.

Because, she said to herself, *I'm the one who really wants help.*

THERE WAS NO answer that day from Atsushi-kun to the message she'd left him.

No reaction to my desperate call for help. Aki realized for the first time that, though she knew his pager number, he'd never actually given her his phone number.

She'd told him all about her problems with her stepfather.

Atsushi had promised her he'd protect her, that he'd never let anything like that happen again.

But these guys—they'll really help me.

They'll stand up to it all with me.

BUT ON THAT January day, when she'd gone over to the nurse's office, wanting to support Masamune, truly wanting to do what she could, no one else had turned up.

It had been so cold.

Looking out of the window of the nurse's office at the pale sky, Aki felt betrayed.

"Ma'am, is it true that Aki has come into school today?"

Outside the door of the nurse's office, she overheard the voice of Misuzu from the volleyball team.

It made her want to run.

The nurse was warming her hands over the portable heater and Aki had clung to her, weeping. "Please, tell her I'm not here. Even if they all come, *please* don't tell them I'm here."

Aki crawled into the small bed in the office, pulled the covers up over her, and lay there trembling.

She did know. She did. That she was behaving badly.

The other girls all had a good laugh, placing prank calls to telephone sex chat lines, but they acted as a group. No one ever did that sort of thing without the others.

I'm not like Misuzu and the others anymore, not at all.

324

I FOUND OUT that the kids in the castle didn't betray me, but that doesn't make it any better.

The fact remains: we can't see each other outside.

"I can be a bit slow, and don't exactly understand all that stuff about parallel worlds, but what you're saying is we can never meet up in the outside world?" Rion said.

"Yep." Masamune nodded.

"You mean we *can't* help each other?"

"That's right. We can't help each other."

THE MONTH OF March was almost over.

Please, make my life a bit more tolerable.

Make my mother stronger.

Please kill my stepfather.

Please take me back to a time when the girls in the volleyball club didn't all hate me.

If none of these wishes can come true, I'm going to stay in this castle forever.

I made up my mind the day before it was all due to be over.

I hid inside the wardrobe in my room, and I waited for five o'clock to come and go.

"AKI-CHAN! AKI-CHAN, where are you?"

I heard Ureshino calling my name, while he looked frantically for me.

I'm sorry, Ureshino.

Everyone, I'm sorry.

I can't do this on my own anymore.

I'm sorry you got mixed up in this.

I don't want to go home.

I don't want to go on living.

I just can't bear it anymore.

AOOOOOOOOOOOOOOOOOOOOOOOO!

Aoooooooooooooooooooooooo!

I heard the howling.

An overpowering light began to fill the castle.

The wardrobe door was being pulled open.

A wolf, with its mouth wide open, was staring at me—

"DON'T RUN AWAY! Come over here! Give me your hand! Aki, *please!*"

"Aki, keep breathing!"

"Aki, it's going to be OK!"

"Aki!"

"Aki!"

"Aki!"

"Aki!"

"Aki!"

I suddenly notice the door is closed.

Someone is banging on it. Over and over, calling my name.

It's—Kokoro.

"It's OK, Aki! Aki-chan! We *can* help each other! We *can* meet! We can see each other again! So you have to live! You've got to keep going, and grow up to be an adult.

"Please, Aki. I'm . . . in the future. In the future, where you are too. Where you're all grown up!"

The voice came closer.

In her confused mind, Aki suddenly thought, *What the hell?*

Kokoro sounded as though she was crying. Crying and pounding on the door.

"The times we all live in—the years—they're all different!" Kokoro said. "We're not in parallel worlds at all. We're all students at Yukishina No. 5 Junior High, but we live in different time periods. *We are all living in the same world!*"

* * *

IT ALL STARTED with something Tojo-san had said.

When are you moving?

The first of April.

Very soon, then.

Can't help it. Dad wanted to move in March, but the first of April is a Saturday this year so he has the day off.

This year.

Something about this statement stayed with Kokoro.

Come to think of it . . .

The other kids in the castle were living through different days of the week. They didn't match.

Nor did the day of the week when the opening ceremony at school was held.

Nor did the holidays—like Coming-of-Age Day.

She should have considered all this earlier.

That the weather was different.

Their shopping centers were different.

As was the geography of their district.

As were their teachers and the number of classes in each school year.

But *the entirety of their worlds* was the same.

SHE FIRST BEGAN to notice it when she was experiencing Ureshino's memories.

That day in January when he thought he'd been stood up by them.

While he was waiting for the others to turn up, Ureshino ate his rice balls. It was a Sunday and he felt content, and contemplated the sky.

Just then Ureshino's mother arrived. Someone was with her. A kindly-looking woman with tiny grey streaks in her hair. Wrinkles formed around her eyes when she smiled.

Ureshino called her "Kitajima-sensei."

She was different from the Ms. Kitajima Kokoro knew. But she knew instantly who she was. She was just much older than the woman Kokoro knew. In Kokoro's reality, Ms. Kitajima was a much younger teacher, with no grey hair or wrinkles.

As she considered this, she remembered something else.

They'd been hanging out in the castle and she was talking to Ureshino about Ms. Kitajima.

She's so pretty, Ms. Kitajima, Kokoro had said.

Pretty? Ureshino seemed to have his heart set on any eligible female within sight—and Ms. Kitajima would certainly fit the bill—and so this reaction was odd. Kokoro had wondered about it for a good long while.

In Ureshino's reality, Ms. Kitajima was not the attractive young teacher that Kokoro knew.

SHE REALIZED THERE was something about Masamune's memories, too, that had bothered her.

They're not going to bail on me. I know it.

He was talking to himself, not to anyone else. His voice was wobbly.

They're gonna come. I know it.

The hand kept rubbing his back.

Something must have prevented your friends from coming.

In this memory, she had much longer hair than the Ms. Kitajima Kokoro knew.

This was, again, an older Ms. Kitajima.

Which is why she wanted to probe each of their memories.

To get them to show her how it was for each of them.

SUBARU'S WALKMAN, FOR example.

Subaru took a music player out of his bag, connected to earphones, a model Kokoro had never seen before, and in the memory Subaru had been listening to cassette tapes. This player was far heavier and sturdier than anything she'd ever seen anyone carrying around with them.

BUT WHAT REALLY confirmed it all for her was her experience of Fuka's memory.

When she played the piano there was a calendar beside her, with the date of her summer piano competition marked in red.

The calendar year was 2019.

Not 2005, which was last year for Kokoro.

AND WHEN SHE entered Aki's memories, she had further confirmation.

Nowadays even students owned cell phones, but Aki communicated by pager. When Kokoro was younger, her mother had had a pager, which she used to keep in touch with her workplace and with Kokoro's father, so she was fairly familiar with how it worked. It wasn't a device to talk on, but to send a one-way message. "Pocket bell" was the Japanese for it, a term her mum used to use.

As Aki had tried to type in a message to the pager, in her haste she'd knocked over a calendar on the table. The calendar read 1991.

If Kokoro matched up all the others' realities, an even clearer timeline would emerge, she was sure.

For Aki, Kokoro was from the future.

For Fuka, Kokoro was living in the past.

I never said you can't meet up, or can't help each other. It's time you people worked things out. Think *about it.*

The Wolf Queen's words were on the nail.

We can *meet.*

We won't look as we do now, we'll be a different age, but it's not true at all that we won't be able to see each other.

"Aki-chan!"

Kokoro opened up the door to the body of the grandfather clock and called out.

A key was hidden behind the pendulum.

She took hold of the key and spied a small keyhole in the back of the clock.

So this *is where it is,* Kokoro thought.

The Wishing Room.

They'd looked all over, and all this time it was hidden in an obvious place.

Kokoro inserted the key into the hole. There was a creaking sound as the back of the clock cracked open.

Kokoro closed her eyes, and made her wish.

Save Aki.

"Please!" she shouted. "Please, save Aki! Please forget that she broke the rules."

Light spilled out.

Not the muddy light from earlier, or the brutal overpowering light.

But a milky, soft light that enveloped Kokoro.

"*Aki!*" Kokoro shouted desperately into the light.

Hang in there.

"We *can* all meet each other!"

Kokoro recalled the scene in *The Wolf and the Seven Young Goats* when the mother goat opens up the grandfather clock where the youngest goat is hiding.

Aki, come out, Kokoro wished, and reached her hand through the open door.

"Don't run away! Come over here! Give me your hand! Aki, *please!*"

She was shouting at the top of her voice.

"It's OK, Aki! Aki-chan! We *can* help each other! We *can* meet! We can see each other again! So you have to live! You've got to keep going, and grow up to be an adult.

"Please, Aki. I'm . . . in the future. In the future, where you are too. Where you're all grown up!"

Kokoro felt something soft and warm.

Someone was grasping her hand.

Kokoro shut her eyes tight, and grabbed the hand back as firmly as she could. *No way am I going to let you go.*

"Kokoro?"

"Yes. It's me, Kokoro!" Her face was wet with tears. Aki's hand. She would never, ever let it go. "I came to get you."

"Kokoro—I'm so sorry. I—"

"It doesn't matter!" Kokoro was shouting, her voice welling up from deep inside her. "It just doesn't matter! You've got to come *baaaack!*"

Her voice cracked.

With every ounce of strength, she pulled the hand towards her.

At that moment—

"Kokoro!" a voice said. Not Aki's, but someone from behind her.

She barely had time to think before she felt a hand on her shoulder. She turned around with a jolt.

It was Fuka.

Fuka, and Subaru, and Masamune, and Ureshino, and Rion.

They'd all come back. Her wish had been granted.

"Is it Aki?" Masamune asked, and Kokoro nodded.

"Yes!"

That short exchange was enough. While Kokoro thrust her hand beyond the clock, the friends took hold of her and each other in a line like in a tug-of-war, and they yanked with every ounce of strength they could muster.

"Heave-ho!" she heard Subaru call out.

"We're not letting go of you, even if it means we all die!"

She felt something slipping.

They all shut their eyes and pulled harder.

This wasn't *The Wolf and the Seven Young Goats*, but more like the Grimms' story *The Enormous Turnip*, Kokoro thought. And suddenly she felt a weight lifted off her.

We can do it, she said to herself.

"Here we go, Aki!"

"*Heeeave-hooo!*" they shouted. The tops of Aki's fingers began to emerge from behind the clock.

The momentum sent them all tumbling backward down the staircase.

AT THE TOP of the staircase, in front of the grandfather clock, lay Aki.

"Aki!" Kokoro shouted, and raced back up the stairs.

"Aki, you idiot!" both Masamune and Rion said. "Seriously, you deserve a good kick in the butt," added Rion.

Aki looked as if she'd just emerged from underwater.

Her face was all wet—she'd been crying so hard and for so long.

"I'm so sorry!" Aki managed to speak through her sobs. Eyes bloodshot, she looked at each of them in turn.

"I'm so sorry. I—"

"You complete idiot!" This from Fuka, echoing the boys. Fuka's face was just as flushed and wet with tears as Aki's. "What are we going to do!" she squealed. "We've used up our one wish—to rescue you!"

"I'm truly, truly sorry. I—"

"Thank God," Fuka said, and clung to Aki's neck in a tight hug. "Thank God you're all right."

Aki's eyes widened, but they were blank. Arms wrapped around Fuka, she gazed at each of them again.

Perhaps she noticed that they weren't actually angry.

She let out a long, deep sigh.

WITHOUT WARNING, THEY became aware of the sound of hands softly clapping.

They knew without even turning around who it was.

They also knew that their last hour of friendship was here. They knew, and they were ready.

Since the wish had been granted, the group would now lose all memory of ever having been to the castle.

The moment of farewell had finally arrived.

"Wolf Queen."

As one they turned to face her.

"Well done, indeed."

She was standing at the bottom of the staircase in the grand foyer, daintily clapping her small hands.

Closure

SUBARU WAS IN 1985.
　Aki, 1992.
　Kokoro and Rion, 2006.
　Masamune, 2013.
　Fuka, 2020.
　Ureshino, ?

THEY CHECKED WITH each other to see what year they were living in and where.

In the trashed Game Room, they spread out a sheet of paper and wrote it all down.

"I don't remember what year it is," Ureshino said, and the rest knew exactly where he was coming from.

Sometimes you could be well aware of the day of the week and the month, but scarcely aware of the actual year.

A stir swept through them as they digested each other's details, particularly the moment they realized that Subaru was still in 1985.

"That's back in Emperor Shōwa's era!" Masamune said, and Subaru replied, "Sure. Sounds about right." But he looked confused, and Kokoro realized even the mention of Shōwa didn't click with him.

Then Subaru said: "Didn't the world end in 1999? You know, after Nostradamus's great prophecy? Whoa. It's a relief to know it didn't." He smiled and no one knew if he was joking or not, or whether he had actually believed it.

"Of course it never ended," Masamune said caustically. "I mean, when you were playing my state-of-the-art video games, didn't you ever think anything was weird? Maybe that the screen was so clear and sharp? Back in your time, Subaru, weren't consoles really simple machines?"

"I never played them much, so I just thought that's what they must be like. You said your friend made the game, so I thought it wasn't on sale yet and you'd got hold of an advance copy or something."

"Me too," Kokoro said. "I did think it was quite odd. The Nintendo DS you had, Masamune, wasn't like the one I have."

Kokoro had convinced herself that, if parallel worlds existed, it would be possible that their gaming devices would not be identical.

"You're talking about the first-generation Nintendo DS, aren't you? The one I was using is the third-generation DS."

Masamune scrutinized Subaru as if studying his features for the first time. "I just don't believe it. Subaru and I are, what . . . twenty-nine years apart in age?"

The paper recording all their timelines was now filled with myriad scribbled calculations.

"You're pretty sharp though, Kokoro, to notice. I never ever thought for a moment that we didn't come from the same time period."

"I can't believe it," Rion said, "but it does seem more likely than the parallel world idea Masamune had."

"Yeah, yeah," Masamune said, frowning a bit. "Sorry I scared you."

"Look, aren't there seven years between each of us?" Fuka laid a finger across each of their years. "Seven might be an especially significant number here. There are seven of us, and the seven hiding places were taken from the story *The Wolf and the Seven Young Goats*."

"You're right."

Once they'd established this fact, all kinds of other things became clear.

For instance, all the different iterations of the shopping center, and the location of McDonald's.

Aki came from Minami Tokyo City of the *past*.

In the future, Careo probably developed into an even bigger shopping mall with its own movie theatre. Just as Masamune and Fuka described it.

"So Ureshino must be from between Aki and Kokoro's years. There's a fourteen-year gap there, instead of seven. So Ureshino should be from the year 1999, no?"

"Eh? Really?" Ureshino looked pensive for a moment, but then shook his head. "Nah, I don't think so. I mean, I was born in 2013."

"*What?*" they exclaimed.

"So that would mean . . ." Fuka said, gazing off as she computed the numbers. "That for you, Ureshino, right now it is 2027. You should have told us that from the start."

"2027! That's really incredible! So you're from way off in the future?" Subaru said, looking stunned.

"I guess I am," Ureshino said, tilting his head.

Listening to this exchange, Kokoro said quietly, "Just wow . . ."

In the 2006 that she lived in, Ureshino wasn't even born yet. It was hard to wrap her mind around it.

"So Kokoro, Rion and I are the only ones with fourteen years between us," Aki murmured slowly. "How come?"

After such prolonged crying, Aki's face was still pale, but Kokoro could sense she was getting back to her normal self. She was relieved that Aki was now contributing. "I've no idea," Kokoro replied after a moment, shaking her head. "It would make more sense if there was somebody in between us . . . It's sort of strange as it is."

"But I can see how it might work," Fuka said slowly, and everyone looked at her. Fuka glanced at Aki, sitting cross-legged on the floor. "Do you remember the last day of February, when there was no one else in the castle? It was just the two of us. We called the Wolf Queen, but she didn't appear either."

"Yeah, I do."

Ah, Kokoro thought. The two of them had had a strained relationship in the early days, but towards the beginning of March she'd noticed how they were getting on so much better, and she'd thought it quite odd, and wondered at what point they'd made up.

"That must have been a leap year."

"Ah . . ."

"Every four years there's an extra day on the twenty-ninth of February. Aki's is in 1992, and mine in 2020, but no one else had one. So for you it was suddenly the first of March, no?"

"You're right . . ."

"We are the only two who gained a day."

Fuka's use of *gained* was a bit odd. As she listened, Kokoro began to work something out.

"Holidays, too," she said.

"Holidays?"

"In January when we discussed what day the school opening ceremony was, we started talking about Coming-of-Age Day, remember? Subaru said it was on the fifteenth, and we talked about how in parallel worlds it would fall on a different day for all of us."

Back then, Subaru and Aki had said:

Coming-of-Age Day is the fifteenth, isn't it? I didn't think it was a two-day holiday.

The opening ceremony's one thing, but I thought Coming-of-Age Day would be the same for everyone.

"So back in Aki's time they hadn't yet linked holidays with weekends? I'd heard that that's how they used to do it."

"Is that really what happened? They moved the holidays?"

"Yeah. It's the Happy Monday System . . ."

"Happy Monday?!" Aki exclaimed, then burst out laughing. "What a silly name. Kokoro, are you playing games with me?"

"No, I promise I'm not! I didn't make it up. It really exists!"

Kokoro wasn't used to being laughed at, and rose to defend herself.

But at the same time she thought, *Good—Aki's quickly getting back to her feisty old self again.*

"One more thing—back in your day, Aki and Subaru, you went to school on Saturdays, didn't you?" Fuka said.

Kokoro was startled. *The system of two days off per week.*

Until third grade in elementary school, Kokoro's school had every second Saturday off. And she'd really enjoyed having an extra day off every other week.

Once Aki had mentioned how she and her boyfriend had been stopped by a truancy officer while they were out in town. Kokoro had thought it was because they looked as if they might have been about to cause trouble, but the real reason was that in Aki's time they still had lessons every Saturday, and she should have been at school.

When it came to this, Aki and Subaru's reactions were different.

"What? Saturday is going to be a day off?"

"Yes," Aki said, "that's what they said—one Saturday a month would be off, but I haven't been to school much so I wasn't really thinking about it." She carried on thinking aloud. "So in the period you're in, Kokoro, you never go to school on Saturdays? Wow—so we really are living in different times."

"Yeah." Kokoro nodded, and suddenly had a new thought. "For you people, are there still No. 2 and No. 4 junior highs in Minami Tokyo City?"

"What do you mean?"

Fuka answered, "They aren't there anymore, because the number of children in the area has dropped."

When Kokoro had made the visit to the alternative School, the teacher in charge there had said the same thing.

She'd said that after the cozy, relaxed atmosphere of elementary school, there were plenty of kids who had trouble fitting in when they started junior high. Especially with No. 5 Junior High, since it had grown so huge due to the reorganization and merging of schools.

Back when Aki had mentioned possibly repeating a year, Kokoro had asked if she planned to move to another nearby school. And Aki had said, *You mean, like No. 4 Junior High?* At the time it had struck Kokoro as odd, since there wasn't a No. 4 school anymore.

"Seriously? Is that right," Ureshino unexpectedly chimed in. He was staring at them, eyes wide. "I always wondered why our school is called No. 5 when there's no No. 4. Now I see. The schools all have odd numbers now, so I thought maybe even numbers were unlucky or something."

"Isn't that an insult to all the even-numbered schools around the country?"

Aki let out a long sigh. "The whole thing is so weird," she said. "You guys are about the same age as me, and we're all so alike, but Kokoro, you and Ureshino—everybody, in fact, apart from Subaru— you're all from the future."

"It feels strange to me too, to think you're from the past, Aki. I just can't get my head around it."

"Come to think of it, though, you and Rion are from the same year," Subaru said suddenly.

He was right.

And now they knew the full story, it explained the uneasy feeling Kokoro had had earlier, that there were just too many dropouts from the same school.

And how though he was also from 2006, Rion, who was actually studying abroad, was still included in the group.

"I think it's because I really wanted to go to Yukishina No. 5," Rion muttered. Exactly as the Wolf Queen had said to him before. "Maybe she summoned me here because I wanted to make friends in a Japanese school. To let me meet Kokoro."

"We really might have met," Kokoro said. Rion raised his head. Kokoro explained, "In the nurse's office back in January, at the beginning of the third semester."

It warmed Kokoro's heart to think that she and Rion were from the same period. Hawaii and Japan—if only the distance hadn't separated them, she might really have met Rion in the nurse's office that day. And yet if he hadn't gone abroad to school, Rion might have been an ordinary kid attending Yukishina No. 5, and would perhaps never have been invited to the castle. You never knew how chance could change things.

"Well, we're all going to forget all this anyway," Kokoro said.

Even if Rion came back to Japan and they passed each other on the street, neither would remember who the other one was.

The very thought was painful to her.

"Wolf Queen." Fuka turned around and looked at the Wolf Queen, who had been sitting silently in front of the fireplace for some time. "How much time do we have left?"

"I'll give you just under an hour," the Wolf Queen said, as if thoroughly bored by them all now. They watched as she got to her feet, the hem of her dress swishing.

"So you'd better get ready then."

THE WOLF QUEEN had arrived among them, gently applauding, and appeared as collected as ever.

Now that Aki had been rescued, the Wolf Queen's dress, which had been in tatters, was back in its usual pristine condition. Before they knew it, the darkened castle was now suddenly bright again.

"Well done!" she said, with a touch of sarcasm.

No one knew quite how to react.

Only Kokoro was brave enough to speak. "Wolf Queen . . ." she said.

The others stared at the Wolf Queen, a look of fear frozen on their faces.

Kokoro hadn't seen the version of the "huge wolf" for herself, so she didn't know the details of what it had done to them, but it was clear the others had experienced something unearthly before they were "buried" underneath their X mark. Just from the intensity of the howls, she sensed it was indescribable, and the kids themselves were not fully conscious of it.

"Why all the grimacing?" the Wolf Queen said dismissively. "Don't worry. Nothing will happen to you. I didn't really want to have to do it, anyway, and I never would have had to, if *somebody* hadn't broken the rules." The Wolf Queen cast a glance at the newly rescued Aki. "Think about what you did!"

"I'm so sorry."

Aki's face was still pale, and she started trembling again. The Wolf Queen nodded, accepting her apology. "Well, you're all safe now."

"Everything's out of kilter," Rion said. "I mean, I was so frightened, scared to death."

The Wolf Queen ignored him and pointed her muzzle towards Kokoro. Somehow she seemed to be smiling. "Well, *you* did well to work out what's going on here. To understand that this is a castle that transcends the rules of time."

"Um." Kokoro nodded, still confused. Her eyes met the girl's through the wolf mask. "You said something that led me to realize it will be possible for us to see each other. We're all at the same school, but from different periods across time."

Kokoro still remembered the question Rion had once asked.

It was the day Aki turned up in her school uniform, and they began to realize they were actually all at the same junior high.

You've done this before, bringing other Little Red Riding Hoods here and telling them they could have a wish granted, haven't you? Were those Little Red Riding Hoods also students at Yukishina No. 5 Junior High? Every few years you bring a group of them here, don't you? Rion had asked.

To his question, the Wolf Queen had replied: *Every few years—I think it's more consistent than that.*

Still cryptic, but she'd meant it literally.

She summoned children here with a fixed number of years between them.

342

Not able to meet? Not able to help each other? Neither one was true. So long as they uncovered the truth.

"The castle will be closing as pre-stated. Unfortunately, that will be today, not tomorrow," the Wolf Queen said haughtily.

They were prepared for this, but even so it was hard to hear.

"So our memories will disappear?" This from Fuka. "Will we really forget absolutely everything?"

"Right," the Wolf Queen said categorically. "As I explained to you all earlier, since you've found the key and the wish has now been granted, you will no longer remember a thing." She gazed at them steadily. "However." She paused and raised a forefinger. "I will grant you extra time."

"Extra time?"

"This is the Castle in the Mirror, where the rules of time are fluid. I can give you a moment of pause, before each of you goes back through your mirror. Be ready, and please make sure you don't leave anything behind."

It was just like the closing ceremony at the end of a school year, Kokoro thought. When the teachers instructed them to make sure they took all their belongings home from their lockers and desks.

"Check your own rooms, and the Game Room," the Wolf Queen said. "From tomorrow you will no longer have access. For now, I have stopped the flow of time outside. You will be able to return to your world by seven o'clock, Japan time. Your parents may tell you off, but they won't be too cross."

It felt a little odd, while surrounded by the scattered ornaments of the wrecked castle, to hear her sounding so concerned for them, but it seemed appropriate. "Don't we have to tidy up here?" Ureshino asked. The pillars were cracked, the walls soiled, overturned furniture and crockery scattered everywhere; the castle looked like it had been hit by a tornado, and they felt uneasy about leaving it like that. Ureshino continued hesitantly, "So, are you OK for us to just pick up our own stuff? Won't it be a huge job for you to clean the mess all by yourself?"

"It won't be a problem, not at all," the Wolf Queen replied, with a dismissive wave of her thin arm. Then she looked more directly at Ureshino. "You're a pretty decent guy, aren't you?"

The group exchanged an astonished look. This moment of humanity was not what they'd come to expect from their wolf.

"OK, I have a suggestion," Ureshino said confidently. "Before we gather up our things, I want you all to come to the Game Room. I'm still super confused by everything, and I'd love you to explain it, Kokoro-chan."

"OK," Kokoro said.

They went back to the trashed Game Room, and Kokoro picked up the sheet of paper on top of the overturned table.

And she began to explain how each of them existed in a different time.

"JEEZ . . . WHAT THE hell?"

Each of them had gone to their room to ensure they didn't leave anything behind, while Masamune stayed in the Game Room, rummaging through the rubble for his video games.

Some of the consoles had been crushed underneath the overturned table and the cases with games looked utterly squashed. Sighing and tutting, he placed them one by one inside his backpack, wondering if he could return them to the manufacturer.

"If I'd known this was going to happen, I would never have brought them."

He continued to mutter and grumble under his breath when he heard his name.

"Masamune."

He turned around to see Subaru at the door. "What d'ya want?" Masamune asked. "Have you finished checking your room?"

"It's OK. I didn't bring much from home. And I didn't use the room much either. I spent most of my time in here playing games with you. Here, let me help," Subaru said, crouching on the rug. "We'll pick up everything together."

As he watched Subaru straightening up a chair which had toppled on its side, Masamune had a strange feeling.

This boy, Subaru, had spent the best part of a year in this room playing video games. One was in ninth grade, the other in eighth, and despite all the hours they'd spent together, laughing and exclaiming over the games, it was still hard to believe that Subaru came from a different age—that he was a junior high student from 1985.

He is now twenty-nine years older than me, thought Masamune.

He plucked the ruined PlayStation 2 from the mountain of rubble. *Damn it*, he thought, *what're ya gonna do with this?* He still had a PlayStation 3 at home, and 4 was launching soon; he knew his dad would buy it for him if he pestered him enough.

He decided he wouldn't bother lugging back the broken TV. It was an old Braun tube TV his father had forgotten about. Masamune had discovered it in their storage shed, and compared to an LCD TV it was unbelievably bulky and heavy. It was no better than some antique.

"Masamune, you mentioned earlier that you had an even newer game console at home? But that it didn't fit the TV terminal. What do you mean?"

"Ah—that's this one, PlayStation 2."

So I even have to explain that, eh? Masamune chose his words carefully. "At home I have a more advanced version of this, PlayStation 3, and that's the device I really wanted to bring over, but they have more sophisticated TVs now and if you don't have one, the plugs won't fit. This retro TV isn't compatible. This PlayStation 2 was actually used by my dad back in the day."

"Really?"

He probably still doesn't get it, Masamune thought, but Subaru was humming, with a smile on his face.

"Do you really understand?" Masamune couldn't help asking.

"Not completely, but it's cool to think that the future will turn out like that," he said. "So your father liked video games too, did he? Is that why you like them so much?"

"Maybe that's partly why."

He and his father rarely played games together anymore, but ever since he could remember he was used to seeing his father collect games. Even now, if he badgered his dad he'd usually buy him whatever games he asked for, since he understood the appeal himself. That's the kind of father he was—and Masamune was thankful.

"You know . . ." Subaru said, as he rummaged through the scattered games.

"What now?" Masamune said.

"I'm thinking of becoming one," Subaru said.

"One *what?*"

"Someone who designs games."

Masamune was on his hands and knees on the floor at this point, but he stopped searching and fell silent. Subaru stopped rummaging too, and caught Masamune's eye.

He sat up. "I've been thinking about it. In 2013, the year you live in now, I'll be, what, forty-three . . . or forty-four? Hard to believe, but a decent age, I was thinking, though to you I'd be an old guy. An adult, in other words." Subaru laughed. "That's why—that's what will be my goal from now on. To become a game designer. Then you can say, 'A friend of mine designed this game,' and it'll be true."

Masamune did not know what to say.

He felt like he couldn't breathe, as if an unseen force was pressing down on his chest. He felt a sharp twinge in his nose, his eyes began to fill with tears, and he looked down quickly.

"What're you talking about?" he managed to say, his voice cracking. "We're all going to forget anything we've said here, so what's the point? It won't stop me boasting."

"You think? Still, don't you want to believe that some things will change, that this is all somehow meaningful? Because I've never had anything I really wanted to aim for, until now."

He spoke so casually it made Masamune wish he could be a bit more serious.

"So if I can find something I'm really keen to do, I'd be so excited. I think I can remember that much when I go back through the mirror, if I will myself to. I promise you. So even if you and I forget each other, you won't be lying. You *do* have a friend who makes video games."

Masamune bit his lip to stop the tears.

"Masamune?"

"Thank you, Subaru," he said quietly, before Subaru could look too closely at his tear-stained cheeks. But Subaru looked relieved.

"Um," he said, nodding. He rested his eyes on the wrecked devices. "Great," he murmured.

FUKA CLOSED THE lid to the piano.

She trailed her eyes around the room with a thankful heart.

Taking her handkerchief out of her pocket, she gave the lid a good wipe.

As she tidied up the rest of the room, there was a knock at her door. "Yes?"

"It's me. Ureshino."

They'd all decided to come together for one last time in the grand foyer, so why was he now outside her door? She opened it just wide enough to see the side of his face.

He was standing in the hallway alone.

"What is it?" she asked quietly.

"Well . . . there's something I wanted to tell you."

His face was flushed and he was clutching his hands in front of him. Before she could even think of what it might be, he said, "The thing is . . ." and looked directly at her. "Fuka—will you go out with me?"

He said it so boldly it surely echoed through the whole castle. Fuka opened the door wide in astonishment. Ureshino looked totally serious.

"You can give me your answer when we go back through the mirrors, but will you think about it and let me know? Even . . . even if you don't remember, it will feel like a drama where two people are fated to be together and one of them spies the other in a crowd. If you see me, something will click."

"Yeah, but . . ."

They lived in different times.

Seven years apart, to be exact. In Ureshino's time, while he was in junior high, Fuka would have already graduated.

"I'm so much older than you—plus, we're going to forget everything anyway."

"But even so, I still like you," Ureshino said. He was dead serious, squeezing his balled-up fists with such force they turned a porcelain white.

Fuka smiled. She was simply extremely happy.

"I understand," she said. "If I see you somewhere, and fate tugs at me somehow, I'll call out to you. Though by then you might be head over heels for someone your own age."

"No way! I like you! I like you *so much*, Fuka!"

They were still talking in the doorway when someone joined them.

"Yeah, yeah, yeah . . . I like you, I like you. Give me a break!"

It was Aki, who'd apparently just emerged from her room. She rapped Ureshino on the back of his head. "Ow!" he cried, rubbing it. Behind Aki were Rion and Kokoro, who was looking flushed, and holding her hands out in a gesture of apology to Fuka.

"Sorry to interrupt," she mouthed.

"What are you saying?" Ureshino said. "From my perspective, Aki, you're an old woman, so there's no chance I could fancy you."

"Try saying that again?" Aki grimaced and she yanked at Ureshino's ear. Fuka couldn't help but smile again.

"Ureshino," Fuka said, "if I bump into you, I might not remember you, but you'll understand why, won't you? If you remember me, then you can tell me the whole story and convince me to go out with you. I can be a bit stubborn sometimes, so I might not believe you."

Ureshino looked stunned for a second.

"Whaaat?" he exclaimed, exaggerating his question. "Is that how you answer me? So cool, so disdainful?"

"God, you really are so annoying, y'know?" Aki said.

And Fuka just felt content that they could all chat like this.

IN THE GRAND foyer, the seven mirrors were each cracked and falling apart. But they had at least been moved back to their original line-up and nailed to the wall. The Wolf Queen had evidently prepared them for their return.

"I had so much fun," Fuka said, as if speaking for them all. Fuka seldom said what she thought, and Kokoro was happily surprised. She felt exactly the same way.

"Yeah," she smiled.

"It was only while I was here that I began to feel normal." Fuka gazed at the group. Behind her round glasses, her eyes looked soft, but also a little sad. "I thought I could never be like everyone else. I was just a loser. So it made me so happy when you guys made friends with me, like you would with anyone."

Kokoro smiled at her candor.

Ureshino spoke up. "But isn't that strange?" Everyone looked a little alarmed, wondering what he was about to say. He sounded indignant. "Fuka, you're not ordinary at all. You're so kind, and so together—you're far from ordinary."

"That isn't what I meant—though I'm really happy to hear that, Ureshino."

"But it's true, isn't it? Ureshino's right." This from Rion. "Whether you're ordinary or not. It doesn't matter. You're a good person, Fuka, and so I wanted to be your friend—that's all there is to it."

It was Fuka's turn to gasp. "Am I wrong?" Rion asked.

"No," Fuka replied in a small voice, shaking her head. "Thank you," she added.

"Now that you mention it," Subaru said, looking over at Masamune. "Masamune, you sometimes called Rion a *dish*. What does it mean?

You said it behind his back so I thought it must be bad. We're out of here soon, so could you tell me now?"

"What?" Masamune said, looking irritably at Subaru, and then at Rion.

"Eh?" Rion said. "What's that all about? Behind my back? That's freakin' creepy."

"Oh, so it *is* something bad, is it?"

"I wasn't saying anything bad. It's just not the kind of thing you say to someone's face."

Back in 1985, in Subaru's world, maybe *dish* wasn't a word anyone used much. For Kokoro, this was vocabulary used by the younger set. It would sound a little weird, for instance, if her parents said it. So that's how their miscommunication came about.

"You used that word too, Kokoro, didn't you?" Subaru asked her. "You said Rion's a dish."

"What?!" she exclaimed. Her ears grew hot. "I *never* said that!"

She really didn't remember, but became so flustered that she broke into a sweat.

"Whoa, that's creepy," said Rion with a huge smile.

"Let's all tell each other our full names before we say goodbye," Subaru suggested. "If we see our full names in each of our worlds, it might trigger a memory. My name's Subaru Nagahisa. *Subaru* is the constellation; *naga* and *hisa* are the characters meaning 'long' and 'a long while.'"

"My name's Akiko Inoue. Inoue's a common name," Aki said, "but the *aki* in Akiko is the character for 'crystal,' and *ko* is just the word for 'child.'" She shook her head, and turned to them. "Honestly, I didn't want to share last names at the start because my mother had just remarried and my last name had changed. And I didn't want to tell you my new last name."

"I'm Rion Mizumori. Mizumori means 'protecting water' and I told you before that Rion is the *ri* in *rika*—science—with the character for sound, *on*."

"I'm Fuka Hasegawa. Fuka's written with the characters for 'wind' and 'song.'"

"I'm Kokoro Anzai. Kokoro's written in *hiragana*, not Chinese characters," Kokoro said.

"You all know my name. Haruka Ureshino. Haruka is the character meaning 'distant.' Ureshino is written with the characters meaning 'happy' and 'field.'"

Masamune had remained quiet throughout. Frowning for some reason, he said, "Aasu Masamune."

"What?!"

They stared at him. They hadn't quite heard properly, and pricked up their ears.

Masamune's face turned bright red.

"Aasu Masamune. The *aa* means 'blue' and the *su* means 'clear water.'"

"Aasu, is that really your name? You're joking, aren't you?"

"I'm not. In 2013 it's a fairly common name. So why don't you oddballs from the past just shut up, OK?"

"Yeah, but *aasu* is how we Japanese say the English word 'earth,' right? So what's all that about?" asked Aki, making Masamune sulkily turn away.

Even for Subaru, his best buddy here, this was news. For her part, too, Kokoro was surprised.

Now that she thought about it, when she was inside Masamune's memories, the Wolf Queen had called him by his full name. And she had thought Masamune was his last name, but she wasn't able to catch the first name.

"So Masamune's your last name, not your first."

"Yeah—which is why I didn't want to tell you. Because I knew you lot would make some smart-arse remark."

"Wow, it's weirder than my name," Ureshino said.

Masamune looked even more annoyed. "Don't say it's *weird*!" he exclaimed.

THEY WERE STANDING shoulder to shoulder in a line.

The cracked mirrors signaled that this was, indeed, their last journey. According to the Wolf Queen, beyond the castle on the other side, the mirrors were likewise shattered.

"Aki," Kokoro said to Akiko, who was standing beside her.

"Yes, Kokoro?" Akiko turned her head sideways to look at her.

"Give me your hand."

Aki uncertainly held out her hand. Kokoro clutched it tightly.

She remembered what she'd seen. The ugly reality that was awaiting Aki on the other side of the mirror.

Her mother and stepfather were part of Akiko's unchangeable reality. Once Kokoro let her small hand go, Akiko would have to return to that world. There was nothing left that Kokoro could do.

"I'll be waiting for you in the future," she whispered.

Akiko's eyes widened.

"I'll be waiting, in 2006, fourteen years in your future. Come and see me, OK?"

Let her understand.

All she could say were a few words that she wasn't sure would ever get through to her.

For several moments Akiko stood silently looking at Kokoro, who had turned her gaze forward. Her hand was still in Kokoro's firm grip.

She nodded. "I think I understand."

She was promising Kokoro she'd come to see her.

"I was terrified, thinking the wolf was going to eat me. I'm never doing anything so stupid like that, ever again."

And Akiko broke into a smile.

"PEOPLE, TAKE CARE now!"

"We will!"

"See you."

"Bye."

352

"Goodbye!"

"Take care!"

"I hope we can see each other sometime."

A chorus of voices in a fugue.

Akiko's voice.

Kokoro.

Fuka.

Masamune.

Ureshino.

Rion.

Subaru.

Their figures merged into the mirrors as they embarked on their final passage.

Back to their own time, to their own reality.

*　*　*

THE RAINBOW-COLORED light spilled into a kaleidoscope that bathed the floor of the grand foyer—then vanished.

Only the little girl in the wolf mask was still there.

She checked that the last vestige of glow had disappeared from each of the mirrors before turning slowly away.

Quietly, she drew in a deep breath.

It's over, she thought in the silence.

After a few moments she heard: "Hi, sis."

The voice made the girl in the Wolf Queen's mask flinch. She turned towards the direction of the voice, to the mirrors where the glow had recently dissipated. Then she quickly looked away.

Rion Mizumori was standing tall in front of his mirror.

He'd been on his way home, but had turned back.

The Wolf Queen had her back to him. She pretended not to have heard.

But Rion wasn't about to give up so easily.

"Mio-chan. Say something."

"Go home." The Wolf Queen did not turn round. "I told you to go back. If you don't go now, you'll never be able to get home."

She felt something would be destroyed if she looked round, so she gritted her teeth and stared at the grandfather clock at the top of the staircase.

Rion had no intention of going back.

"I had my suspicions from the very first day."

30 March.

"The day the castle is due to close is the anniversary of your passing."

HIS OLDER SISTER Mio had said, *If I'm not here anymore, I'll hope for one single wish for you, Rion. I'm sorry you've had to put up with so much.*

He remembered her gentleness.

I want the same as you—to walk to school together.

"Honestly, I was planning to get hold of the key tomorrow and ask for a wish. If Aki hadn't done what she did, I was going to ask everyone to let me wish that my sister could come back home."

The girl whose face was hidden behind the wolf mask.

She had made this castle for him, using every ounce of strength she had left.

Once Rion had had this realization, he couldn't shake it.

The junior high in Japan he'd wanted to attend.

The friends he'd wanted to have.

"It's exactly the same," Rion said. "This castle is just like the doll's house you had in hospital."

The exquisite doll's house bought by her parents lay next to the window in her hospital room for weeks.

As it was a doll's house, there was no running water. You couldn't use the bathroom. And there was no gas.

But there was electricity, since they'd installed tiny light bulbs through all the rooms.

None of the other utilities worked in the castle, but you could still play video games. And you could flick a switch and there would be light. He was never sure why electricity was the one thing they had.

The dolls she played with all wore dresses like the one the Wolf Queen had on now.

The doll's house his sister loved so much.

The seven children welcomed into it.

The search for the key that followed the story she had read to him over and over, *The Wolf and the Seven Young Goats*.

And the day the castle was scheduled to close, 30 March.

Not 31 March.

The fact that this was the anniversary of her death had to be significant.

This castle was prepared just for him.

The Wolf Queen had told them she'd invited other groups before, but he knew that wasn't true.

The group she had invited was unique.

"Mio-chan."

The Wolf Queen didn't reply.

Rion carried on speaking.

"The only year missing is 1999. You brought a kid from every seventh year, but 1999 is the only year where there is no representative. Between Aki's time and mine is a gap of fourteen years, twice the other ones."

He fairly hurled this at the Wolf Queen's back, since she refused to turn and face him.

"You and I are seven years apart in age."

His sister had died at thirteen, when Rion was six. Her first year of junior high. She had never worn the school uniform for Yukishina No. 5 Junior High that hung on the wall in her hospital room, not even once.

The memory was so painful, as if his chest was being ripped open and his heart was being wrenched out.

"So—1999 is *you*, isn't it? The girl who wanted to go to Yukishina No. 5 but couldn't."

The Wolf Queen's back seemed to tremble, ever so slightly. But her shiny, toy-like little shoes were planted firmly on the floor.

When had she created all this?

In her last year of life, she'd mostly kept her eyes closed, as if sleeping. Even little Rion thought it better that she sleep if she was in that much pain.

Was it then? he wondered.

Eyes closed, asleep, she had come here every day.

If I'm not here anymore, I'll hope for one single wish for you, Rion.
I want to be able to walk with you to school.

Rion said this innocently enough, his one modest wish.

If I do go back to that school, then I want the same as you—to walk to school together, Rion, and to play with you.

His sister had said it. This is surely what she had wished for.

His sister had always loved making up stories, and this castle and the quest for the key were exactly the kind of thing she would have come up with.

The Wolf Queen still didn't turn around.

She seemed resolved not to face him, no matter what.

Rion knew well how strong she was; she would not give in.

"At first, I thought my dead sister had come back since she wanted to see me. But when I saw the way the seven-year timeline seemed incomplete, I finally understood. That you must be traveling here from that hospital room, too. Your reality is still in that room with me when I was six, isn't it?"

Rion's voice began to crack as he fought back tears.

"You were coming over here every day back then, weren't you?"

He gazed around the castle.

"That last long year—you spent it in here, in this very doll's house, together with me and all the others."

356

He finally began to understand what her last words to him really meant.

Rion . . . I'm sorry I scared you. But I had a good time.

On that day, when he was just six, he'd thought she was referring to her frightening him by dying. But she wasn't. Those were the true feelings of this Wolf Queen who now refused to turn and face him.

His sister had meant the words *I had a good time* for this Rion, the one here now.

The next day, the castle would close forever.

30 March.

The day she died.

My sister will leave me. The Wolf Queen is about to die.

"You did this all for me, didn't you?"

He choked now on his words; he couldn't finish them though he was trying.

Rion and his sister were seven years apart in age.

So there was no way they would ever go to school together, even if she hadn't been sick. Rion was now thirteen years old.

A freshman in junior high, the same age his sister was when she died. That had to mean something.

She'd built this castle expressly to meet her brother when he reached the same age as she had been on the day of her passing.

But not just Rion.

She'd gathered other children from seven-year intervals, none of whom attended school. Mio had always been good at making up stories. Like the premise for a fairy tale, she decided on the rules, and played with them all according to the rules of her game.

Within the castle the Wolf Queen was free, vibrant and full of life. She'd appear out of thin air, as if weightless, then disappear, playing with them all just as she wished, and obviously having a wonderful time of it.

Rion looked at his sister in her frilly dress. He broke down.

Her hair was still long, her hands pale, yet plump and supple.

Not the thin hands that Rion had come to know. "I'm glad I could see you."

That was what he wanted her above all to know.

Rion smiled at her back. "I was so happy you came to see me in this way. I'll make it through without you somehow. I'll let people know what I want to do, and if I don't like something—well, I'll let them know. I regret now that I didn't tell Mum and Dad how I really felt."

Over this last year and a half, Rion had come to understand that it wasn't entirely because she wanted to distance herself from him that his mother made him go abroad to school. She'd recommended he study overseas, yet she never stopped worrying about him, evident from all the presents she brought when she visited, and how she'd taken him her homemade cake.

"Do you ever feel like you want to come back?" his mother had asked.

Maybe she hadn't been lying when she'd said she wanted to give him the opportunity to develop his talents. Maybe she truly believed it would be for his own good. *Yes, I want to go back to Japan*, Rion had thought, and his mother hugged him.

"I know, I know," she said.

I'm the one who gave up and swallowed back down my words, he thought. *If only I had persisted with her, she might have come to understand how strongly I felt.*

"Mio-chan."

The Wolf Queen still didn't respond.

His sister, who'd given him so much warmth, so many precious memories, wasn't coming back.

"Since this is the end, could you listen to one more thing I'd like?"

Mio had always had a soft spot for her little brother. He had such fond memories of that.

She remained facing away and he continued to address her back. "I want to remember this," he said. "I want to remember it all. Remember the others, and remember you. I know you might say that's impossible, but still I want to."

He waited in silence, but the Wolf Queen didn't respond.

Rion turned towards the mirrors. Inside himself, he whispered to his sister, *Farewell.*

He reached his palms out to the mirror.

Then she spoke.

"I'll do my very best."

He turned around to see her, but the dazzling light from the mirror made his field of vision melt, and the shapes in the grand foyer began to fade. The Wolf Queen was no longer visible.

Something flickered before him. The Wolf Queen was in front of him and their eyes met. She slowly removed her wolf mask and smiled.

Or at least it seemed that way.

✳ ✳ ✳

APRIL 7, 2006

As Kokoro left home punctually, her mother called out, "Will you be OK? Do you want me to go with you?"

"I'm OK. I'll go by myself," Kokoro said.

Last night she'd told her mother over and over again, but she still seemed worried. *It's only to be expected*, Kokoro thought, but she had made up her mind.

Today was the first day of the first semester of eighth grade for her at Yukishina No. 5.

She was able to go confidently to school because she'd understood that this school wasn't the only place she belonged.

Moé-chan had moved on to another school. But her words to Kokoro remained strongly etched in her memory.

It's only school.

She knew now there were other worlds, other places she could go.

If she didn't like her school, there were always the No. 1 and No. 3

junior highs nearby. She knew she'd make it. She could go anywhere. It wasn't as if it was always going to be easy. There'd always be people she disliked. That reality wasn't going to go away.

There was a person who'd said she didn't have to struggle if she didn't want to.

That's why she'd decided to go back.

Back to school.

THE CHERRY TREES were in full bloom and their blossoms fluttered silently to the ground. A light wind was blowing.

As Kokoro walked through the school gate, she held her hair down in the wind. She was a little anxious—it would be a lie to say she wasn't—but she'd set off to school today with her head held high.

She heard a voice from somewhere in front of her.

"Hey."

Eyes narrowed in the blustery wind, Kokoro looked towards the voice. The fallen blossoms stopped swirling and her field of vision began to clear.

She saw a boy straddling a bicycle, and he was looking in her direction.

He was wearing the boys' uniform for Yukishina No. 5 Junior High, the school badge showing clearly on his chest.

The embroidered name tag said *Mizumori*.

I feel as if—I know his name, Kokoro thought. Her eyes widened.

Because she sometimes had a dream.

A dream of a transfer student arriving.

And among all her many classmates he noticed her, and a smile as dazzling as the sun spread over his face. He said, "Good morning." And he smiled.

Epilogue

AS SOON AS the child entered the room, she knew: *The time has finally come.*

She wasn't sure why she was so certain.

But her heart trembled, and whispered to her.

You've been waiting for this day for a long, long time.

The pain that recurred so often—the feeling of her arm being yanked hard—came back to her.

Akiko Kitajima was a member of the NPO *Kokoro no kyoshitsu*. As well as serving as a counselor for several local schools, she had been involved with this alternative School from its inception.

Like many of the children who came to it, she'd also attended Yukishina No. 5 Junior High.

There was a time back in junior high when Akiko had stopped going.

It was in the autumn of her third year, while at her grandmother's funeral, that Akiko first met Ms. Samejima.

Samejima-sensei. Yuriko Samejima-sensei.

She'd lived in the neighborhood, near Akiko's grandmother, since the days when Akiko was very young, and had apparently helped Akiko's grandmother with her shopping and other errands. Ms. Samejima was quite an intense lady, and at the funeral she wailed far more loudly than any of the deceased's own relatives. Akiko and her family were taken aback, for Akiko's grandmother had never mentioned this friend. When Ms. Samejima came up to Akiko and asked, "Are you Akiko-chan?" Akiko was in for an even bigger surprise.

They may have never heard a word from Akiko's grandmother about Ms. Samejima, but she certainly seemed to know all about Akiko.

She took her hand and looked intently at Akiko. "I hear you've dropped out of school?" she said, holding her hand even tighter. "You poor child," she said, tearing up.

Ms. Samejima had never met Akiko's mother before, but she didn't hesitate to speak her mind. "You've never paid her any attention," Ms. Samejima said, and Akiko's mother paled and stared at her.

"Who do you think you are?" she fired back. "What gives you the right to speak to me like this?"

Samejima-sensei's response could not have been more brazen.

"I am this girl's grandmother's friend, that's who I am. Akiko, your grandmother was always so worried about you. And she asked me to help you if anything ever happened to her. She told me this as her last request, and that's why I'm saying what I'm saying."

Ms. Samejima ran a little school for kids who found they couldn't keep up and were starting to drop out of school, all for a low monthly fee. She urged Akiko to visit it, but Akiko refused, thinking the old lady was a busybody.

But Ms. Samejima didn't give up so easily. She took Akiko to the school she'd dropped out of and convinced the teachers to let Akiko repeat the year. "Let her study hard for one more year," Ms. Samejima said, "and then she can decide if she wants to go on to high school, or what it is she wants to do. I'll supervise her all the way."

And with that, the deed was done. She would repeat her final year.

But still Akiko could only see her as a busybody middle-aged woman butting in where she wasn't wanted. She was sure that even if she repeated the year, it would all end up as it had before. She had zero desire to go back to school.

At least that was her attitude until April, when her extra year of school began.

As she was about to start her second time around in ninth grade, she finally decided to allow Ms. Samejima to help her.

She knew she was in trouble. She couldn't keep up with schoolwork. She didn't even know what it was she didn't know.

And she simply felt that this was the time to ask for help.

And she started to want to study again.

She'd thought there was no one who could help her, but now she saw that there was Ms. Samejima, offering a hand. It came as a sudden realization.

That was when she started to feel a sharp pain running down her forearm.

It felt as if someone was pulling her arm hard.

SO AKIKO GRADUATED from junior high one year late, moved on to high school, and during that year her long-held wish came true: to enter the education department of a university. Ms. Samejima got in touch with her, with the news that she was starting an NPO. She planned to rent a larger building than her little juku had been using, and to create an alternative Free School where children who couldn't—or wouldn't—attend regular public school could go.

The Free School was named *Kokoro no kyoshitsu*, Classroom for the Heart.

She invited Akiko to help out.

"I'd be happy to," Akiko replied. She was overjoyed that Ms. Samejima needed her, and since she planned to be a teacher herself, the experience she might gain there would certainly come in useful.

She first met Dr. Kitajima in 1998, a couple of years after she began to assist at the school. Akiko was a junior in college by then.

Dr. Kitajima was a caseworker at a nearby general hospital, and he learned about the alternative School and got in touch. He was hoping to take the in-patient children at his hospital who were falling behind. He'd also be very grateful, he said, if some of the teachers could visit the hospital.

As Akiko found herself more drawn to his calm smile and his gentle manner, she had a premonition.

I might end up marrying him.

Kitajima—she repeated his last name to herself, and each time she did, the feeling inside her grew stronger.

ONE DAY, AKIKO encountered a young girl at the hospital. Dr. Kitajima had brought her into the courtyard outside.

She was a tiny girl with a lively personality. Akiko heard she was a first-year student in junior high, even though she seemed much younger. Her gaze, though, was very adult. The meds she was on had made her hair fall out, and she now wore a cap. She'd officially entered Yukishina No. 5 Junior High, though she had yet to attend a single day.

Her name was Mio Mizumori.

Akiko would never forget the encounter.

That year Akiko and Mio began classes once a week.

"Akiko-sensei, I'm so looking forward to this."

The girl was a bundle of eagerness. A well of curiosity.

Every time Mio's large eyes gazed at her, Akiko sat bolt upright, goosebumps spreading across her. As long as this girl called her "Akiko-sensei," she wanted to continue to spend time with her, and teach her. To be a teacher her young pupil could be proud of.

So there are children like this in the world, she thought.

Meeting Mio had a tremendous impact on her.

Mio wanted nothing more than to go to school, but she couldn't. She wasn't pessimistic or gloomy at all, but instead was eager to absorb and learn everything she could. More than a few times her iron will spurred Akiko on, made her feel *she* was the one being rescued.

The experience touched Akiko immensely.

She always thought she understood the feelings of children who couldn't attend school, who couldn't make it, didn't fit in—the ones who stuck out. But she hadn't. As she worked towards her goal of becoming a teacher, as she helped out at the alternative School, she'd been so sure of it, deep down. But she was wrong. Her own circumstances back in junior high, and the situations of each of the children she met now, were unique. Not a single one was the same.

When Akiko was a senior in college, Mio passed away.

A light spring rain was falling on the day of her funeral, and Akiko stood by her grave, blank and crying, and as she did, she looked at Mio's little brother. Seeing him standing there, she could hardly breathe. Her heart fluttered as she recalled Mio's voice, calling her Akiko-sensei. She understood how very precious her time with her had been.

What she wanted to become was, perhaps, a bit different from the usual public school teacher.

She wanted, as much as she could, to continue her connection with the alternative School. And to be the kind of person who could get close to all the children, to meet their own individual circumstances and needs.

She moved on from graduate school, got married, and changed her last name. As she worked with the alternative School a thought arose in her, before she even realized it.

Now it's my turn.

Why she felt that way, she had no idea.

But from long ago she'd always had a scene etched in her heart. And a strong, sharp pain she felt in her arm.

The memory of someone yanking her, hard.

I was rescued.

There are children somewhere who, trembling, and at the risk of their own lives, pulled me by the arm and brought me back into this world.

It's OK, Aki.

Grow up to be an adult.

I'm in the future, where you are too.

Children who said these words to me, kept me tethered to the world, gave me the chance to grow up.

Their faces weren't clear, but somehow she always saw Mio's image overlaid on them.

Why, she didn't know. But this thought came to her, every time the stabbing pain in her arm returned.

Now I'd like to pull those children by the arm.

KOKORO ANZAI WALKS slowly towards the room. Lips pale, eyes darting around uneasily.

When Aki sees the girl, she knows instantly. The time has finally come. Why, she can't say.

It feels as if she's been waiting a lifetime for this moment.

The familiar sharp pain in her arm comes back, as if it is being yanked hard.

What sort of trauma has this girl been exposed to? What sort of struggles has she faced? Akiko has no idea. But still her heart swells at the thought.

"So Kokoro, I understand you're a student at Yukishina No. 5 Junior High School?"

"Yes."

"I went there too," Aki says.

I've been waiting for you, a voice says inside Aki. *It's OK, grow up to be an adult.*

HANGING ON THE wall of the Free School, a small rectangular mirror reflects the young woman and the girl. A beam of sunlight catches its edge, and there is a tiny flash of rainbow colors. *Hm?* Aki thinks, and she has the feeling that in the mirror, sitting there, are she and the girl, as they used to be, back in junior high.

A cool spring breeze carrying the scent of green grass blows gently in, caressing the surface of the mirror, dissolving the rainbow-colored light. The light slowly, softly envelops them both, Kokoro and Aki, as they sit there, face to face.

Reading Guide

EREWHON

About the Author

© YOSHIHIRO KAMIYA

MIZUKI TSUJIMURA lives in Tokyo and is a well-known author of bestselling mystery novels in Japan. Her groundbreaking novel *Lonely Castle in the Mirror* combines elements of Japanese fantasy with highly relevant themes of emotional wellbeing and friendship. It won the coveted Japan Booksellers' Award, voted by booksellers as the book they most like to sell, and became an instant No.1 bestseller in Japan, selling over half a million copies. Tsujimura has also won the Naoki Prize for her work. Rights have sold across the world.

About the Translator

PHILIP GABRIEL is Professor of Japanese literature in the Department of East Asian Studies, the University of Arizona. He is the author of *Mad Wives and Island Dreams: Shimao Toshio and the Margins of Japanese Literature* and *Spirit Matters: The Transcendent in Modern Japanese Literature* and has translated many novels and short stories by the writer Haruki Murakami and other modern writers. He is the recipient of the Japan-U.S. Friendship Commission Prize for the Translation of Japanese Literature (2001) for his translation of Senji Kuroi's *Life in the Cul-de-Sac*, and the 2006 PEN/Book-of-the-Month Club Translation Prize for his translation of Murakami's *Kafka on the Shore*.

Discussion Questions

These suggested questions are to spark conversation and enhance your reading of *Lonely Castle in the Mirror*.

1. In Japan, there are many *futoko*—children like Kokoro and her friends who refuse to go to school due to circumstances that impact their mental health, and whose families must choose between homeschooling or sending them to "free" schools that don't result in any academic accreditation. How is mental health treated differently in Kokoro's community than in your community? How do you feel about those differences?

2. What are your memories of your first attempts to make friends and figure out your place in your school and your community? Did you ever find yourself in a situation similar to that of Kokoro and her friends?

3. Some of the people in Kokoro's life treat her as an independent human being with her own thoughts and wishes, while others, such as her homeroom teacher Mr. Ida, seem to want to impose their own ideas on her. How could her family and friends better support her? What kind of help would be useful to you if you were in a similar situation?

4. Kokoro comes to new understandings about the other students in the castle and her classmates at school over the course of the book. What did you find most surprising or interesting about how her views changed? Do you remember meeting someone in your life who really shifted your perspective?

5. The other students in the castle notice that Ureshino is "in love with being in love," and he can't help but fall in love with each girl in turn. How would you have handled that kind of awkward

situation? What's the most awkward thing you have ever had to deal with in a group of friends or schoolmates?

6. Which of the students did you relate to the most? Why? How would this book change if a student other than Kokoro was the main character?

7. This book was originally written in Japanese. How do you imagine that your experience reading it in English might differ from reading it in the original language? What kinds of considerations would you take into account if you were translating someone else's writing into another language?

8. Many readers of this story have commented on how quietly it moves through Kokoro's daily life, paying close attention to the many small obstacles she faces from one moment to the next. How do you feel it compares with a traditional Western novel, which would ordinarily follow a dramatic rise of action and then reach a swift conclusion? How does the novel's structure impact how you experienced the themes and emotional journey of the story?

9. *Lonely Castle in the Mirror* references many fairy tales, including "Little Red Riding Hood," "The Wolf and the Seven Young Goats," and others. Why do you think the author chose to use fairy tales to tell this story? Why do you think she chose these specific fairy tales?

10. The wolf-girl sets strange rules that range from utterly mundane, such as what times the children are allowed to visit the castle, to the whimsical and even the terrifying, such as the risk of being eaten up for staying past the curfew. If you could have your own castle in a mirror, what rules would you set, and who would you invite?

11. Each student has the opportunity to search in the castle for a key that can grant one wish. If you could have one wish, what would you wish for? What would you have wished for when you were younger?

Publisher's Note

According to a recent UNICEF report, Japanese children were ranked second-to-last in an international survey assessing children's mental health across thirty-eight developed and emerging countries. While Japanese children were ranked first in physical health and often live in relatively prosperous economic circumstances, instances of bullying in schools, as well as difficult relationships with family members, lead to a lack of psychological well-being.

The popularity of *Lonely Castle in the Mirror* in Japan, where it scooped two prizes and became a bestseller, is testament to its power to heal and to open debate.

Resources

There's no shame in asking for help when you, or someone you know, are having a hard time. All of these resources are confidential and can be accessed free of charge.

United States

988 Suicide & Crisis Lifeline: Call or text 988, or chat online
Crisis Text Line: Text "HOME" to 741741
National Sexual Assault Hotline: Call 1-800-656-4673 or 1-800-656-HOPE
National Domestic Violence Hotline: Call 1-800-799-SAFE (7233) or text "START" to 88788
National Teen Dating Abuse Helpline: Call 1-866-331-9474 or text "START" to 88788
National Eating Disorders Association: Call 1-800-931-2237

*AVAILABLE 24/7

Substance Abuse and Mental Health Services Administration Hotline: Call 1-800-662-4357 or 1-800-662-HELP

The Trevor Project: Call 1-866-488-7386 or text "START" to 678678; for LGBTQ+ youth

Trans Lifeline: Call 1-877-565-8860, in English and Spanish; staffed by trans people

Canada

National Suicide Hotline: Call 988

Talk Suicide Canada: Call 1-833-456-4566 or text 45645 from 4 p.m. to midnight

Kids Help Phone: Call 1-800-668-6868 or text "CONNECT" to 686868, in English and French

Trans Lifeline: Call 1-877-330-6366; staffed by trans people

National Eating Disorder Information Centre Helpline: Call 1-866-633-4220 or, in Toronto, 416-340-4156, or chat online

WAVAW Rape Crisis Center: Call 1-877-392-7583 or chat online

Hope for Wellness Help Line for Indigenous Peoples: Call 1-855-242-3310 or chat online, in English, French, Cree, Ojibway, and Inuktitut

Missing and Murdered Indigenous Women and Girls Crisis Line: Call 1-844-413-6649

Wellness Together Canada: Call 1-866-585-0445 or text "WELLNESS" to 741741, in English and French

Drug Rehab Services: 1-877-254-3348